WHIRLWIND

As Europe stands on the brink of war, Elizabeth discovers love and passion with Julius at her aunt's home in Berlin. When the couple witness the terrible events of Kristallnacht, Elizabeth is horrified to find that Julius appears to approve, and returns home distraught believing the man she loves is a Nazi. When she discovers she is pregnant, Elizabeth gives her baby up for adoption and tries to forget, building a new life as a dutiful wife and mother. Ten years later, with peace in Europe, Julius journeys to England, hoping that Elizabeth has waited for him. Can they be together at last? ...

WHIRLWIND

WHIRLWIND

by

Eileen Stafford

Magna Large Print Books
Long Preston, North Yorkshire,
England.

British Library Cataloguing in Publication Data.

Stafford, Eileen
  Whirlwind.

  A catalogue record for this book is
  available from the British Library

  ISBN 0-7505-1319-5

First published in Great Britain by Severn House Publishers
Ltd., 1997

Copyright © 1997 by Eileen Stafford

Cover illustration © Len Thurston by arrangement with P.W.A.
International Ltd.

The moral right of the author has been asserted

Published in Large Print 1999 by arrangement with Severn House
Publishers Ltd.

Magna Large Print is an imprint of
Library Magna Books Ltd.
Printed and bound in Great Britain by
T.J. International Ltd., Cornwall, PL28 8RW.

For Paul and Carol

With love

ACKNOWLEDGEMENTS

Much has been written about the Second World War and its aftermath but it is often difficult to understand how ordinary people felt during those horrendous years. Several books have been of inestimable value in my research. Two which stand out are *Hearts Undefeated—Women's Writing of the Second World War* and *Frauen—German Women Recall the Third Reich* by Alison Owings. The writings of Christobel Bielenberg were also extremely helpful.

The video *Bristol at War* brought the past powerfully to life, enabling me to recall many of my own early memories. For details of the Luftwaffe attacks on the Bristol Aeroplane Company in September 1940 I turned to the book *Target Filton* by Kenneth Wakefield. My thanks also go to the War Graves Commission for the help I received in locating graves of Luftwaffe air crew buried in England.

Finally, many thanks to my husband, and to my friends in the writing group, for their constant encouragement. I am also grateful to Dot, my agent, for her never-failing support.

E S, 1997

'The whirlwind of war had caught up all our lives ... the old landmarks had disappeared and the new ones were not yet clearly defined.'

Constance Goddard

PROLOGUE

November 1989

Elizabeth woke early. She pulled on her dressing gown and went downstairs to make a mug of tea and to let Caro into the garden. She cradled the mug in her hands, carried it back to bed and sipped it rapturously. The first mug was always the best of the day. She turned on the radio, and upset some of the scalding liquid over the duvet as the disembodied voice made its incredible announcement.

'The Berlin wall is no more. At the stroke of midnight the twenty-eight mile scar cutting across the city was breached by rejoicing crowds. They poured through the checkpoints, and danced on the top. Where border guards once shot to kill they are now looking on indulgently. It appears that East Germans are now free to travel to the West unimpeded.'

Hardly knowing what she did, Elizabeth finished the tea, turned off the radio and remembered. She was back in Berlin and it was another November. She would never forget that wonderful afternoon or the hideous evening that followed, the day that changed her life.

She went downstairs again and opened the

15

garden door, for she knew that Caro would be waiting impatiently to be let in. She patted him, gave him a large bone-shaped biscuit, but he was not deceived. He sniffed at it dubiously and then took it from her hand and crunched it into small pieces all over the new kitchen carpet.

She went into the sitting room, turned on the gas fire and the television and watched the breakfast news. She sat quite still, riveted by the pictures that were flashing across the screen before her disbelieving eyes. The Mayor of Berlin was saying that the people of Germany were the happiest in the world today. Germany would be united again.

For a moment she felt fear and then her heart leapt. He would be free at last. He would come. Surely he would come now.

A great love was always there in the background of the mind ready to spring into new life at the right time. And now must be that time.

CHAPTER 1

1938

Elizabeth wrapped Christmas presents for her German cousins and thought of the cauldron of emotions she had left behind in Berlin. Ever since she had returned to England she had wished, in spite of all that had happened, and in defiance of her better judgement, to be there still in the stimulating atmosphere of her aunt and uncle's sumptuous home. Berlin was vibrant and volatile, a place of sudden terror and sometimes death, but of excitement too ... and the man she loved was there.

She sat back on her heels in front of the fire and brooded miserably on the enigma that was Julius and the events that had caused her to come back to England so abruptly. She could hear his voice as real, as clearly as if he were here beside her, but the mystery that surrounded him was as unresolved as ever.

Her mother took the brightly-wrapped parcels and examined them one by one before putting them into the box with her own gifts. 'Emmi, Werner, Hans,' she said reading the labels. 'Is there one for Julius?'

'No.'

'But you usually send him a little something.'

'Not this year.' Elizabeth tried to sound as

17

though the giving or not giving of a present to Julius was of no matter whatsoever. She noticed a flicker of satisfaction cross her mother's face. Louise Benson had never been very partial to the young German.

'Any special reason?'

'No,' Elizabeth said again, with deliberate carelessness. Silently, in her head, she added, *yes, a thousand times yes. I love him and I shall probably never see him again. I left my heart in Germany along with the horror and the fear.* She longed to scream the unspoken words at her mother, but she said nothing. Julius of the shining blue eyes and the curling blond hair, the attentive, loving ways. Julius, the childhood friend of her cousins and herself, the man she loved to distraction, and would never have.

'Very well,' her mother said. 'I'll fasten the box and we'll get it in the post.'

Elizabeth hardly heard. She was suddenly back in Berlin and it was a cold November afternoon, the ninth, a Wednesday, the day that had changed her life.

'Would you like to walk a bit?' Julius had said after lunch on that day, deliberately directing his question only at her.

She had glanced at him quickly, had seen the warmth and eagerness in his eyes, could still see it. 'That would be lovely. I'm so full of Aunt Sophie's cooking that I need to walk for hours and hours.' Had she needed a reason to accept that invitation? Of course not, but certainly an excuse for the sake of the others. Her three cousins had been in the room. Emmi

18

had looked at her and grinned. 'Not me,' she said. 'I've a book to finish.'

Werner and Hans had shaken their heads. 'You two go and exercise for all of us,' Werner said.

They had walked through Uncle Heinrich's beautiful acres down to the lakeside, to the old summer house set amongst tall pine trees. It was stone-built and very beautiful, but cold and damp now in November. Julius had pushed open the door, held out his hand to her and they had gone inside. The mustiness contrasted powerfully with the sweet scent of the pines.

Thinking about it afterwards, Elizabeth frequently wondered if she had known what would happen. Her upbringing had been strict, her morals virtuous and still firmly in place, but all her mother's teaching had vanished as suddenly as frost before sunshine. After the first passionate embrace he had held her at arm's length, had looked at her hungrily, but with hesitation. It was she who had pulled him close again. She thought of it now with shame.

Their lovemaking was fumbling, awkward and later full of guilt. Yet it was for Elizabeth a magical hour, both painful and glorious, the awakening of her senses and her heart, a moment that, remembered, caused tears to flow in loneliness and anguish so often afterwards.

They had swung back to the house hand in hand and she had been deliriously happy. She thought then that nothing mattered but their love, that no one could ever part them. Now she realised how wrong, how naive she had been.

'I want to marry you,' Julius had said, but there was a hesitancy in his voice that she had chosen to ignore. 'I've never loved anyone else, Elizabeth. Will you always remember that?'

Mesmerised by what had just happened to her, Elizabeth had found nothing odd about those last words. Marry him? Of course she would. Marriage to Julius would be heaven on earth! She had turned to look at him and was filled with the greatest joy she could ever remember. Unable to find words to express her happiness, she had squeezed his hand in unthinking acceptance. The brief thought that she would have to leave England permanently caused her few misgivings. Her relationship with her parents had always been slight, her affections given, since she was quite small, to her German family.

'It might be a long time,' Julius said quickly. 'There are matters to sort out and ... and things you don't know.'

What was he talking about? Hadn't he just asked her to marry him? 'What things?' she said, suddenly uneasy.

'I can't talk about it, Elizabeth. Not yet. Would you trust me?'

'Of course I will, but surely we can tell the others?'

'No. Not yet. Not until it's safe.'

She was shocked by the sudden intensity in his voice.

'Safe?'

She remembered wanting to shout her new-found happiness aloud for everyone to hear and she could still feel the chill of disappointment that had enveloped her like a great rain cloud, but Julius had stopped, taken her in his arms again, kissed her as passionately as before.

'I can't explain now, but I promise that later you'll know everything, and I'll buy you the biggest diamond in the world! Until then let's keep our love as our own precious secret.'

He had smiled reassuringly, and with his arms tight around her she had managed to banish her sudden disquiet.

'You do love me, Elizabeth?' There was anxiety now in his voice. 'And you trust me?' he repeated.

'Yes. I trust you.'

But those promises were soon to come crashing down in disarray, for the most perfect afternoon of Elizabeth's life was to be followed by an evening of total horror. The screams and the terror of that Berlin night were burned into her brain for ever.

'I should like to go into town,' Julius had said after dinner. 'The shops in the *Kurfürstendamm* are quite beautiful after dark.'

Elizabeth longed to be alone with him again. She had nodded casually, trying not to look too pleased in front of the others.

She preferred not to remember the rest, but the pictures in her mind refused to be banished, would come to her at all times; most frighteningly in the night, but also while she was out shopping in the safe English streets, or at meal times, and often when she was

21

sitting before the fire with the flames flickering comfortably and her father lighting his pipe. And when the wind blew smoke down the chimney and into the room, then the smell in her nostrils was not the pleasant solacing odour of safety and home, but the reek of terror, the stench of fear.

'We'd better get this to the post office, then,' her mother said. She carefully dripped sealing wax onto the knots of the string which she had tied around the parcel. 'I hope it reaches Germany intact.'

Elizabeth was brought abruptly back to the present. 'I'll take it, if you like,' she offered.

'Thank you,' Louise said gratefully. 'I've a lot to do. I keep thinking of poor Sophie over there with that awful *Herr* Hitler. I can't help worrying about her.'

'She'll be all right,' Elizabeth said. 'With Uncle Heinrich making important things like munitions or something in his factory you can be pretty sure that she'll be perfectly safe.'

Her mother obviously didn't notice the irony of her reply. 'I hope so,' she said. She fetched a bottle of black ink and a pen with a thick nib. 'Will you write the address?'

Elizabeth nodded and wrote, in large capital letters, her aunt and uncle's name and address, and then BERLIN, GERMANY.

She put the parcel into a big wicker basket and left the house, glad to be alone, unwilling and yet driven remorselessly to relive again in awful detail the events of that frightful night.

22

The parcel she was carrying, the choosing and wrapping of the presents for the cousins, the deliberate omission of anything for Julius, all these things forced her to recall, in ever greater detail, the night she wanted so passionately to forget. As she walked through the pleasant, tree-lined streets of the opulent Bristol suburb where her parents lived, the quietness seemed suddenly to fade and she was back in the noise and excitement of Hitler's Germany, with Julius.

Berlin—October 1938

It was three months earlier when Julius von Brandt strode through the autumn streets and pondered his membership of the select group of students, all of whom had vowed to put an end to the Third Reich. At their clandestine meeting today it had been stressed yet again that to be a dissident was highly dangerous, and this allegiance must be a carefully hidden secret, unknown even to one's nearest and dearest. Outwardly they must be seen as good and stalwart members of the party, exemplary National Socialists, always ready with a *Heil Hitler* whenever necessary. Only thus could they successfully plot the downfall of their impossible *Führer*.

Julius gritted his teeth in frustration and thought of Elizabeth. How could an English girl possibly fall in love with a Nazi? How could he deceive her into thinking he was one?

He had only recently realised that his feelings for her were no careless or passing infatuation. He wanted to marry her, wanted these wretched political problems to vanish so that he could finish his medical studies in peace. Peace! That was a laugh. Only last week Hitler had marched triumphantly into Czechoslovakia. God alone knew where it would end. And what were Britain and France doing, for goodness' sake? Didn't they realise that amidst the euphoria in Germany there was an ever-growing band of dissenters like himself?

And he must keep all these thoughts concealed, hidden, especially from cousin Hans with his enthusiasm for the wonderful Third Reich and all its obscenities. But from Elizabeth too? Dear God in Heaven, how was that to be accomplished? She was coming to Germany in November. His heart beat more quickly and he wished for more maturity and wisdom than his nineteen years had so far bestowed.

November 1938

Elizabeth had always been curious about Julius and his relationship to her aunt and uncle, and as her feelings for him subtly changed from friendship to love, so her curiosity grew. There were so many mysteries. But that afternoon in the summer house she had put her worries aside as well as her principles, and nothing but her love for Julius and his for her had any importance at all. In the evening of that day she still felt a glow of contentment.

They wandered hand in hand through the brightly-lit Berlin streets. There was a general air of prosperity and careless delight. People were well dressed, laughing, remarking on the fashions in the windows, the furniture, the paintings. The grim happenings that she sometimes read about in the newspapers seemed a thousand miles away.

But then suddenly everything appeared to change before her eyes. It was as though some evil force had been let loose upon everyone, a Pandora's box of wickedness suddenly exploding. The laughs became jeers and shouts, the bustle and brilliance turned into a holocaust of fear. She heard the smashing of glass, watched in horror and disbelief as shops were ransacked, and more terrifying still, she saw the protesting shopkeepers beaten and dragged away in full view of the acquiescing police. There was complete disbelief written on the victims' faces at first, followed by panic and horror.

'What's happening?' she screamed to Julius. 'Do something!'

Then she saw the child, a small terror-stricken face, a face which was destined to haunt her for years to come, a little girl in a blue dressing gown. The child was clinging to her father, was snatched from his grasp, pushed angrily to the ground and the man beaten senseless with a bloodied truncheon. He was hauled into a rough cart, and the child, no more than three or four surely, struggled unsteadily to her feet screaming to the uncaring, even assenting crowds, screaming with outstretched arms for her daddy. Then she fell again onto the bloodstained cobbles.

Julius rushed forward still holding Elizabeth's hand and they pushed through the crowd together. He reached the child first, pulled her gently to her feet, said something in rapid German, but she screamed again, tried to get away from him, and then there was the woman pushing towards them, gathering the little girl into her arms, clutching her fiercely, comforting her, covering her with kisses. Elizabeth saw the anguish in her eyes as the cart with its pathetic occupants trundled off amidst the jeering onlookers.

It was at that very moment that Julius seemed to change too. He stood quite still for a moment in the middle of all that senseless violence and proclaimed in loud ringing tones, 'They are Jews, only Jews. Don't worry about them, Elizabeth.'

At first she could not take in the import of what he had said. His words made no sense at all to anything she believed of him, and as his remark sank into her numbed brain she looked up at him in total stupefaction. The woman and child heard those frightful words too and Elizabeth had one last glimpse of the frightened mother and of the little girl's fair hair and blue dressing gown, streaked with her father's blood. The woman stared at them both for a moment with angry, accusing eyes.

Julius pulled Elizabeth away, guided her over the glittering wreckage and into a quieter side street. She wanted to run from him. Anywhere, just to get away from such an obscenity as he had uttered, but he held her hand in an iron grip and she couldn't free herself.

Somehow they managed to get back to the safety of Aunt Sophie's house, to warmth and coffee and a seemingly impossible normality. But neither said anything during the whole of that frightful way home.

Later, still trembling, she looked into the faces of both Julius and her cousin, Hans, as they talked about the events of the evening, and she knew, with rising horror that there was, if not total assent to what had been done, a grudging acceptance that it was necessary. Germany must be rid of its undesirable aliens, they said. She thought of her grandmother in Bristol, her father's mother, despised for being Jewish. When she was small her mother had always discouraged visits. The horror she had just seen suddenly had a shaming and more personal face.

In bed that night, tense and frightened, cold in spite of one of Aunt Sophie's enormous feather quilts and a big stone hot water bottle, a multitude of fears and doubts chased through her sleepless brain. 'I want to marry you,' Julius had said just a few hours before. That golden afternoon seemed a whole world away now. How could she ever have contemplated such a thing? How could she marry a German, a man who approved those frightful obscenities? *Does he really approve? Perhaps he is merely saying those things because of Hans?* Her thoughts turned then to very English Aunt Sophie, her mother's twin, who had bravely married Uncle Heinrich in spite of fierce family opposition back in 1919. She thumped her pillow angrily and allowed a flood of bitter tears to flow unimpeded onto the bedclothes. *I should never have given myself to Julius as I did. How could I have been so foolish, so wicked?* Eventually, when the distant church clock chimed five, she slept.

Julius, too, was considerably shaken by the events of that fateful day. How could he have spoken those hideous words? *Jews, only Jews!* Dear God, could he ever forgive himself? Said, of course, to disguise his subversive activities, but still horrendous in his own ears, and how terrible then to Elizabeth?

The following day he had to pass through some of the devastated streets on the way to college. He kept his eyes cast down in shame. Of course, he told himself firmly, if he hadn't noticed the cynical face of one of Hans's SS cronies watching him as he had rushed to pick up the pathetic little girl, he'd have kept his mouth shut.

But it was a feeble excuse. Being a conspirator was sometimes too difficult for sanity. Pretend to be a Nazi, they had told him. He shuddered at the very idea. It went totally against every shred of decency he'd ever known. But if Hitler was to be disposed of he'd have to do it. He glanced at the shattered windows, scrunched over the glass. If the unthinkable happened and none of the plots were successful, what would happen to his beloved Germany? And the Jews? He had some good friends who were Jews. They were to be resettled, apparently! That was a sick joke.

He caught sight of a dressmaker's model standing crookedly, her hair singed, and her feet lost amidst a heap of wreckage. He paused for a moment and thought of Elizabeth. That wonderful time in the summer house now seemed a hundred years ago, a dream. How could he have been so irresponsible? She was the girl he wanted to marry one day. She deserved respect and he had treated her like a ... he swore and passed along the street trying to ignore the paltry efforts being made to board up the ravaged buildings.

He clenched his fists and vowed to do everything he could to overthrow this monstrous regime that had his country in its grip. When Hitler was dead, then and only then could he begin to live, to marry Elizabeth. For now he must do the best he could to persuade her to keep their love a secret held in trust for happier times.

That same morning, Elizabeth woke suddenly and knew quite clearly what she must do. She would return to England as soon as it could be arranged. With the broken glass and the stench of fear in its streets, Germany had lost its glamour. All her hopes were shattered, and she felt that her life lay in ruins like the pitiable Jewish shops.

She had intended to spend some months in

Berlin perfecting the language before university next year, but all that was past. Cousin Emmi was to have had time in England too. It was a sort of exchange. Her mother and her aunt had always been close, sharing their children.

All those plans had perished now in the ruins of *Kristallnacht*. For so, she learned later, that night had been dubbed Crystal Night: the night of the broken glass and the broken lives.

Aunt Sophie, perhaps guessing something of the shock and turmoil in her niece's heart, managed to sort out the travel arrangements as quickly as possible. She asked no questions and Elizabeth merely said that she felt that she should be home for Christmas after all.

In spite of her wish not to talk alone to Julius any more she gave in to his pleading and they went into the garden together the following evening, keeping to the well-lit paths around the house.

They walked in silence for a little time, then she said briefly and without preamble, 'I'm going home to England as soon as Aunt Sophie can arrange it.'

He stopped suddenly and she too paused and turned round to look at him. His features were in darkness, the light shining brightly from the window behind.

'I still love you, Elizabeth,' he said quietly. 'Nothing has changed.'

'Everything has changed.'

'Things are not always what they seem,' he said. 'If you could trust me, if you could wait ...'

He reached for her hand but she dashed it away roughly. 'Wait? For what? To see more Jews beaten senseless while you and your friends laugh? No, Julius, never.' She felt her anger rising and she turned furious eyes upon him. 'I know what I saw and heard, Julius,' she said savagely. 'Nothing will ever blot the memory of those things from my mind. And you are part of it all, you are German, you acquiesced, didn't you, as all your countrymen and women seem to do? I see Germany as it really is now. The blinkers I had always worn have gone, and, God help me, I see you clearly too. There will probably be a war soon between your people and mine. How can I stay? How could I ever be your wife as you suggested yesterday? And my grandmother is Jewish, yes Jewish.' She pulled off one of her gloves and thrust her hand towards him. 'There's Jewish blood in me, Julius, in these veins, just like we saw spilled all over the cobbles. You can't have a Jewish wife to spoil your so wonderful Aryan line, can you!'

He flinched in horror at what she so obviously thought of him. Nothing was happening as he had intended. He wanted to yell at her that he was not a Nazi, never had been, that he wanted the downfall of Hitler more than anything in the world. All his noble ideals to keep his secret from her became suddenly dust and ashes. Wasn't his love for this girl more important than patriotism? 'I don't care a damn about your Jewish blood,' he declared loudly.

A window was suddenly closed above them

and both looked up in alarm.

'I hope Hans didn't hear you say that,' Elizabeth said.

But it was Sophie who had heard, who had closed the window noisily to warn them. She rushed down the stairs to the back door and opened it, illuminating them with a sudden rush of light.

'Thankfully, Hans is listening to his wireless on the other side of the house,' she said. 'Otherwise you might have had some awkward questions to answer, Julius.'

He shrugged his shoulders. 'I'm not afraid of Hans.'

'Then you should be. He's my son, but he's also an informer. I'm deeply ashamed to say so. Just be careful.' She gave them both an enigmatic look and quickly went inside again, closing the door quietly behind her.

Elizabeth stared after her and shook her head, tried to recover herself a little. 'It's no good, Julius, is it? No good because there is too much between us, too many barriers. Last night showed me that.'

He was silent, brought abruptly back to reality by Aunt Sophie's warning. His love for Elizabeth was just as strong as ever. He knew that nothing would ever change that, but he had been reminded how dangerous his mission was, and that Elizabeth must be kept safe and must not be harmed by any association with him and the dangerous things he had to do.

'Only for now,' he whispered. 'The barriers will come down eventually. Wait for me

Elizabeth, and trust me. I love you. Remember that.' He wanted to kiss her, to wrap her in his arms but she pulled away from him.

'I'll write to you. That's all I can promise,' she said, and then she turned from him and went into the house, leaving him outside in the dark and cold of the November night.

Elizabeth avoided Julius for the whole of her remaining few days in Germany but when they said goodbye, when she solemnly shook his hand in front of all the family, she knew that the precious hour in the summer house would colour her whole life. *Julius, my very first love ... Do you really approve of such obscenities as I have seen? Probably not, but you are German. I love you. I love you Julius and I want to stay with you for ever. Is history repeating itself? Am I copying Aunt Sophie by falling in love with a German as she did? No, of course not. I will never marry you, Julius.* Aloud she said, 'I shall think of you all at Christmas. Have a lovely time. I might come back in the New Year if things are better.' She knew quite certainly that she would not.

As the train pulled out of the station she stood at the door and waved, and as soon as it was safe to cry, tears poured uncontrollably down her cheeks. Would there be a war between her country and theirs? Dear God, not again, not another war.

She sat and thought about all the things that had led to today and the hopeless tangle of their lives, events which had brought two families together in two different countries.

33

Her mother and Aunt Sophie had been inseparable until the unthinkable had happened back in 1919. Sophie had disgraced herself and the family by marrying a German too soon after that other war, the Great War as it was called. As if such a terrible catastrophe could possible warrant the word 'great', she thought. Little contact had been allowed between the sisters for some years, but Sophie's genial and prosperous husband, Heinrich, had gradually been accepted by his English relatives, and when the parents were dead and the children grown a little, the visits had begun.

Elizabeth, an only child, had adored her German cousins from the very first time they met. She loved their sprawling, comfortable house on the outskirts of Berlin with its old-fashioned and faded luxuries and its servants to do all the disagreeable tasks. And there had always been Julius as well, a glamorous two years older, an added bonus. She had idolised Julius. She was never quite sure what his relationship with the family was, but he appeared regularly every holiday time and very occasionally spoke of his mother who lived in Dresden, a town, he informed her, that was outstandingly beautiful. She had once asked him why he visited her aunt and uncle's home so often and he had looked at her with a strange, secret smile on his face and said that it wasn't to be talked about. He had no father, apparently, and Uncle Heinrich appeared to be very fond of him. So the mystery had remained. She had always been glad when he was there.

And now there was the further mystery to add to the other. How could he approve of Hitler's terrifying and dreadful excesses, how could anyone? Had he meant those terrible things he had said? Could she be in love with a Nazi? It was unthinkable.

In the first-class compartment of the half-empty train, she stared at the swiftly passing countryside and remembered the fun of past holidays when they were children. There had been frequent bonfires and picnics in the woods. They had swum in the lake and skated on it in winter beneath a frosty star-filled sky. There was snow such as she seldom saw in England, endless games and, of course, ponies to ride. Finally there had been the growing realisation of what Julius meant to her. Had that really all come to an end?

She arrived in England to a bleak November day, grey and cold, and with the newspapers full of reports of the rising hysteria against Jews in Germany. Every time she read an account of more restrictions and atrocities, the memories of Crystal Night returned, and with them, to haunt her, thoughts of what had gone before, what she now saw as a betrayal of her country as well as of herself and everything in which she believed.

She sometimes recalled too how she had, much earlier, listened to her cousins talking about the rise of Hitler, how she had reacted to the marches, the excitement of a resurgent Germany, and had, to her eternal shame, felt a tingle of elation now and then. It was infectious, this rampant nationalism.

England—December 1938

When she posted the Christmas parcel to her cousins, Elizabeth smiled disarmingly at the lady behind the counter who was staring suspiciously at the address. 'Germany? You got friends there then?'

'Relations actually,' Elizabeth said. 'My aunt and cousins.'

'Hope they're not Jews!' The woman looked at her over ugly, steel-rimmed spectacles.

'No, they're not Jews.'

'That's all right, then.' She stuck a great number of stamps onto the brown paper and dropped the parcel into a box on the floor. 'It's not very nice for Jews now in Germany with old Adolf Hitler on the prowl.'

'No,' said Elizabeth. 'It's not very nice.'

On Christmas Eve, Elizabeth looked bleakly at the sparkling tree which her mother had placed in the sitting room. Its tinsel glittered, reflecting all the colours of the dancing flames, usually a comforting cheering sight, but now yet again reminding her of the broken glass, the terrifying fragments sparkling on the pavement in the lamplight of a Berlin night ... and the little girl in the blue dressing gown.

Sophie Kleist had long ago become reconciled to the frequent presence of Julius in her home. Now that he had left school and was studying in Berlin his visits were shorter, but more frequent. At least her husband had found him a room in the city and she was grateful for that. She could not easily have accepted his permanent residence. Although he was always charming to her, often bringing flowers or a small gift of exquisitely wrapped chocolates, he reminded her constantly, even now, of the existence of Helga, his mother, Heinrich's mistress. For nearly twenty years she had known about Helga, about her husband's visits to Dresden, had smelt the heavy cloying perfume on his clothes, had seen the triumphant, satisfied look in his eyes when he returned. He would always kiss her fondly after these visits, and, just like his bastard son, present her with some expensive gift in compensation.

'I can't imagine how you put up with it,' her sister had said frequently during the early years, and always the answer had been the same. 'Because I love him still, and I love Emmi, Werner and Hans too much. I should lose them, of course, if I left. Heinrich would see to that. And how could I manage all the practical difficulties anyway? Even if there was some way of escaping with them to England he would have followed us, taken them back somehow. I could never have subjected them to so much misery and uncertainty.'

37

So she had stayed in her adopted country, had endured the fact of her husband's infidelity but on one condition only. No one must know. When Julius was old enough to understand the truth, he had been sworn to secrecy. His mother must never come to Berlin. Those wishes had been respected and the family had been told that Julius was a distant cousin, a fatherless orphan whom their father was unofficially adopting. His mother was an invalid it was asserted and was unable to travel. All lies, of course, but they sufficed and Sophie had been able to keep her pride and her self-respect. She sometimes wondered if her children suspected the truth, but if they did they kept their council and nothing was ever said.

Heinrich was a jovial and popular man, an affectionate father and an extremely generous and loving husband. In the great feather bed he made love to Sophie enthusiastically once a week, and, to her own secret mortification, she enjoyed his boisterous attentions. At least he still found her attractive. His mistress couldn't entirely satisfy him. It was a small comfort.

The only other person who knew the facts was, of course, her twin sister. Louise, Elizabeth's mother, had first met Julius when he was about eight years old and she had obviously been suspicious. She had looked at Sophie questioningly, and had quickly guessed the truth. So she had told her sister everything, had talked bitterly of the beautiful Helga von Brandt, the long-time mistress in Dresden. She had confessed to secret tears and anger,

38

especially over the final outrage, the frequent presence in her home of this handsome love-child of her husband's.

Louise had been incredulous at first and had wanted to face her brother-in-law with her indignation and fury, but the child's charm, the father's undoubted charm too, and Sophie's insistence that she had accepted the situation and wanted no showdown, had gradually won. 'It is the German way,' Sophie had said. 'If I want to keep Emmi, Hans and Werner, I must submit.'

The grief and anger of those early years had faded considerably. Sophie seldom cried, seldom felt affronted now. Heinrich's prosperity and loving care for her made up somewhat for the increasingly frequent visits he made to Dresden. She was only pondering on it all afresh because of her niece's hasty departure. She had noticed the way Julius and Elizabeth had looked at each other, had always wanted to be together, preferably alone together, and she feared for both of them. What strange pre-ordained irony had cast these two into this ill-matched love affair? For that was what she feared it was. And why had Elizabeth rushed home so unexpectedly? Could it have been the horrors of *Kristallnacht,* or was there more?

Sophie was in her garden tidying up various shrubs, secateurs in her earth-covered hands and a full wheelbarrow beside her waiting to be taken to the bonfire heap. To work with ordinary, elemental things eased her mind, helped her to sort life out a little when her thoughts were troubled. But now there were other larger problems too. Sometimes she had to remind herself that the dilemmas of her family were as nothing compared to the greater agony of her husband's country. No amount of hard work in garden or house could alleviate the sickening feeling in the pit of her stomach, the certainty that there would soon be a war between England and this Germany which she had come to love.

She looked up at the darkening sky and imagined English bombers flying in anger over Berlin, imagined her own Werner in the *Luftwaffe* flying fighters. Saw Hans in his gloomy uniform. How could she and Heinrich possibly have produced a son who wanted to be in the SS?

And Julius. After all these years she actually admitted some affection for her rival's child, this unacknowledged step-son. He was obviously not a Nazi as he pretended to be. There was always a reluctance in his *Heil Hitlers*, a frown on his handsome face when he heard the fanatical shouts in the streets. Yet perhaps he too wanted a pure, purged Germany? She couldn't be sure. She shuddered for Elizabeth, for herself, and for the Jewish families she knew.

She pushed the wheelbarrow with difficulty over the soft, rain-soaked lawn and tipped the contents onto the heap. Perhaps there would he some winter sunshine tomorrow to dry the branches a little and to bring a morsel of cheer to her spirits and to the grey December garden.

She had no idea how it would all end and suddenly she longed for the hills of Devonshire where she had been brought up, for the wild tors of Dartmoor. She thought of her sister's cottage in its little Dartmoor village. Merricote. She had spent a holiday there years ago. For a few moments of pure fantasy she imagined herself running away to hide beneath its old slate roof, secure from Hitler, from war and strife, from all the traumas of her life, safe within its sturdy stone-walled rooms and in England again. For the first time in many years, Sophie was homesick.

Dresden—1938

Helga von Brandt put the last touches to her Christmas tree. She knew that Julius would be home tomorrow to spend a few days with her. He was a good son. She sighed. It was hard being a mistress, the other woman. She thought of Heinrich and all the years she had been here for him, all the years she had received his largesse, his love, and for what?

This flat was hers. When her parents disowned her because of her affair with Heinrich, he had given her the deeds, so there was security, at least. That, and a small income for life, and her son. She had Julius. He was worth all the suffering. And freedom of course. She had freedom. She was no obedient *Hausfrau,* she hadn't to wash Heinrich's shirts and socks! She laughed to herself, a little hollowly. Perhaps there were a few advantages to being a mistress after all. She wondered what present Heinrich would send her? And what would he give to his English wife? This Sophie whom she had never seen, and whom she often envied with such jealousy and resentment that she felt sometimes it would quite engulf her. Sophie had his name, his other three children, the position, the respectability.

She stood up, brushed bits of tinsel and pine needles from her skirt and said the name to herself, *Sophie Kleist, Sophie Kleist.* She stood in front of the ornately framed mirror and glared at her reflection. Then she said aloud, 'Well, I have kept my family name, the name with the title, von Brandt. I am Helga von Brandt and my son is Julius von Brandt. Much better than just Kleist.'

Julius arrived the following day. He always spent this special time with his mother rather than in Berlin with his father and the family he had come to regard as his own. He knew that Werner, his half-brother, suspected the truth, but he had never voiced his doubts. They were good friends. As for Hans, he was much too taken up with his efforts to be a good member of the party to bother about much else, and Emmi was sweet and innocent, too childlike and trusting to doubt her father's explanation. What about Aunt Sophie? Like Elizabeth he had taken to calling her this when he was quite small, before he knew that Heinrich was his father, and his mother merely the despised mistress.

Then his heart beat more quickly, for his

thoughts turned to Elizabeth and he was filled with despair. She had gone back to England so unexpectedly and with such anger. He still felt guilty for what had happened that afternoon in the summer house as well as for his behaviour in the evening. He should have acted more honourably on both occasions.

In his mother's presence he made a great effort to appear cheerful, tried to make her happy. They had always been close and he watched her as she unwrapped the presents he had brought. Emmi, sweet Emmi, believing the tale that this unknown woman, Julius's mother, was an invalid, had knitted and carefully wrapped an exquisite bed-jacket.

'She must be a kind girl. In other circumstances I should have liked to know her.' Helga held up the lacy garment. 'I shall treasure this, Julius. And I must thank her. I shall write.'

There was perfume from Heinrich, the most expensive, the most exotic available, as always hidden from the rest of the family and passed to Julius surreptitiously just before he left. The present that was openly given was a hamper of food delivered from one of Dresden's most opulent stores.

By the second day of his stay Julius was aware of his mother's frequent puzzled frowns whenever she looked at him. His efforts to keep his unhappiness hidden were obviously not achieving much success. After they had eaten, after the maid who came in each day had cleared away and had left them for the night, they sat either side of the comforting fire and Julius

43

knew that he was about to be questioned. He didn't mind, needed a confidante in fact, and his mother was the only person he really trusted. She would never betray him, never criticise.

'There's something troubling you,' she said. 'I can see it in your eyes. It makes me unhappy too, Julius. Is everything well with your father? You haven't had any disagreements?'

'No, Mother. Nothing like that.' He stared into the glowing coals and was silent for a long time before replying. Then he said slowly, 'You remember the English cousin, Elizabeth?'

His mother nodded. 'A pretty girl. You have often talked of her and I have seen her photograph.'

'I love her. I wish to marry her. We were together when the Jewish shops were attacked. It was the most frightful thing I have ever seen. She went back to England almost immediately.'

There was much more he would have liked to say but Helga leaned forward and touched his hand gently. 'An English girl is a risk, my son, but if you both love each other truly you'll survive the problems.'

He had expected her to remonstrate with him, to tell him that it was impossible.

Instead she said, 'Had you ever thought of going to England while there is still time?'

He stared at her in amazement. It was the very last thing he had thought to hear. He shook his head. 'And desert Germany now when anyone who can still think clearly should be working—' he lowered his voice, '—for the downfall of Hitler?' It was a relief to say it. His mother was the only person to whom he could voice such things.

'That's what I fear most,' she whispered. 'That you might be imprisoned or taken to one of those fearful concentration camps that I've heard about.'

CHAPTER 2

England—January 1939

A new year. Elizabeth glanced at the empty pages of the diary her mother had given her and shivered. She flicked through the pages to August. A baby. Julius's baby! She had never thought it could happen when you only loved someone once, when it was the very first time. It was too awful, too much of a punishment. And, of course, no one must ever know that the father was German. That at least was one thing she could do for this child, keep its origins concealed. Julius must never know either, must never have any claim on his misbegotten offspring.

He had written, of course. In each letter he told her that he loved her and hoped that she would return to Berlin. He asked her forgiveness, and she could only guess that he was referring to his remarks about the Jews. He couldn't write openly of such things for fear of his letters being intercepted. She understood

45

that. He agonised over her sudden return to England and her coldness to him during those last days. But the horror of the night of the broken glass remained with her and her replies so far had been brief. The long letter she wished to send was too difficult to write, and now with this further dramatic and frightening complication to her life she doubted if she could ever bring herself to commit to paper all her deepest feelings.

She told him merely that as it looked very likely that their two countries would soon be at war it would be foolish to make any plans for the future. The words were wrung from her, and every time she took up her pen she felt that she was howling silently inside. What might have been, or might one day be, had little importance now, however. What actually was had vastly more significance.

She knew that she must tell her mother soon about the baby, and she dreaded the telling. Eventually, with much trembling, she made her momentous announcement at breakfast one morning in early January. 'I'm going to have a baby,' she said quickly and without preamble.

Louise Benson looked up from the newspaper, replaced her cup in its saucer with exaggerated care. 'What did you say?' Her voice was cold, full of disbelief.

'A baby. I'm expecting a baby.'

There was a terrible silence in the room, a wall of antagonism and mistrust between the two women.

'Are you quite sure?'

It was not the question that Elizabeth had expected. She nodded. She often thought her mother resembled a cat, not the amiable sort, but more the wild variety ready to scratch and pounce. She felt like the victim, a trembling mouse or terrified bird already disabled and waiting for the final blow.

'My God, I don't believe it,' Louise said. 'After all we've done for you.' Another silence and then, in a strangled voice, 'Who?'

'I can't tell you who.'

They sat looking at each other across the tablecloth, its whiteness perfectly matching the pallor of their frozen faces. The stillness in the room was frightful. Only the clock on the mantelpiece made any sound as it sonorously ticked the moments away.

Then Louise came slowly to life, now seeming more like a programmed mechanical doll. Her eyes and voice were full of fury and distaste. 'I thought you had more sense. I never imagined you could be so stupid. I trusted you.' She clasped her hands tightly together in anger. 'How in God's name are we to tell your father? The shame of it will kill him. He'll insist on knowing who was responsible. You'll have to marry, of course.'

The staccato sentences sounded like gunshot to Elizabeth. She shook her head. 'I can't.'

Fresh alarm spread over her mother's face. 'Not a married man?'

'Please don't ask me. I can't tell you who it was and I definitely cannot marry him.'

'You've been in Berlin of course. It's not one

47

of your cousins? Surely not. That's filthy incest.'
'No.'

Louise threw back her head in sudden triumph. 'Then it must be that boy Julius whom your uncle dotes upon. I never liked him. It takes one bastard to father another!'

There was real venom in her voice and Elizabeth felt her senses reel until she was numb with shock. What was her mother talking about? 'What do you mean?' she managed.

'I've kept my mouth shut until now for the sake of my sister. Her so-happy marriage is a complete lie. Your uncle has a mistress, a woman living in Dresden. Julius is their son and that beast, Heinrich, yes, your dear Uncle Heinrich, insists that Sophie has him in her home for part of every school holiday. It's been going on for years.'

Elizabeth clapped her hand over her mouth in horror. 'Oh no. How frightful. I don't believe it.'

'Well, you had better believe it, my girl, because it's true. Sophie found out just a few months after her marriage, but by then she was expecting Werner and there was nothing, absolutely nothing she could do about it. Our parents were against the marriage in the first place. They wouldn't have had her back here. Later, after they died and she had a little money of her own and some independence, she discovered that she would lose all her three children if she decided to leave Heinrich. She's endured the humiliation ever since.' Louise's lips curled in disgust.

48

Elizabeth, pale and shocked, tried to come to terms with what she had heard, with this frightful new revelation. Things began to fall into place and she was filled with pity for her aunt. She had always liked Aunt Sophie, 'loved' would be the better word, and if she was honest she was more at ease with her than with her own mother. Although they were twins, Louise was cold and distant, while Sophie always seemed to have her arms outstretched ready to hug. And what had she, Elizabeth done? Given herself to the youth who was the cause of her aunt's pain, and she was now, horror of horrors, going to have his baby, thus compounding all the misery of the years of betrayal.

She looked at her mother with tear-filled eyes. 'Perhaps I should get rid of it?'

Surprisingly Louise shook her head. 'No. That would be a sin,' she said piously. 'There are plenty of couples wanting babies. You'll have it in secret and then it must be adopted. We can tell our friends that you've gone away to college. No one need know the truth.' Then, as another thought struck her, she added, 'And you're to say nothing about it having a German father. Adoption might be difficult if that ugly fact is discovered.' Suddenly Louise was her normal organising self again, although her face was still white, her forehead creased in an unpleasant frown. She stood up, folded her napkin and put it neatly on the table. 'Your father's position would be untenable, of course, if any of this should be known in the school. He would be removed from his post immediately. You are to

49

be very careful.' Her eyes swept the comfortable room, the playing fields visible through the long window.

For a second Elizabeth thought again of the golden hour in the summer house. Nothing had mattered then except Julius and their love for each other. Her father's job in this highly respectable English public school had been the last thing on her mind. She was deeply ashamed.

Then she had an idea. 'Could I go to Merricote?' she said tremulously. *Merricote, lovely little Merricote the house in Devon where I could be at peace.* Her father had bought it when he was offered a school house. Some holidays had been spent there, and occasionally Aunt Sophie and the German cousins had come to stay, but never Julius. There were no memories of Julius at Merricote.

Her mother turned a look of pure outrage upon her and she flinched. 'Merricote? What are you thinking about? All the inhabitants of Kellworthy would discover your disgrace in no time at all. You know what a small place it is. I should never lift up my head there again. No, you'll have to go somewhere where we aren't known. There are plenty of establishments around the country for fallen girls like yourself. I'll make discreet enquiries somehow. They'll arrange the adoption and you'll come home afterwards as though nothing had happened.'

Elizabeth shivered. She rose from the table and went to stand with her back to the fire, but there was little heat in it for it had not long been lit.

'Of course, you could be wrong,' her mother said. 'I shall make an appointment with a doctor whom we don't know, and we shall say nothing to your father until it is confirmed.'

'Does he have to know that it's Julius's?'

'Leave that to me. It might be better if he doesn't. He would be so outraged that he might decide to go to Germany and face your uncle.'

'No!' Elizabeth almost shrieked the word. 'They must never find out, especially not Julius.'

Grim-faced Louise nodded. 'You're right for once, I suppose. I don't want anything to hurt my sister. I'll think about it.'

Elizabeth knew that she would have to conform to whatever scheme her mother devised. There was no other way. Rebellion was useless. *In any case, what have I to rebel against?* she asked herself angrily. *I've brought this disaster on myself and I suppose I must consider that I'm lucky to have a mother who'll help me deal with it.*

After her mother had marched from the room Elizabeth continued to stand in front of the uncomforting fire. Adoption! Of course there was no other choice, yet the very word filled her heart with ice. Then her lips set in a determined line. *I don't want this baby,* she told herself firmly. She turned and stared at her reflection in the mirror above the fireplace. She glared at the pale face which stared back at her. *Yes, I do want it. I want to keep it, to tell Julius that I'm having his baby, to marry him.* The conflicting thoughts chased each other through her head and then she spoke aloud as if to give more weight to the statements that she must make herself believe if she was to get through the next terrible months. 'No,' she said. 'This baby will be German and I shall always know it even if no one else does. He'll remind me constantly of *Kristallnacht*. I shall think of the little girl in the blue dressing gown, of you, Julius, and those frightful things you said.'

She had whispered the words and now she firmly closed her mouth again and spoke her thoughts silently once more to her reflection, for they were too awful to voice aloud. *Baby? What baby? This thing you carry is merely an encumbrance. Keep telling yourself that and it will be easier. As Mother said, there are plenty of people waiting to adopt newborn babies, nice little English babies. Born in England, it will be English. There is no question of your keeping it, no question of marrying Julius. He is the enemy now. There's going to be a war.* She gave her image one more withering look, and then strode out of the room, determined to get on with her life whatever frightful decisions her mother might make for her. She would be rid of her burden by August. Very convenient. Maybe she would be able to get a place at university for September.

Berlin—March 1939

'So, she is definitely not coming for Easter?' Julius tried to sound as though it meant little to him.

Sophie looked again at the letter which had just arrived. 'She says that she cannot come. That she is going away to college.'

'Is there an address?'

Sophie glanced up at him in surprise. 'Of course. Just the usual one, the school.'

He could contain his impatience no longer. 'May I read the letter, Aunt Sophie?'

'Certainly.' She passed it to him and he hoped that she had not noticed his eagerness. He carried it to the window and read the loved handwriting, scanned every line for mention of himself, but there was nothing. She had not written to him for many weeks and still he wrote faithfully into the void. He told her of ordinary things mostly, but tried to hint of his hopes for the future, for their future together. He longed to tell her of his other hopes and dreams too, dreams of a Germany free and happy again, with all fear gone from its towns and villages. Sometimes he gave in to his yearning, but always the page ended in the fireplace, its tell-tale words blazing and curling until no censor could decipher any of the forbidden and dangerous dreams.

Sometimes he seemed to feel her with him, in his arms. *I love you, Elizabeth,* he said silently, in English. *Please, understand what I truly am.*

Weston-super-Mare—Spring 1939

There were daffodils along both sides of the circular drive and a great cedar tree dominating the front of the house. *My prison for the next endless months!* Elizabeth saw nothing of the beauty of the old mansion. She merely registered the tiny barred windows, the thick stone walls and the greyness of the sky which completely matched her despair.

The taxi pulled up at the front door and she sat quite still, as though all this was happening in some dream world in which she had no part. Her mother was already out of the vehicle and saying something to the driver before she managed to force her reluctant legs to do her bidding.

'No. Don't wait. I shall walk back to the station.'

The brusque words jerked Elizabeth from her state of non-being. So this was it. She was being dumped here to pay for her sins. That glorious, iniquitous afternoon seemed so long ago now. Berlin had become a distant memory full of conflicting images, excitement, tension, fear and death. When she closed her eyes she could still sometimes see the little girl in the blue dressing gown, the broken glass, the horror of *Kristallnacht*. In her nightmares she heard the screams. And there was Julius too of course. *'Jews, only Jews.'* The words sounded obscene, terrifying. Sometimes, in dreams, she saw him jerk his arm upwards, holding it rigidly in a Nazi salute and she heard him repeating the *Heil Hitler* of the power-crazed crowds. Yet when she awoke, distraught and sweating, she always reminded herself fiercely that it was cousin Hans who frequently made that frightful obeisance,

54

never Julius. Why did she impute these evil things to Julius in her dreams when she had to admit that she had never actually witnessed him make them in reality? Perhaps, she reasoned miserably, it is because I need a reason for my rejection of him and his baby.

Strangely, his letters had stopped coming, and although she was bewildered and dismayed by this, it also strengthened her brave resolutions a little. He had obviously put her right out of his mind. Perhaps he had found someone else, some blue-eyed creature at that precious university of his, a girl with long blonde plaits flowing down her back, the apparent uniform now of all Hitler's precious Aryan maidens! Maidens! Elizabeth frowned, ashamed of her own lost virginity.

The driver took the one small suitcase and grinned at her, and as her mother strode imperiously to the front door he winked at Elizabeth. 'Any time, Miss,' he said. 'Happy to oblige.' He touched his cap, winked again and climbed back into his cab. 'Harry's cabs, always ready!'

Elizabeth watched as he drove out of the gates and she wondered grimly what he meant. Was there some double meaning in his jovial remarks? Were all the inmates of this 'Home for Wayward Girls' somehow debased, easy pickings? She set her lips in a grim line, straightened her back, and glared at the retreating vehicle before picking up her suitcase and going to stand beside her mother at the still firmly shut front door.

In spite of the constraint between them,

Elizabeth was glad of her mother's presence during the first difficult moments. She felt defenceless, a condemned prisoner.

After the seemingly endless formalities had been concluded and various papers signed, Matron delivered her final blow to freedom. 'You will be allowed to receive letters, but they will be opened by myself or one of the staff before they are handed to you, and you must put your own letters for posting in the box in the hall, stamped but unsealed. That is one of our most inviolate rules.' The voice was rigid, severe and there was no smile on the thin lips. 'Your mother can leave now.' She turned to Louise. 'You need not worry, Mrs Benson. Your daughter will be looked after and closely confined here until the baby is six weeks old and we have arranged the adoption. Then she will be allowed to leave.'

Elizabeth counted rapidly in her head. A prisoner until the end of September at the very least! Dear God, how to survive those endless weeks?

For a moment Louise looked slightly taken aback and Elizabeth, noticing the expression on her mother's face, wondered for one brief second if there was to be a last minute reprieve, but no. Louise drew on her gloves. 'Then I shall go, Elizabeth, and I hope you will be a credit to your father and to me, and make up for the unhappiness you have caused us.' She walked to the door which Matron had opened for her. 'I shall visit you in a few weeks' time.'

There was no hug, not even a brief kiss or

a smile. Elizabeth stood motionless until she had gone, then she retrieved her suitcase and followed the girl who had been summoned to take her to the common room where she must wait for further instructions.

Meanwhile her mother walked slowly down one side of the circular drive and for a moment wondered if she had done the right thing. But of course she had, and if all those letters from that contemptible Julius von-something-or-other were anything to go by, not before time too. She wished he would stop writing. It had been a bit disconcerting, intercepting the post every day before Elizabeth could get her hands on it. That was ever since she'd known about the baby of course. Unprincipled youngsters who behaved in such a disreputable fashion couldn't be allowed the freedom to correspond any more. Well, there wouldn't be any problem now. At first she had been inclined to burn them, but that hadn't seemed right somehow. She was superstitious and had heard that to burn letters brought ill luck. So what to do with the things? Bury them? They might, horror of horrors, be found by the school gardener.

In the end she decided that they would all go under the floorboards at Merricote. The very next time she went there she would hide them properly and forever. Someone might find them one day, of course, in the distant future, but it wouldn't matter then, and at least she would not have brought bad luck on herself by burning them. She knew just the place.

Julius would have to stop writing soon anyway.

There was going to be a war with Germany and letters wouldn't be allowed. No fear of him coming here either. That had been one thing she had dreaded. Sad about poor Sophie, of course, being in an enemy country, but she'd made her bed by marrying that German scoundrel, Heinrich. She'd just have to go on lying on it.

In keeping the letters from Elizabeth, Louise decided that she had probably saved her daughter from a similar fate. And with Heinrich's bastard son, of all people!

With all her remaining doubts banished, and with a self-righteous glow, Louise walked briskly back to the railway station and took the next train to Bristol. By the time she was once more in the respectable security of her husband's school she had assured herself that she had made absolutely the right decisions about everything.

Isobel MacDonald was jolly, with sparkling brown eyes. There was a brightness about her, and a sense of mischief too, that Elizabeth found intriguing in this dismal place.

'Welcome to Eldorado,' she said.

Elizabeth tried to smile. 'Thanks. I believe we're in the same room.'

'Along with ten others. And silence after ten o'clock, so make the most of now.'

It was the evening of the first day and the first chance Elizabeth had found to speak at length to any of her fellow inmates. One hour of recreation was allowed from eight until nine.

The room was bare of ornament. Chairs

were set uncompromisingly around the walls and a long, scrubbed wooden table dominated the centre. Some books and a few religious magazines had been placed upon it. 'For our improvement and edification,' Isobel said. 'I'd rather knit.' She glanced down at the piece of work in her hands and shrugged her shoulders. 'Blue, of course,' she said. 'If it's a girl it's to be adopted. A boy we keep! Not fair, but that's life. How about you?'

Elizabeth immediately liked Isobel. Perhaps they would be friends. She needed a friend. 'Adopted, whichever it is,' she replied. 'I want to forget as soon as I can.'

'Difficult, I believe. We aren't allowed to talk to the girls who've already produced. They live in the other wing, but I've seen a few tears now and then.' Isobel came to the end of a row, put her knitting down in her lap and consulted her much thumbed pattern. After some counting and concentrated frowns she started a new line and looked up. 'Want to talk? It helps sometimes.'

Elizabeth nodded bleakly. 'Perhaps.'

'The usual I suppose? Parents ashamed and all that?'

'Absolutely horrified. My father teaches in a boys' school. You can just imagine the outrage and disgrace, can't you!'

'One of the boys, was it?'

Elizabeth wanted to laugh hysterically. 'No. Not one of the boys. Someone I shall never see again and must put out of my mind.' *Why am I telling such lies? I long for Julius every night of my*

59

life, but a different Julius, an English Julius. An impossibly stupid dream. She got up and went to the table, selected a copy of *The Christian Herald* and took it back to her seat. 'I'd better look as though I'm doing something. I'll never want to knit baby clothes.'

'Sorry, old thing. They'll force you to, I'm afraid. We have to make a complete layette, everything.'

'Even if it's to be adopted?'

' 'Fraid so. That's the rules.'

'Never.' Elizabeth shook her head. 'I couldn't. I try not to think of it as a person, just as something I have to get rid of.'

'Why didn't you then?'

'Oh, not like that, not kill it. Just get rid of it. Give it to someone who wants a baby.' Recently she had begun to feel tiny tell-tale movements inside her body. They disconcerted her, and when she said or thought any uncaring thing about her child she felt rebuked. It seemed to her as though the baby was aware of its ultimate rejection, could hear her words, understand her thoughts. She told herself that this couldn't possibly be, was quite fanciful, yet at these moments her guilt was always renewed. 'Tell me about this place,' she said quickly to her new friend, trying to change the subject. 'And about yourself.'

'Nothing very exciting about me.' Isobel smiled. 'My parents live in Yorkshire, have a big house, servants. I "came out" last year, did the round of social things, was presented and all that. Then I fell in love with someone

60

quite unsuitable, forgot that I should always say "No", and the result you see before you.' She scowled at her bulging stomach. 'And before you ask, he's married.'

Elizabeth had guessed that this girl was somewhat different from most of the others. Her cultured voice betrayed her. 'Why did your parents send you here?'

'The usual reasons. They wanted somewhere as far away as possible. Somerset seemed a good choice.'

'Yet they're going to take the baby?'

'Not as mine of course. I haven't any brothers and the estate is entailed. It must go to a male heir. Unfair again. My mother intends to say he's hers. I've no idea how they'll manage the subterfuge. They don't take me into their confidence. Father was a barrister before he inherited, though, and anything he wants he usually gets.' There was an edge of bitterness to her voice and Elizabeth felt the beginnings of sympathy.

'But how will you feel, knowing he's yours and not being able to ...?'

'Cuddle him, feed him?' She shrugged her shoulders again. 'I don't know. He'll be my little brother. I'll go away, probably. Get married. Have some more babies one day.'

'I don't think I could do that.'

'No choice, absolutely no choice.'

For a time they were silent and Elizabeth disconsolately turned the pages of the magazine and stared at the advertisements for boot polish, the latest gas cookers, and for Pear's soap to keep your complexion baby-soft. *Baby-soft! No, please no. Don't let me think about the softness of babies!* She frowned angrily at the badly-drawn likenesses of the slim, happy-looking girls who were acclaiming the benefits of all these desirable things. They looked as though nothing could disturb their tranquillity and poise.

Isobel glanced across at the magazine and grinned. 'Just let them have a few weeks in this place,' she said. 'They wouldn't look so pleased with life.'

'What's it really like here? Is everything as bad as it looks?' Elizabeth hoped desperately for a denial, for some shred of cheer.

'Worse! What do you want to know?'

'Anything.'

'Right, then. It's a sort of cross between a convent and a prison. We get up at five-thirty. You'll be given a job first thing tomorrow. I started with responsibility for cleaning the grates out, laying the new fire, fetching in the coal. Never done such things in my life. They had to teach me how to make paper sticks. Can you make paper sticks?'

Elizabeth shook her head. 'The school servants did all that.'

'Well, you take a sheet of newspaper, roll it up tightly like a long pointer thing, then twist it round and round so that it stays put. You lay about four of those in the grate, put a few real bits of wood next, then small pieces of coal on top. After that you pray that it'll catch.'

'You do that every morning?'

'Nope. Not now. Matron liked my patrician

tones.' She laughed again. 'I was chosen for the most honoured accolade. You now see beside you the top personal maid of Mere House. I'm Matron's special servant. I have to look after her clothes, her room, carry up her food and do all the other things that she deems beneath her. It sounds easy but believe me, I'd go back to doing the fires any day.'

Their conversation was cut short by the strident ringing of a bell.

'Supper now, bread and jam and a cup of tea, then prayers.' Isobel rolled up her ball of wool and stuck the needles through it. 'This is where we have to cleanse our souls yet again. We're scum, my dear Elizabeth, absolute scum. We have to atone every evening!'

Elizabeth stared at her new friend, then rose, put her magazine back on the table and wondered how on earth she was to survive the next five months.

"My Dear Elizabeth,

I hope you are well, as we are here. We heard today that final plans for the evacuation have been made. The whole school, lock, stock and barrel, is to move next month to a country house in deepest Wales. What a place to choose! I dread it but I suppose that we have to make sacrifices now that war looks certain. Of course it means that you'll be on your own more or less. Once we've left here it will be a long way to visit.

Under the circumstances I think that when your 'trouble' is over you had better consider finding a job instead of trying to get a place at University or coming to us to live again. Everything will be at sixes and sevens both here and in the new accommodation and I've no idea at all what amount of space we'll have. We probably won't be able to give you much help financially either, although of course we'll do our best. In the last war women were needed for all sorts of work and I suppose it will be the same now. How about working on a farm? That might suit you. You always liked animals and you'd get board and lodging.

I'll fit in a visit before we leave here and we'll talk about arrangements then.

Your loving mother,
Louise Benson."

Elizabeth's hand shook with suppressed rage as she read the letter for the second time. *And why does she have to sign herself, Louise Benson, as if I had forgotten my own mother's name?* She stuffed the offensive piece of paper into her apron pocket. *My 'trouble'! That's what this baby is to her, to me, to everyone.* She felt a sudden stab of pity for her baby, rejected even by its grandmother. Grandmother! Elizabeth felt a glimmer of sarcastic amusement at the picture this word evoked. Then she took the letter out again, tore it into shreds, added them to the dustpan that lay on the ground at her feet, and angrily continued sweeping the yard, her first job of the weary day.

Visitors were allowed once a month and then only if vetted and approved by Matron. No men friends. Even fathers were frowned upon, as if the whole male sex was suspect.

'Not exactly suspect,' Isobel said one afternoon when she and Elizabeth were lying on their beds during the hour of bedrest which was obligatory during the last two months of pregnancy. 'I think it's more that we are the temptresses and might corrupt their pure little minds.'

'Looking like this!' Elizabeth glanced at the ungainly mound beneath the quilt. 'I feel I'll never be attractive again.'

'Rubbish. I'm going to get out of here and tempt them all I can and then say no at the last minute, make them suffer a bit.' Isobel laughed grimly. 'Until I find Mr Right of course. Men get off scot-free and we are labelled the seductresses and sinners. Not only do we have to bear months of hell in this hideous place, but all the blame is reckoned to be ours. Quite monstrous. Most girls here have been betrayed and left in the lurch by a member of the superior and self-satisfied male sex.' Her voice was full of contempt.

Elizabeth's bed was at the end of the row and she turned her face to the wall, feeling salty tears on her cheeks. There was still no word from Julius. Was he like all the rest of them? Had he really deserted her? Yet she reminded herself that the decision to part had been hers alone. She was assailed by a moment of doubt but then she remembered the strutting confidence of the roaring Berlin mobs, the hideous Nazi flag, the fear in the streets, and she knew that she had, after all, made the right decision. She could never have stayed, never have become a *Hausfrau* in Hitler's Germany.

Sometimes, when in sleep, she heard the screams of *Kristallnacht*, felt the terror, and she had called out in German. The first time she did this Isobel had told her the next day, had whispered that she shouldn't speak German or she might be suspected of being a spy. 'You could be put in an internment camp for enemy aliens!' she had said dramatically.

'I'm as English as you are.' Elizabeth was indignant, but slightly fearful also, and her face had been suffused with guilty colour as she thought of the German blood that must run somehow in her body, in her baby's body, mingling with her pure English heritage, and dear God, with that trace of Jewish blood bequeathed from her father's mother. What was she handing on to this small creature whom she was to bring into the world? A battlefield? And who really was Julius? What sort of man lived behind those handsome German features? What kind of father had she given to her unborn child?

'Why do you speak German?' Isobel had asked. 'And so fluently too. At least it sounds fluent to me.' She had stared at her almost suspiciously.

'I have German cousins,' Elizabeth replied. 'My mother's sister married a German. I used to spend my holidays with them in Berlin.'

'Better keep quiet about it,' Isobel advised sternly. 'German sounds a bit like Dutch if you don't know either language, though. I shouldn't think anyone here is clever enough to speak anything but dear old English.' She laughed disparagingly. 'Best say that it's Dutch if you must shout out in your sleep.'

CHAPTER 3

England—Summer 1939

When the roses were in full bloom and the water-lilies were opening their waxen flowers on the fish pond behind the house, Isobel's baby son was born. Elizabeth noticed the roses particularly because she had asked if she could take a few buds to her friend in hospital. The request was firmly refused. No fraternisation whatsoever was allowed between those who were still waiting for their babies and the girls who had already produced. No reason was given for this strange regulation, but there was no way to break the rules. As soon as Isobel returned she was whisked straight to the annexe across the road.

So it was that Elizabeth had no idea what to expect, and when the first colicky pains seized her one night she wondered what she had been eating. She lay in her hard, unyielding bed clutching the blanket in rigid hands and trying not to cry out. She groped her way downstairs and out into the privy in the yard but no relief was to be found there. By morning she was convinced she was about to die, but Matron, summoned by one of the other girls, took one look at her and grinned. 'This is what it all comes to, my girl,' she said, gloating evilly. 'It'll teach you not to be so easy next time.'

In the cottage hospital just up the road she was bidden to have a bath. *A bath? How can I have a bath in this state with these searing pains ripping my body apart every few minutes?* But she did as she was told, lay in the steaming water and, to her surprise, was comforted a little. She was then given a flowing white gown open down the back and a label was fastened around her wrist.

After that she was told to climb onto a high bed and she was left completely alone with only her ignorance, pain and terror for company. The day passed in a confusion of alien sights and sounds and then the nightmare hours of darkness followed when she seemed to float in and out of consciousness, aware only of the fierce agony of her body.

'Bear down. Push.' The voices came from a long distance, from a tunnel of darkness. *What are they talking about?* She could not recognise her own voice or the screams that she uttered. *Who is making those frightful noises?*

Then there was another sound. She came from the depths of horror to the height of ecstasy in one glorious moment. Her body was at peace and they were offering her a cup of tea.

A cup of tea? Gentle arms helped her to sit up a little and she saw a small, angry face. It was all she could see in the confining wraps. They held the shawl closer, placed the little wrinkled scrap near. She felt the tiny hand, fingers so small, and she was filled with a rush of protective love. No one told her about the pain and no one told her about the glory either. But it was only fleeting. She turned her head away. 'A little girl,' they said. 'You have a lovely little girl.'

Every day in hospital Elizabeth fought against loving her child. *She is German, her father is German, soon to be the enemy. His blood is in her veins. She is to be called Kristall because I never want to forget that fact, or the day when Julius betrayed me and everything I hold dear. It will help when the child must be given away.*

'Kristall? How do you spell it?' The nurse looked puzzled. 'It's a pretty name, but unusual.'

'It's spelt K-R-I-S-T-A-L-L,' Elizabeth said.

'But I thought it was C-R-Y-S-T-A-L like my mum's best set of cut-glass fruit bowls?'

'That's the English spelling.'

'Then what's the other?'

'It's ... it's Dutch,' she lied. 'Dutch for glass.'

The girl looked bemused. 'Oh well, you can always call her Chrissy, I suppose. My little sister's Chrissy, short for Christobel. Nice name, Christobel. Why don't you call her that?'

Elizabeth turned away and sighed. The baby was pulling at her breast, the milk flowing satisfactorily into the tiny mouth and she was filled with the most conflicting emotions she had ever known. It was her mind that was now a battlefield. *I mustn't love this child. I have to give her up to strangers. Kristall! What does it matter what I call her? They'll change it. She'll be Mary or Jennifer or Pamela. To me she will eventually become just a memory, a memory that will bring back thoughts of a man I want to forget and a golden afternoon in a Berlin garden. An afternoon followed by an evening of terror, and an image that will not go away. Another little girl, a terrified child in a blue dressing gown.*

The golden days of summer, a scorching summer such as the people of Weston seldom beheld, and the beach was crowded with trippers making the most of the last few weeks of peace. Pathetic donkeys worked overtime giving rides to excited children and hefty adults, and the tradesmen rubbed their hands with glee at the profits they were making from their candy floss and toffee apples.

But the weather only brought the girls of Mere House intense discomfort. Their pregnancies became more unendurable, the time spent in the airless ward of the local cottage hospital seemed unbearable, and their babies were over-dressed, over-heated and fretful. One of the few bonuses of the relentless heat was that, once back in the dubious comfort of the home with the care of their babies entirely in their hands, the endless washing could be dried outside. There were no grates to be cleaned or fires to be laid

70

either, apart from the enormous kitchen range of course. This hungry monster was always belching forth unwelcome warmth and fumes and there was a strict rota of slaves, as they called themselves, to minister to its needs.

Most of the girls were so caught up with their duties and their own predicament that they failed to notice the preparations for war going on steadily all around them. A few locals were digging holes in the hard, sun-baked earth of their gardens for air-raid shelters and some of the older inhabitants gossiped and complained to each other constantly about *them Germans who was going to upset the apple cart all over again, as if once wasn't enough.*

Sometimes Elizabeth would overhear some such remark or see the preparations and then she would look at her baby with increased guilt and sorrow. She would think of Germany and the family she loved, Aunt Sophie especially. Then she would try to blank the vivid picture of Julius from her mind yet again. For Germany *was* Julius. In her thoughts she could never disentangle him from his background however hard she tried.

But there were other things that disturbed her too. Isobel's baby had been born just three weeks before Kristall and she could see her friend's devotion to him growing deeper day by day, and with it her misery.

'I shall have some more babies,' Isobel said one day as she cleaned the exquisitely rounded bottom of her little son. 'I shall marry one day and have lots of babies like I told you. I've discovered that I ...' She paused. 'Well it was pretty awful having him, but they say it's a piece of cake the second and third times.' Her voice was tight, full of emotion, and suppressed anger too. 'I think I'm a natural mum. Sounds soppy, but I really like babies.'

Elizabeth thought of her own hours of ignorance and agony. She certainly didn't intend to repeat the experience in a hurry. She said, 'Why didn't they warn us? About the pain and all that?'

'And have us worrying our heads off for months? No. I think I preferred to remain in ignorance. Anyway, isn't he worth it?' She tucked the thick towelling nappy around the baby's chubby legs and bent to kiss him.

Elizabeth watched her grimly. Her own baby was asleep in the austere room they called the nursery. 'You're getting too fond of him!'

'Yes. *Getting fond* isn't quite right. I adored him the moment they gave him to me.'

'You're not supposed to.'

'He'll be my little brother when I get home. I suppose sisters can love baby brothers. Do you know what my mother has done?'

Elizabeth shook her head.

'Worn some padding inside her clothes. I told you that she intends to pass him off as hers, but somehow I never thought she'd go that far. They'll adopt him officially of course, but as far as the servants and neighbours and even most of the relatives are concerned, he's her baby.'

'I don't believe it, about the padding I mean.'

'True. It's absolutely true. I'm sworn to secrecy. Now, of course, I've told you. You could blackmail us!' She attempted a laugh. However serious the moment Isobel could usually manage some humour.

'Right-ho. I'll remember that when I'm broke!' Elizabeth tried to match the jocular tones. Then more thoughtfully, and suddenly pitying herself, she said, 'You don't have to give him up like I do, though.'

'That's where you're wrong, my dear Elizabeth. My mother won't allow me to touch him when we go home. She has said as much. There'll be a nanny, of course.' Isobel carefully fixed the nappy pin, pulled the winceyette nightgown down and wrapped the baby in his shawl. 'Back to the nursery then, my lad,' she said. She cradled him closely in her arms and Elizabeth saw tears in her eyes. She immediately felt her own eyes filling too in sympathy, and with their shared misery.

With every day that passed Elizabeth felt the bond between herself and her child deepening. The baby had Julius's blond curls and bright blue eyes. She was reminded of him whenever she bathed or fed this tiny scrap, this miniature feminine version of the man she still loved. She tried to tell herself firmly that she would be glad when the adoptive parents arrived, would welcome the day when she handed the baby over. Perhaps then she could lay the memories of Julius to rest forever and start a new life.

Every minute of the day was busy now and

she was glad of this. There was no afternoon rest, no hour to lie on the bed and think, and although her weary body longed for relaxation, she knew that to keep busy was the best remedy for her increasing anguish.

There was so much washing, vast quantities of it, and all to be done by hand, the nappies must be soaked and then boiled, swilled many times, put through the mangle and finally hung out to dry on one of the numerous washing lines at the back of the house. There was an endless mound of clothes and bedding too, for every time the baby was wet the cot sheet and vest must be changed. And there were four-hourly feeds, rigidly kept, with no deviation allowed. If a baby awoke before the set time he would have to cry miserably, setting all the others off in a discordant cacophony of sound.

'Why don't you keep her?' Isobel asked one night when the ten o'clock feed had just been completed, and the babies put back in their cots.

'How on earth could I manage that? I need to earn a living, and my parents would disown me completely.'

'You might be able to get a job as housekeeper or something,' Isobel said vaguely. 'I've heard that it can be done now and then.'

Elizabeth flopped on her bed and shook her head. 'Don't imagine I haven't thought about it, but no. It's quite impossible. Anyway, I want to forget the past completely, make a clean break.'

Isobel looked at her sadly. 'Forget her father,

you mean, don't you? You never talk about him. I'm not sure that's the best way to forget. It just buries all the hurt. Sometimes it's better to tell someone, get it all out. Does he know he has a daughter?'

Elizabeth gritted her teeth. 'No, and he never will,' she declared. 'He has no part in my life any more and I shall never see him again. Please God, Kristall will never know anything of him either.'

'Sorry, old thing. I shouldn't have asked.' Isobel sounded contrite. 'Has Matron said anything about prospective—'

'Parents for Kristall?' Elizabeth cut in. 'Yes, as a matter of fact she has, just this afternoon. That's why I'm so weepy and edgy.' She looked steadily down into her lap unwilling to meet her friend's eyes. 'Eminently suitable, apparently.'

Brenda Sawyer was bubbling with excitement. This was the day she had been longing for. The letter had come at last. There was a suitable baby ready for them. Her arms wouldn't be empty any more. Not her own baby, of course, but that was of little consequence now. She would be a mother. Hopefully there would be no more contempt from her neighbours and relations, no more pitying remarks and glances from her friends. The splendid pram in the front room would have an occupant, the vast quantity of pink baby clothes she had knitted over the long, weary months of waiting would be seen fluttering from the clothes line.

They had specified a girl right from the

75

beginning. She couldn't contemplate bringing up a noisy, boisterous little boy. David hadn't been so sure about this, but she had overruled him. 'It must be a girl,' she'd said firmly. 'A girl or nothing.'

'We wouldn't have had a choice if ...' He got no further. She had frowned at him severely.

'A boy of our own would have been different,' she had said. 'But if it has to be a little stranger, then it must be a girl.'

And now there was a baby girl waiting for them. Brenda looked at the letter again. Would they come next Sunday at four o'clock to see her? If they liked what they saw they could take her immediately. The mother was a pleasant girl, the letter continued, well-educated and well-spoken. She had refused to disclose the name or any details about the father but it could be reasonably assumed that he was respectable and from the upper classes.

With those assurances comfortably in place Brenda and David had no misgivings. David spent much time on the Saturday servicing his motor car. He had saved some petrol for this important journey. He filled the tank and put a can in the back in case of need. When he had finished Brenda cleaned the inside. 'Got to have everything spick and span for our daughter,' she said.

'Decided on a name yet?' David asked as they drank much needed cups of tea after their labours.

'I'll read you the list again.' Brenda fetched a card from her handbag. 'I keep adding to it, but nothing takes my fancy.'

'I like Margaret,' David said. 'Nice and plain and ordinary.'

Brenda frowned and chewed the end of her pencil. 'Good enough for royalty, but the princess is always called Margaret-Rose, and that's too much of a mouthful.'

'What about Dorothy after my mother?'

'No fear.' This spoken with feeling. 'Let's just wait and see what her ... let's see what they call her already.' She had been about to say, *her mother*, but those two words stuck in her throat. She, Brenda Sawyer, was the mother. She didn't want to acknowledge any other.

Elizabeth packed Kristall's clothes, all carefully washed and ironed, into the paper carrier bag that had been given to her. There was a shoe-box provided as well for the special things. 'That's for baby to have when she's grown a bit,' Matron said. 'If her new mummy and daddy allow it, of course.'

'What should I put in?' Elizabeth opened the box and stared at the tissue paper that had enclosed a pair of someone's flat sensible shoes. There was a little picture of them on the outside. She tore at it distractedly.

'Something you want to give her. No photographs or messages of course, but a gift perhaps for when she's older, and the best little garment you've made.'

Elizabeth finished tearing off the label and then sat down and stared at the empty box for some time. When she was alone she took the silver bracelet that she always wore, held it in the palm of her hand, ran her fingers around its shining tracery of leaves and then placed it in an envelope. On the outside she wrote, *For Kristall when she is grown.* She laid it reverently at the bottom of the box and added two lace-trimmed handkerchiefs. Julius had given her the bracelet and inside was engraved her name and his and the date: 25/12/37. And also in smaller letters the precious message, *Ich liebe dich.* In parting with this symbol of their love she felt that she was acknowledging the ending of it. Perhaps one day their daughter would read those words, *I love you,* and would know that her parents had loved each other, that she was not the result of some casual and uncaring union.

In giving this gift she was assuaging her guilt a little, for it was a symbol of the past that she treasured deeply. She remembered receiving it. Julius always spent Christmas in Dresden with his mother and she had been in England when she had opened this special present. She recalled that moment so clearly now. As soon as she had seen the words she had quickly slipped the bracelet onto her wrist so that her mother should not see. It had never left her arm since that time, until now, until she placed it in the box for Julius's daughter. Perhaps it was at that moment nearly two years ago, she reflected, that her feelings for Julius had begun to change from the gentle sisterly affection that she felt for all her German family into something more, a love that was to have its flowering a year later, and its final fruition in the birth of this baby whom she was so soon to give up, Kristall whom she had vowed not to love, and whom she now adored.

Her final gift to her daughter was the christening gown that she had bought and painstakingly embroidered. It was a beautiful thing that she had found in a second-hand shop in the town. She had washed it carefully, and then added her own personal touch, a pattern that she had worked out first on paper and then transferred to the delicate fabric, a letter J interwoven with an E. Her name and that of Julius, entwined for the last time. She had taken a perverse pleasure in this labour of love, for as such she saw it, but tears had frequently fallen onto the tiny stitches, and when it was completed she had washed the little garment again, ironed it with meticulous care, and then folded it so that the golden thread that she had used was the first thing to be seen when the tissue paper was unwrapped.

She had kept the garment carefully hidden while she worked upon it. It was a complete denial of everything that she had tried to believe, everything that she had declared to Isobel and to herself. *Why am I doing such a sentimental thing?* she had asked herself, and then supplied the answer. *To expunge my feelings of guilt, of course.*

And now, as she packed the box, Elizabeth derived a further small grain of comfort from what she had done. Julius would never know that he had a daughter, Kristall would never know anything of Julius, but his initial on the gown, and the bracelet that had been his gift were tokens of love between the three of them. *Even if she never has these things, never sees them, the giving of them makes me feel better. I can think of her wearing her father's bracelet one day, imagine it on her arm, and it's a link between the three of us.*

Sunday morning was the first Sunday of October, a day of autumn sunshine, leaves just beginning to turn, and yesterday's papers telling of thousands more conscripts called up, but Elizabeth was aware of none of those things. This was her terrible day, the day she knew she would remember with guilt and remorse for the rest of her life.

She was given her instructions after breakfast. The last feed was to be at two o'clock. After that Kristall was to be dressed in her prettiest dress, placed in the cot in the special reception room, and left.

The fact that four weeks ago war had come officially to England, that Germany was now the enemy and that Julius was the personification of that conflict, made little difference to Elizabeth. Since she had been here in this desolate place, her own unhappiness had prevailed over any feelings of patriotism or real interest in what was happening in the world outside. The events of the past weeks had merely strengthened her resolve never to say anything that might reveal her baby's German blood. Yet she still loved Julius, still, to her own shame yearned for him while despising all that he stood for.

'They are arriving around tea-time.' Elizabeth

heard the words through a cloud of misery.

'Must I meet them?' She stared at Matron who was sitting impassively behind her large desk, the very picture of starched and insensitive officialdom.

'Not unless they especially request it.'

'Are they ... are they likely to do that? I don't think I could bear it.'

'You are to remain in the adjoining room until they have gone.'

This was the ultimate cruelty and Elizabeth wanted to pick up the heavy inkwell that was within a hand's reach and throw it at the woman, wanted to run to the nursery, snatch Kristall from her cot and escape into the bright October day, into freedom and peace.

Peace? There was no peace. She stood quite still, fists bunched, teeth clenched, and tried to assume some control.

'I know how you must feel, but it is for the best. We have chosen the new parents very carefully. Your baby will have a good life. The husband has an important job at the Bristol Aeroplane Company and so won't have to join up. They have a pleasant little house, a good income, and the wife longs for a baby.'

Still Elizabeth did not speak. All her powers of logical thought and movement appeared to have deserted her. She was in some sort of frightful vacuum or dream.

'Your mother is coming for you tomorrow morning. You will be able to start life afresh without anyone knowing of your wrongdoing. Meanwhile, I must ask you to sign this form.'

The voice was a little kinder but still firm, a voice that was used to obedience.

Elizabeth glanced at it, couldn't read a word for the tears which blurred her vision, then she turned and groped her way to the door, walked along the corridor to the nursery and entered, brushed her tears away angrily and looked at the row of austere little cots. Entry here was forbidden except at feeding and changing times but she went straight to her own sleeping child and knelt on the floor beside her. She gazed at the baby, at the fuzz of fair hair, at the delicate features and tiny fingers, and tearless now, tried to imprint every detail onto her anguished mind.

'Another half an hour to go before feeding. You should not be here. You will disturb the babies.'

Elizabeth stood up, looked disdainfully at the nurse in charge, picked Kristall from her cot and marched towards the door. But the woman was quicker. She shot across the room barring her way. They stood glaring at each other.

'You bloody well won't keep me from my own child.' Elizabeth had never used a swear word before in her life and colour rushed to her face. She felt a surge of triumph, but it was quickly extinguished. Kristall opened her eyes, stared at her mother and her tiny face puckered in distress. She started to wail and Elizabeth's distraught mind imagined sudden hostility in the baby features.

'There you are. You've upset her.'

Defeated Elizabeth slumped down on one of the nursing chairs that stood in regimented lines around the walls of the room. She cradled the baby lovingly in her arms, rocked her gently but the wails increased in volume until, dismayed, she wanted to shake her instead.

'Feed her then,' the nurse said impatiently. 'For goodness' sake shut her up before all the others start. As it's your last afternoon I'll make an exception.'

Elizabeth undid her bodice and pressed the baby's angry mouth to her breast and after a time, as the milk flowed, a look of contentment took the place of distress and Elizabeth began to relax a little. But when the baby was replete she was filled with dread and terror. This was the last feed, the very end! How could she do it? How in God's name could she give her precious child away for ever?

'When you've washed and changed baby you must go to the clinic and get yourself bound up, and you mustn't drink any liquids for the rest of the day.' The words were cold, decisive, brooking no argument, allowing no emotion. Robot-like Elizabeth obeyed. She had been warned about this last frightful procedure. Breasts that were full and yearning for a tiny suckling mouth were agonizingly painful, sometimes for days. It made the parting a thousand times more fraught.

Just before four o'clock she returned to the nursery, dressed Kristall in her prettiest frock, tied a pink ribbon around the shoe-box, and placed baby, box and bag of clothes in the special cot in the reception room. She kissed the tiny face and walked rigidly out of the room. *I am walking away from my baby for ever and I am doing it for her, for her, for her. For myself as well, and for Julius.*

'She's beautiful,' Brenda Sawyer said. 'Absolutely beautiful.' She turned to her husband. 'Don't you think so, David?'

'Yes, my dear. Whatever you say.'

'But look, look at her. She's like me. She's fair. She's our baby, our own dear little baby.'

'The mother has to sign the forms of course,' Matron said discouragingly. 'She won't be your baby officially until that's been done.'

Brenda brushed the unwelcome words aside. 'But of course she'll do that, especially if you tell her how absolutely perfect we are for each other, what a good home the baby'll have.'

'I have already done that.'

'What a strange name.' Brenda glanced at the words that Elizabeth had written on the lid of the shoe-box. 'Kristall. I like it, actually.'

'We haven't decided on a name yet.' David sounded apologetic as if their failure to choose a name somehow discredited them as parents.

'How about keeping Kristall, dear? It's nice. Funny spelling though. Kristall with a "K". It means good quality glass, doesn't it? You know, the cut kind.'

David nodded. 'Yes. A pretty name. We couldn't do better than that.'

'Much classier than Margaret in spite of

the princess being Margaret-Rose. Can I pick her up?'

Matron nodded. 'Of course. But first do you want to see the mother?'

Brenda had been bending over the cot, her finger clutched in the baby's tiny fist. She disentangled herself and stood up. 'Most definitely not. I am her mother now.' Then, as an afterthought, 'And please, Matron, do not tell the girl that we intend to use the name Kristall. You never know, it might lead to her finding us. Tell her that ... that it will probably be Dorothy, after my mother-in-law.'

'No need to say anything at all,' Matron said.

Elizabeth, in the adjoining room heard only a buzz of voices, no distinct words. The walls of the old house were thick, the doors solid mahogany. She sat quite motionless in the armchair provided for this very purpose and twisted her handkerchief between her anguished fingers. How much distress had these walls witnessed? What unhappy ghosts haunted this room?

She heard footsteps in the corridor outside and still she sat frozen in hopeless immobility. Then there was the sound of tyres on gravel, a car going down the drive, and she was alone, quite alone, with all of her life stretching ahead, empty and futile. She had turned her back on the man she loved and given her baby away and her own mother was coming for her tomorrow.

CHAPTER 4

Germany—October 1939

'England will soon fall or capitulate. You can be sure of that.' Hans had just come in from a party meeting and he was glowing with well-being and enthusiasm.

'Perhaps.' Julius looked up from the newspaper. 'They haven't been invaded or beaten in any war since 1066, though. It might not be such an easy walk-over as you imagine.'

'Rubbish. They're not prepared and their leader's a blockhead. We'll be in London in no time.' Hans grinned at Julius. 'If the *Führer* had been at the helm the last time we shouldn't have lost, shouldn't have been so humiliated. Think what he's done for Germany since he came to power.'

Julius thought. He thought of *Kristallnacht*, he thought of the little girl in the blue dressing gown, the child he had tried to save and then denounced on that terrible night. He thought of Elizabeth in England, and now that war had been declared between Britain and Germany, as inaccessible to him as the sun and the moon.

Sometimes, in moments of despair, he wondered why he hadn't taken his mother's advice last Christmas to go to England while there was still time. But that was not an option

86

now. Even if he had gone, he mused, he would probably have been shut away as an enemy alien and suspected of being a spy! That would have been the final irony!

No, Elizabeth was far better off without him. Before September there had been letters from her mother to Aunt Sophie. From these he had learned that she had a place at college, and there were hints of a new romantic attachment too. And all his letters to her had remained unanswered. That could only mean that she wished to finish with him for ever, despised him totally. He clenched his fists in frustration and wondered how he was to manage his life in the coming months, how to put Elizabeth out of his mind, and also how to avoid fighting for the Fatherland and the cause he didn't believe in.

'The *Führer* is a good man,' Hans said cutting into Julius's thoughts. 'He loves children and animals, especially dogs. Anyone who loves dogs has to be honourable.'

Julius laughed hollowly. 'If you believe that, my dear Hans, you'll believe anything.' He was not in the mood to be careful today.

Hans stared at him and Julius was immediately aware of the unpleasant frown that creased his brow. *A foolish thing to say. Although he is my half-brother there is no affection between us. Perhaps he would like to see me gone from here. Informer? Yes, I am sure he is. Even his own mother thinks he is. How could I come to criticise Hitler so blatantly. Am I becoming too unguarded?*

Emmi breezed into the room, unwittingly saving the situation with her constant good

87

humour. 'What do you believe, Hans?' she asked, having overheard Julius's last words. She smiled at them both quite innocently.

'I just said that *Herr* Hitler is a good man. He dotes on children and dogs. Julius doesn't seem to agree.'

Julius quickly shook his head. Now was the time to make good his thoughtless blunder. 'You mistake me,' he lied. 'I merely meant that loving dogs doesn't automatically mean—'

'Stop arguing,' Emmi broke in. 'I like people who are fond of animals and if it's true about *Herr* Hitler and his pet dogs, everything'll probably be all right and he'll see that no harm comes to all those Jews who've been rounded up. I believe there were some children amongst them, and no doubt a lot of them have dogs. They're being resettled somewhere. Can't think why, but I suppose it's for the best.'

Julius marvelled at the cleverness and the simplicity of her reply, but did he hear a trace of sarcasm? Could Emmi possibly be sarcastic?

Hans made some non-committal grunt and left the room.

'Well done, Emmi dear,' Julius said when he was sure that the door was firmly closed. 'Was that a very clever remark or do you believe it?'

She glanced uneasily at the door and then whispered, 'No, I don't believe it, I'm sorry to say. I fear for the Jews very much, and Hitler's dogs must be Gentile ones! But you must be more careful what you say, Julius. I'm frightened of Hans. He's fanatical, and therefore dangerous. Have you heard the latest?'

'No. What?'

'He intends to join the SS if they'll have him.'

'*Liebe Gott!* I knew he was an enthusiastic party member, but the SS! What does your mother say?'

Emmi shrugged. 'What can she say? She's horrified, of course, but she dare not openly oppose the idea.'

'We'd better shut up too.'

'In front of Hans I am a good party member,' Emmi said. 'We must keep our doubts to ourselves and not give the smallest hint of them in this house.'

'Or anywhere,' Julius added. He gave Emmi a brotherly kiss. 'Don't worry about me. I've years of studying before I qualify. That should keep me out of trouble. Hopefully it will keep me out of the forces too. We shall no doubt need all the doctors we can get.'

Emmi was not convinced. Being a medical student was no guarantee of safety, rather the reverse, she thought, but she didn't voice her doubts. 'Then concentrate on your studies, Julius, and you'll be one less to worry about,' she said dubiously.

But Julius did not concentrate on his studies as Emmi and his mother hoped. In the parks and gardens of Berlin and Munich where he trusted there were no listening ears other than sympathetic ones, he and his friends mostly students, planned and worked. Hitler must be liquidated. He tried not to think of Elizabeth.

89

His love for her was buried deep in his heart, put aside, probably for ever. Their worlds were too far apart now.

The carefully planned Munich bomb exploded disastrously, killing innocent bystanders in the *Büergerbraukeller* and injuring a great many more. Julius listened to the announcement on the wireless in his father's home and he was relieved that Hans was not there to see his clenched fists and the despair in his eyes. Hans would be triumphant, full of zeal to catch the traitors who had perpetrated such an outrage.

Emmi was in the room too and she put her knitting down on her lap and stared at Julius. 'So our beloved *Führer* is safe,' she said loudly.

He said nothing, but he knew by the way she looked at him, that the words were spoken for ears other than his. She was as devastated as he was. So this was the end, the end of his hopes of freedom, probably the end of him and his friends too. A wash of fear swept over him. The SS were not known for the gentle handling of their opponents.

In Dresden the following weekend his mother was more hopeful. 'The generals are bound to act soon,' she said. 'There are plenty of high-ranking Germans opposed to Hitler. There will be a *coup d'état* soon, mark my words.'

Julius looked at her in surprise. 'I thought you wanted to keep out of all that.'

'I do, of course I do. I am only a woman and

have no thoughts on the matter.' She attempted a laugh. 'And your father will make a lot of money out of the war.'

Julius thought of the factory and its dubious products. He stared into the swirling grey waters of the Elbe, the great river that swept through Dresden. He and his mother had come out here to talk where there would be no listening ears. In the beautiful gardens bordering the river there was comparative seclusion.

'I sometimes wonder about the morals of living so comfortably from the proceeds of Heinrich's work,' Helga continued.

Julius was jolted from the comfortable complacency that he had accepted ever since he could remember. 'There's little choice for you, Mother, but what about me?'

Helga stopped and turned to look at him. She put her hand on his arm. 'You are young. Concentrate on your studies. Forget your conscience. Sometimes it is the only thing to do, the only way to survive. I want you alive, Julius. You are all I have.'

He put his hand over hers, pressed it affectionately and wondered if perhaps she was right about denying one's integrity and principles. But it was too late now. He had set his course, pledged his allegiance. Already a number of his friends had been arrested on suspicion of being involved in the latest ill-fated coup.

The following week there was an early morning knock upon the door of his Berlin flat. Julius was taken to a prison for dissidents,

91

a concentration camp called Dachau.

In Wales Elizabeth tried to come to terms with the loss of her baby, tried to make plans for the future, tried to accommodate herself to her parent's life. It was only for a short time, she told her mother. She wouldn't be a burden on them for long.

Louise Benson had surprised herself by feeling a slight twinge of loss over her unseen and unacknowledged granddaughter. She had refused to go to Mere House after the baby had been born, that is, until she was assured that the adoptive parents had safely departed with the child. Now that it was too late she wished that she had plucked up courage to take one quick look. Richard had always wanted another baby. Perhaps ...? Occasionally, she was filled with despair at the chance which she had allowed to slip from her hands, the chance to try again with a granddaughter. She had never been able to achieve a satisfactory relationship with her only child.

She and Richard had collected Elizabeth and were giving her a temporary home in the little cottage that had been allocated to them in the school's evacuation premises. 'There's not much room,' she had said grudgingly. She silently nursed her frequent and uncomfortable remorse, and would not allow Elizabeth to suspect even a glimpse of it. It would be easier when the girl left. Without her daughter's haunted eyes constantly staring at her she might find it possible to forget. 'You can stay until something is arranged,' she said. What the 'something' might turn out to be, she had no idea.

'Do you think you will hear from Aunt Sophie?' Elizabeth asked when she had been in Wales for a few days. 'Are we going to get any news from Germany? There's been nothing since war was declared.'

Louise looked at her sharply and shook her head. 'I doubt it. I contacted the Red Cross, told them that Sophie and I are twins and that I hoped to keep in contact, but they can't do anything. Not yet anyway.' She was examining the letters which had just dropped through the box. 'One for you,' she said.

Elizabeth's heart leapt. After all this time was he actually ...?

'From that friend of yours I think. At least the postmark is Yorkshire.' She peered at it more closely before handing it over. 'You said she lived in Yorkshire, didn't you?'

Elizabeth's disappointment only lasted for a second or two. She had missed Isobel when she left Mere House with her baby. She seized the letter and ripped it open.

Eventually she looked up at her mother. 'She suggests that we try to join the Land Army and get a posting together.'

Louise sniffed derisively. 'I know I suggested it, but I've been thinking since then. I should think you'd be better in one of the Forces. You'd be an officer with your background and as for that posh Isobel,' she nodded towards the letter in Elizabeth's hand. 'She's gentry. Why on earth does she want to go into the Land Army?'

93

Elizabeth laughed, her spirits suddenly rising. She looked down at the letter again. 'She's always lived in the country, likes the open air, knows about animals, rides horses.'

'Oh well.' Louise shrugged. 'You do whatever you like. It would be too dirty and rough for me, but you're both young. How are you going to manage it?'

'We have to go to a recruiting office. She says that we'd better go together if we want to be on the same farm. She suggests that I go to Yorkshire for a few days. Her father will arrange it all.'

Louise breathed a sigh of relief. She wouldn't be required to do anything. Elizabeth would be away, the last disastrous ten months or so could be forgotten, and she could return to the peace and comparative quiet of being a Housemaster's wife in one of England's most reputable public schools. The letters to her erring daughter from that disturbing Julius had stopped arriving and there would certainly be no more now, thanks to *Herr* Hitler and his war. She had a great pile hidden away in a locked drawer of her bureau. She was grateful that Richard had always allowed her a degree of privacy, that he never interfered in anything she did and that consequently she had been able to secrete the letters away from him. Dear man, he had no idea about anything really apart from his beloved school, had not enquired any further into the fatherhood of Elizabeth's child once she had told him that she refused to name the man. All that remained now was to bury the letters beneath the floor at Merricote. One day they would go down there for a holiday and she would be rid of them for ever.

Thinking of the letters again and with her heart lifting at the prospect of Elizabeth's departure, she assured herself that it was a good thing after all that the baby had been adopted by strangers. What on earth had possessed her to have that fleeting desire to hold a little one in her arms again? Absolute foolishness!

She wished that the letters were burned to ashes but she remembered too well the fortune teller who had declared to her that fire was dangerous, that to burn possessions, and letters in particular, would bring bad luck. It had been like an omen, reinforcing what she had heard before. She would never burn Julius's letters however much they haunted her.

She returned her mind to the matter in hand. 'How will you get to Yorkshire?'

'Train I suppose. Isobel suggests next week. Is that too soon?'

'I shall be sorry to lose you,' Louise lied. 'But of course you must go. We might have enough petrol to take you to the station. I'll ask your father.'

Elizabeth looked with amazement at Corndon Hall, Isobel's family home. It stood outside the town of Matsworth on a slight rise, and as she climbed from the motor car in which she had been collected from the station she stared up at the twenty or so windows that were set in straight lines across the front of the house. They were all decorated with regulation strips of brown paper in case they should be shattered by some enemy bomb.

Isobel laughed at her dazed expression. 'They used to take a lot of cleaning,' she said. 'The windows, I mean. One of the maids did nothing else. We don't bother now that they're all covered with pretty patterns.'

Elizabeth wondered what to say. It was the kind of moment when one groped for some inconsequential remark and nothing presented itself. She had known that Isobel's home was large, but had never imagined anything like this. And to add to her unease there was the little boy somewhere inside those forbidding walls, Isobel's baby son whom she must acknowledge merely as Isobel's little brother. She had been invited only on condition that she kept the secret strictly to herself.

Later that evening when the two girls were alone Elizabeth said, 'So, honestly, how are you managing?'

'With difficulty.' Isobel lit a cigarette and puffed wisps of smoke that rose in irregular circles towards the ceiling. 'I don't see much of Oliver. He has his own rooms and a nanny. Even my mother doesn't spend much time with him. That upsets me really. He's going to miss out on ...' she paused, 'on love, I suppose.'

Elizabeth looked at her in surprise. Isobel was usually merry, full of jokes, ready to minimise the problems and find something funny in

96

any situation, but there was no brightness now.

'The nanny is very satisfactory,' she continued dully. 'At least he'll get some mother-love from her.'

Was there cynicism in her voice? Elizabeth thought so, and thought too of her own baby in another woman's arms. How could they both bear it? Only with endless work to displace the hurt.

'Light me a cigarette,' she said. 'I'll try again.'

They sat for a time in companionable silence, sharing their unhappiness. Elizabeth had only smoked once before and she coughed and her eyes filled with smoke-induced tears that hid the real ones which were trying to struggle through. 'I think we both need to get on with life,' she spluttered eventually. 'To do some war work as quickly as it can be arranged.'

But it was not to be arranged as speedily as they hoped. At first they were told to help out with the evacuees, and then when it was learned that they had good Higher School Certificates, they were told that they must go into one of the women's Forces.

'No,' Isobel insisted. 'It's the Land Army for me. I've always been an outdoor type, and we need all the food we can get, don't we?'

Elizabeth wouldn't have minded the Forces, the Wrens for preference. The uniform was jolly nice, but she was swept along in her friend's enthusiastic wake, and eventually their names were entered for a month's farm training.

'Go home and we shall tell you as soon as there's a vacancy,' the woman in the recruiting office told them.

Then came the big freeze, the coldest winter in living memory and as snow fell in never-ending blizzards, the girls, marooned in the comfortable oppression of Isobel's home, toiled from morning to night doing whatever needed doing. The roads were rivers of glass, and the fields, after a brief thaw and then more fierce frosts, were glittering mortuaries for frozen animals.

The two great shire horses were harnessed to improvised sleighs and food was carried to remote cottages. The village was completely cut off and Elizabeth, swathed in numerous sweaters and an assortment of coats, gloves and ludicrous knitted pixie hoods, wondered if life would ever assume any normality again. She swept snow endlessly, helped to dig animals out of their potentially icy graves, lit fires, chopped wood, and frequently wondered what had led her to accept her friend's invitation to come to this wild and desolate part of England.

It was February before the thaw finally came. The dirty, melted snow-water ran in torrents from the hills, filled the rivers, flooded the village street and even forced itself into the Hall itself, but by the middle of March the floods had subsided, the birds were singing again, and the endless blinding white of that terrible winter had given place to the greens and browns of new life in hedge and meadow.

And at last, at the beginning of April, Elizabeth and Isobel were on their way to their first placement, a farm in Gloucestershire. The great freeze had changed everything. No time now for Land Army training school or any other such luxuries.

'You get to bed early,' the farmer's wife told them on their first night. 'Got to be up at four for the first milking.'

Once more Elizabeth wondered why on earth she had chosen this unbelievable course for her life.

In Dresden, Heinrich faced a distraught Helga. 'Get him out,' she screamed hammering his chest with her small hands. 'For God's sake, Heinrich, use your influence. They've taken Julius to some frightful concentration camp. Dachau! Get him out before they—' She sank onto the sofa and burst into frantic weeping. Eventually she managed to achieve a brief moment of control. She wiped her eyes and stared up at him. 'I heard, Heinrich, I heard that they have killed some of them, some of the students ... garotted them!'

England—1940

Brenda Sawyer looked at her sleeping baby and wondered whether she should take her away to the country.

'It's up to you, dear,' David said. 'I don't

99

want to lose you both, but I don't want you bombed either.'

'Nothing's happened so far, no bad air raids or anything. Perhaps it'll all be over soon. I'll stay a bit longer anyway. Couldn't leave you here all on your own.'

David smiled affectionately at the two of them. Ever since they'd fetched baby Kristall, Brenda had been a different person, happy and fulfilled, bubbling over with confidence and cheeriness. Those were just the attributes he needed in a wife, especially now that he had such a demanding job. With all the rush to make more and more aeroplanes he'd no energy left when he came home at night. No energy for anything in fact, but that didn't matter now that Brenda was over her anguish about not having a baby. And Kristall was perfect: slept all night, hardly cried, was pretty with bright blue eyes that smiled at him on the few occasions when he was persuaded to hold her.

Jolly good thing they'd been accepted by the adoption people, and no trouble over signing the final papers either. Sometimes he felt sorry for the unknown mother having to give up such a lovely kid, but mustn't think like that, of course. Brenda was Kristall's mother now, a much better mum than the real one, a young flibbertigibbet of a girl, most likely. Unmarried too, of course. He shook his head. Disgusting what the young got up to nowadays. He'd have to see that Kristall didn't know about *that*. Bad blood sometimes will out. Better not say anything along those lines to Brenda. She'd have

100

a fit, never would hear a wrong word spoken of the baby.

'If Jerry bombs fall anywhere it'll be London,' Brenda said optimistically. 'Bristol should be pretty safe, and we've got the shelter.'

CHAPTER 5

'Gosh,' Elizabeth said, 'I've never been so exhausted in my life. Four weeks of sweated labour and not enough time off to get further than that seedy old village.'

'And now two whole days of bliss,' Isobel added. 'What'll we do? Any ideas?' They had both thrown their dungarees onto the floor and were stretched out on their beds in a mixture of fatigue and euphoria. 'At the moment all I want to do is sleep.'

'Me too.' Elizabeth clasped her hands behind her head and stared at the ceiling with its smudged brown stains and ancient cobwebs. 'But not really. Not here anyway, and tomorrow morning I bet we'll be as lively as crickets. Let's go somewhere.'

'How about London?' Isobel propped herself up on one arm and reached for her cigarettes.

'I wish you'd give up those things.' Elizabeth wrinkled her nose in disgust.

'You should persevere. They're the sign of enlightened womanhood.'

'Rubbish. I've tried, but the attraction eludes

me. They're horrible!' Then she sat up abruptly. 'What did you say? London?'

'Yes, London. We could stay at my parents' flat, go to dances, well, one dance anyway, and see *Gone with the Wind* if you liked.'

Elizabeth felt a great rush of excitement. 'I've never been to London.'

'Then it's high time you went, my dear child. Right. That's it. London here we come.'

'How'll we get there?'

'Hitch a lift to the station. Should be easy. Got anything decent to wear?'

'Nope. Nothing suitable at all. I'll buy something. Hope we won't be bombed.'

Isobel grinned at her. 'Shouldn't think so. Jerry seems too busy conquering poor little Holland to bother about us. Not much seems to be happening over here so far.'

Elizabeth thought of Germany and shivered. Visions of Werner came into her mind. He was probably in the *Luftwaffe* by now. Bombers? He'd wanted fighters, but Aunt Sophie had written just before the war to say, sadly, that it was to be bombers after all. Could he actually be dropping bombs on Holland and France? And would she really one day look into the skies and imagine him up there, the enemy, just as all Germans were enemies now to everyone in England. He was gentle, fun to be with, wouldn't hurt a fly. She heard his laugh, remembered the times they had played together as children, how she had longed to have him for brother instead of cousin. How on earth could he justify flying bombers?

And then, inevitably, she thought of Julius. Was it so long ago that they had stood on the Berlin railway station and looked at each other with all their love in their eyes and none on their lips? She remembered sitting in the train that took her away from everything she held most dear, and how she had thought that her world was ending, almost wished she could make an end of herself too!

She had worked so hard during the past weeks that her weary body had given her mind few chances to brood, and as soon as she went to bed each night she was fast asleep. It was something to be devoutly thankful for. But now there was to be a little while of relaxation and maybe the memories would come flooding unwillingly back. She didn't want that. She jumped up quickly and started rummaging in the cavernous built-in cupboard that held the few things they had brought. 'I heard that we've got to wear something white in town,' she said.

'White?'

'You know, for the blackout. So that we'll be seen and not knocked down before ...'

'Before Jerry bombs us!' Isobel laughed. 'Awful to be killed by a London taxi. A German bomb would be much more exciting.'

Elizabeth continued her searching and tried to feel amused by her friend's remark, but the word *Jerry* always distressed her. She knew that she must get used to it, but it was derogatory, like *Kraut*, *Boche* or *Hun*, and, of course, it was meant to be. Yet all those names hurt. Her mind was crowded with memories of so many good Germans, Emmi of course and Werner and lots of her cousins' friends whom she had come to know over the years, and there were the servants in her aunt's house who had always been kind to her when she was little. And yes, perhaps Uncle Heinrich too, in a way. Even his long-standing dalliance with his mistress, Julius's mother, couldn't make him evil surely? Why couldn't people see that wickedness was more to do with a nation's leaders than with individuals?

She sighed. One day she would talk to Isobel about all these things, tell her about Julius perhaps. It would be wonderful to confide in someone at last. She knew that she still called out in German occasionally in her sleep. Thankfully, the farmer and his wife believed her when she said it was Dutch. Holland was a great little country much to be admired even though it had fallen to the dastardly Boche!

'I haven't got anything white,' she said emerging from the cupboard. 'I'll have to buy a scarf or a hat.'

'Same here. Let's get something to eat and an early night. Then up with the lark and London, here we come!' Isobel stubbed out her cigarette, leapt from her bed and threw on the dress that the farmer's wife insisted should be worn for supper each night. Trousers were strictly for the fields and cowshed.

Elizabeth did the same and began to experience a glimmer of excitement. Perhaps at last she was going to feel carefree again.

She hardly remembered what that was like.

First Lieutenant Philip Gibbons was also looking forward to leave that weekend and he, too, headed for the capital. On Saturday night he danced repeatedly with a fair-haired girl with a strange, remote look about her, as though she had suffered some recent calamity or loss. But you hadn't to look far for disasters in wartime in spite of this being, at the moment, a bit of a phoney war.

She was wearing a frock of some soft clinging material and her figure showed through it, slim and almost unbearably vulnerable. She aroused in him neither immediate passion nor lust, but more ... he groped for a word, *protectiveness*, perhaps. She looked in great need of cherishing. He often felt like this about women in spite of his mother's decided lack of any vulnerability. Perhaps it was because of it he thought. Bossy, strident females like his mother made him cringe.

Both intrigued and challenged, he made efforts to amuse her, to bring a sparkle to her eyes.

'I can't believe that you're a land girl,' he said when she had amazed him with this piece of information. They were dancing a very sedate waltz. He suddenly had to revise most of his first impressions.

'It's too dark to see my hands,' she replied. 'No amount of Snowfire Ointment will heal the damage.'

He laughed and gently pressed her hand, which lay small and warm in his. 'It doesn't feel rough to me. What made you choose the land? Wouldn't one of the services have been more suitable? The Wrens, for example.' He thought of some of the smart young female officers he knew, winced a little, and held her more securely. Too smart and too uppity for words, some of them. On second thoughts maybe the Land Army was a better bet!

'The Wrens uniform is nice. Better than scruffy old dungarees,' Elizabeth said. 'I must admit that I was tempted.'

He grinned into the darkness for the lighting had been dimmed for this dance. 'I can't imagine you in dungarees at all.'

'Well, it's what I wear most of the time, I'm afraid.'

'You haven't answered my question.'

'About why I chose to look after animals rather than people?'

'I suppose so, if you put it like that.'

'I like animals.'

'That's not a proper reason.'

'It was because of my friend. She absolutely refused to do anything else. She's been brought up on the land and we wanted to be together.'

Isobel was dancing with a young man in RAF uniform. Every time their paths converged the girls grinned at each other and Philip had noticed this. He looked across at Isobel and her partner. 'Farmer's daughter?'

'Yes and no. Her parents are very rich, big house, horses, hunting, shooting, all that sort of thing.'

'Ah. I see, or rather, I don't see.' Philip

106

thought of the girls his mother had tried to force upon him. None of those would have lasted long in the Land Army. 'I've heard that land girls are treated pretty abysmally. I'm surprised that you stick it.'

'We manage. We have to feed the nation you know.'

He laughed. 'Very noble. Husband? Boyfriend?'

'No husband, no boyfriend, no brothers and no sisters,' Elizabeth said. 'Some cousins. You ask a lot of questions.'

'Sorry.' As the music came to an end and he led her to a table at the edge of the room she caught Isobel's eye again and winked. She felt suddenly like a schoolgirl at a first dance, wonderfully free and slightly wayward. The word sprang into her mind catching her unawares. That was what she had been labelled for almost a year of her life. Well, perhaps that was what she was, not good and respectable at all, but wayward. But in future she would be hard as nails, quite ruthless. No man should ever take advantage of her again. On second thoughts the likeness to a schoolgirl wasn't at all correct. She was older and wiser now and forewarned was forearmed. She knew what men were like.

She looked at her escort as he pulled out a chair for her. Now that the lights were brighter again she could see his dark hair brushed sleekly back and his brown eyes smiling at her. He wore the uniform of a naval officer and her heart thudded annoyingly. It was a long time since she had been in the company of a man like this. The characters around the farm were either very old or very young. Their nails were dirty, their manners non-existent. 'Thank you,' she whispered. 'I don't know your name yet?'

'Philip Gibbons,' he said. 'First Lieutenant.'

For a second she expected the quick click of the heels, the German stance, and then she laughed aloud. Not only was this the first acceptable man she had met for a long time, he was in fact the first British officer she had ever talked to. Hard as nails? Could she really be that? It wasn't in her nature at all. Well, she'd try, but it looked as though it might be a losing battle.

He stared at her, wondering why she had laughed. All his efforts to make her do so had failed until now. 'Something funny about my name?' he said, amused.

'No, of course not. It's a splendid name. I'm Elizabeth Benson.'

When the music started again it was a quickstep. Her favourite. Julius had taught her how to do it. Philip held out his hand to her and they started to dance, but for a second it was Julius's arms that held her. She was back in Germany and it was the University Ball.

Philip held her firmly. He was a good dancer, had always enjoyed dancing. He felt protective again, a good feeling. His arm tightened around her. 'You dance very well,' he murmured.

'Thank you.' She opened her eyes and was in England again, in London, dancing with a British officer and he was smiling at her. And

108

that night, when the taxi dropped them at the front door of Isobel's parents' flat, she allowed him to kiss her and promised to write to him, to meet him again perhaps before he went back to sea.

Isobel came in later. 'Well, how did it feel?' she said as she stirred Ovaltine in the tiny kitchen.

Elizabeth, in borrowed dressing gown and slippers, had padded out of the bedroom to join her. 'Strange. Good on the whole. How about you?'

'Mine was okay, married though. Wife pregnant and in Cornwall. He's stationed somewhere near London. So that's it. Trust me to pick another unavailable character!'

'There are plenty more around. Next time lucky.' Elizabeth took a sip from the steaming cup that Isobel had handed to her. 'Thanks. Mine is a First Lieutenant, name of Philip Gibbons, and, by all accounts, highly eligible.'

'So, are you going to see him again?'

Elizabeth propped herself on the kitchen stool. 'I'll probably meet him once more. He asked me if I would, but then, of course, he'll go back to sea and it might be months before he gets any more leave. It's all very casual.'

'Perhaps he'll write?'

'Possibly.' But Elizabeth thought of the letters that Julius had promised. She was still perplexed by the sudden silence after those first few passionate outpourings that she had received from him in Bristol. Until war had been declared there had been occasional snippets of information from Aunt Sophie, and she knew that he was well, hadn't had any frightful accident or anything like that. 'Men are only after one thing though, aren't they?' she said, a trace of bitterness creeping into her voice. 'Although I can't say that my handsome Lieutenant was very riddled with passion when he kissed me goodnight. He's a splendid dancer though. I enjoyed that.'

Isobel grinned and lit a cigarette. 'The lust will come later,' she said. 'Have a smoke and don't be so depressing.'

'No, thank you.' Elizabeth wrinkled her nose in disgust, but the tobacco smell reminded her of Julius, as it often did. Suddenly she wanted to tell Isobel everything. The burden of secrecy was becoming too great. She opened the biscuit tin instead and pushed the nondescript biscuits around.

'They're all a bit stale I expect,' Isobel said.

Elizabeth found a Petite Beurre and nibbled it distractedly. 'Yes they are.' She frowned at the biscuit and then looked straight at Isobel. 'Kristall's father is German,' she said. 'And I still love him.'

'My God!' Isobel stared at her in amazement. 'And you've managed to keep a frightful secret like that all this time! I can hardly believe it.'

'It's been hard. I've longed to tell.'

'So that's the reason for the German you gabble in the night.'

'Are you very shocked?'

Isobel was thoughtful for a moment. 'Perhaps.

Stupid of me, but yes, I suppose I am shocked. I don't know quite what to say. I had no idea. Gosh, it must be bloody difficult for you. I can understand all the mystery now though. Want to talk about it?'

'He was a friend of the family, a sort of relation. Julius von Brandt. He was almost always there. We played together when we were small. He asked me to marry him.'

There was such a silence then between them that Elizabeth could almost hear Julius's voice in her head, could see his anguish when she had told him that she was leaving for England, that she could never be his wife.

'Why didn't you?'

'It was Crystal Night. Mean anything to you?'

Isobel frowned and searched her memory, then suddenly she recalled the things she had heard, the newspaper reports, fairly meagre but shocking nevertheless. 'Yes. I read about it. All the Jewish shops being attacked. Gosh, Liz. You mean you were actually there?'

Elizabeth nodded. 'It was dreadful. We saw ... well, I don't want to think too much about it or the nightmares will come back. Julius said something so awful that I knew straight off that I couldn't marry him, couldn't stay in Germany any longer. It was as simple as that, a sudden clearing of the starry-eyed state I'd been in until that minute.'

'What on earth did he say?'

'Something about the Jews. I suddenly realised that if he really believed those frightful things it

111

made him part of everything that was going on in Germany. Until then I'd blinded myself to most of it.'

'And you came home and found yourself pregnant!' Isobel took a long draw on her cigarette, inhaled deeply. 'My God! What a frightful thing to happen. Poor old you.'

'And perversely I discovered that I was still in love with him whatever he said and believed. But that didn't mean that I could marry him.' She shook her head and felt tears threatening. 'I absolutely couldn't live in Hitler's Germany. My mother insisted on the baby being adopted, and until she was born I wanted that too. That was why I decided to call her Kristall.'

At first Isobel looked mystified, but then understanding began to dawn. '*Kristallnacht!* Kristall! Well, of all the things!'

'So that I'd be reminded of what he said that night and so that it would make the parting with her more bearable,' Elizabeth explained. 'It's strange,' she continued thoughtfully. 'I've always disliked uncertainties, always wanted to have everything settled, cut and dried so to speak. Calling her Kristall in my mind from the beginning made me absolutely sure that I would never keep her.'

'It's a pretty name if you don't know anything of its origins.'

'Her new parents will have changed it most probably. But she'll always be that to me. Everything I felt about Germany, about Julius, even about my baby was encapsulated in that name, Kristall.'

112

'It was a brave thing to do,' Isobel said quietly.

'What do you mean?'

'You were making a statement and it was something you couldn't easily go back on.'

'That was just the point. I needed to be quite sure that I had done the right thing. The name reinforced it.'

'I'm not like you,' Isobel said. She dumped her cup in the enamel bowl in the sink and swirled water into it. 'I don't like certainties, I prefer not to be totally sure about things. I like taking risks and hang the consequences. I should have been afraid of changing my mind. Thanks for telling me about Julius and Kristall though, Liz. I'll be as silent as the grave, of course.'

Elizabeth breathed a sigh of relief. It was good to have shared her burden, though why Isobel should think her brave she couldn't imagine. She felt anything but brave. 'Thank you for listening,' she said. 'I think I'll have another go at one of your revolting cigarettes again.' She finished the biscuit, put her cup into the bowl beside the other, took the dishcloth and washed both, placed them on the draining board, dried her hands and accepted the cigarette that her friend had delightedly lit for her.

'Bravo. Thought you'd come round to it in the end. It'll do you good.'

'I doubt it, but it might calm my frayed nerves.'

Both girls laughed.

'We ought to get some sleep,' Isobel said.

'I'm tired as hell and we've got to get back to that bloody farm tomorrow. Think I'll try one of those stale biscuits now.' She took one from the tin. 'It's a pity you like things to be all hunky-dory,' she said thoughtfully. 'Nothing's cut and dried in wartime. There are absolutely no certainties at all.'

When David Sawyer came home one day from work and told his wife that the first bombs of the war to fall anywhere in England had landed on Canterbury, she shook her head dubiously. 'Near London,' she said. 'Canterbury is near London isn't it? I always said they'd bomb over there. Bristol'll be all right. No need to worry.'

David shook his head in despair at his wife's stupidity. Never looked at a map, never read a book, why on earth had he married her? 'Perhaps we ought to think about you going away somewhere with Kristall,' he said hopefully. 'What about your sister in Wotton-under-Edge? You'd be safe there.'

'No fear. She wouldn't want us. We've got the shelter. I'm staying.' Kristall was sitting on the floor in her playpen surrounded by toys. 'Who's a lovely girl then?' Brenda cooed at her daughter. 'Wouldn't want to leave Daddy would we? Not to go to rotten old Wotton-under-Edge with Aunty Molly would we?' The baby picked up a rattle and waved it obligingly. 'There you are, see. I told you she doesn't want to leave you.'

David suffered a hearty kiss on the cheek from his wife.

114

She took a starched white cloth from the drawer beneath the dining room table and spread it out on top of the green baize one. 'I was lucky enough to get a whole half a pound of sausages today,' she said. 'There was a long queue, but I had Kristall in the pram and we enjoyed ourselves, didn't we, lovey? The time passed quickly what with all the people to talk to, and it was worth it. Mind you I expect they're half full of bread.' She put worn but sparkling knives and forks on the table, and went into the scullery. 'They're in the oven,' she called through. 'Sausages are always nicer in the oven, and we've got some nice veggies from next door's allotment.'

'That's nice, dear,' David said politely. *Nice* he thought, what a nice word it was. It summed Brenda up perfectly. She was a thoroughly *nice* person. He didn't deserve her at all.

Julius stared at the stone walls of his prison in disbelief. There was a wooden bench and in the darkest corner an empty, stinking bucket. The window was small and barred and too high to see through. It was the stuff of nightmares, of old tales of the Middle Ages, not of a modern civilised State. Civilised! He thought of the Jews and laughed hollowly. If this could happen to him, a good Aryan with, on the surface anyway, a faultless pedigree, what would be the fate of those others not so blessed?

Hours and days passed in a miasma of silence and non-being. He had no idea how many days. The silence was one of the worst things to bear, a terrible suffocating stillness that held indescribable fears, fears that were made more hideous by the ominous sounds that penetrated the thick walls from time to time.

He spent many hours pacing the small cell, four strides across, four back, again and again like a caged tiger. Sometimes he would collapse on the bench and the shivering would begin again. He had been given no blanket and only had the clothes he was wearing when they came for him. The December cold bit into his bones and the shivering increased until it felt that his whole body was one quivering mass of icy terror. Then the pacing again and finally a fitful sleep.

They brought him bread three times every day, and water in a tin mug. Sometimes they carried away the bucket and brought it back empty but not cleaned so that the smell became part of existence, an all pervading cloud of stinking repugnance. And there were the interrogations, a succession of nightmares that left him reeling and sometimes only semi-conscious.

Then one day there was a small delivery. He was to go to Berlin they said. He was taken to a shower room where, to his amazement he found hot water and soap. He was told to shave and to put on the clean underclothes that were provided. Was this perhaps release? His spirits rose. But then the chains appeared and nothing was said, no explanation.

The train journey was frightful, taken at night and with two SS guards either side of him. He thought of Hans and wondered where he was now? Doing something similar to this? Too awful to imagine that someone you knew so well, a half-brother, in fact, could descend to such depths. Escape? Might it be possible? Of course not. His mind jumped disjointedly from one thing to another, often to Elizabeth. Dear God, if only they were together in some free, miraculous place. He must be feverish. No such Eldorado existed anywhere in the world. There was no freedom any more. They would shoot him if he tried anything.

The Berlin prison was pure luxury compared to the last one, a mattress on the bench, some filthy blankets, a little more food, cheese occasionally with the bread, an apple now and then. And he could actually see through the tiny, barred window. But see what? An exercise yard with prisoners who looked as frail and emaciated as the very old and dying inhabitants of a charity hospital he had once visited with his mother. Yet these people were young. He could see their hair, fair or dark but never grey, and sometimes they would turn their faces towards his window and he would see they were young faces on bodies a hundred years old. Mostly they were women. The few men in the prison exercised at different times, in small groups, carefully watched, and never with him. He was allowed no time outside at all. Fresh air was obviously too good for anyone suspected of criticism of the Fatherland.

Heinrich Kleist paced up and down his thickly

carpeted living room just as his son paced in so different a place.

He knew that he was well thought of, his factory turning out the products of war that Germany needed, and would need in ever greater quantities for the conquest of Europe. His family was almost beyond reproach too, one son in the SS, another in the *Luftwaffe*, a good pilot. The only cause for suspicion might be Sophie. An English wife could be a disadvantage, but she had taken German nationality and was, to all intents and purposes, a good German *Hausfrau*.

So, how was he to accomplish Julius's release? He could never face Helga if he failed. He thought of the students who had been executed. It was a nightmare that haunted him, caused him to cry out repeatedly every night in his sleep. He always awoke both sweating and yet shivering with fear. Damn it, he loved Julius more perhaps than his other two sons. No reason for this. It was just one of those curious facts of life, nothing to do with Helga or Sophie. Of course Julius had taken his mother's name, von Brandt, so he would have to acknowledge him officially as his son. Perhaps he should have done it long ago.

Heinrich lit a cigar, frowned at his reflection in the great ornate mirror above the fireplace and made his plans. He knew the right people, and now the authorities had moved the boy to Berlin there was possibly more hope.

The following day he walked through the Berlin streets and thought about his life. He

118

was proud of being German, proud of his war record. He had fought for the Fatherland in the last war and had been ashamed of the terms of the peace that had been signed in 1918. Adolf Hitler had a few excesses of course, but that was to be expected in any great leader. On the whole he was good for Germany, would see it rise to become a great power again if only a few young fools like his mistaken Julius could be made to see the truth and the error of their ways. He was determined that as soon as he had procured his release he'd take him in hand, privately instruct him about a few things, get him into the factory perhaps instead of allowing him to continue his studies. Universities were always seats of sedition.

He strode purposefully towards his interview at Gestapo Headquarters in the *Prinz Albrechstrasse* and tried to feel optimistic about the outcome.

It was a sombre building and there were rumours that many murky deeds occurred there, but Heinrich was inclined to put talk like that down to scaremongering. He looked at the flight of stone steps at the front and for one betraying moment wondered if they had been designed to deter, or at least intimidate unwelcome visitors. But as he puffed upwards he told himself not to be so fanciful. This was what Helga would have thought, and probably Sophie too. He was behaving just like a weak woman, and that was something that Heinrich Kleist certainly was not! When he reached the top he squared his shoulders and pushed the door open.

Inside he was greeted by yet more stairs.

Somewhere in this place Julius was probably incarcerated. He had no information about his exact whereabouts. In spite of himself he shivered at the silent coldness of it. There was a deadly chill in the air and it was obvious that the sun never penetrated these thick walls.

He reached his destination at last, a room to which he had been directed, and there he sat down in the company of others. With immense shock he saw that two of them were chained at the ankles and their shoes had no laces. They were emaciated and their faces had an empty look, a hopelessness that he had never seen before. He was at once deeply ashamed of his rather corpulent figure, the result of Sophie's excellent housekeeping. Ashamed too of his expensive clothes and general air of prosperity. One of the prisoners looked at him and Heinrich tried to signal his sympathy, attempted to read something in the man's eyes, but they were blank, conveying nothing.

After an interminable length of time, for, unwilling to take out his gold watch and heavy chain, he had no idea of the passing of minutes or even hours, the two prisoners were ordered out and he watched in increasing dismay their weakness, their efforts to keep upright, to put one chained foot in front of the other. As the older man stumbled he sprang to his feet but was motioned sternly to sit down again and he surprised himself by obediently doing so. This place was affecting him already, destroying his sense of identity, making him feel guilty even though he knew he had no reason to be any such thing. He gritted his teeth. Years ago the Security Police had not been menacing like this. Could there possibly be any truth after all in the tales of their increasingly sinister activities? He felt the beginnings of fear, an emotion of which he was singularly ignorant.

'*Herr* Kleist?'

He rose again, but more slowly this time. It was a woman who addressed him. He looked at her severe hairstyle, her expertly made-up face with its no-nonsense expression, and he imagined that he could see cruelty in the blue eyes. He bowed slightly. 'I am Heinrich Kleist,' he said formally just as though they had been introduced at some social function.

'Follow me, please.'

He followed and found himself eventually in a smaller room. There was a desk with two chairs behind it and one other chair to which he was directed. He put his hand to his forehead to shield his eyes from the bright spotlight that was shining fully onto his face. The woman left him there alone before he had a chance to ask for the light to be switched off. He closed his eyes and felt his self-confidence melting away.

By the time a man came into the room and seated himself behind the desk he could feel the beginnings of a headache, the blinding migraines that he had begun to experience lately. They were always accompanied by jagged flashing lights and these, added to the fierce light in the room almost blinded him. He could see nothing of the man behind the desk.

At the end of an hour of interrogation he was

exhausted, but managed to stagger to his feet. He hardly grasped the words that signalled the end of the interview.

'In view of your patriotism, *Herr* Kleist, and your contribution to the war effort of the Fatherland, your son will be released. However, he will not be allowed to continue his studies but will be delivered to the *Bewährungskompanie. Heil Hitler!'*

'What is the *Bewährungskompanie?'* Helga demanded.

Heinrich had driven to Dresden the very next day. He was still suffering, still dazed and exhausted from his visit to Gestapo Headquarters, felt now that he was fully in sympathy with Julius and was completely disgusted with his youngest son, for how could Hans become one of *those.* But all this must remain hidden. For the sake of his family he must continue to be a good party member, his *Heil Hitlers* as enthusiastic as they had always been. His doubts would be his own private burden. 'It is a section of the Army,' he said. 'A special unit.'

'Doing what?' She frowned at him.

'I am not sure,' Heinrich lied. How could he tell her that this release was almost as terrible as a death sentence? He had made enquiries about the activities of the *Bewährungskompanie.* It was a branch of the Army that did the most dangerous jobs, like laying or clearing up minefields. That was all anyone would tell him. Much had to be left to the imagination.

'Why can't he continue his studies?'

'Can anyone now?' Heinrich said. 'All our young men are needed for the services.'

Helga got up and put her arms around his neck. 'Thank you for trying, Heinrich,' she said. 'Perhaps we shall see him soon. Perhaps he will get leave.'

Heinrich fervently hoped that Julius would not visit his mother until he had recovered a little. If he looked anything like the other pitiable victims of Hitler's precious Gestapo then Heaven forbid that Helga should see him.

CHAPTER 6

'Do you know what day it is today?'

Isobel nodded. 'Yes I do, as a matter of fact. It's Kristall's birthday.'

With milking finished for the morning and the eighteen cows settled in the far meadow, the two girls had been directed to clean out the ditch where water normally flowed from a spring into the duck pond in front of the farmhouse. Usually a winter job, now, in August, this must be done again because the summer trickle was blocked by a prolific growth of greenery.

'Got to keep the ducks happy in wartime,' Elizabeth said with a sardonic grin as she pulled at a large dandelion and then prised the reluctant root from the ground with a fork. She looked belligerently at it, and then blew the seeds, counting as she did so. 'One, two, three, four! I loved doing that when I was small.'

'You're spreading the things.'

'I know I am.' She threw the plant down to join the others. 'Well, they need a chance don't they?' She straightened her back and stared into the cloudless summer sky. 'I think about Kristall every day. Do you think the pain will ever go?'

'In about a hundred years,' Isobel answered. 'Or perhaps when we've other children.'

'I wonder if that'll really make any difference?'

'I hope it will.' Isobel was cutting back some brambles and every now and then she paused to pull the long branches from her clothes.

'I wish I knew what she looks like now. She'll be walking, won't she?'

'Probably. Oliver is.'

'At least you can see your baby now and then. I wouldn't even know if Kristall was dead.'

'Don't be such an idiot. Of course she's not dead.'

'Well, I wouldn't know, would I?'

'I'm not going to answer that stupid question. She's having a lovely birthday party and she's well and happy.'

'How can you possibly know that?'

'I don't. But it's the most likely thing, isn't it, with those loving parents you were told about? So stop being melodramatic and morbid.'

Neither spoke for a time after that and only the occasional expletive broke the silence as particularly vicious thorns penetrated Isobel's thick leather gloves. Suddenly she said, 'Pity

124

you couldn't meet your Philip again while he was on leave.'

Elizabeth shook her head. 'He's not *mine* at all, and no, I don't think it was a pity really. His letters are quite enough for now, thank you very much!'

Then suddenly, from far away, they heard the sound of aircraft, the unmistakable and ominous throbbing that heralded yet another daylight raid.

'Here comes Jerry again,' Isobel said. 'Predictable as ever. No point in being serious about anything in wartime.'

Elizabeth gazed at the approaching planes. In the distance they looked beautiful, like a flock of silver birds, and she wondered, as she always did, if Werner was amongst them, the enemy? And Julius? Had he joined up too? He had never said which service he would prefer. Maybe training to be a doctor counted as a reserved occupation in Germany, but somehow she doubted it. It was easy to imagine him flying. It made each raid even more poignant.

'Do you know what they are?' Isobel asked. She dropped the sickle and shaded her eyes. 'Heinkels? Junkers?'

'No idea. Probably Junkers. My cousin thought they were good. Good! That's an irony!' Suddenly she felt a flow of water around her galoshes. 'Look,' she said, transferring her gaze from sky to feet. 'The water's running quite strongly again now.' She stepped out of the ditch. 'At least we've done something to please someone this morning.'

'The ducks! I hope they lay us plenty of eggs as a reward.'

'I don't like ducks' eggs.'

'Nor do I much.'

They both laughed, picked up their tools and went to the back door of the farmhouse, where they knew cups of tea and enormous hunks of seed cake would be waiting for them for elevenses.

Molly Crewe, the farmer's wife, greeted them sourly as always. Then she groped in her apron pocket and brought out a grubby looking letter. 'Another one,' she said reluctantly. 'Want it now or shall I keep it till dinner time?' She waved it about, tantalising, and then held it against her flat chest and attempted to rub the accumulation of paw marks and grease from the envelope with her sleeve. 'The cat walked over it,' she said, 'and then Mister picked it up when he was spreading 'is toast.'

'I'll have it now, please,' Elizabeth said, irritated as always by this maltreatment of her post. There had been a constant stream of letters from Philip Gibbons, each one full of the small unimportant details of his days. His ship would probably be going to the Far East he told her. He wasn't allowed to say much more about that of course. Secret, he said. He always finished by telling her that he had fallen in love with her at first sight and that this was quite out of character and had never happened to him before.

She replied fairly regularly too, but always casually, keeping the relationship relaxed and informal. 'I like writing,' she had told Isobel. 'I always wanted a pen-friend.'

Isobel had laughed at her. 'No need to make excuses.'

Elizabeth rubbed her hands on her dungarees and took the letter from the grudging fingers of Molly Crewe. There was an old wooden bench and a table of sorts in the yard and they carried their tin mugs and cake over to it.

Elizabeth flopped down and stared at the envelope. 'He'd have a fit if he could see the state of it,' she said. She turned it over and looked at the naval crest on the back. 'Perhaps our dear Molly is jealous. Maybe she thinks that I'm trying to be above myself having letters from an officer.' She laughed, ripped it open and unfolded the page of thick and beautiful paper inside. 'At least I know she hasn't steamed it open. It's too clean for that.'

She read slowly to the end and then passed it over to Isobel. 'He's got leave. Two weeks in Bristol, wants me to meet the parents.'

Isobel read it too and grinned mischievously. 'Gosh, Liz. This is it then. Lucky you.'

'Lucky? Not at all. I told you I don't want a serious relationship. Doubt if I ever shall. Loads of girls write to men in the services just to cheer them up. That's how I thought of it.'

'Love at first sight!' Isobel said. 'How romantic. Do you really think it was?'

'No idea. Perhaps. I'm not in love with him.'

'You like him, though?' Isobel had finished her cake and was trying to make the crumbs

127

stick to her fingers so that she should not waste any.

'You're eating earth along with cake,' Elizabeth said. 'No one would ever think you'd been brought up posh to look at you now. Of course I like him. That's not the same as loving though, is it?'

'Could be.' Isobel licked her fingers one at a time and stared at them thoughtfully. 'I believe that love can grow.'

'I'm not prepared to take the risk.' She drained her mug. 'I should like a nice undemanding friendship. That's all.'

'Silly girl. Men don't want just that. Especially in wartime.'

'So, what should I do?'

'Go to Bristol. See him, talk to him, be honest with him.' Isobel grinned. 'See how you feel. No hanky panky mind!'

'Don't worry, once bitten twice shy.' She realised that Molly Crewe was hovering near the back door and stopped abruptly. 'Come on. Look at the frown. Our time's up.'

'The potato field for the rest of the morning,' the farmer's wife ordered loudly. 'And this afternoon as well. Get 'em all up before they'm green. Mister 'ave dug 'em and taken some, but I sometimes thinks 'e's blind as a bat the number 'e leaves just lying. Lorry's coming for 'em tonight, so see you don't miss any.'

Elizabeth carefully folded her letter and returned it to its grubby envelope. She grinned at it and remembered its writer's immaculate uniform, his smooth hands undefiled by any contact with mother earth, the feel of his arm around her when they had danced, and his charming smile. Her parents would absolutely love him. She got up, stretched her back in anticipation of the hours of irksome toil ahead and fetched the baskets that were stacked in front of the barn while Isobel carried their mugs and plates to the kitchen door.

On their way to the potato field Elizabeth said, 'I feel like I'm in a play, or perhaps like a puppet and someone else is pulling the strings. I was so much in love with Julius, and thinking about Kristall always makes me think of him too. They're bound up together in my mind, but occasionally I can't see him clearly any more. That frightens me.'

Isobel stopped to pick an early half-green blackberry and chewed it absently. 'It shouldn't frighten you. In fact you should be glad. The sooner you get over him the better all round. I hardly ever think of Oliver's father now.' She spat out the remains of the blackberry.

'But you weren't in love with him.'

'Not quite true. I thought I was at the time.'

'Do you think that love can fade?'

'Of course. It's happening all the time. Mine certainly did. If it was ever there in the first place!'

Elizabeth shook her head. 'I can't imagine not loving Julius. I feel a bit like Catherine in *Wuthering Heights*. Do you remember what she said of her feelings for Heathcliff?'

'I think so.' Isobel frowned. 'Wasn't it

something about *being* Heathcliff? I always thought the idea a bit far-fetched actually.'

'Oh no. I read it at school and saw the film too, with Laurence Olivier. I remember those particular lines. In fact I quoted them in my School Cert exam, got a distinction.' She chuckled. 'I can recite them to you if you like.'

'Go ahead. My pleasure!'

Elizabeth paused, dumped the potato baskets on the ground and leaned over an old farm gateway. She stared dreamily at the folds and peaks of the distant hills.

' "What were the use of my creation, if I were entirely contained here? My love for Linton is like the foliage in the woods: time will change it I'm well aware, as winter changes the trees. My love for Heathcliff resembles the eternal rocks beneath: a source of little visible delight, but necessary. I am Heathcliff! He's always, always in my mind: not as a pleasure, any more than I am always a pleasure to myself, but as my own being." '

'Wow!' said Isobel. 'You are a romantic, aren't you! You really believe all that?'

'If you mean do I believe that love can be as deep as that, yes I do. If I marry anyone else in the future it'll be a flimsy insubstantial thing compared to my love for Julius.'

'Fiddlesticks.' Isobel walked on. 'Sorry, but I'm a realist. You'll marry some glamorous chap in uniform, have babies, and Julius will just be a dream.'

Elizabeth gathered up the baskets and strode after her. 'Wrong, wrong, wrong, although I wish that I could believe you. Have you considered that perhaps no one will want to marry either of us when we confess our murky pasts?'

'Don't confess then.'

'Maybe I won't. It's a frightful secret to keep though.'

'Not that frightful, and in your case, comparatively easy I should think.' Isobel stopped at the gate to the potato field and wrestled with the string that bound it to its granite post. 'Why does this silly gate have to be fixed so securely? Only mugs like us would want to go in and pick potatoes.' She glanced with extreme disfavour at the rows of toppled plants and brown earth.

'Just to annoy us probably.' Elizabeth stood watching. 'I shall agree to meet Philip, just this once,' she said. 'I suppose it's embarkation leave, so I won't see him again for ages, years perhaps.'

Isobel won her battle with the string and triumphantly pushed open the reluctant gate. 'That's a bit pessimistic of you. The war might be over sooner than you think.'

'Joke, joke,' Elizabeth said. 'Remember I've seen Hitler's Germany, the fanatical crowds and—'

'And your cousin is in the *Luftwaffe*,' Isobel finished for her. 'Best shut up about that. Come on, let's get these bloody potatoes picked up.'

And I'm in love with a bloody Kraut, Elizabeth said to herself angrily. She threw the potatoes into the basket with extra venom. *A Kraut, a Hun, a Jerry. And I'm going to Bristol next month to see Lieutenant Philip Gibbons, RN who must never, never find out about any of those things.*

Brenda had made a cake for Kristall's birthday. She had decorated the icing sugar top with dolly mixtures, had carefully placed one red candle in the centre, and the inside was soft sponge. 'So that she and her little friends can have some,' she explained to David. 'I've saved up the ingredients for ages. I'm asking three little girls and their mummies. Will you manage to get some time off, dear?'

David sighed. A first birthday party might be important, but not really vital to the war effort. Making aeroplanes must surely have a far higher priority. He had just come in, was concerned about the headlines he had seen outside the newsagents, and he was tired. The latest German strategy apparently was to bomb the airfields. He thought of the great Bristol Blenheims that he was helping to turn out as fast as possible at Filton. Pity the pace couldn't be speeded up even more, give the Jerries some of their own medicine. David sometimes wished that he was working on Spits and Hurricanes, lovely glamorous little machines, all Britain had, really, between it and the bloody Jerries up above in their murdering crates.

He clenched his fists angrily. How could Brenda calmly talk about birthday cakes and

132

the like when they were on the brink of invasion, when the *Luftwaffe* intended to bomb them all to Kingdom come? He put his newspaper down on the table and glanced at the headlines. RAF bombers were attacking targets in Germany. About time too.

'A cup of tea, dear?' Brenda said. 'Kristall's in bed. I managed to get her off early tonight. It's her big day tomorrow.'

She came to take his light summer overcoat from him and he watched her as she put it carefully onto its hanger and carried it to its appointed place in the cupboard under the stairs. A good-looking woman still, shapely but not really fat. Probably because she hadn't had kids of her own. Pity about that. He'd have liked a son that was really his. Kristall was okay, but it wasn't the same, somehow. Brenda didn't seem to mind though, she doted on her. He made an effort to smile indulgently. Perhaps it was a good thing after all, that women, well some women anyway, were like this, only thinking about their own little world. They weren't supposed to be concerned much with war. War was a man's game. Just as well, probably, if they kept the home fires burning and all that, like they did in the last one. 'You'll have to save me some cake,' he said. 'I couldn't possibly get time off for a birthday party.'

Tuesday, August 20th! The important day had arrived. Between giving Kristall mouthfuls of mushed-up cereal, Brenda tore off yesterday's date from her Promise Calendar and revealed

133

the Scripture verse for today. 'Can a woman forget the babe she bore?' she read dubiously. 'Yea, she may forget yet will I not forget thee, saith the Lord.' She frowned at it. Not a very happy choice, not a good omen either. She wasn't a religious woman but liked to have a thought from the Good Book to see her through each day. Today's verse made her think of that girl, the one she tried to banish from her mind, Kristall's natural mother. Mother! Occasionally, in her more generous moods, she endeavoured to feel some shred of gratitude to this unknown girl who had provided her with the baby she had yearned for. Today perhaps she could manage a few charitable thoughts. Perhaps the girl was thinking about the day last year when she'd given birth to her baby? Maybe she was wondering how she was, how she looked? What a frightful thing not to know what had happened to your child! Brenda shed a sentimental tear or two and spooned another helping into her daughter's waiting mouth. Kristall banged the wooden tray of her high-chair in delight, spluttering food all over it. Brenda smiled at her indulgently, wiped up the debris, and bent to give her a watery kiss.

The party was a great success. The children who had been invited, all girls of course, were dressed in their prettiest frocks, the jelly and sticky cakes were consumed fairly eagerly and vast amounts of precious food ended on the floor. Brenda didn't mind at all. She had carefully spread one of David's dust sheets beneath the large dining room table.

'Do you want any more?' one of the mothers said, and when Brenda realised that it was children she was referring to and not jelly she smiled as serenely as she could. 'David would like a little boy, but boys are troublesome aren't they!'

The woman looked doubtful. 'You've just got to have what the good Lord sends,' she said piously. 'I've got two girls. It would be nice to have a change. I'd like a boy, trouble or no.'

'My Robert is an angel,' another mum contributed. 'Better than this little madam.' She indicated her two-year-old daughter who was beneath the table picking up bits of squashed cake. 'Boys aren't always a problem. Perhaps you'll have a boy next time.'

Brenda nodded. 'Perhaps,' she said. She wouldn't tell any of them that Kristall was adopted, not ever. It was a secret to be strictly kept.

'What a pretty name Kristall is,' a third mum said as she helped herself to a Marmite sandwich. 'How did you come to choose it? Does it mean anything special?'

'Cut glass,' Brenda said. 'It sparkles and chimes. We had some tumblers for a wedding present. They're in the cabinet in the front room of course. Too precious to use. But I always liked it, the word I mean.'

'But that's spelt C-R-Y-S-T-A-L, isn't it?'

Brenda was immediately defensive. She had no idea why her daughter's name should be the wrong spelling. In fact she had often wondered why she hadn't realised this and used the proper

135

letters for the christening. 'We like the other spelling,' she said. 'It's more unusual.'

The woman looked doubtful. 'With a "K" is foreign, isn't it?' she said, 'the foreign word for glass? I've seen it spelt like that somewhere.'

Brenda had had quite enough of this conversation. She couldn't stand criticism or any probing that might lead her to say something she would regret. 'Now for the birthday cake,' she announced, determined to change the subject. She took a box of matches from the mantelpiece and lit the one candle. 'Happy birthday to you,' she began, and they all joined in, 'Happy birthday dear Kristall ...'

She watched her little daughter's excited face and chubby dimpled arms outstretched towards the flickering light and was supremely happy, the doubts of a minute ago banished.

But that evening after Kristall was asleep she stood in the pinkly decorated room and quietly opened the cupboard door and stared at the shoe-box on the top shelf. She reached up and edged it towards her and then took it down and opened it. She often did this. It was a sort of secret penance for not having been able to give David the son he wanted. Inside was the christening gown which she had refused to use. She traced the embroidered letters with her finger, a J and an E. She knew what they stood for: Julius and Elizabeth. Those two names were engraved inside the silver bracelet that also lay in layers of tissue paper in the box. There were some other words too that she couldn't read. One day she would pluck up courage and get a

136

magnifying glass and work out what they said. David would be able to see them. He had better sight, but she had never had the courage to ask him and he hadn't noticed them. He wasn't too interested in things like that. She sighed. His aeroplanes seemed to be more important to him than anything lately. Well, perhaps that was a good thing really. We had to get this war won hadn't we!

The bracelet was in an envelope and on the outside was written, *For Kristall when she is grown*. To be honest it gave her the shivers, as though a couple of ghosts had some part in her baby's life. Yet she couldn't bring herself to dispose of it. It could be sold, of course, but Brenda knew that if she did this she would always feel guilty. If ever, God forbid, the truth came out, Kristall would certainly ask for details of her birth. How could she face her grown-up daughter and tell her that she knew nothing? The bracelet would be on her conscience for ever. The shoe-box and its contents were a great burden to her, but at least she had done nothing wrong. Everything was intact, tied up with the pink ribbon. She would put the box away in a safer place soon where Kristall wouldn't easily find it. Maybe she would always keep it hidden, but at least nothing would be destroyed or given away. She would keep everything safe, a salve to her conscience, even if never revealed.

Before she retied the ribbon she looked again at the two names. She put her finger over the three words engraved after the names and rubbed gently but however hard she squinted she couldn't make out the tiny letters. The date was clear though, 1937. That was a long time before Kristall was born, longer than nine months. What did it mean? She didn't want to think about it. And the name, Julius, unusual, almost with a foreign ring to it, like Kristall. Why had she kept that name? Dorothy or Pauline or Margaret-Rose after the princess might have been much better. Not Elizabeth after the elder princess of course. Certainly not Elizabeth. That was the girl's name. It would have been tempting fate too much to call her that. Still, it was too late to do anything now. Like it or not, Kristall it would have to remain.

She heard the front door open and quickly put the box back onto its high shelf. She glanced at her sleeping child, kissed her softly and went downstairs. 'That you, dear?' she called knowing quite certainly that it could be no one else.

'Of course it's me,' David answered with a *frisson* of his usual irritation.

'We had a lovely party,' she said. 'And I've saved you a piece of birthday cake.'

David had completely forgotten that it was his daughter's first birthday today.

Guilt hung heavily upon Louise Benson. She was plagued with doubts. Had she treated Elizabeth badly? Should she, after all, have allowed her to keep her baby? Would Elizabeth judge her harshly in later years? Had all her reasons and decisions been wrong? The agonising thoughts chased around in her head constantly, but it was the letters from Julius that plagued her most. She had brought them with her to Wales, was terrified that they would be discovered and her treachery revealed, longed to burn them but was too scared to do so because of the bad luck that had been foretold.

To add to her misery, she hated Wales, detested the great mountains that rose in wild and frightening grandeur almost from the edge of the school playing field. In Bristol there were civilised places to walk and pleasant shops. She had loved the Clifton Downs, the graceful span of the Suspension Bridge, and the road around the sea walls where she could look down onto the Portway below and watch the motor cars that seemed just like the little Dinky toys they sold in Woolworth's.

Here in this outlandish place there was no Woolworth's, no paths to walk on, just these great glowering mountains; savage, untamed places where she was afraid to set foot. And the little apartment that had been allocated to her and Richard was too small to swing a cat round. Not that she had a cat—nasty, smelly things always catching mice and bringing them into the house half dead or half eaten.

Louise was weighed down with her own self-imposed misery.

'How about a visit to Merricote?' Richard suggested one day at the end of June. 'School breaks up soon and we could go there for the whole of August if you like.'

Her spirits rose a little. Merricote, their little Devon cottage, just outside the pretty village of

Kellworthy. Much more civilised than Wales.

'That would be lovely,' she said. 'Could we manage a few days in Bristol on the way? There haven't been any air raids to speak of yet. A waste of time, all this evacuation, if you ask me.'

Richard nodded. 'We'll stay for a week or so in a boarding house or hotel in Clifton and you can visit all the old haunts. I'll make some enquiries.'

Two weeks later Louise was busy packing for the journey to Devon. There was a large trunk to be sent on in advance. Ever since Richard had suggested the holiday she had begun to feel better, but she knew that only when the letters that troubled her so much were in some final secret resting place would she really begin to throw off her depression. Now was her chance to get rid of them forever. She would bury them beneath the floorboards at Merricote.

She took the letters, in their carefully wrapped and sealed envelope, from her underwear drawer where they had been concealed for the past dreary months and put them on the bed where they lay, accusing her. Then she took several pairs of knickers and, holding the envelope gingerly as though it would burn her fingers, she wrapped the knickers around it and put it right at the bottom of the trunk. She sat back on her heels and stared at it and a frown crossed her face. If Richard ever discovered what she had done, how she had deceived Elizabeth, he'd be furious. He must never find out. He'd despise

140

her. Lately she frequently despised herself.

Feverishly, she piled clothes on top, her own and Richard's in reckless abandon, the more the better. Hopefully out of sight would be out of mind and when they were hidden somewhere beneath the floor at Merricote, please God, she'd be able to forget them for always.

The trunk was waiting for them when they arrived in Devon in the middle of August. Louise looked at it in some concern, but its sturdy ropes were still in place. No one had tampered with it. Soon her worries would be over. She'd hide the wretched parcel, and Julius what's-his-name would be buried forever along with his plaguing letters.

Richard hauled it upstairs, struggled with the ropes, opened the lid and grinned at her. 'Can I leave you to unpack?' he said innocently. 'I want to have a look at the garden, see what's to be done.'

She smiled sweetly at him, 'Of course, dear,' she said. 'And then we'll have a nice cup of tea. Mrs Tremaine has left us food and things in the scullery.'

As soon as she heard the back door close, she grovelled in the trunk throwing clothes everywhere. Her hand closed over the parcel and she held it timidly for a moment before putting it at the bottom of the largest drawer of her dressing table. This piece of furniture had always been hers. Richard wouldn't look in here. Then she tidied the room and went downstairs.

That evening he walked to the pub in the village. 'You don't mind do you, love?' he asked. 'I won't be long. Bobby Tremaine'll be there. I need his help tomorrow to knock the garden into shape.'

'Don't rush,' she said. 'I've lots to do.'

The board in the attic bedroom came up easily. She wrapped the letters in further paper and then in a piece of muslin. With superstitious care she wedged the parcel behind one of the ancient joists well away from the opening. She replaced the board and pulled the old rug over it so that her secret was completely hidden.

She stood up and a great load of guilt and worry dropped from her, buried beneath the floorboards along with the repugnant love letters. Just like Christian in *Pilgrim's Progress*, she thought. He lost his burden, didn't he! Not quite in the same circumstances, but never mind. The similarity appealed to her, made her feel virtuous somehow. No one would ever find them until some distant time when they were all dead and gone and the house fell down. Its sturdy stone walls had been here for at least three hundred years and would no doubt last for another couple of hundred.

Before leaving the room, Louise glanced at the boxes of Elizabeth's toys which had been stored here years ago. The sturdy little pram which she remembered had been a Christmas present stood beneath the window and there were a great number of dolls. She picked one up, a large baby doll with a chipped *papier maché* face and a flannel nightdress that had been Elizabeth's

142

own. The doll was frayed and shabby with years of much loving. Louise cradled it in her arms for a moment, then placed it quickly in the pram, tucked the dusty eiderdown around it and turned away. Angry with herself for the unexpected rush of sentiment, she gave one last quick look around to make sure that everything was in order before closing the door firmly behind her. Then she went downstairs to the kitchen. She could allow herself a cup of hot milk with a dash of brandy and honey now surely? The letters were dealt with. She could relax at last.

CHAPTER 7

September 1940

'Stupid to go to Bristol now that we'm in the thick of it,' Molly Crewe said when Elizabeth asked for a few days leave. 'Best stay here in the country where 'tis safe.'

Surprised at this concern for her security, Elizabeth grinned. 'Don't worry about me, Mrs Crewe. I'll be all right. Most of the bombing is in the East and the Midlands, and anyway I know Bristol. I was brought up there, remember.'

'That don't mean a thing. If your name's on one of Jerry's bombs then you're for it wherever you was brought up.'

The total absence of logic in this remark amused Elizabeth. 'I doubt if anyone has bothered to put my name on a bomb,' she said. 'I'll be back safe and sound by the weekend, you'll see.'

Molly sniffed doubtfully. 'Well if you'm quite set on the idea Jim'll take you into Little Hending along with the eggs, Wednesday being market day.'

Elizabeth clambered eagerly from the train at Temple Meads Station, pushed through the jostling crowds and felt both excitement and a glimmer of nostalgia. This was her town, where she had been born, brought up, gone to school. Her last memories of Bristol were of those miserable weeks before she went to Mere House, but there had been many happy years before that.

The school house which had been home for as long as she could remember was closed now, waiting for the end of the war, waiting for some distant golden age when they could all go home. Most of the furniture had been sheeted down her mother had said. No, she couldn't stay there, not even for a couple of nights.

'You would be welcome to stay with my family,' Philip had written and she had speedily replied that, thank you, but she would do no such thing. Her grandmother lived in St Pauls and she would go there. She must visit her anyway. *Best keep my independence, no commitments, no two-day scrutiny.*

He was to meet her outside the station, but

144

first she must go to the ladies' room, comb her hair, rearrange her hat and compose herself. It was a dreary place with a huge cracked mirror over an empty fireplace full of used cigarette packets and other disagreeable looking rubbish.

She stared at her reflection, dabbed some powder onto her cheeks and carefully applied the bright red lipstick that Isobel had insisted was high fashion. She had kept this hidden in her handbag until now. Molly and Jim Crewe would have a fit at the very idea of lipstick and there was no need either to give the wrong impression on a train crowded with servicemen. But the garish slash of vermillion now instilled a little confidence, a momentary bravado. She took out an old handkerchief brought especially for the purpose, put it carefully between her lips and pressed them together. That would stop the lipstick from smudging apparently. Isobel had insisted on the importance of this manoeuvre and they had laughed at the implications.

She looked with some satisfaction at the blue suit she had chosen for the journey, a soft rayon with a straight skirt and a jacket with wide shoulder pads. White blouse, black gloves and a little black hat completed the outfit. She had bought the whole lot in London on that last visit and it had been carefully folded in tissue paper and packed away in her suitcase on top of the old wardrobe until yesterday.

She smoothed the soft leather of her gloves. They felt sensuous and rich. She adored gloves. They hid the tough, work-roughened hands that she was so ashamed of. She had always disliked her hands anyway, too big, too square, peasant's hands. But yes, on the whole she felt that she was presentable enough as long as no one saw the broken nails and the earthy stains that couldn't be removed however much she scrubbed.

She tried her hat several ways, finally decided on an especially rakish angle, frowned nervously at herself, and then slung her gas mask and bag over her shoulder, took up her suitcase and walked, with some trepidation, towards the station entrance.

Philip Gibbons was waiting for her, handsome and smiling. He held out both hands to her and she put her suitcase down, allowed herself to be kissed on each cheek, wondered about this, and was quite lost for anything sensible to say.

'You look ravishing,' he said. 'I suddenly realised that I hadn't seen you in daylight.'

She grinned at him. 'I hope I pass muster, then.'

'Absolutely A-1! How about me? The same applies. Do I pass too?'

She looked him up and down. He was in uniform. What magical things a uniform could do for a man! It flashed through her mind that she had never seen him in civvies. He was handsome anyway of course but as a naval officer, well, he was quite breathtaking. *Mustn't be blinded by gold braid.* 'Absolutely A-1,' she repeated.

He picked up her suitcase. 'I've got the jalopy,' he said. 'Stored up all my petrol ration.'

'Is that legal?'

'No idea, but there won't be much more from now on so let's make the most of it, get around a bit.'

He led the way to the vehicle and she stared in admiration. It was an open top model all gleaming black paintwork and sparkling chromium trim.

'My goodness, it's beautiful. Some jalopy,' she said.

'And it goes like a bomb.' He put her suitcase on the back seat.

'Like a bomb?'

He laughed. 'Rather an unfortunate figure of speech in the circumstances, I suppose. You'll need a scarf to keep your hat in place.' He produced a large square of silk, folded it expertly into a triangle and handed it to her.

She looked at it suspiciously, was aware of a heavy cloying perfume, and, interpreting her thoughts, he said, 'It's my mother's. I ran her down to Weston-super-Mare yesterday. It was lovely. I thought we might go tomorrow if the weather holds.'

Weston-super-Mare! Mere House! It was the last place on earth she wanted to visit. She could feel the colour drain from her face, and for a moment, as she settled herself in the passenger seat she felt quite dizzy with shock and remembered pain.

He hadn't noticed. 'It's an Austin "10" of course. Father bought it for me just before the war. Jolly wizard bit of machinery, four-speed gearbox with synchromesh on second, third and

147

top gears. I shall be very sorry to lay it up when I go back to sea.'

What was he talking about? Synchromesh? What on earth was synchromesh and what importance could it possibly have when the words 'Weston-super-Mare' caused her mind to fill with only one thing: a baby with fair hair and Julius's blue eyes, a tiny helpless scrap crying for her ... Kristall!

Weston-super-Mare, oh, please no!

'We'll take a picnic to Weston tomorrow, have it on the beach.'

And she could say nothing, could find no words of disagreement.

He took her silence for approval. 'Not much traffic,' he said. 'Petrol's only for doctors and the military and so on now, so we should have a pleasant drive.'

She tried to achieve a little calm, to attend to what he was saying, to banish the disquieting memories. 'Farmers get an allowance,' she said. 'Dyed some colour or other so that they can't sell it on the black market.'

'Do you have any on the farm? Got a tractor?'

She shook her head. 'No. Jim Crewe couldn't even drive a motorbike, let alone a tractor. He's got a horse for ploughing and things and for pulling the trap to market. That's how I managed to get to the station this morning.' Then, with her composure returning, she added slowly, 'Do we have to go to Weston tomorrow?'

He turned to look at her. 'No. Not if you

148

have any other place in mind. I like it though. Bracing and healthy and all that. Mother wants to retire there one day in her old age. Is there anywhere else you would prefer?'

She tried to think quickly. 'Clevedon? Severn Beach?'

He frowned. 'Neither are as nice as Weston. What have you got against the place?'

'Nothing,' she said.

After lunch they walked on the Clifton Downs, looked at the Suspension Bridge, so familiar to Elizabeth. 'Our house was near here,' she told him. 'I love this part of Bristol.'

'Jerry seems to love Bristol too at the moment,' Philip said as the sirens wailed dismally. 'Come on. We'd better get to a shelter.'

She sat close beside him in the stuffy and crowded semi-darkness, and wondered what on earth had made her accept his invitation. Tomorrow would be dreadful, and the meeting with his parents afterwards even worse. How to escape? She heard the menacing throbbing planes overhead, then the shriek of falling bombs in the distance.

'Filton again,' a man said. 'Bloody Jerries. The workers are sitting ducks in them flimsy shelters. Poor sods. Glad my missis ain't there.'

Elizabeth shivered, looked at the shadowy frightened figures around her and thought of Werner. *What would all these people say if they knew that I was wondering about my cousin, feeling concern for one of those pilots up there raining bombs down on us all? And even worse, that I*

149

had given birth to a German baby! Then she remembered something from a year ago. Mere House and Matron telling her about Kristall's adoptive parents. *A responsible job with the Bristol Aeroplane Company,* she had said.

She sat up straighter, tense and frightened. Supposing the father was killed? Supposing Kristall had no one? Tears started to her eyes and she brushed them away with her gloved hand, pink face powder smudging on the sleek black leather. *Don't be so stupid, so melodramatic. She'd have her mother, wouldn't she? Mother? I am her mother! How can I go on with this pain, gnawing away at my insides like some insidious cancer. Will it never go away? Perhaps I must marry, have another baby to supplant the one abandoned.* She could feel Philip, the warmth and strength of him beside her, almost a comfort, a consolation. *Perhaps I could do it.*

They walked across the Suspension Bridge in the afternoon sunshine almost as if there had been no bombs, no death and destruction just a few miles away on the other side of the city. He took her hand and smiled down at her. She hadn't realised how tall he was.

'Not frightened now?'

'No, but it was horrible. Do you think they hit their target?'

'The BAC? Perhaps. We shall know soon enough. But worrying can't help anyone. Sounds callous, but that's war. How about some tea and cakes to cheer us up?'

'I might manage one.' They crossed back again

150

to the Clifton side, found a small restaurant and she began to relax a little. *If only I could tell him ... I've had a baby, the father is German.* The words stuck in her head just as the sticky icing sugar on the custard slice she was trying to eat, stuck to her teeth.

'Perhaps you'd like to see a film?' he suggested. He wiped his fingers carefully on the linen napkin. 'By the way, if you put that thing on its side and slice it downwards it's easier to manage.'

She had made quite a mess. Yellow custard and horrible mock cream had oozed all over the plate. She hoped that he was looking at the cake and not at her hands. 'Too late to tell me now,' she said, and they both laughed. Conversation was becoming easier. If you concentrated on silly inconsequential things the serious concerns of life faded a little, she thought.

'Mustn't get it on your smart suit.'

She abandoned the remains, drank her tea, poured him another. 'The weather's too nice to go to the pictures, but if *Gone with the Wind* is on anywhere I might be tempted.'

'I thought you had seen it.'

'Yes, in London. It was wonderful. I cried buckets.'

'We could go to see *The Wizard of Oz.*'

She wrinkled her nose. 'How about the zoo?'

'Right. Splendid idea. We can walk there if you like.'

Elizabeth had always loved the zoo. It had been one of her favourite places when she

151

was little. She looked down at her feet and was thankful that her shoes were comfortable. 'I should like that very much,' she said.

He dropped her at her grandmother's house in St Pauls later that evening. 'Eight o'clock,' she had told him. 'I haven't seen my grandmother for a long time and can't arrive too late.'

She knew that he had been a little surprised at the location. This part of Bristol was poor, working class. His parents lived across the Suspension Bridge in a big house backing onto Leigh Woods. She would see it tomorrow when he took her there for dinner.

Elizabeth felt guilty about her grandmother. She couldn't remember her mother ever visiting. She had always spoken disparagingly of the fact that her mother-in-law was Jewish, almost despised herself for having married a Jew. 'A half-Jew actually and not practising of course,' she always declared vehemently to anyone who found out, as if this somehow minimised the supposed disgrace.

Her father had gone to see his mother regularly in spite of the displeasure that these visits provoked, but he had seldom taken Elizabeth with him. She remembered her mother's various ploys to keep her at home and wished now that she had resisted, had made more effort. As she grew older it would have been possible.

Esther Benson was small and dark with greying hair fastened into a bun at the nape of her neck. She greeted Elizabeth affectionately and after a moment's pause they hugged each other.

'Well, how you've grown,' she said, and they both laughed. 'Come in, my dear and have a cup of something and later on we'll have a nice old gossip.'

Elizabeth felt a glow of warmth towards this friendly little woman and wondered how much they had each missed through her own shameful neglect. It was another grief caused mostly by her mother's hardness.

'Perhaps we can get to know one another better now that you are grown-up,' Esther said.

Elizabeth nodded. 'I do hope so, Grandmother.'

'I'll show you your room and leave you to unpack while I put the kettle on.'

Was there a trace of embarrassment? Perhaps, but no reproach. Elizabeth followed her up the narrow stairs and into a small room at the back of the house. It was bright and airy. The bed had a patchwork quilt and two teddy bears sitting jauntily upon it.

'Your father's,' she said. 'I wanted to give them to you when you were little, but your mother wouldn't have them.'

Elizabeth picked up the bears, cuddled them in her arms, thought of Kristall. 'Thank you for putting them on my bed,' she said. 'I've never had a teddy bear. Lots of dolls, but no teddy.'

'Then they are yours now. Don't be long with the unpacking. I'd like to hear about that handsome young man who brought you. If you want to tell me of course.'

'I think I would,' Elizabeth said.

When she was alone she stared out of the window onto the row of back yards, all tiny, some clean and neat like her grandmother's, some squalid. Feeling suddenly pensive she thought about her life, her father's climb up the social ladder, his 'good' marriage and her mother's rejection of this lovely old lady who might have been such a comfort and bulwark to them all. She thought of the splendour of Aunt Sophie's home in Berlin, a slightly shabby splendour to be sure, but a palace compared to this. She remembered *Kristallnacht* and the women she had seen hounded and beaten, women like her grandmother. She thought of Julius. *Only Jews.*

How much could she confide in this Jewish grandmother? Could she tell her about Julius, even about Kristall? And *Kristallnacht?* No that would upset her too much. Perhaps another time, but for now, just a little, go slowly.

'So, are you going to marry him?' Esther said later when they were sitting in the cosy back room with Ovaltine and home-made biscuits balanced on their knees.

Elizabeth had told her about the first meeting with Philip and his frequent letters. 'Do you think love at first sight is possible?' she asked. 'That's what he says he feels.'

'It happened to me and your grandfather,' Esther said. 'We met one day on the Downs. I'd lost my hat. It had blown over the cliffs down onto the Portway. I was so upset.' She paused, took a sip of Ovaltine, and smiled to herself at the long-ago memory. 'He insisted on taking me to the haberdashers in Clifton and buying me another one then and there. That was very forward and daring of him of course in those days, but I fell in love with him that very minute.'

Elizabeth felt a tingling happiness from head to toe. It was a perfect story. 'And did he fall in love with you too?'

Esther nodded. 'He told me a week later that he had done so as soon as he saw my wind-blown hair and my distraught face! We were married just a year after that.'

'And he didn't mind that you were Jewish?'

A shadow crossed the older woman's face. 'He did and he didn't so to speak. I had to give up my beliefs, accept his God, his way of life, but in those days a woman would do that. You followed your man. You had no thoughts of your own, or were not supposed to have.'

'And you lost your family too I believe?'

'I was cast out by my father for marrying a non-Jew. I was considered to be dead. Even my own mother disowned me.'

'That's awful.'

'I accepted it because I loved Oswald so much.'

Elizabeth wanted to ask whether the sacrifice had been worth it, but she did not dare. Instead she said, 'So love at first sight can be genuine?'

'Of course it can, dear. If he loves you and

155

you love him, then marry him. Giving love is the best thing of all, especially while this old war is on and there's so much suffering and hate.'

Elizabeth lay in the spotless little bed later that night and thought about her grandmother's words. *Giving love is the best thing while this war is on.* Perhaps she was right. Why not give some love and get a large dose of it back? And if she didn't have over-much at the moment for the giving, well, it might come. At least Isobel assured her that it would. And love at first sight wasn't just pie-in-the-sky, an imagined thing. It had worked for her lovely grandmother and it could work for her too. It was one-sided of course, the love was mainly his at the moment, but that was all to the good. Did she want to get married? Yes, perhaps. She had changed her mind! She wanted to escape the back-breaking toil of the Land Army, wanted to be cosseted and protected for the first time in her life, just like Cathy in *Wuthering Heights.* Cathy had married Linton when her heart was totally given to Heathcliff. Perhaps you had to settle for second best when the man you truly loved was completely lost to you.

And of course she wanted babies! She hugged the two teddy bears in her arms, thought of having Philip's baby, a baby who would be wholly hers, whom she could keep for always. And then she fell asleep to dream, for once, neither of Julius nor of Kristall, but of a little, unknown scrap who was crying out for her to love.

156

Philip came for her at eleven o'clock, as they had arranged. He was wearing flannels now and an open-necked shirt with a cravat knotted at the neck. Yes, he was just as handsome. Her heart gave a little lurch and she invited him into the house, introduced him to her grandmother, saw him stare at the Menorah on the mantelpiece with its seven candles.

'So, you have a Jewish grandmother?' he said later as they drove away.

'Yes.'

'But you are not Jewish, are you?'

She shook her head. 'No. My grandmother had to renounce her religion and bring my father up as a good Christian. She married out, as they say.'

'And now she has gone back to her roots?'

'Why do you say that?'

'The seven branched candlestick above the fire, the candles which have obviously been lighted.'

'It's a Menorah. Yes, she has taken her faith again. Perhaps she never truly lost it. She kept her promise to my grandfather until he died. As soon as she was free she became Jewish again.'

'One is always Jewish. It doesn't change if you change your beliefs.'

She looked at him in surprise. 'How do you know that?'

'It's a matter of race. That's partly what Hitler can't stand, another race, and an incredibly clever and successful one, making such inroads

157

into German society. I'm not too sure that we want loads of Jews taking all the best jobs over here either, to be honest. You know what's going on in Germany of course?'

She felt cold in spite of the sunshine. Her hands were clenched tightly on her lap. Was Philip as prejudiced as Julius? No, he couldn't be. Not here in England. 'Yes. I know what's going on in Germany.'

He looked at her keenly. 'Have you been there?'

She nodded. 'Before the war, yes.'

'Same here. I went to Berlin with my parents for a holiday.'

She breathed a sigh of relief. He saw nothing odd in her admission then. *But, I have a baby, a German baby.* The words sprang into her head unbidden, as they frequently did, a singular warning. What would his reaction be if she should speak that confession aloud? She couldn't begin to imagine.

All the way to Weston they talked about light-hearted insignificant things, laughed a lot, and she felt as though she was living in a bubble that might burst at any moment.

He parked the car on a fairly deserted stretch of grass at the top of the beach, spread out a rug beside it, took a picnic basket from the back and smiled at her. 'You have to admit that Weston is very pleasant,' he said. 'What had you against it yesterday?'

She took a deep breath, settled herself on the rug. 'Just an irrational feeling,' she lied. 'The mud perhaps. I have never liked the stretch of mud between the sand and the sea. It seems menacing, waiting to get you.'

He opened a bottle of something which fizzed enticingly and poured her a glass. 'What a fanciful girl you are.'

She closed her eyes and downed the champagne in one long draught, heard sea gulls in the summer sky reminding her vividly of Mere House.

'I want to marry you.'

The words seemed to come from a long way off. She opened her eyes and looked at him. He lit a cigarette and she saw that his hands were trembling.

'I shall be sailing shortly. It'll probably be a long haul. I'd like to know that you are here for me, that there's someone wanting me to come home safely. If I know that, then I shall be confident of coming back alive.'

He took a small parcel from his pocket, opened it and she saw the sun glittering on diamonds. She had never been more amazed, more humbled in her life. 'I couldn't, Philip,' she whispered. 'It's much too soon. We shouldn't make anything definite.'

'There's not a lot that can be definite in wartime,' he said, 'but we could make our pledge to each other. It's a sort of superstition I have. Like riding into battle with your favours fluttering in the wind.'

In her present mood she couldn't keep up with his flights of fancy. 'Now who is being fanciful? What are you talking about, Philip?'

He smiled at her, kissed her gently. 'I suppose

I'm a bit of an old romantic,' he said. 'But I need to know that you are here, like an anchor, waiting for me, praying for me.'

'Praying? I don't know that I believe in God any more.'

'Just positive thoughts sent out every day, thoughts and prayers sent into the unknown.'

Elizabeth looked at him and was strangely moved. Here was a very extraordinary man. Could she learn to love him? He was as different from Julius as Weston-super-Mare was different from Berlin. Two places utterly diverse, opposed, at war. Could she pledge her life to this man whom she had only known for such a little time? Could she, could she, when there was always that shadow of another? Yet she had always said that she liked certainties, wanted everything assured and established, hunky-dory as Isobel persisted in calling this enviable state.

He took the ring from the box, took her irresolute hand, placed the diamonds on her fourth finger. The ring fitted perfectly. An omen? Superstition seemed to be in the air. She looked at it, twisted it on her finger.

'You will marry me, then?'

'I'll wear your ring for you,' she said. 'And I'll pray for you, Philip, for your safe return. That's all for now. We may not be the same people after the war.'

He ignored this last remark. 'My mother will be delighted,' he said. 'The ring was my grandmother's.'

Her happiness was suddenly and inexplicably threatened, a little cloud forming on the horizon

160

of an otherwise agreeable day. She had no explanation for the feeling of greyness that rushed from nowhere to swamp her. Resolutely, she tried to banish it. No irrational weaknesses should be allowed.

They finished the picnic, raced each other along the beach, laughed, took off their shoes and paddled in the muddy sea, packed up the crockery and remains of the food, drank the rest of the champagne, and then drove towards Bristol again and the visit that she dreaded.

The house stood in its own grounds with a circular drive that immediately reminded her of Mere House. There were two great cedar trees on either side of the lawn and a hideous monkey puzzle in the centre. Philip pulled up outside the splendidly intimidating entrance, and Elizabeth stared in awe at the great stone pillars and the two marble lions guarding the door.

She half expected a uniformed butler to greet them, but it was Philip's father who opened the door, reaching it before Philip had time to find his key. He smiled at her, a large loose-limbed man with a firm handshake and kindly eyes. 'Welcome to Westleigh, my dear,' he said after she had been introduced. 'We've heard a lot about you.'

Mrs Gibbons was another matter altogether. Thin, with pursed lips and grey hair firmly arranged in a victory roll at the nape of her neck, she held out her hand to Elizabeth in a reluctant manner. 'You are in the Land Army I believe,' she said. 'Very noble, I'm sure.'

They walked in the garden at the rear, drank

161

sherry in the sitting room, and at half-past-six it was suggested that Elizabeth might like the use of a bathroom and guest bedroom in order to wash and change for dinner. She had been warned about this, had brought a crêpe de Chine dress and smart shoes, and she accepted the offer gratefully. After a quick bath in the meagre amount of water that wartime restrictions allowed, she sat in the beautiful bedroom and tried to relax. Philip was to announce their engagement at this meal. What had she done? What on earth had she done?

The ring was back in its box in his pocket again. 'We'll keep it a surprise for the parents,' he had said just before they reached the house. 'I'll present it officially to you after dinner.' They had pulled into a field gateway and she had removed it from her finger, handed it to him, and wondered if she really wanted it back again. But she had refused to entertain those rebellious thoughts almost as soon as they came into her head. *Of course I want Philip's ring. It is the passport to security and position and respectability. It is what I wanted years ago, what we all longed for at Mere House, a man's ring, a man's name! Shame on us for needing those things. How angry Isobel would be, but Isobel is the exception.*

She stayed in Bristol for another two nights, going back each evening to her grandmother's house, taking a perverse delight in the difference between the poverty of St Pauls and the opulence of Westleigh House and its neighbourhood.

162

'I think it would be better if you don't tell the parents that your grandmother is Jewish,' Philip said on the day after the dinner party.

She looked at him in amazement and dismay. 'Surely they don't ...' She had no idea how to finish.

'They're not anti-Semitic or anything, but they wouldn't like Jewish blood in the family.'

She had almost given him back his ring. 'I thought that not liking Jewish blood was Hitler's prerogative.'

'A lot of Brits feel some sympathy with his ideas as long as they don't go too far.'

She remembered that he had said something of this before.

'Like smashing Jewish shops, like concentration camps?' she said.

'Most of that is propaganda.'

'I was in Berlin on Crystal Night!' She couldn't help herself, had to say it. The pictures in her head were too vivid to be ignored.

He turned to look at her, concerned, and she hoped, ashamed.

'Is that so?'

'Yes it is. I saw it with my own eyes. And now I don't want to talk about it, Philip. But please don't make any excuses for Hitler's treatment of the Jews. Don't condone such fiendish excesses.'

'Of course I wasn't doing that!' His voice was full of indignation and alarm. 'My mother is of the old school. She has very firm, very entrenched ideas.'

'I hope you don't take after her.'

'You will have to help me not to.'

They were walking on Brandon Hill. He pulled her down onto one of the seats with a view right over the city. 'She has been a great influence in my life. I had almost everything I asked for when I was a child as long as I did just what she wanted, accepted her views about everything. Even going into the Navy was her idea, but I think she regretted sending me to Dartmouth when she discovered that I was becoming independent at last.'

Elizabeth looked at him, thought what a complex character he was. 'I doubt that I can ever vanquish your mother,' she said, and then wondered what on earth she meant by that word, 'vanquish'.

'Was it really only a holiday?' he said suddenly.

She had no idea what he was talking about. 'Was what a holiday?'

'Germany. You said you were there on Crystal Night. That was 1938 wasn't it?'

'Yes. I wanted to perfect my German.'

He turned to her in surprise. 'You speak German?'

'Yes. Quite fluently as a matter of fact.'

'Any special reason?'

'My mother's sister married a German. I used to visit her and my cousins frequently.' She waited for his surprise, perhaps even disapproval.

After a moment's silence he said, 'And now?'

'We hear nothing, of course.'

'I'm sorry. It must be difficult.'

'Yes it is, very.' *Is this the time to tell him about Julius? Is it necessary? Yes, it is necessary. To my peace of mind.* 'I had a German boyfriend.'

She could feel the sudden tenseness in him. If there had been no disapproval before it was there now.

'My God, Elizabeth! Why did you have to tell me that? I think I would rather not have known. I hope you don't mean a lover?'

'Perhaps,' she said. 'But the past is over and done with. It's now that matters. The present and the future are the only important things.'

He was silent for a long time. Then he said, 'I don't want to think of you with anyone else. It burns me up. I want to believe that I'm the only man in your life.'

Alarm bells rang in her head. Was she going to marry a jealous man? Surely not. 'There is no one else,' she said. 'No one else at all now, Philip. You need have no fears about that.' *And that is true, quite quite true.* She put her hand over Philip's and smiled at him. 'I wouldn't have taken your ring if that were not so,' she said.

Some of the uneasiness eventually left him. 'I suppose I am the jealous sort,' he said, 'and of course you're right, the past is the past. Don't tell me any more and don't mention it again.' He put his arms around her and kissed her on both cheeks.

'Why do you kiss me like that?' she asked. 'In the French way?'

'I like France,' he said with a smile. He kissed her on the lips. 'Better?'

She nodded. 'Much better.'

Jim Crewe, complaining sorely at having to take the pony and trap out on any day but Market Day, met her in Little Hending. 'Don't know why folks have to go gadding about,' he moaned. 'Never been further than twenty mile meself and all the better for that!'

Back in the farmhouse and in the privacy of her bedroom she unpacked her best frock and put it carefully in the skimpy wardrobe. She was sitting on her bed looking at the ring on her finger when Isobel came in from the fields.

Isobel grinned at her broadly. 'Gosh, it's good to have you home. You've no idea how awful it's been here all on my own.'

'I can guess.' Elizabeth waved her left hand about so that the ring flashed in the late afternoon sun.

Isobel stared as if hypnotised. 'Gosh, Liz, you don't mean ...?'

'Yes, I've gone and done it! Taken his ring and said I'll pray for him.'

'You'll *what?*'

'Pray. P-R-A-Y. He's a strange character, talked about knowing he'll come back if someone wants him to.'

'Well, I'll be jiggered! I never thought you'd go as far as that.'

'I didn't go as far as anything. I stayed very demurely with my grandmother each night. What do you think of the ring, then? Impressive, isn't it?'

Isobel came over to have a look, took her hand and gazed at the flashing diamonds. 'It's

166

beautiful. Must have cost a packet.'

'He's rich.'

'That's not why you're going to marry him though?'

'Of course not.'

'Why then?'

Elizabeth shrugged. 'I've been thinking about that all the way home on the train. He says he loves me. He's nice to be with, interesting, well-educated, a gentleman. I want to be looked after, mollycoddled, and more than anything I want a baby, one I shall keep, that no one can ever take from me again. I want more than one, Isobel. I want lots and lots of babies.'

'Do you love him?'

'I told you, I like him very much.'

'And do you think that you'll be happy settling for second best?'

'You told me that I would didn't you?'

'Perhaps I did. God, am I to blame?'

'Don't sound so depressing. Of course you're not to *blame* as you so tactfully put it!'

Elizabeth got up and stared out of the small window at the darkening garden. 'I know what true love is, Isobel, and I don't suppose I shall ever find it again. I know what it's like to love a man with all my heart and being, but he's German, isn't he? There's a terrible war between us, and he's probably dead by now. Don't tell me not to marry Philip. I must forget Julius. You're always telling me that I should. I need a man in my bed and babies in my arms. Maybe I'm being foolish, but that's how it is.' She turned and stared at her friend. 'He's going back to sea, of course. I might never see him again.'

'So you won't have a man in your bed and babies in your arms, will you?'

'No, and I won't be mollycod.iled and looked after either. Not while the war is on anyway.'

'Bloody war,' Isobel said. 'What about Kristall?'

'He will never know. I told him that I once had a German boyfriend but that was all.'

'He didn't ask questions?'

'Tried to. Was he my lover, he said? I fudged it, didn't give an answer and in the end he told me that he didn't want to know. So that's that. Kristall is firmly part of the past, not the present or the future.'

'Good for you. I hope it all works out.'

'It will. But I'm not worrying about anything. Like I said, the end of the war is a long way off. We might all be dead.'

'Cheerful,' Isobel said. She bent down and rummaged amongst the accumulated chaos beneath her bed and came up triumphant with a biscuit tin in her hands. 'Have one of these,' she said. 'Our post office lady smuggled them out to me in exchange for a couple of those ducks' eggs that we don't like.'

'Thanks.' Elizabeth ate the biscuit and brushed crumbs from her skirt onto the floor. 'You know me, Isobel. I like everything to be settled and secure, hunky-dory so to speak. I like to know where I'm going even if I never get there!'

Isobel let out a great guffaw of laughter.

'Well, my dear Lizzy, I don't know whether to hope you get there or not. Depends on a lot of things, but right now I know exactly where I'm going and that's down the garden to the lavatory. Oh, for a nice civilised one, inside and with a flush.'

'Plenty of those in Philip's posh house,' said Elizabeth.

CHAPTER 8

France—September 1940

Werner, now in occupied Chartres, sat uneasily with his fellow officers at the day's briefing. He listened in dismay. Bristol was to be the target, the Bristol Aeroplane Company at Filton, to be precise. A new phase in the air war was about to begin. The aim now was to destroy the British aircraft industry and particularly that which was concerned with fighter production.

He sat stoney-faced and knew that, of course, it made sense. British Spitfires and Hurricanes were admired and feared by the *Luftwaffe*. In his lumbering *Heinkel* he had often been amazed by the agility and speed of the little aeroplanes which swooped out of the sky, guns blazing. He had seen many of his comrades succumb to the accuracy of their fire and the manoeuvrability of their brilliant Rolls-Royce engines. These engines were made at Filton he was being told.

The factory must be destroyed.

'Should have done it weeks ago,' his friend said as they walked to their aircraft.

'I suppose so.' He shrugged his shoulders and drew deeply on the cigarette which would be the last before he returned ... if he returned.

'Only suppose so?'

'I've been to Bristol. Nice city.'

His friend turned to look at him enquiringly, almost suspiciously. 'Thought you looked a bit down in the mouth. How come you were in Bristol?'

'My mother's sister and my cousin live there, or did.'

Silence. A cold uncomfortable silence. 'My mother is English, was English,' he said, quickly correcting himself.

'Bad luck. Must make things difficult.'

'A little.' He tried to sound non-committal. He'd been foolish to mention it, of course, but the briefing had been a shock. He'd known that it would come one day, the order to bomb a place he knew rather than the anonymity of London or a military target, but he'd constantly pushed it to the back of his mind. When he'd joined the *Luftwaffe* he'd hoped to fly fighters. That would have been fair combat. He marched on towards his aeroplane, thinking about the little *Messerschmitts* that were to protect him, wishing they were Spits.

'Well, I don't suppose they'll be working in an aircraft factory,' his companion said.

What was he talking about? 'Who won't?'

'Your aunt, your cousin.'

'No. No, I don't suppose they will.' He shivered, imagined Elizabeth making aircraft parts in the factory he was about to bomb. Surely not? Please God not.

His thoughts turned to Julius. Elizabeth and his half-brother were always together in his mind. They'd been in love, of course. And now Julius had been arrested because of some foolish indiscretion, some disapproval of the State! Students in Munich had been hanged for speaking out against the *Führer*. Surely that was not to be his half-brother's fate? Werner hated the war, hoped that those in power would move against Hitler soon and bring the whole miserable business to an end. He had become more and more aware lately of the depravity of the country he loved. Innocent civilians were arrested just for tuning in to enemy wavelengths now, and God only knew what happened to them after that. There were frightful, unthinkable rumours whispered fearfully here and there. What kind of regime was he fighting for? The thought troubled him deeply. Did he really want Germany to win? Too late now though to defect, to do anything but get on with the job, however frightful it appeared to be. Best not to think too much.

He stood watching the ground crews refuelling, and then took to the air. It was a beautiful day, perfect for locating the target accurately, splendid for bringing sudden death and destruction. He forced his bitterness and anger to the back of his mind, looked fleetingly at the blue of the sky and prayed that Elizabeth

171

and Julius would live, would meet again, would find happiness one day in spite of all the forces loaded so formidably against them.

The bombers with their escort of fighters flew in perfect formation to Cherbourg then across the Channel which sparkled blue and silver in the morning sunshine. Werner tried to banish his early memories of holidays in Bristol. The City of Churches it was often called. He hoped the inhabitants were praying now. He tried to concentrate only on delivering his bombs accurately and returning to France alive.

When the command came, *Bombenschachte auf,* his only thought was relief that he personally hadn't to open the bomb doors. The British fighters, the Spitfires and Hurricanes that they had expected and feared, had failed to materialise, the bombs were away and there was no more to do but to get his aircraft safely back to base.

But if the fighters for once had been tardy, the gunners on the ground below were not. The explosion was terrifying, immense, and the aircraft went into a spin. Werner gripped the controls but could do nothing, gave the command to bale out and then found that it was too late. In a fearful fireball his aeroplane crashed to the ground, and the country for which he had once felt some kinship and to which he had just brought such monstrous terror and death, received him and became his resting place.

Kristall always knew that she could do anything she liked with her mother. Her fourth birthday confirmed this opinion.

'We can't have a party, lovey,' Brenda said. 'The rations aren't enough and Mummy's too tired.'

Kristall's eyes filled with angry tears. 'I want a party. I want jelly and cake and my friends and presents, and jam sandwiches.' She beat her small fists on the table. 'I'm going to have a party.'

Brenda sighed. Where did this child get all that determination and brains, yes brains? If it was her own little girl she'd be sweet and easy-going, but there must be bad blood somewhere in this one. Ever since David had been killed in that frightful daylight air raid on Filton, nearly three years ago now, she'd had trouble with Kristall, even wondered sometimes, guiltily of course, if adopting a child had been such a good idea after all. She looked helplessly at the determined, screwed up little face, and a bit more of the love that she'd had in such abundance in the early years seemed to slip away out of the window.

Perhaps David had been right. He'd never been over fond of Kristall, forgot her birthday, seldom played with her. He'd wanted a boy. Brenda thought of David and brushed the ever ready tears from her eyes, remembered the day back in that awful autumn of 1940, when she'd watched the planes that were to kill him flying overhead. They often came in the daylight then, usually on the way to somewhere else, London way or up North, and occasionally they were ours. She couldn't really tell the difference. She'd been putting some washing on the line that day, could remember the warm September sun shining in her eyes as she looked up. There were such a lot of them and in perfect formation. They couldn't be Jerries to be flying like that without our boys trying to get them surely? Yet the throbbing engines sounded ominous. She had shaded her eyes and continued to marvel at the sight. Then suddenly she heard the gunfire, Purdown Percy, the big ack-ack gun doing its stuff. She hadn't waited to see or hear any more, had dropped the washing, grabbed Kristall from her pram and rushed inside to the doubtful safety of the cupboard under the stairs. David had said that was the safest place. Even if the house collapsed, the stairs were strong, better than one of those Morrison shelters that sometimes gave way, and certainly more comfortable than a damp, chilly Anderson in the garden.

She had called the cat into the cupboard and the three of them had waited, quite calmly at first, for the All-Clear. Her next-door neighbour was in her cupboard too. The walls adjoined and she could hear her talking to her small dog, also cuddled in the companionable darkness.

Then she had heard the wail of bombs falling, followed by the explosions that were almost a relief because if you were still alive then you had survived that bomb, at least. 'They sound a bit close,' she had called through the wall. 'Suppose they're after Filton,' her neighbour had shouted back tactlessly.

David did not come home at his usual time. She had begun to worry, and in the early evening she had been told the news. A direct hit on the air-raid shelter full of workers, all killed. It still made her shudder to think of it. David had been there, had died instantly.

She had taken some time to adapt to widowhood, would have liked to do some war work, but with baby Kristall to look after it was out of the question. It was a few months later that the trouble had started. She couldn't imagine that Kristall missed her daddy. There had never been a close bond between them.

Perhaps the fault was in herself. Brenda had tried to find a reason for Kristall's increasing tantrums, hoped that she would grow out of them, but instead they became worse.

'She needs a dad,' Bill Hodgson repeatedly told her. 'Could do with a wallop now and then. You're too soft, Brenda.'

And Brenda was inclined to agree with him. Bill was the milkman, a widower, no children, came to see her frequently of an evening as well as delivering the milk each morning. She usually managed to find something for his horse too, a carrot top or even, now and then, a precious sugar lump. A real comfort was Bill, bucked her up no end.

And now it was Kristall's fourth birthday! Amidst the noise and excitement Brenda, feeling ashamed for having given in so helplessly to her

175

daughter, thought of previous parties. The first had been lovely, apart from David forgetting all about it. The second was almost fun too, but the third had been frightful with Kristall throwing a tantrum, lying on the floor, being sick, the other children going home early.

And now here they all were again. No tantrums this time though because Brenda had been careful to do everything to please her demanding little daughter.

At the end of the afternoon, when the other children and their mothers had gone home she looked around at the chaos of her parlour, stared at Kristall's angelic and uncaring little face and burst into tears. This day should be a happy one, but it wasn't. Of course, she reminded herself, as she rubbed at her eyes with her best lacy handkerchief, she hadn't actually given birth herself on this day so there was nothing personal to celebrate. In fact it was the one day in the year when the unknown woman who was Kristall's first mother intruded into her thoughts.

It was while she was in this state that Bill Hodgson arrived. He took one look at the disorder of the room, at the little girl sitting amidst it all playing with the assortment of toys that were strewn over the floor, and his lips set in a determined line.

'Like me to take over would you, love?' he said.

Brenda straightened her hair, stuffed her handkerchief into her sleeve and looked up at him gratefully and with a little shock. He

176

had never called her 'love' before. 'Yes, please,' she murmured.

'Right. The first thing is you, Miss,' he said to the child. 'Up to bed.' He picked up the surprised Kristall in his sturdy arms and carried her, wailing and protesting, upstairs. He set her down at the lavatory door. 'In there,' he directed. 'Then wash your hands and get yourself into bed.'

She stared at him, knew at once that she had met her match, puckered up her mouth in the beginnings of a wail, then did just as she was told. When she reappeared she stood beside her bed, big tears in her eyes. 'Can't undress,' she wailed. 'Want Mummy to do it.'

'You've worn your mummy right out,' Bill said. 'Come here.' He roughly undid the buttons at the back of her now grubby party frock. 'Into bed in double quick time or you'll get a wallop.'

When he went downstairs again there was no sound from the bedroom. Brenda had made some efforts to clear up and she looked at him in amazement and gratitude. 'How on earth did you do it? I have to lie down with her every night until she's asleep.'

'More fool you,' he said. 'A bit of stick now and then. That's what that kid needs.'

Brenda shook her head. 'Not a stick, Bill. I could never allow that.'

'We'll see.' He sat down on the red plush armchair that had always been David's and lit his pipe. The belligerent mood was set aside. 'Marry me will you, Brenda, love?'

Of course she would marry him. She'd been wanting him to ask her for long enough, was weary of managing on her own, needed a man about the place to tell her what to do. 'Yes,' she whispered. 'I'll marry you, Bill.' She wiped her hands which were red and rough with all the washing up and went over to him. She kissed him gently on the small bald patch on the top of his head.

He looked up at her and laughed, put his pipe down in the grate and stood up, put his arms around her and hugged her tightly. 'Let's make it soon,' he said. 'I've been lonely since Madge died with only the horse for company.'

'As soon as you like,' she agreed, wondering for a second whether she could replace not only Madge, whom she had never met, but the horse, whom she had. It was wonderful to be wanted and to be hugged like this though. No one else needed her.

Well, perhaps Kristall did, but only for her own ends, and if she was honest David hadn't needed her exactly. He'd always been too clever for her, had been irritated by her stupidity. Brenda was well aware that she was a bit stupid when it came to learning and all that. Bill would suit her nicely, not too brainy, but good with the milk round, a steady income, and best of all, he'd take Kristall in hand. Not that she'd let him smack her too much.

She returned his enthusiastic kiss and then pushed him away. 'You'll have to wait till the wedding,' she said coyly. 'No hanky-panky before, mind.'

He grinned, sat down again, took his pipe and relit it. 'Of course not, woman,' he said. 'What do you take me for? And now how about a cup of tea? I've brought you a bit of Jersey milk. Left it by the hall-stand.'

Brenda hadn't noticed the big quart bottle of rich, creamy-yellow milk. A real treat that was. 'Lovely,' she said, and she kissed him again. Life with Bill was going to be fun.

She put the kettle on the gas stove and went to fetch the milk. He'd cheered her up, lifted her right out of her depression. She felt better than she'd done for years. Why, there might even be a baby of her own. She'd heard that sometimes, when there was no child, the fault was the man's. Perhaps it had been David all along. Of course the woman was always blamed, but maybe ... the thought gave her a little flutter of pleasure. An ordinary child, a boy or girl like her and Bill would be wonderful, better than the rather frightening, brainy little stranger Kristall had become. She immediately felt guilty, put the milk down on the bottom stair, ran lightly up to the back bedroom and opened the door quietly. Kristall was asleep, her golden hair strewn over the pillow, tears wet on her cheeks. Filled with remorse, Brenda leaned over her, brushed the tears away gently with her finger and kissed the soft baby cheek. She must try harder, try to love her more, persuade Bill to be a good dad to her. She tiptoed to the door, stood for a moment and wondered about Kristall's real father. He hadn't really come into her thoughts very much until now. Was he clever? Probably.

Right out of her class. Julius he was called. It was inside the bracelet. Did he know he had a daughter?

She pulled the door so that it was almost shut but not quite, put Kristall's little slipper in place to prevent it from banging and walked thoughtfully down the stairs to Bill and her new life.

Germany—1942–3

Julius's seemingly charmed time in the treacherous *Bewährungskompanie* had come abruptly to an end. But it was not his mother, not Helga, who first received the news, but Sophie.

After three years of this terrible war, she was becoming used to disaster. There had been a similar dispatch a long time ago, how long she hardly remembered, when her own son had been lost somewhere over England. This second telegram caused the earlier grief to come surging back. She remembered crying for weeks over Werner's death, both for him and for the manner of his going. There was no glory in bombing civilians, nothing that she could be proud of, and it was her own dear country that he had damaged and which had, quite justifiably, killed him. How ridiculous war was. How had he come to fly bombers? He had always said that he wished to be a fighter pilot. Fighters would have been more acceptable to her, but bombers!

And now Julius! But not killed, both legs

180

blown off! He had been more honourable than Werner. The thought gave her immense grief. Julius had tried to do something about that monster, Hitler, and his evil plans, while her own two sons had betrayed her, Hans in the SS, Werner bombing England.

But what a hideous thing to happen to Julius. And she must tell Heinrich. She knew that it would drive him straight into Helga's arms, for this was their child, the loved son, and just as he had comforted her when Werner had been lost, so now he would comfort his mistress. She tried to replace her hatred for this other woman with sympathy, and to some extent she was successful. They were both mothers, both must come to terms with the frightful things that this war was doing to their children. She must keep her hatred only for the Third Reich and all its machinations.

She had been just as horrified as the rest of the family when she knew, after his imprisonment, that Julius had been sent to the *Bewährungskompanie*. It was the section of the Army reserved for those known to be troublesome, a convenient and outwardly respectable way of disposing of rebels, not as controversial as outright execution or a living death in a concentration camp, but highly dangerous and therefore almost as terrible. One did not usually survive too long in the *Bewährungskompanie*. That Julius had been unhurt for such a long time had seemed almost a miracle.

Sophie kept the telegram in her pocket until

Heinrich came home from the factory and then, pale-faced, she handed it to him and watched his tortured expression as he read. She wondered for the thousandth time, how it was that this misbegotten child of his was the favoured one.

He looked at her with anguish in his eyes. 'I must go to Dresden,' he said. 'I must tell Helga. I shall stay for a time.'

She nodded. 'I'll put some things together for you,' she said. For once she felt no bitterness at his going.

The following day, Helga and Heinrich stood together beside Julius's hospital bed. He was unconscious, a great arc supporting the bed-clothes in the place where his legs should have been.

'Is there any hope at all?' Helga had not yet been able to cry but she brushed her hand over her face. 'And if he does recover, Heinrich, how will he bear it?'

Heinrich was supporting her, his arm around her waist and his other hand holding one of hers firmly. He was as devastated as she, his face contorted with anguish, but he willed some of his strength into her and into the boy on the bed. 'He is my son,' he said. 'He will be able to bear it.'

Consciousness came to Julius in waves, rising and receding and with it, helplessness. He tried to sit up, pushing with his elbows at the hardness of the bed. But he couldn't rise an inch and fury took the place of fear. What the hell was he doing here? Why couldn't he move? 'I'm going back,' he shouted, but where or to what he had no idea and then the room faded and blackness overwhelmed him again.

He opened his eyes hours or days later and saw his mother and father standing beside his bed. What were they doing? Heinrich had his arm around his mother, damned careless that, something never to be done in public. He closed his eyes again and the troublesome sight disappeared.

A nurse brought two chairs. 'I think he will come round soon. They usually do.' She smiled encouragingly and Helga and Heinrich sat down close beside each other. Helga took Julius's hand in hers and then at last the tears flowed. 'My only child,' she whispered. 'He's my only one, Heinrich.'

And Heinrich flinched remembering her pleading years ago that they should have more children, and his unwavering decision that on no account must they bring more illegitimate offspring into the world. Cruel? Had he been cruel to her and was that why he loved her and this boy so much? Was there guilt in it? He closed his eyes, bent his head, and had nothing to say.

There were more operations during the following days and Helga stayed. She sat for hours at a time and only returned occasionally to the hotel room that Heinrich had arranged for her close to the hospital. Heinrich came and went, his work, his other family claiming much of his attention, his heart in the hospital where

183

his son was struggling between life and death.

But Julius did not die. Christmas and New Year came and went and he knew nothing of either. He lay for days in a drugged stupor, waking now and then, as the morphine began to wear off, to monstrous surges of pain in the legs that were not there. Then there was the comfort of yet another dose and another blessed time of oblivion.

Helga knew that he had no idea, no conception whatsoever of what had happened to him and as the moments of consciousness became longer so did her anguish.

'I've told him,' the surgeon said, 'but it meant nothing. Perhaps you or his father should help him understand.'

She tried to feel grateful to this man, yet achieved only bitterness. His skill had saved her son, but now she was left to do the almost impossible. *Help him to understand!* How? How could anyone do such a harrowing and frightful thing?

Eventually it was Heinrich who managed to do the impossible and convey the truth to Julius's drugged mind. But the knowledge only penetrated slowly and not as one hideous piece of unbearable fact.

But one day, weeks later, he surprised and delighted Helga. 'They'll give me tin legs,' he said. 'I've heard that there's a British prisoner of war with tin legs.'

She was pushing him around the grounds of the hospital in a wheelchair and she stopped, suddenly hopeful. The misery of the past months began to fade a little. 'Prisoner of war?' she said vaguely.

'Yes, he flew fighters apparently, was shot down, baled out, and new legs were dropped by parachute for him, from England.'

Julius had heard this amazing piece of information from one of the nurses who had been on duty when Douglas Bader had been brought in. At first he had not believed it. A legless pilot? Impossible! But she had assured him that it was true, but that it was not to be talked about. No one wanted to make a hero out of a British flier, but nevertheless it was a bit of news that might cheer Julius. She had taken an inordinate risk.

Cheer him! He thought of little else, and since that moment had begun to get well. He told his mother as much as he knew.

She went on pushing. 'A wonderful story,' Helga said. Privately she wondered if the whole thing had been made up for her son's benefit.

'You don't believe me, do you?' Julius turned to look up at his mother and grinned at her. 'It is absolutely true, I assure you, but not to be talked about. And if he can do it, so can I!'

Helga, for a moment, caught his mood and for the first time in weeks felt a little light-headed. 'Fly Spitfires?' she said.

He shook his head. 'No, get about on tin legs. Perhaps they'll let me go back to university.'

'No, Julius. Not that, please.'

'I thought you would want me to do something safe and worthwhile?'

Helga shivered, her mood of flippancy

185

disappearing rapidly. 'Safe, yes,' she said. 'But students are suspect. They do dangerous things.'

'You're talking about the Munich plot?'

'Ssh!' She walked more quickly, pushing the wheelchair along the path towards the lake where daffodils were just opening and birds were busy with nest building. Here they would be away from the threatening hedge. 'Bushes have ears,' she whispered.

Julius laughed. 'Don't worry, mother. It probably wouldn't be Munich anyway. And not for ages. The war might be over by then.'

'Over? How?'

'I have no idea.' The war hadn't figured much in his mind for a long time.

Helga shivered in the chilly April breeze. 'Let's go in, Julius. Mustn't get cold.' With difficulty she manoeuvred the ungainly vehicle around on the narrow path. 'You know that Berlin has been bombed?'

'Yes, I heard.' Then, suddenly trembling, he said, 'Any news from England?'

'Nothing. How could there be?'

'I just thought perhaps the Red Cross might get something through to Aunt Sophie.'

Helga knew that he was still thinking of Elizabeth. Sometimes in his delirium he had called out in English, called her name, had said things that had made her both embarrassed and frightened. She hoped the nurses had not understood, and each time he had done this she had replied quickly and loudly in German willing him to stop. Usually the words had petered out in a stream of meaningless sounds. There were informers everywhere, probably many Nazi supporters on the nursing staff who would happily see their patient restored to health only to be taken off to a concentration camp and yet more horror. Helga shivered. One of her friends had recently been arrested merely for listening to foreign broadcasts.

'I don't think it's possible to get any news from overseas,' she said. Then more gently, 'Forget her, my son. There are other girls, plenty of nice German girls who would—'

'Want a man with no legs?' He fumbled with the thick rug that covered him, angrily pulled off his gloves and lit a cigarette. 'I don't suppose even that damn British flying genius has managed to find a woman who'd want only half a man.'

In spite of his anger Helga smiled to herself. Perhaps he was coming back to life again. She was quite sure that if the authorities allowed him to live he would properly and triumphantly survive. He would never allow himself to become a permanent invalid. Heinrich was right. Julius was his son, had inherited his determination and courage.

'What was his name?' she said.

'Who?'

'Your legless pilot.'

'Bader. Douglas Bader. German name funnily enough.'

'So it is. And I expect he has a nice wife waiting for him in England.'

'Then he's damn lucky.'

187

'And so will you be.'

Julius grunted and twisted around to put his hand on hers as it rested on the handle of his chair. 'Sorry, and sorry you have to do this.'

'I like doing it,' she lied. It was the last thing in the world she wanted to do. It broke her heart. 'One day you might have to push me.'

'And how will I manage that with no legs?'

'As easily as your English pilot flies his Spitfires.'

For the first time in months they laughed together.

England—1943

'Wish I could get a nice fat chicken for our wedding,' Brenda said. 'Not much chance of that though.'

Bill gave her a hearty peck on the cheek and grinned. 'You never know what I might manage. A bit of extra milk here and there and a few eggs works wonders.'

The service was to be in the parish church and Brenda hoped that Kristall would behave herself. She'd made a lovely bridesmaid's dress out of some parachute silk, trimmed it with a bit of old lace that she'd salvaged from a frock of her mother's and put a frill on the bottom so that her everyday shoes would not be seen. No money or coupons for new shoes.

Not many brides went to their weddings nowadays with a bridesmaid all dressed up so lovely, but then it wasn't many that had

188

such a pretty daughter as Kristall. Not good mind you, but pretty, yes certainly pretty as a picture with those big blue eyes and golden waves. She'd do her hair up in rags so that it had real Shirley Temple ringlets for the day.

'I don't know why you want to go to so much trouble with the kid,' Bill said. 'Spend the time on your own rig-out. That would be more sensible.'

'I've got my dress ready,' Brenda declared. She had no intention of telling him that it was the same one she had worn for her wedding to David all those years ago. She'd still got the same slightly dumpy figure but no more inches added anywhere, thank goodness, so it fitted. It had cost a pretty penny and had been packed away carefully in layers of tissue paper ever since so it was as good as new. If she dyed it a nice blue no one would guess the truth. She was a bit worried about the dying, but the instructions on the packet assured her that it could be done, and next week, when she had a completely free day she was going to attempt it. After the wedding it would do for an ordinary 'best'. She wasn't likely to get married for a third time, and with the rationing it was silly to keep anything packed away.

So Brenda went to her wedding resplendent in a rather streaky blue frock, a wide-brimmed straw hat bought years ago at the seaside and now trimmed with a piece of net curtain, and a small bunch of flowers arranged as best she could to look like a bouquet. Kristall, who loved dressing up, was for once almost perfectly

189

behaved. She walked behind her mother with carefully measured steps, gave her the home-made silver horseshoe at the correct time, threw confetti with delight, and not until she was quite sure that no one could see her did she frown and put out her tongue at her new father's broad back.

Elizabeth's mother, constantly homesick for Bristol, had managed to persuade a friend to send her some local newspapers from time to time. So it was that a week later she stared in fascinated horror at the photograph of a burly man and his fawning bride. It was the bridesmaid's name that had caught her eye. 'Kristall,' she read. *'The four-year-old bridesmaid with the unusual name, looked just like Shirley Temple with her pretty dress and golden ringlets.'*

With heart pounding and a face from which all colour had drained, Louise stared spellbound at the likeness of the child. It could have been Elizabeth who was looking up at her, accusing, angry, for there was no smile on the little girl's features.

She carried the newspaper to the window so that the light fell brightly upon it. Yes, there was no doubt. Even without the name she would have known, but the age and the unusual name made it doubly certain. This was her own rejected granddaughter. So they had kept the name Kristall. Elizabeth had been sure that it would be changed. She must never know that it had not.

A great wash of shame and misery swept over

190

her, and then like a returning nightmare, the quandary. What to do? She could certainly never bring herself to destroy the photograph, tear it up or put it onto the fire. There was only one thing to be done. It must be added to the letters from the child's father, *that Julius*. She must keep it hidden and safe and then put it away under the boards at Merricote, the boards that would hopefully keep their secret until she was dead and gone. She and Richard had planned to spend Christmas at Merricote this year, just the two of them. It should be easy enough to add one more item to her package of sins!

She fetched scissors from her work basket and carefully cut the picture out along with the account of the wedding. Then she hid it in her underwear drawer, destroyed the rest of the newspaper in case Richard should ask what she had removed, and feeling distraught and shame-faced, tried to concentrate on making some potato cakes from one of the wartime recipes that she hated. Anything to please Richard and ease her tortured mind. But the little girl's angry and miserable expression haunted her and refused to be banished. Yet there was nothing that she could do about it, absolutely nothing.

Christmas 1943

Bill Hodgson was quite determined that the kid shouldn't get the better of him, but he didn't want his new marriage messed up either. He'd make an effort to be firm but kind, try to win her confidence a bit. She liked animals Brenda had told him, always on about a dog. Well, he had a soft spot for animals too, but it didn't make sense to have a dog in wartime, what with meat hardly to be had and nearly everything on the ration. He'd go down the Hay Market and talk to one of his mates who had a scruffy little pet shop there. Perhaps there was something else a bit smaller she'd like for Christmas. *Kristall*—daft name. What on earth had persuaded Brenda to choose something like that? Sounded snooty, uppity, out of their class. Still, her first bloke was clever wasn't he? Worked on designing aeroplanes. A bit above a milkman.

So it was that on Christmas morning Kristall found a large package waiting for her beneath the paper chains that festooned the kitchen.

'Go on then, love. Open it.' Brenda, hair still in curlers, and woollen dressing gown belted tightly around her waist, watched her daughter, praying that she'd be pleased. She was desperate for some peace on this special day.

Kristall looked at the parcel suspiciously. It was tied up with string and she could see that there was a wooden box underneath for the brown paper wasn't quite big enough. A card hung from it and she took this off first and stared at it. 'To Kristall, with love from Mummy and Daddy.' She read the words aloud. They were easy words written big, but she could read lots now, not just those. Then suddenly funny noises came from the box, funny squeaking noises. She looked at her mother and back at the box and as realisation dawned she ripped at the paper and stared through the wire at the tiny frightened little creature cowering in the back corner.

'It's a guinea-pig,' Bill said. 'A very young one, six weeks old so he'll tame easy. I've made the cage nice enough for indoors. Too cold to keep a guinea-pig outside in winter.'

'Your daddy got it for you,' Brenda said proudly. 'Nothing to do with me. I don't like animals. But he persuaded me. As long as you keep it clean you can have it in your bedroom. No smell mind!'

Kristall was quite still for a moment and then she opened the cage door and put both her hands into the box. A pet! She'd always longed for a pet. Could her new daddy, whom she hated, really have done such a nice thing?

She put her hands gently around the little animal, felt the terror-stricken, fast-beating heart, lifted him out and cradled him gently against her nightdress. Then she looked from one parent to the other and smiled. 'I'm going to call him Henry,' she said. 'And soon he'll be my best friend and he'll love me.'

'She smiled at you,' Brenda said later to Bill. 'She really smiled at you.' For the rest of the day Brenda was moderately happy. Bill had managed to get a goose from goodness knows where. She didn't ask any questions. He gave her a string of pearls, not real of course, but nice, and she had given him a pair of socks and a pullover that she'd been knitting secretly for ages, all made from wool unpicked from one of David's jumpers, washed and rewound and made up in a different pattern. She was very pleased with her industry and Bill had no idea that it was second-hand wool. He'd kissed her and put the pullover straight on.

Perhaps things were going to be a bit better now. Perhaps the guinea-pig would work a miracle on her difficult, brainy child and they could be a proper happy family.

When they were in bed that night and he'd made love to her in his energetic boisterous way, he seemed disinclined to go straight to sleep as he usually did. 'Think it worked?' he said. Then with a laugh, 'The guinea-pig I mean?'

'Of course it did, love. She's been as good as gold all day.'

'She's not a bit like you is she, placid and that? Suppose she takes after her first dad.'

Brenda's heart gave a little lurch. She hadn't told Bill about the adoption, had been frightened that he might reject her. No man wanted a wife who couldn't have kids, after all, and he'd be sure to think that it was her fault there'd been no baby. She knew that he wanted a second family, his two sons being grown up and in the Army.

And now she suspected that her dream might be coming true. She was three weeks late. It must be that, surely, never been late before. So perhaps she could tell about Kristall. It was now or never anyway. She'd better get it over with. 'She's adopted,' she said nervously.

It took a moment or two for her words to sink

in. Then he pulled away from her, sat up in bed. 'What? What did you say? Adopted? When? It's a bloody lie. I don't believe it. Why didn't you tell me?'

She tried to calm him. This was awful. She could feel his whole body tense and angry. It was a sudden and terrifying reaction, much stronger than she had expected. It filled her with dismay and an overpowering fear. She'd never seen this side of him before. 'It's all right, Bill,' she said. 'It wasn't me what couldn't have children. It must have been David.' She moved closer to him, put her hand on his but he pushed her away.

'Who are her parents then? Must be real riff-raff? My God, Brenda, what a bloody stupid thing to do, take a baby that's not yours. No wonder she's like she is, full of bad blood. Might be criminal, anything.'

'They told me that she was middle-class and her mother was very respectable.'

'Respectable! That's a laugh. Some bloody tart more like. And what about the father?'

'She wouldn't say anything about the father.'

He got out of bed, switched on the light, and stood glowering down at her. 'Well, now I know why Kristall is like she is. She's bad through and through. No wonder her mother gave her away.' He clenched his fists. 'Wish we could give her away too. Could we send her back where she came from?'

Brenda was crying now, loud heart-rending sobs. 'Course we couldn't,' she said. 'She's adopted. It's all legal and that.'

'Then we're stuck with her. I'll be more strict than ever. Beat the bad blood out of her. Guinea-pig indeed! What a fool I was.'

'Don't take it away from her, Bill. Please.' Brenda had seen the happiness that the little creature had given. 'Please, please, Bill.'

'We'll see about that. It depends on how she behaves. Damn silly name, Kristall. Where'd she get that from?'

'She came with it. I kept it.'

Bill sniffed derisively. 'Stuck with that too, then.'

Brenda wiped the tears from her eyes, tried to compose herself. She had to say something to take away some of his outrage. 'Bill,' she said. 'I think I'm in the family way. I think we're going to have a little one of our own.'

He looked at her again, doubt now mingling with the anger. And to Brenda, watching him anxiously, it seemed to take a hundred years before some of the thunder went out of him. Then he put out the light and clambered back into bed beside her. 'Are you sure?'

She nodded. 'I think so. Will that make everything all right?'

He kissed her roughly. 'When we've got our own kiddies it won't matter about Kristall will it?' He was gentler now, concerned for her. 'Can we? I mean if you're expecting can we go on ...?'

'Course we can,' she murmured as she gathered his big bulky body into her grateful and welcoming arms once again. 'As often as we want.'

Neither of them heard the footsteps on the landing. Kristall went back to her own room, icy cold with terror. What did it mean? Something bad certainly. She knew a bit about adoption. It came in stories sometimes. Her mummy wasn't her mummy at all, then. It was someone else, someone called a bloody tart. What was a bloody tart? And why had this, this tart, given her away? Because she was bad through and through that Bill-man had said. She'd never call him Daddy ever ever again. She went over to the little cage where the frightened guinea-pig was cowering in the corner. She pulled him out and into her arms. 'Henry,' she sobbed, stroking him gently, 'I do love you. Will you love me even if I'm bad as bad?' She felt some of his little oval-shaped droppings fall into her hand and she put him back gently. Mustn't get Mummy cross by keeping him in the bed. He'd mess it all up.

But she wasn't Mummy at all. They wanted to send her back somewhere. She brushed tears away and remembered something else. Kristall was the name her ... what could she call her? ... her tart-mummy had given her. Perhaps she was a princess like the little girl in the story book. She must cry without making any noise so that they didn't come. She didn't want them any more, ever. She pulled Henry's cage up close to her bed for comfort and burying her face in the pillow, cried herself quietly to sleep.

CHAPTER 9

Kristall—September 1944

'We can't have that guinea-pig in the house when your baby brother arrives,' Mummy said. 'Animals spread germs.'

And the next-door neighbour said, 'Your nose will be properly put out of joint when your baby brother comes.'

And nasty Bill-Daddy said, 'You just behave yourself, my girl, when the baby comes, or I'll take that blessed guinea-pig straight back to the shop. You mark my words.'

That made Kristall really, really frightened. She didn't like Bill-Daddy one little bit. Mummy said she must call him Daddy, but in her head he was always Nasty-Bill-Daddy, and she tried not to say Daddy out loud very often. It occurred to her one day that she must have a real daddy somewhere. Her school friends said that everybody did, so as well as a tart-mummy she had a daddy. Perhaps he was a prince or even a king with a golden crown. One day she'd find him.

She hated this horrid baby who was coming to live with them soon, hated him almost as much as she hated Bill-Daddy. Where was he coming from anyway? How did they know he was coming and why were they making such a

198

fuss about it? He seemed to be very important. And why was her nose going to be put out of joint when he came and what did it mean? She looked at her little nose sometimes in the mirror, stroked it with her finger and hoped it wouldn't hurt or look funny if it really happened. The questions and worries went round and round in Kristall's head all the time.

Her fifth birthday had come and gone, and now that she was at school it was a bit better. She was top at reading and sums and the teacher was always nice to her. She liked Miss Webb very much and sometimes wished that she was her mummy. Every day when she got home she rushed upstairs and told Henry all about everything. He was bigger now and quite tame. In fact when he heard her come in he would stand at the front of his cage and make funny little welcoming squeaks. She usually had a few dandelion leaves or some carrot tops for him and she'd take him out and cuddle him for a bit, stroke his soft whirly fur and even let him run round the room sometimes. He liked to run all around the edge next to the skirting board and under her bed and then he'd come up to her again for another dandelion leaf. Henry was her very favourite person and nice Miss Webb came next.

Mummy and Bill-Daddy didn't want her any more. She knew it was because she was adopted, and if ever Bill-Daddy did anything nasty to Henry she'd run away and never come back. When she thought about it she always cried. It was too awful to imagine. But Miss Webb said that the Lord Jesus in the sky loved animals. Kristall got down on her knees every night and prayed that He'd keep Henry safe. She wasn't quite sure how He'd manage it from right up there, but He was magic wasn't He and could do anything?

At the beginning of September Mummy disappeared and Kristall was left with awful Bill-Daddy. She hated that, and hardly spoke to him at all. She could wash and dress herself, go to school on her own and put herself to bed. He cooked her food and that was all. At mealtimes they sat opposite each other and ate, mostly in silence, and in the evenings he went out. 'I'm going to see your mummy,' he always said after tea. 'Don't get up to any mischief while I'm gone, mind.'

One day she came home from school, ran upstairs to tell Henry that she'd come top in 'problems', and then stood quite still at her bedroom door. There were no welcoming squeaks, nothing, just a trail of sawdust on the floor.

'Where is he?' she shrieked almost falling down the stairs in panic.

'Out in the back lav,' Bill said. 'Baby's coming home tonight and your mum don't want any smelly animals in the house.'

She rushed past him, out into the yard to the disused lavatory and there he was, there was the cage sitting on top of the wooden seat. 'Henry,' she sobbed. 'I thought ...' What she had thought was too terrible to say. 'Henry, I do love you,' she whispered. Her heart was beating furiously and she had scattered dandelion leaves and grass all down the stairs and right through the house.

'Get in here and clean all this mess up pronto,' Bill shouted at her. 'Or he goes tomorrow. Is that clear?'

Her mummy came home in a motor car. Kristall had never ridden in a motor car and here was Mummy all grand with Bill-Daddy helping her out, and in her arms was ... was the baby. Kristall's face creased in a scowl of pure hatred. She put her hand onto her nose to see if was all right and not out of joint.

'You've got a little sister,' Mummy was saying. 'Come and give her a kiss.'

'No she doesn't,' Bill-Daddy said, pushing her away. 'Got germs probably. Don't touch her.'

Kristall ran inside, through the house and out to the back lavatory. She threw her arms round Henry's cage. 'We'll run away,' she sobbed. 'As soon as I'm a bit bigger I'll run away and find my real mummy and daddy and you'll come too. I'd never leave you to them.' Henry squeaked his alarm and then went on nibbling the carrot that she'd sneaked earlier from the vegetable rack in the scullery.

It was a horrible evening. After tea the baby had to be fed. They wouldn't let her see that. Then Mummy put a dreadful smelly nappy to soak in a bucket. Disgusting.

When the meal things had been cleared away Kristall sat down at the table to draw a picture to take to school. She was glad the summer holidays were over. She'd hated those four weeks.

She chose the black crayon from her pencil-box and did jagged lines angrily all over the sky. She wished she could do them like that on the baby's silly red face. But if she did, it was Henry who'd be hurt. She shivered with misery and fear. She couldn't think what Bill-Daddy might do to her precious guinea-pig if she did anything to the baby. She'd have to be as good as good for Henry's sake.

Suddenly she looked up from her picture. 'What's her name?' she asked. 'Has the baby got a name yet?'

Mummy and Bill-Daddy were sitting each side of the empty fireplace having a smoke. 'We're calling her June,' Mummy said.

Kristall knew that it wasn't June now. It was September 1944. Her teacher had made them all copy it from the blackboard today and she'd said something about praying for our brave soldiers in France. Kristall was going to add that to her prayers for Henry tonight. Jesus was strong enough to look after them as well probably.

'Why?' she said. 'I don't like that name.'

'What you like or don't like has nothing to do with it,' Bill-Daddy said. 'Your mummy has chosen it because of the landings in June.'

Landings? What on earth did he mean? The landing was the place upstairs by the bedrooms.

'Our brave soldiers landed at a place called Juno Beach back in June,' Mummy said. 'That's why your sister's name is going to be June.'

It sounded daft to Kristall and she added another jagged line to her picture. 'Why is mine Kristall?' she said suddenly.

'God only knows,' said Bill-Daddy. 'Stupidest name I ever heard. You came with it.'

Came with it! Kristall remembered then that she'd heard them talking about this on that awful night when she first learnt that she was adopted. Her first mummy and daddy had chosen *Kristall* for her! She knew that it meant lovely sparkling glass, much better than dull old June!

Elizabeth—1945

Elizabeth knew that memories of Crystal Night would haunt her forever. Because her child had been conceived on the afternoon of that day, and in Germany, the memory was even more poignant. She was not prepared, however, for the avalanche of anti-German feeling that descended like a great vicious cloud, and greater than ever before, on a January day more than six years later. The Red Army had discovered Auschwitz! There had already been tales of a place called Maidenek, but Auschwitz confirmed the earlier hard-to-believe reports.

Newspapers were full of the latest terrible stories, frightful harrowing things that no one could imagine really happening in twentieth-century Europe. Everyone she met, everything she read, posed the same appalling questions. Who were these people who could do such things? How could ordinary men and women allow it to happen? They were like us weren't they? Not wild savages but civilised, cultured. Germany was the home of great music and art wasn't it? How then? A war yes, that was acceptable. It was the way of the human race unfortunately. But mass murder of the most despicable kind, killing children too, babies!

She and Isobel sat in the small picture-house in Little Hending and stared in horror at the screen. There were few pictures to back up the statements but the reporter vowed that they were all true. The Russians had taken photographs, he said. They were too terrible to show.

There was hardly a sound from the shocked audience, just a sniff and a gasp of disbelief here and there, a suppressed sob now and then. Once outside in the cold winter night, the disgust, the hate broke forth. 'Kill the bastards, bomb them to death, kids and all. The only good German is a dead 'un.'

The fierce comments went on and on and Elizabeth and Isobel, stunned into silence, hurried away, round to the back of the building where they had left their bicycles. They cycled the five miles to the farm hardly speaking, the pale flickering of their lamps making small yellow beams of light through the eerie country lanes. Occasionally an owl hooted, some frightened night creature rustled in the hedge or ran across their path, and the death screams of a hunted rabbit seemed appropriate to what they had just heard.

And Elizabeth was screaming too, but inside,

silently. She thought of her grandmother and her own Jewish blood and then perversely she thought of Julius. Julius, with his gentle ways, his kind sensitive hands, his smile. How could Julius be one of those? How could he be a child murderer, a torturer hounding men and women to their deaths in gas chambers, crematoria? Of course he could not be. And Werner, her cousin, even Uncle Heinrich, Emmi, lovely kind Emmi, and Aunt Sophie? How was Aunt Sophie managing to live in a country that had done such monstrous unimaginable things?

'Do you think they knew?' Isobel said at last. 'The ordinary German people I mean?'

They had reached home and she opened the barn door and propped her bicycle against the stone wall inside.

'I've no idea.'

'Wasn't there a resistance?' she insisted. 'I mean, your Julius knew about Crystal Night didn't he? And so did hundreds of others.'

'Don't call him *my Julius,* for goodness' sake. He's not that any more and never can be.' Her voice was sharp, full of hurt. 'It was too dangerous to protest.' Elizabeth remembered the fear, the constant looking over one's shoulder to see who was listening to the odd careless remark, the pressures to join the party and the penalties if you didn't. She had also seen the fanaticism in the eyes of Hans, the cousin she had never trusted. It was a madness, a passion, shared by thousands, a betraying, vicious thing.

'Dangerous or not, they should have spoken out. Perhaps Hitler wouldn't have remained in

205

power if they had.' Isobel's voice was indignant.
'It's easy enough to say that here. We've always been free to say what we like.' She leaned her bike against Isobel's and followed her friend across the yard and into the farmhouse. 'And most people worshipped Hitler in the early days. It's difficult to believe now, but I saw it first-hand. He was almost a god to them. He'd rescued Germany, brought jobs and prosperity.' She took off her coat and put it on a hook inside the door. 'Then it became a police state,' she said, warming to her subject, 'and it was too late. Open disagreement on any level just wasn't possible. I knew that much even before I left in '38.'

'Maybe,' Isobel replied suddenly losing interest. 'Thanks for the lecture. Anyway they'll be able to speak out soon won't they? Then they'll all be anti-Nazis.' Her voice was cynical. 'Gosh it's cold. Hurry up and shut the door.'

'Film any good?' Jim Crewe looked up as they entered the kitchen. It was warm and full of smoke from the inefficient chimney and from his pipe. 'Western was it? I always likes a good shoot up. Enjoyed *The Oregon Trail* a few years back.'

'No, not a western.' The newsreel had almost blotted out thoughts of the film that they had gone to see. 'Just a soppy thing that you wouldn't have liked,' Isobel said.

'Were there pictures of that concentration camp on the news?'

'One or two.' Elizabeth waved her hand in front of her face in a feeble effort to fan away some of the obnoxious haze and then made for the door again. She didn't want to talk just now, couldn't bear to relive any of the things she had heard and seen. 'Eye-witness reports mostly. They were bad enough without pictures.'

'Ought to be rounded up and shot every last one of 'em. I treat my animals better'n that.'

'I should hope you do,' Isobel said. She stood for a moment warming her hands at the fire.

Jim sniffed derisively, took another draw on his pipe. 'Missis have left the kettle on for your bottles. She've gone up.'

In the back scullery they filled their heavy stone hot water bottles and Elizabeth cradled hers, woollen-wrapped, in her arms as she went upstairs followed closely by Isobel. She wished tonight that she had a room to herself, hadn't to share. She could see Julius clearly again now. There was a time when his features had faded from her mind, when he seemed to be receding from her life, but now she was back in pre-war Germany, could see and hear the terror of that night, saw once more the little girl in the blue dressing gown. Had she been taken to one of those unspeakable camps? Had her little slippers been added to the pathetic pile of shoes?

It was too dark in the bedroom to read, for upstairs in the farmhouse there were only candles. Elizabeth got into bed as quickly as possible, pulled the thick eiderdown around her neck and lay watching the flickering light dancing on the wallpaper. She wondered how she could banish the hideous pictures that her

207

mind had made from the reporter's words, how to sleep without seeing emaciated corpses being shovelled into mass graves, and the heap of children's shoes. That was the most terrible thing. *All that was left*, the Russian soldier had said.

Then suddenly she thought of Philip. 'Do you think they'll hear about it abroad?' she said. 'Our troops, I mean, and at sea?'

'Probably, but not for a bit.' Isobel gargled, brushing her teeth with water from the china jug that they filled each day and set on the marble washstand. She spat carefully into the enamel pail and then replaced its lid. 'Why do you ask?'

'No reason.' Was there a reason? Elizabeth suddenly felt a chill sweep through her. Strangely, she felt personally defiled by the German atrocities as if part of the evil was in herself.

She knew that Isobel would laugh if she confessed to these outlandish feelings, so she remained silent. She thought of Philip, visualised him at sea, confident, giving orders, coming home, kissing her, marrying her, taking her into his arms ... But then, intruding on that picture came Julius and her heart leapt. Julius, the betrayer, Julius, the Nazi, Julius, the man she loved.

Isobel got quickly into her narrow bed on the other side of the room, shivered at the coldness of the sheets and blew out the candle. 'You'll be married soon and then Germany and all its dreams and horrors will fade completely. I still can't understand why you've waited so long. You could have married on that last leave of Philip's. You always said that you wanted to get away from here, that you wanted to be cherished. I remember that word. I thought it very decadent.'

Elizabeth, still thinking of Julius, of Germany, said dreamily, 'I don't suppose I shall ever forget Germany. I've asked myself the same question though lots of times. Why do I stay here slaving away every day when I could have been Philip's wife long ago and living in the lap of luxury?'

'Beats me,' said Isobel snuggling further down in the bed and pushing the hot water bottle down to her cold feet.

'I like it here,' Elizabeth stated. 'I've become very fond of the place. In fact it'll be a wrench to leave.'

'Do you realise that we've been here for more than four years? That quite takes the biscuit.'

'We've helped to win the war. Think of all those ships we lost in the early convoys. They were bringing us food I suppose. Well, we've contributed our bit. With all our efforts they hadn't to bring so much.'

Isobel yawned. 'Perhaps you're right. Roll on your wedding anyway though. I can't wait to leave.'

'You don't have to.'

'Stay here without you? No fear. The war can't last a lot longer can it? They don't need us now. I intend to have some fun.'

Sophie was in her kitchen peeling potatoes. There was precious little to eat now in Berlin and she was grateful that she had ordered a large quantity to be stored in the cellars after last year's harvest. With so many mouths to feed, potato soup with a few carrots and a morsel of stock was usually the main meal of the day. There were no servants to help now. They had mostly been drafted to work in factories, and three poor souls had been killed in the bombing.

She tried to peel the potatoes as thinly as possible for nothing must be wasted. Berlin was in ruins, mercilessly battered night after night by waves of enemy bombers, not enemies at all to Sophie of course, but deliverers! When she heard the Allied planes she was always overcome with both fear and excitement in almost equal measure. Surely the war would end soon. The way things were going, Germany couldn't hold out much longer, surely? She would be free again, free to go home. Dear, dear England! How she longed to be there. If she survived! So far, the house, Heinrich's house, for she refused to call it hers any longer, had not been damaged, but it was crowded now, crammed with bombed-out families, friends who had lost everything.

All her children were away. Werner had been shot down over England. Strange somehow, her favourite son buried in English soil, almost as if he belonged there and had returned home. A

210

fantasy, she knew, but a comforting one. Emmi was nursing and Hans was probably on some battlefield somewhere. They had not heard news of him for a few months now. His activities in the SS had so disgusted her that in her secret thoughts he had almost become the enemy. Yet she wept and prayed for him every night.

Heinrich came home occasionally but spent much of his time in Dresden with Helga. Not that this mattered so much now. The old hurt had almost disappeared. His factory had been bombed to smithereens, and a good job too. He would never say just what he had been making but it was something sinister and not to be talked about, she was sure. She saw Julius now and then. He was getting about fairly well on the tin legs that had been made for him, but needed a stick. At least he was saved from the Forces. In spite of the tales she heard about the famous British flier who had no legs, the authorities had not suggested that Julius was capable of any further war work, and so far had left him alone.

Today he was coming to Berlin to have a small adjustment made to one of his legs and in spite of everything she felt a little glow of pleasure at the thought. He was a nice boy even if he was her rival's son. He'd always been pleasant to her, and since his accident she had felt sorry for him. After all he was on the 'right' side wasn't he! One didn't dare mention any such thing of course, but she knew. Perhaps one day in the future she might be able to help him a little.

She cut the potatoes into chunks and piled them into the large pot of stock that was simmering on the stove. Yesterday she had managed to get a bag of bones and the stock was rich and brown. She put in a pinch of salt and a few dried herbs, rather stale now, but better than nothing. Then, as Julius was coming, she added one of her precious onions.

'Can I stay here tonight?' he asked her later that evening when he had appreciatively finished his substantial bowl of stew. 'The hospital has been damaged, but they say they'll be able to see me tomorrow, all being well.'

'Of course,' Sophie said. 'Where else? We're crowded out of course. You'll have to sleep on the floor, but I'll find some cushions.'

He smiled at her. 'The floor will be fine.'

The next day, the unthinkable happened. Julius and Sophie stared at each other across the breakfast table as the news came through on the crackly wireless set. Dresden had been bombed! More than just bombed, annihilated! For the first time in almost five years of war Sophie felt mounting shame as she listened. Beautiful, exquisite Dresden, the treasure of all Europe, was in ruins. And worse than that, countless thousands of innocent civilians killed. What could the Allies have been thinking of? She shook her head in horror. Then suddenly the horror became personal. Heinrich was probably in Dresden, with his mistress, with Julius's mother.

'My mother,' Julius said. 'Dear God, my mother!'

'And your father! I think that Heinrich is there too.'

Julius reached across the table to Sophie, held his hand out to her and she put hers in his larger one for comfort. There was no embarrassment or awkwardness between them any longer. They had always avoided mentioning those two names in the same breath, but now, in the magnitude of the greater tragedy, lesser concerns lost their power to wound.

'I'll have to get there somehow,' he said. He reached for his stick and struggled to get up. 'The leg will have to wait.'

Sophie watched him hobble across the room, wanted to stop him going, but knew that nothing on earth would keep him here. She knew too that he would accept no help. She saw his determination and marvelled at his bravery and rapidly returning strength. At the door he turned and looked at her. 'I'll let you know as soon as I can,' he said.

For his sake she prayed that Helga would be alive.

England

When, one February morning, the news of the bombing of Dresden was announced in triumphant headlines in Jim Crewe's newspaper, Elizabeth felt physically sick.

'The bastards deserve it,' Jim said with relish.

213

'Pity it's not the whole bloody country.'

'It almost is,' Elizabeth said.

'Jolly good job, then. You a spy or something?' He eyed her with suspicion.

'No. But Dresden was beautiful.'

'So was Exeter.'

Of course, of course. Tit for tat. Elizabeth ate her toast in spite of rising distress. A long morning lay ahead. *Julius, were you there? Are you alive still or just a statistic, one of the thousands of dead? Killed, roasted to death in the fireball which we delivered on St Valentine's day? Your mother lived in Dresden. You promised to take me there. You never did.*

When she had time to read other newspapers she found that she was not alone in her disquiet. Dresden could be compared to Florence the reports said, an old town full of magnificent eighteenth-century baroque and rococo art and architecture, a treasure house of Dutch and Flemish paintings. Julius had said something of all this.

'You've been very solemn lately,' Isobel said when they were working together the following day. 'You haven't said a dicky-bird all morning.'

'What does *rococo* mean?' Elizabeth asked. She must concern herself with something other than Julius.

'Highly decorated, I think, very beautiful, scrolls and shells and things. It was pointed out to me when I was taken to Italy years ago. I didn't care much about it in those days, preferred to visit an ice-cream stall. Why do you ask?'

214

'Just Dresden.'

'Oh yes, nasty business.'

'Did you ever go there?'

'Never. And it's too late now. How about you? Your relations must have taken you.'

Elizabeth shook her head. 'No. Julius often said that he would, but we never got around to it. His mother lived in Dresden.'

Isobel stood up straight and leaned on her shovel. 'Gosh, Liz, that's awful. I'm sorry.'

'There's nothing I can do, no way I can find out if any of them are still alive.' Elizabeth pulled her scarf more tightly around her neck against the keen February wind. 'Berlin has been bombed to smithereens too.'

'You're not saying we shouldn't do that, surely?'

'No, of course not. We've got to end the war somehow. It's just all so bloody stupid.'

'Philip will be home on leave soon though won't he? That should cheer you up.'

'Yes,' said Elizabeth. 'It should cheer me up.'

Germany

Between Berlin and Dresden there lay more than a hundred miles of near chaos. For weeks it had not been easy to travel between the two towns, but now it was almost impossible. Unable to walk easily for more than a few yards, Julius constantly cursed his legs. When it was obvious that there were no trains, no public transport of

215

any kind, in fact, he stood beside the road and hoped for a lift.

Eventually it came and when, some uncomfortable hours later, the truck driver reached the outskirts of Dresden, he climbed stiffly out of the cab and stood staring in shock and disbelief at the heap of ruins that had, only a few days before, been his own beautiful city. He wished that he had been here, that he had died too. He wanted to lie down on the rubble and never get up. It was more desirable surely to have been a victim than to witness this terrible, unimaginable devastation.

He could see no building standing, nothing with any resemblance to anything that had been before. At first he thought that no living thing could be alive and then there was a movement, and a tattered and grime-covered figure emerged from what must have been a cellar beneath the rubble of a still smouldering building. Whatever it was, for it could hardly be called human, it glanced in his direction. He could feel eyes boring into him. He took a step forward, held out his free hand. 'Can I do anything ...?' His words sounded feeble as if they came from someone else, from a long way off. He felt too clean in spite of the long journey, too tidy to be in such a terrible place. 'I wasn't here,' he managed. 'I've come to find my mother.'

The creature laughed, a horrible sound that he thought he would remember forever, and the blanket that had been covering her from head to toe slid from her shoulders. 'Would you recognise a heap of ashes?' she said, 'for that is what they are, all of them, everyone, ashes, burnt to ashes.' Then she burst into tears and crumpled onto the ground at his feet.

Unsteadily he tried to reach her, but his stick fell and his legs seemed to go in opposite directions. He cursed quietly, tried to pick up the stick, but it had fallen close to her and she grabbed it, held it out to him. 'Tin legs,' he said.

She got up, stared at him, and without saying anything they stumbled together as far as they were allowed through the still smoking streets. Here and there the roads were narrow pathways between mountains of rubble, but mostly they had to clamber over the debris and often the dead, or bits of the dead. Julius almost fell many times. The girl held his arm, helping him with every step. 'It's no use,' she said eventually. 'The only place that's safe is the river bank. You know, where we used to get the pleasure steamers. Some little buildings are still standing and if there's any food to be had it'll be there. I think they bring it up the river from Meissen.'

They came at last to the waterfront, a once favoured place where there had been boats and gaiety and beauty. Julius had often walked there with his mother. Now it was his turn to weep, all the pent-up emotions of the past few days suddenly finding release.

She held him in her arms then, allowed him to cry until the remorseless sobbing eased a little. 'Where were you?' she whispered. 'How did you escape?'

'Berlin. It's bad there too, but nothing like this. Why did they do it? Why bomb Dresden?'

'No one knows. We had nothing here but refugees from other places. People trying to escape the Russians. They are mostly all dead now, burnt to nothing. Even facing the Russians might have been better than a death like that.'

They found a place to sit and when he had collected his thoughts a little he realised that she spoke in 'high' German, the speech of the articulate, the educated classes, that she was young, and beneath the grime and rags she might even be pretty. 'What do they say about the Russians?'

She shivered. 'That their soldiers rape and steal, that often they kill. It was the Red Army which discovered the concentration camp in Poland, and we ordinary Germans have to pay the price of their outrage and disgust.'

'Do you believe all that? About Auschwitz, I mean?'

She nodded. 'I don't want to believe, but I've heard such terrible stories.'

'Our armies did frightful things in Russia too, to Russian women and children.'

'So they rape and kill us.'

He nodded. 'The British won't do that.'

'So I've been told. How can you be so sure?'

He didn't say, *I was in love with an English girl. Was? Am I still?* He said, 'They haven't suffered like the Russians. We didn't invade England, did we? When we're liberated I hope it will be by the British or the Americans.'

'Liberated?'

He looked at her in sudden alarm. That was not a word one used of the triumphant, conquering Allies.

But she shook her head. 'It's all right. I'm no Nazi, no informer, and now I know where you stand too. Shall we stay together for a bit? All my family are dead. I'll help you look for your mother.'

Julius felt suddenly comforted. He put his arm around her and she snuggled close to his side. She was like some small frightened animal finding welcome refuge.

'What is your name?' he asked gently.

'Liesel,' she murmured. 'Just Liesel. That's enough for now. I don't feel that I have any other.'

Elizabeth—1945

In March, Elizabeth, almost twenty-five, and in spite of herself, sometimes still a little in love with a dream and a memory, awoke to her wedding day. She was staying at Westleigh. Mrs Gibbons had insisted upon it, and insisted also upon making most of the arrangements for the wedding. She had organised the reception and invited a great number of guests. Elizabeth and her parents had been consulted politely, but not involved very much. It was all very rushed because Philip was to sail for the Far East shortly.

'But it's the bride's mother who usually does

everything,' Louise had complained. 'Not the bridegroom's.'

'I know, but Philip's family are paying nearly all the bills, so I suppose they must have their way.'

Louise had realised that there was nothing more to be said and she had given in as gracefully as she could. In spite of all the shortages and rations it was to be a big wedding and thoughts of the ever-increasing amount of money that would be needed to pay for it had at first terrified her. The offer from the Gibbons family to pay most of the expenses had been received with secret relief, but outwardly with self-righteous protest.

And now the actual day had come. Yesterday afternoon Elizabeth had walked through the gardens with Isobel. 'My last day of freedom,' she had said. She had linked her arm through Isobel's and thought how comforting it was to have such a good friend. 'How long is it since we first met? Six years? How time flies.'

'Almost exactly six years,' Isobel replied. 'I remember the day you arrived at Mere House. You were so miserable, so hopeless.'

Elizabeth had laughed bleakly. 'Weren't we all?'

'I suppose we were. We've changed a lot since then, thank goodness.'

'And now I am to be Mrs Philip Gibbons, a completely different person. Will Elizabeth Benson exist any more?'

'Not Mrs *Philip*, please. Mrs *Elizabeth* Gibbons. You should not give up your identity. If my turn ever comes I certainly shall not.'

'But it's usual. Most women do and are pleased about it. It shows they've been successful in the marriage stakes, captured a man and all that.'

Isobel had frowned in severe disapproval. 'Not you and me, Lizzy. We're new women. We believe in our rights. We just borrow our husband's name for a time because it's convenient. Beneath, we are still who we were born.'

'That's rather a new-fangled idea isn't it?'

'Rubbish. Of course it's not. I hope you're not going to become one of these poor things who are just echoes of their husbands.'

'I've discovered that Philip likes to lay down the law. He takes after his mother. Mrs Mildred Gibbons is as formidable as a battle-axe, as you have no doubt seen.'

'Yes, I've seen.'

'He has a jealous streak too that I've only recently detected. It's flattering, of course, but rather frightening in the circumstances!'

'Stop worrying. He'll never find out about Kristall.'

'Have I been very deceitful?'

'For goodness' sake, Lizzy, of course you haven't. How many affairs do you think he's had? Do men feel guilty if they don't confess to every conquest, every child they've fathered? No of course they don't. Remember Mere House, remember all the girls there, most of them abandoned by worthless, philandering males. No, my dear Lizzy, you have nothing to be ashamed of. Hang on to that conviction like grim death.'

They grinned at each other and walked in silence for a while and then Elizabeth, wanting to change the subject remarked, 'What a beautiful garden this is. Look at the daffodils. There must be thousands over there in the orchard. They seem to be growing wild. Some of them are still in bud. I suppose it's because of the cold February.' She wandered over and picked a small bunch. 'There were daffodils at Mere House when I arrived. It's strange. I remember them quite clearly, and I remember my sorrow when they faded.' Silently she said, *just as my dreams must fade, just as my thoughts of Julius and Kristall must be buried away forever now, and not to be resurrected next year like the daffodils!*

That had been yesterday, and now, on her wedding day, the dream had not gone, had sprung, unwelcome and unbidden to life as soon as she opened her eyes. Angry with herself she jumped from bed and pulled on her wrap. 'I love Philip very much,' she affirmed aloud to her reflection in the long mirror, believing that if she said it enough times it would become fact. 'Yes, I truly love him and I am determined to make him happy, to be a good wife in every way I know. And yes, I shall be Mrs Philip Gibbons if that is what he wants.' Then, chuckling a little at the remembrance of Isobel's disapproval of this idea, she pushed bare feet into slippers and padded quietly downstairs to make herself a fortifying cup of tea.

The kitchen was spacious, dominated by a long scrubbed wooden table and a comforting Aga. Elizabeth drew a chair close to its warmth and drank her tea. Was she happy about today? Yes of course she was. The past was over and the dreams would fade. Kristall would always have a place in her heart, but a very secret place, and Julius must disappear.

She had known Philip for more than four years now, most of them, it was true, spent apart, but a naval wife must expect such things. She had become used to the idea. She smiled to herself. It was the best of both worlds surely, a good marriage, financial security, and a certain freedom too! Was there anything more to want? They had already bought a house, a pretty place in a village outside Bristol. 'Convenient for mother,' Philip had said, and then had added quickly, 'and for your family too, of course. They'll come back to Bristol after the war I presume?'

She had tried not to mind too much about the first reason for his choice. Bristol was home after all, the place in which she had been born and brought up. *But has he chosen that particular village so that his mother can keep an eye on me? Is this another sign of his jealousy? No, of course it isn't. I must stop thinking like this and concentrate on the positive things.*

There would be babies. They both wanted babies. And animals at last, a dog. She thought of the pets she had always yearned for but never been allowed to have. Did you get married just to have babies and animals, a house, a background, a firm base for your life? Perhaps you did. After five years of war and a broken heart yes, you certainly did.

The sound of a key in the back door lock disturbed the peace of the quiet kitchen. Of course, seven o'clock. The staff would be early today.

'Morning, Miss.' Mrs Maunders, one of the dailies, let herself in, pulled off gloves and heavy tweed coat. 'Cold out there,' she said unnecessarily. 'Any tea left in the pot?'

'No, but the kettle's hot.'

'Always is with one of they Agas. Wish I had one. Ready for your big day then?' she added, with a knowing wink, as she pottered about, brewing herself fresh tea, tidying around busily.

Elizabeth blushed and rose to go back to the chill but welcome privacy of her bedroom. 'Not quite,' she said.

She crept quietly upstairs unwilling to wake anyone yet, needing to be alone for a little longer. Her mind leapt forward to tonight and she was glad that she had already slept with Philip. Each time he came home on leave he had wanted to get married, but for some reason, not quite clear even to herself, she had refused. When it was a short leave they would meet in a country hotel conveniently situated near a small halt on the railway line between Liverpool and Gloucester. 'We are as good as married,' she would say. 'I am Mrs Philip Gibbons for forty-eight hours.'

There in the large, lumpy double bed, she would allow him to make love to her, his gentle and considerate lovemaking somehow purging a little of the guilt she still felt.

'I would like to know that you are secure,' he had repeated every time he came home. 'There are a mighty lot of U-boats out there. The survival rate isn't very high on an Atlantic Convoy, you know. Why won't you marry me?'

For reply she always held him close in her arms, comforting, giving him some of her considerable strength. 'Soon,' she usually said. 'On the next leave or the one after that.'

Freedom was precious. With Philip's wedding ring on her finger she would belong to the Gibbons family and, especially, to his formidable mother. With his engagement ring she had respectability, a firm reason for saying 'No' to opportuning GIs and others, the best of both worlds in fact.

And of course there was, though there should not be, in the deep recesses of her heart, an abiding fragment of a dream. But now ... now she told herself that she had finally and firmly set aside that fantasy. The U-boat menace was at an end, the war would soon be over and there were no more reasons to prevaricate. Although Philip intended to make the Navy his career, peacetime would be far different from war.

It was only the past which belonged to Julius. She would never forget him and the baby she bore and gave away. Kristall would have a little secret place in her heart for ever, but other

225

children would come and heal the wounds. The future was Philip's. She would go to her wedding day joyfully today.

'I am an actress in a play,' she said later to Isobel as she struggled into her elaborate wedding dress. 'A play written and designed by my mother-in-law.'

'Don't be so daft,' her friend told her. 'And she's not your mother-in-law yet.'

'Only a couple of hours to go.'

'You are young and beautiful and you are marrying a rich and highly eligible man and about a million other girls would like to be in your shoes.'

Elizabeth laughed and looked at the little silver shoes that her mother had produced. They were a bit tight, but lovely. It was the 'something old' Louise had declared, for they had been hers years ago when she had married Richard.

'You're right, of course,' Elizabeth said. 'I am very lucky.'

The day passed in a whirl of elegance and style. She left the church on Philip's arm beneath an archway of swords and gold braid. She smiled at her parents and saw tears on her mother's face, but she knew that they were tears of joy. At last she had done something to please them both and she was filled with a glow of satisfaction and happiness.

Click, click, went numerous cameras. She smiled, took a silver horseshoe from a little girl, kissed her gently and thought for a moment that it should have been ... no, of course it should not. One didn't have wedding tokens from one's daughter.

The spring sunshine enveloped her, she smiled at Philip, stood with him for more *click-clicking*, with her parents, then Isobel, then alone, and at last it was finished and they drove to the splendour of the reception in an ancient landau that had been taken out of storage, restored and polished to some of its old glory for the occasion. It was pulled by two lovely greys borrowed from wealthy friends, friends of Mildred Gibbons of course, of course. But it didn't matter. Elizabeth was, for the most part, content.

CHAPTER 10

Philip insisted on carrying her over the threshold. *What a nice, romantic idea. I hope that I am not too heavy! All that farmhouse stodge!*

So here they were at Merricote. She had told Philip that it was her very favourite place, and of course that was true, but privately she knew that she had chosen it partly as a statement of something, independence perhaps, or maybe a sudden valuing of her own family. There had been altogether too much of his. This was hers, a place that her mother-in-law knew nothing of, had never seen, a house of childhood memories and happiness.

227

A local woman was to cook and clean for them for the week. Apart from that they would be alone. 'We can really get to know each other properly,' she had told a delighted Philip. 'Forget the war, forget everything but us.'

The first night of the honeymoon had been spent in a Bristol hotel, and today they had motored down, using some petrol carefully hoarded by Mr Gibbons and proudly presented to them, amidst great laughter, a valuable wedding present.

During that golden week the sun shone for them and the earth, warming a little after the bitter February cold, put forth early wild flowers here and there. Hand in hand, Elizabeth and Philip roamed the Devon lanes, seeing daisies whitening the fields where not so long ago there had been snow. Birds were busy choosing nest sites, carrying odd things in their beaks, blackbirds singing around the garden.

Twice they drove onto the wastes of Dartmoor, where it was still cold, a bitter wind sweeping around the tors and making conversation nearly impossible. And at night they lay in the big double bed, cosy, warm, secure, on the whole happy with each other in this quiet peaceful place where neither war, nor family, nor even dreams of the past were allowed to intrude.

Elizabeth was glad that they had made love before, pleased that there were no surprises in store for her. She was relaxed and totally at ease with him, and he appeared to be the perfect husband, attentive, loving, treating her like a piece of delicate porcelain. The feeling was a novelty and she made the most of it.

He organised everything, was confident and totally in charge, made all the decisions, always determined what they should do although nominally consulting her first. Of course, he was a naval officer, wasn't he, a man of action and command. She must expect this. It was the result of his training and his career. While he was at home Elizabeth considered that this state of affairs was quite acceptable. His long absences at sea would give her all the opportunity she needed to live her own life, to assert herself. She fell in with all his suggestions, all his plans, and when they made love she prayed desperately that it would result in the baby she so much wanted.

The week passed quickly and then he was back in Plymouth with a multitude of things to do before he went to sea again. Elizabeth, alone for long hours in a Plymouth hotel, for their house was not yet ready, had time to think, to reassess her life. Had time to read the newspapers again.

The Allies had crossed the Rhine. Cologne was taken, the war couldn't last much longer. She saw pictures taken from the air of the devastation of German cities, of Berlin, and some of the old worries came back to plague her. Had her German family survived? And if they had, how would Philip react to them? And of course, when the war ended she would have news of Julius.

The year 1939 seemed so long ago. Peacetime! What was peace like? How could one live without excitement and fear? Would peace seem boring?

She shivered in disgust with herself when her thoughts went along these lines and recalled Auschwitz, thought of the hideous things the war had done to so many.

And in April she listened in horror to Richard Dimbleby's golden voice reporting yet another unbelievable atrocity. The British Army had discovered the obscenities of Belsen! This time photographers recorded the monstrous truths and later she saw it all for herself at the cinema. Few details escaped the cameras. Everyone could now see the piles of skeletal corpses, the living dead peering with spiritless eyes at their rescuers, the remains of the gas chambers and crematoria. There could be no doubts any longer, no denials of the things that Germany had done, and the outrage, the fury, increased. For Elizabeth there was the added burden of personal shame, for she felt part of it. She thought of her little daughter, and of the German inheritance she had bestowed upon her so thoughtlessly back in 1938. She was glad that Kristall would never know.

Then Hitler was dead and Elizabeth remembered Hans, his stiff Nazi salute, the *Heil Hitlers* of which he was so proud and so fanatical. Where was Hans now?

Berlin fell, was a mass of rubble. She gazed in horror at the photographs in the press and vividly recalled its glittering prosperity before the war, the bright lights, the times she had walked down the *Unter den Linden* with Julius, shopped in the *Kurfürstendamm,* stared up at the massive Brandenburg Gate, a mighty triumphal arch built nearly two hundred years ago. What remained of all that? Would she ever go to Berlin again and relive those memories?

Did she want to remember? Perhaps she did. But would Philip allow her to do so? Wouldn't it make him think of her past? He wanted no reminding that she had once had a German lover. She tried to shrug her misgivings angrily away. *I have survived a war in which millions have perished horribly. I should be horse-whipped if I feel one glimmer of self-pity.*

She was thinking about all this one day as she walked on Plymouth Hoe. She stared at the ships, serene and still now, for the sea was calm and held no menace today. Then she looked at the distant horizon and spoke aloud to the empty sky. 'Don't leave me alone too much, Philip,' she whispered. 'I thought it would be nice to have a husband in the Navy, to be free much of the time, but I was wrong. I need you to fill in the gaps, to keep the ghosts at bay.'

A woman with a dog stared suspiciously at her. Elizabeth laughed a trifle grimly and walked swiftly on.

The house they had bought on the outskirts of Bristol needed extensive renovations and when Philip eventually sailed Elizabeth moved into a small hotel nearby to oversee the last of the work and to choose furniture and curtains. Now she felt tired, nauseous every morning, needed a rest.

I think it has happened, she wrote to Isobel in early May. *A baby! How about a few days at*

Merricote, just you and me?

So, when the whole country was crazy with joy over Victory in Europe, she was back in her parents' little stone-built house rejoicing that she had an additional reason for celebration. 'Is this a sign that I am completely absolved?' she said. They were sitting in the garden surrounded by the glory of lilac and hawthorn in full bloom, red campion and wild hyacinths in the hedge bottom where the gardener had allowed them to grow undisturbed, and more formal rows of tulips in one of the carefully tended flower beds.

Isobel laughed. 'Absolved? From what? Funny word to use. Sounds religious.'

'I feel religious just now. Grateful for everything, for the baby, and the end of the war, and I think that at long last I'm nearly free of the past.'

'I said that you would be, eventually.'

'Yes you did, and I was determined not to believe you.' Elizabeth was knitting a tiny matinée coat. She put it down on her lap and stared at the swallows diving and wheeling in the sky. 'Do you think they've flown all across Europe to get here?' she said thoughtfully. 'Is that the way they come? Over Germany?'

Isobel looked at her and laughed. 'I shouldn't think so. Italy I believe. Picture the map. Germany wouldn't be on their route.'

'No of course not. I'm just being fanciful.'

'That's allowed in your condition.' She trailed her hand on the grass beneath the deck-chair, picked some daisies. 'So Germany is still there in the background, then?'

'Yes, but not as a threat any more. Not to me I mean, and not to anyone else now, either.'

'I suppose your aunt will come to England soon?'

'If she has survived. Poor Aunt Sophie! I loved her a lot you know. My mother hasn't heard yet. You've seen the pictures of Berlin?'

'Yes. Terrible. A deserved fate perhaps, but that doesn't make it any better.'

'No it doesn't.' Elizabeth finished the line she was knitting, rolled her wool and pushed the needles through the ball. 'Let's go and do something else,' she said. 'We've been sitting here long enough.'

'A walk?'

'Good idea. And tonight I should like to turn out the attic. There are some old toys of mine up there. Would you help? We might find something for your Oliver. I remember that I had a lot of boy's toys when I was small.'

'Lovely. I always enjoy rummaging around in attics.'

'I hope you don't mind spiders. There are lots of them up there. They terrify me to death.'

'I quite like spiders, as a matter of fact,' Isobel said.

As long as Elizabeth could remember, the attic had been used only for storing the family's unwanted clutter. It had a small window with a view over fields and woods, and a cupboard built into a space between two of the walls. There was a dilapidated armchair, a doll's pram, a rolled-up Union Jack, and a multitude of boxes, most of them now with their contents spilling over the floor.

Elizabeth sat back on her heels and surveyed the chaos she and Isobel had made of the room. She picked up a lorry, pushed it back and forth along the moth-eaten rugs. 'My father bought me this. He wished I had been a boy.'

'You had plenty of dolls too. More than me.' Isobel was also sitting on the floor with three dolls cradled on her lap. 'I only remember having a couple.'

Elizabeth glanced in their direction. 'I suppose I did. My mother liked making their dresses.' She put the lorry down and reached for an engine and tender that stood proudly on a circle of track which she had just put together. 'It goes nowhere,' she said. 'Doomed to go round and round depressingly forever. Would Oliver like it? You could buy more lines probably and make it more fun!'

'I couldn't possibly deprive you of it,' Isobel said. 'You might have a boy.'

'What would you like, then? There must be something amongst all this.'

'Some books perhaps. Strangely enough my mother isn't keen on books. I grew up intellectually deprived. I don't want Oliver to suffer the same fate.' Isobel jumped to her feet, placed the dolls carefully back into their pram and pulled a further box from the cupboard. It was too heavy to lift and she dragged it towards the window. As she did so the floor creaked and moved a little. 'Loose board,' she said. 'It nearly tripped me up.'

'It's a very old house,' Elizabeth said, 'sixteenth century, I think. All the floors are a bit uneven.' She got up and pulled the carpet back. 'This board isn't fixed at all.'

Isobel abandoned her box of books and came to look. 'There's a space between it and the next board,' she said. 'It doesn't seem to fit properly. Shall we see if it comes up? It could be a secret hiding place. You might find something exciting, a fortune perhaps, gold and jewellery from the Civil War. They often hid things didn't they?'

'Not in attics! No harm in looking though.'

'Weren't there priest's holes?' Isobel said.

'He'd have been a jolly small priest to hide down there.'

'I didn't mean there, stupid!' They both laughed and Isobel gingerly raised the board. It came up quite easily and she stood it against the wall and stared down at the lathe and plaster beneath. 'Fascinating how they built these old houses,' she said. 'But no treasure and no dead mice or anything as far as I can see. Just cobwebby old dust.'

'We'd better try and put it back a bit more firmly.'

'I'm going to have a good look while it's up though.' Isobel knelt on the floor and felt further along beneath the joist. 'There *is* something. A piece of material.' Carefully she pulled out a parcel wrapped in muslin. 'What on earth?' She handed it to Elizabeth. 'It doesn't look very ancient to me.'

'Should I open it?'

'Of course.'

Elizabeth carried it over to the old armchair, swept the assorted clutter from its seat and sat down. She took off the outer layer and the paper underneath, and then she stared as if it had indeed been a decaying body that she had found for she was looking down at writing she knew, at German stamps on dusty, yellowing envelopes, at a ghost, a dream coming alive before her eyes. And there was a separate envelope with no address, no name. In a trance she withdrew the photograph and hardly understanding saw a little girl, a little girl called Kristall. Scowling. At a wedding.

She stared at it for a long time and then handed it to Isobel. 'Kristall. It says it's Kristall ... I don't understand.' Silence between them, then, 'Dear God. It's Kristall. It's my baby!' The room spun around her. She was going to faint. She snatched the photograph back, held it against her breast. 'It's really Kristall.' She went to the window, held it to the light, traced the small defiant face with her finger. 'I don't believe it. They've kept the name I chose. Kristall, the same spelling, the German spelling. Oh God, I chose that so that I would be able to reject her, so that I'd remember *Kristallnacht* and ... Isobel, do you see what this means? They've kept her name!'

The pile of letters, held firm in a stout elastic band, slid to the ground and she leaned down and picked them up, put the photograph aside, feverishly tore off the band and opened the top one. And read.

Was it a dream? Was it a nightmare? Would

she awake and find herself in her husband's arms? She read another and then another, heard the loved voice, the pained voice asking why she had not replied to his letters, telling her that he loved her above everything, that he would come to England if she asked that of him, even to become an enemy alien. He would face prison for her. *Please, please, reply to me, my darling Elizabeth.* Then he lapsed into German, and she read the words aloud in the language she had tried to forget but had not forgotten. The sentences sprang easily to her lips and she replied to him aloud as if in a time warp. More than six years too late!

Tears streamed down her face like rain and Isobel came to her, took the letters from her, laid them aside, knelt on the floor in front of her, held out her arms to her, and Elizabeth sat there sobbing until the May sky began to darken. Then Isobel led her downstairs to the kitchen, told her to sit down in the old wooden rocking chair and a few minutes later put a glass of something hot into her hands.

'I don't want anything.'

'Drink it. It'll do you good.'

Elizabeth sipped, and felt the burning liquid like fire inside her. 'What is it?'

'Brandy and milk and honey.'

Obediently she drank until the glass was completely empty, and some life and feeling returned.

'Where have you put them?' she said. 'I didn't dream it all, did I? Are there really letters from Julius and a photograph of ...'

237

'No, it wasn't a dream. I'll get them.' Isobel went back to the attic, groped her way over toys and paper and boxes, retrieved the letters and returned to the kitchen. She put them in Elizabeth's hands.

Elizabeth stared at them again, and with the first shock receding now, some of the incredible implications began to dawn on her.

'They've used the name I chose,' she said again as she read the words beneath the wedding photograph. 'She's really and truly Kristall. That's what they call her. I ... Oh, dear God, Isobel, I can find her now. There can't be many Kristalls in Bristol.' She shook her head in bewilderment. 'But how did this come to be here, in the attic at Merricote, hidden away with these letters of more than six years before? How on earth ...?'

Isobel was filled with fear. The church where the photograph had been taken was clearly named, the district where they lived and even the surname. Yes, it would be easy to trace Kristall now.

'I can't think how they got there,' she murmured, thinking that, of course, it must have been Elizabeth's mother.

'It can only be my mother,' Elizabeth said confirming her thoughts. Her voice was full of contempt. 'Only my mother would be capable of such a barbarous thing. How could she do it? How could she live with herself afterwards?' She spread her hands in perplexity, the letters and photograph lying together on her lap, accusing, condemning. 'I never want to see her again.

238

She's ruined my life, changed the whole course of it, and not just once but twice, remember. She forced me to give Kristall away knowing all the time that Julius was the father and that he wanted to marry me. I remember my utter misery when, as I thought, Julius stopped writing. I'll never forget those days. And it was *her* all the time. I can hardly believe it! How could any mother do that to a daughter?'

Isobel took a deep breath. 'Because she loved you. Because she thought it was best for you to forget the past, to start a new life, and that of course is just what you have done. I was watching her on your wedding day. She must have felt completely justified. She looked triumphant, and now I understand why.'

'Triumphant for herself. Triumphant because she had a respectable daughter at last who had toed the line and made a good marriage. My God, Isobel. Don't ask me to forgive her. Ever.'

'Then it'll consume you. No one can live with hatred like that.'

Elizabeth felt rage threatening to overwhelm her in rising waves. Even her friend was now included in it. 'I don't believe that you are saying these things to me,' she shouted. 'You're on her side.'

'I'm on no one's side. Try to think for a moment. He was German, a terrible thing then, and more than that, he'd been a thorn in her sister's life for years and years, the mistress's son. She and your Aunt Sophie were very close, you said. So Julius was the enemy twice over.'

239

'And I had betrayed my family and my country by falling in love with him? Is that what you are saying?'

'That's how she saw it, obviously.'

'And my baby was going to be born into a sort of battlefield with all that alien blood in her veins.'

'Not only alien blood but a constant reminder of your uncle's infidelity. What was his name?'

'Uncle Heinrich.'

'His adultery. His betrayal of her sister.'

Elizabeth was silent, trying to digest the unwelcome words, trying to reject them, trying not to acknowledge the tiniest mite of excuse for her mother's deceit.

'Cling to the fact that she did it all for you,' Isobel persisted, 'and if she was wrong, well, she must have suffered a hell of a lot. Why did she hide these letters instead of burning them? Have you thought of that? It would have been more sensible to put them straight on the fire.'

'You say that she's suffered! Just think what she's done to us. Julius could have come here to England in 1938. It was just possible then. We could have married and lived peacefully right through the war.'

'That's pie in the sky. He'd have been interned for the duration.'

'So what? He'd be alive, wouldn't he, and I'd have Kristall.'

'Alive yes, but totally embittered probably, and he might have—'

'Oh, shut up, Isobel. Stop being reasonable and sensible, for goodness' sake. His letters have

240

reminded me of all I've lost. You can't imagine. I can hear his voice speaking those words ...' she glanced down at the letters on her lap '... just as if he was here in this room.'

'But he wrote them more than six years ago, Lizzy. Six years. Six years of war. It's all in the past and you have a new life. And so, probably, has Julius. I know I sound cruel, but—'

'Yes, you do. Bloody cruel and callous. Because of my mother, Julius is probably dead. I want to rush out to Germany right now and find out, find him, if he's alive.' She slumped in the chair, some of the spirit gone out of her. She felt hopeless and alone.

Isobel sighed. 'Oh Lizzy, Lizzy. You don't know what you're saying. Have you seen the pictures of Germany just now, bombed to smithereens, of all Europe in chaos, ragged refugees and starving, displaced people trying to get to places that don't exist any more? You can't go rushing off to Berlin just like that. And have you forgotten something?'

'What? Nothing else matters but finding Julius. I'll join the hordes trekking through Europe if I must. I've got to find him, Isobel. Don't you see? I must find him somehow.'

'You *have* forgotten haven't you! You're married to Philip, expecting his child. You love him and he adores you. What will it do to Philip if you do such a mad thing? Julius is part of the past. You have to let him go, Elizabeth.'

There was a long silence then, and eventually Elizabeth fumbled for her handkerchief, wiped her face and raised grief-stricken eyes to her friend. 'And if I can do that, if it's possible to do that, what about my baby? What about Kristall?'

'You mustn't even think of tracing her. She's not a baby any longer and she doesn't belong to you any more. She has a new life. She knows nothing about you, probably doesn't even know that she's adopted. Think about her happiness instead of your own. And Philip doesn't know she exists. He might reject you, and then what could you offer Kristall? Only another rejection!'

Elizabeth stared down at the photograph again. 'I shall put it in a frame,' she said. She rose, fetched scissors from her knitting bag and carefully cut around the defiant little figure. Then she walked out of the room as if in a trance, took the photograph of her parents' wedding day, cut it from its silver frame and tore it into pieces. Then she carefully placed Kristall's mutinous little face in the centre of the frame, found sticky tape in the desk, and sealed it up again.

'I'm going to bed,' she told Isobel.

She stood in the bedroom and stared at her parents' double bed, the bed in which she and Philip had made love on their honeymoon only a few weeks ago. She opened the window letting in the sweet night air. There was a lilac bush beneath the window and she leaned far out, breathing its wonderful, healing scent. The war and all its horrors seemed a million miles away, but Julius had been resurrected, had traversed

242

the distance and the years, his letters bringing renewal of the longing and the rapture she had hoped was gone. It could be a fierce, destroying thing if she allowed it to be, with power to threaten her marriage and her life.

Now, in a quieter mood she thought about the reasons she had left Berlin, left Julius. She had thought him a Nazi. There was nothing in the letters to disabuse her of that idea. There could not have been. She remembered the censor, the fear of betrayal, of death if you resisted the regime in any way. Perhaps she had been wrong about Julius. Could she have been? Had she rejected him out of error? The thought was too horrible to contemplate and she would never know unless she sought him out. And that was impossible.

Of course Isobel was absolutely right. Six years was a long time. She undressed slowly, brushed her teeth, climbed into bed, hugged the spare pillow in her arms, and because Philip had made love to her in this bed only a few months ago she tried to think of him instead of Julius. But the misery in her heart blotted his image right out of her mind.

She lay there hour after hour listening to the owls calling from the wood beyond the garden, hearing the rustling of various night creatures below and the bats in the roof over her head. In the distance she could hear the church clock chiming every quarter-hour, always five minutes late. By the time it had reached four o'clock she could feel a weariness overcoming her, turmoil giving way at last to sleep.

She awoke with a deadening sense of loss, but as the day wore on, as she talked to Isobel, walked through the woods at the river's edge and thought about the baby she was carrying, a change began to creep into her heart.

'Finding the letters has been a sort of watershed in my life, a catharsis,' she told Isobel when they were sitting in the garden after tea. 'In some strange way that I don't understand, they have defined my thoughts, brought things to a head. You've helped too. You'll never know how much. You've talked sense, shocked me into seeing things as they are.'

'I'm glad about that, then.' Isobel was slightly embarrassed by this praise.

'Those old pages, the German words, the musty smell, have made me realise how much in the past it all is. Philip and the new baby are the present and the future. Julius is the past.'

'Then perhaps you might find it in your heart to forgive your mother?'

'I don't know, Isobel. I honestly don't know. That may be asking too much.'

'And Kristall?'

'Like you said, I could offer her nothing. She has her own life and that doesn't include me. She'll always be in my heart and I shall treasure the photograph. That's all. Perhaps one day in the future ... who knows? But for now I shall do nothing.'

The following morning the postman propped his bicycle at the gate and walked cheerily up to the front door. 'Two letters today,' he said handing them over to Isobel who had opened the door before he reached it. 'Nice day for a picnic.'

'Picnic?'

'School kids in the village are having a Victory party. Thought you'd have known about it.'

Isobel shook her head. 'No we didn't. I'll make some cakes.' She looked at the envelopes. One from the new man in her life and the other for Elizabeth, from Wales. 'A letter from your parents,' she called doubtfully up the stairs. 'How are you now?'

Elizabeth had slept late and she came down wearing her father's dressing gown, the cord knotted firmly around her waist. Isobel handed her the letter.

'I don't know that I'm ready to read it yet.'

'As you wish. I've made some tea.'

Elizabeth looked at the envelope in surprise. 'It's my father's writing. He never writes.' She took the silver knife that lay on the hall table and slit it open. There was one closely written page inside. She gazed at it, slightly bemused, and then started to read.

'My dear Elizabeth,

As you know, your mother intends to come to Merricote for a few days shortly. I shall come with her and we shall therefore only be able to stay until Monday. I have managed to have my classes covered for that day.

Your mother does not know that I am writing this letter but I wanted to warn you in case you should be shocked by her appearance. She is very ill. For a long time she said nothing to me, but she has become increasingly weak over the past months and was forced to see a doctor recently. Tests have told us what I already guessed.

I am sorry to give you this bad news, but I want you and your friend to act as though nothing is the matter. We are looking forward to three pleasant days.

From your loving father.'

Elizabeth passed the letter to Isobel and waited for her to read it. She was still reeling a little from yesterday's momentous events. Now here was something else, another tragedy to grapple with. 'Perhaps it's worrying over me and my misdeeds that has made her ill. Perhaps everything is my fault.' She walked into the kitchen and slumped at the table. 'My mind won't function properly any more. I was just managing to achieve some sort of composure again and now this. What can be the matter? Yesterday I had such murderous thoughts towards her and now I'm quite devastated. Please God, she doesn't die!'

Isobel poured two cups of tea. 'Perhaps your father is overreacting.'

'My father never overreacts.'

'It may be her heart. People live for years with bad hearts.'

'He says she looks ill. That means only one thing to me.'

'Don't give up so easily, for goodness' sake,' Isobel said. 'We must make sure they have a lovely weekend. I'll help you all I can.'

'Thank you,' Elizabeth said. 'You're the best

friend I've ever had.' And then, to her pleased surprise, she longed for Philip ... not for Julius but for Philip. Why wasn't he with her? Of course, she knew why. She was a sensible, capable service wife, wasn't she? But how could she get through life with a constantly absent husband? *I wish you'd give up the Navy ... I need you, Philip.*

What was Isobel saying? In the midst of all these traumatic events in her life, what on earth was Isobel talking about now? Elizabeth dragged her mind back from all her harrowing problems. Something about helping with a Victory tea party, making Victory cakes, washing up? *Isobel, dear, dear Isobel! Whatever should I do without you?*

Germany—1945

'But she has a sister in England who is dying. A *twin* sister!' The little Jewish woman stood angrily before a British officer in occupied Berlin. 'She is British. She must go to England soon or it may be too late.'

The man looked her up and down. 'And you say she hid you, saved your life.'

'Yes, and my daughter too. She kept us in her cellar for two years. She sacrificed her own food for us, risked her life all that time.'

He shuffled some papers on the desk. 'Frau Sophie Kleist. Damn stupid thing to do, marry a German.'

'There are some good Germans.'

247

He glanced at her again with renewed interest. 'That's an odd thing for a Jew to say.'

'Some resisted Hitler and died for it.'

'Of course. Well, I shall look into your request. Transport is difficult. Everyone wants to get to England.'

'Or America,' she said, half under her breath.

'You? Is that where you wish to go?' Silently, he thought, God, what she's been through! Two years in a cellar! He shook his head slowly in disgust. Not as bad as a gas chamber, though. Must be a brave woman, this Sophie Kleist.

'I'm a doctor,' the shabby little person in front of him announced. 'There's a lot I can do here just now.'

'Very noble, I'm sure. Your English is very good. We may be able to give you a job.'

'Thank you. I should like that. But we are not talking about me. I came on behalf of Mrs Sophie Kleist, remember!' She stressed the *Mrs*.

He stared at her again and then rose, indicating that the interview was at an end. There was a long queue of hopefuls outside in the corridor waiting for his time and sympathy. 'Come back tomorrow,' he said.

'Very well, and I can tell Mrs Kleist you will arrange transport for her, can I?' she persisted.

'I'll do my best.'

Autumn 1945

A Royal Air Force plane of Transport Command eventually took Sophie home, or nearly home.

248

Emmi was with her. There had been much more pulling of strings, many visits to various departments of the newly designated British Army of The Rhine and at last it was done, visas obtained, places secured. The testimony of the Jewish doctor had been important. To hide a Jew in Nazi Germany was a deed worthy of respect and reward. Everyone said so. Sophie was a heroine.

And now they were on their way. It was autumn, the war completely over, Japan vanquished, the Berlin ruins being cleared literally stone by stone, brick by brick, by the well-named rubble women, the *Hausfraus* who had survived and who were put to this work by whichever victorious army was in control of their zone.

Sophie and Emmi, excited, grateful, and to their own surprise full of nostalgia too, flew over the devastation of Germany, towards a new life. Heinrich was dead, likewise Helga, both burnt to a cinder in the Dresden fire-ball. Hans was in prison for war crimes. Sophie had not enquired into just what crimes he had committed, but was grateful that it was an American prison, not a Russian one.

And Julius? He and the girl, Liesel, appeared to be looking after each other. Sophie had left them in charge of the Berlin house. It was in the British zone of Berlin, thank goodness, and had not been damaged too much, either in the bombing or the ferocious street-by-street fighting which had followed and which had left most of the town in ruins before it fell to the Allies.

Sophie had liked Liesel. She seemed good for Julius and he needed someone just as badly as she appeared to need him. He was grateful for the refuge of the Berlin house, mainly to keep Liesel safe from the rampaging, raping soldiers of the Red Army.

Sophie sat in the big, lumbering aeroplane and shuddered at the things he had told her. Few female survivors of the Dresden bombing had escaped the next onslaught. The town had been taken by the Russians, battle-weary, sex-starved men who believed that all German women were their right. They had gone from house to house shouting 'Frau, Frau.' It was said that they would batter to death any man who tried to defend a wife or daughter, or even a mother, for age was no defence. And Liesel had told her that she had seen a little girl of twelve or thirteen screaming, blood running down her legs, raped repeatedly and viciously. 'They are punishing us for Hitler's crimes,' she had said.

Sophie looked across at Emmi and thanked God that she had been lucky enough to escape, that her fluent English had helped and that now she was safe and on her way home. Home! Wonderful, wonderful, safe, happy England. She would never leave it again!

Her thoughts returned to Julius and Liesel. Had Liesel been raped too? She had said nothing of her own treatment at the hands of the Russians, but Julius had been protective, had put his arm about her when she had been talking about all those terrible things. They had escaped eventually and with much difficulty, to

250

American or British lines, Sophie wasn't sure which, had managed to get to Berlin and, as with Emmi, it was Julius's fluent English which had helped. He was working with the British Army as a translator. Sophie hoped that he would be able to keep the house for now. It had been his father's after all. Berlin was more ruin than town and most of the few surviving buildings had been commandeered by the occupying forces, but Sophie had made her claim, stated that she was British by birth, that Julius had suffered monstrously for his stand against the Nazis and that she wished him to take charge of her house in her absence. The British Commanding Officer had listened to her politely and had told her that he would see to it.

So now she was free! Free at last from all the responsibilities and cares of those terrible years.

As the aeroplane flew over the Channel she fell asleep and only awoke when they touched down on precious English soil.

Bristol—Autumn 1945

Sophie and Emmi came straight to Bristol, to Richard and Louise's flat in Clifton. It was spacious and airy, overlooked the Avon Gorge and the graceful span of the Clifton Suspension Bridge.

The two sisters had embraced tearfully, each taking in hungrily the features of the other, but

251

it was Sophie who was most shocked by her twin's appearance. After the past terrible years in Germany it was surely she who should be the thin, emaciated one, Sophie thought.

Elizabeth listened in horror to the tales her aunt had to tell and longed to ask more about Julius. He had only been casually mentioned so far. Eventually the moment came. They had finished dinner, Richard was helping Louise with bath and bed, and she was sitting before the fire with Sophie and Emmi, large mugs of cocoa in their hands.

'Tell me more about Julius,' she said hoping her voice sounded completely casual.

'You know that he lost his legs?' Sophie said, just as though it was his wallet or his watch. 'I wrote about it back in June, as soon as we could send letters again.'

Elizabeth jumped to her feet spilling some of her cocoa into her lap. Shock waves coursed through her body. 'No, I didn't know. You don't mean both legs? Oh no! We never got that letter.'

'It was a long time ago,' Sophie said quickly. 'He's been very brave and he's managing very well. He has false ones. Don't look so stricken.'

Stricken! What a word to use. In spite of her determination that Julius had no part in her life any more she still thought of him often, and he was still the father of her first lost child, for so she thought of Kristall now. She had remained true to the resolutions she had made back in May, that she would do nothing about contacting Kristall and that Philip was the only man in her life. But no legs! Julius with no legs! It was unthinkable. She wanted to gather him into her arms, to look after him forever.

'He was imprisoned for working against the Nazis,' Sophie was saying. 'I thought you knew. Then he was put to work in the *Bewährungskompanie,* a sort of punishment section of the Army devoted to clearing mines and such like.'

'I thought he was a Nazi!' The words were wrung from her. It was the biggest mistake of her life.

'Oh, my dear child, was that why you rushed off so quickly, why you didn't write to him?'

Elizabeth nodded, tears streaming down her cheeks now. 'He said terrible things on *Kristallnacht.* I thought ...'

'He had to join the party, to pretend to be an enthusiastic supporter of Hitler in order to plot his downfall. He couldn't tell you, or anyone. We were all afraid of Hans.'

'Does my mother know all this?'

Sophie shook her head. 'If you didn't get my letter then she doesn't know, of course. Perhaps we shouldn't tell her. I don't want to say anything to upset her now. Julius gets about very adequately on his false legs and now that he has Liesel I think that everything will go well for him.'

'Liesel?' Elizabeth felt her knees wanting to buckle beneath her. What further shocks were in store? She groped for a handkerchief, wiped at the chocolate stains on her skirt and flopped down into the chair again. 'Who is Liesel?'

'A Dresden girl. They are living in my house. I've more or less made it over to Julius for now. He's working as a translator for the British. Liesel is very pleasant. I liked her and they are good for each other. They said something about going back to Dresden one day, but at the moment it's in Russian hands so it's not easy.' Sophie shuddered, remembering. 'I hope they won't.'

So that was it, then! Elizabeth was silent, still staring at her aunt as she digested this last piece of news. She guessed that Aunt Sophie had been aware of the love affair blossoming in her comfortable Berlin home all those years ago, but she probably thought that it had been merely a little passing thing, a teenage romance like so many others, of short duration and of little matter. She knew nothing of the existence of Kristall, of course. She wouldn't be so happy to talk about this Liesel if she did.

Julius and Liesel, Julius and Liesel, Julius and Liesel! The names went round and round in Elizabeth's head, a refrain of bereavement. She thought she had dealt with this loss months ago, but obviously not. And now there was no choice to make any more. It was over, over, over. A good thing. Of course it was a good thing. Julius and Liesel, the perfect couple, a wife to look after him. Elizabeth saw in imagination a pretty, fair-haired Aryan girl, long blonde plaits hanging down her back, competent and fulfilled, just like the hundreds she had seen in the Munich festival years ago, Hitler's cheering maidens!

254

She clenched her fists and felt like a balloon from which all the air had suddenly been released, a thing deflated, flat and empty. With great effort she forced herself to smile. 'That's good then, isn't it?' she said. 'That Julius has someone to look after him. I mean, it must be frightful, with no legs.'

She wanted to laugh hysterically but Sophie smiled at her. 'He heard about Douglas Bader. You remember? The famous Battle of Britain pilot who flew Spitfires and Hurricanes in spite of losing both legs in an accident. I don't think you need feel too sorry for Julius. He's very proud and doesn't accept help easily, and certainly not pity.'

Suddenly Elizabeth thought of the previously strained relationship between Julius and this brave little aunt of hers. Sophie was talking of him with no bitterness at all and yet he was the mistress's son, the constant reminder of Uncle Heinrich's adultery.

Did Sophie perhaps read her thoughts? For she said, 'I became very fond of Julius. He was almost a son to me during the last months. With Werner dead, and Hans ...' She paused and looked into the fire. 'Hans has forfeited all my respect, Elizabeth. I shall always love him, but that a son of mine could be in the SS ... it's been the greatest grief of the war for me, I think.'

Elizabeth put her mug down in the grate and reached across and grasped her aunt's free hand. 'He's suffering for it, isn't he? In prison, you said. Perhaps he'll repent.'

'Repent! What a lovely, old-fashioned word. Perhaps he will, but can I ever forgive? He did nothing bad to me personally, of course, but ... the concentration camps and all that?'

Emmi had said little so far. Now she smiled at her mother and at Elizabeth. 'Julius made up for it, somehow. He suffered for working against Hitler. We were proud of him. We still are.'

'Although we dared not show that we were of course.'

And I dare not show it either. I dare not say how I feel, how I felt, must say nothing about the existence of Julius's daughter! For quite different reasons my pride in him and my love for him must remain a secret too. Forever!

Lying in bed that night in total despair, Elizabeth wondered how she was to get through the rest of her life knowing how unutterably foolish she had been. How could she ever have thought that Julius was a Nazi? And now, how was she to put this preposterous mistake behind her and start afresh? Yet she must. For the sake of her unborn child she must do it. She had rejected her first child because of her insane blunder, she must not ruin the life of the second for the same reason. And her mother? She would say nothing at all, would make her remaining days happy ones.

Louise died on a grey November day just a few weeks later. They were all with her, Elizabeth kneeling on the carpet beside her bed, holding her hand, bending close to hear the last whispered words.

256

'It'll be all right now,' Louise said, not knowing what she said. 'I did the right thing, didn't I?'

'Of course you did.' Elizabeth stroked her hand gently, reassuringly.

'I've always loved you,' Louise murmured. 'I did everything for you. Was I wrong?'

Elizabeth kissed her damp forehead. Did she know that the letters had been discovered? No, she couldn't possibly know. This was delirium, past guilt surfacing. 'No, you weren't wrong,' she whispered. 'I know that you love me, and I love you too, Mummy.' She used the childhood word and it was the last thing Louise heard. Nothing more was said between them, but there was reconciliation at last. The only grief Elizabeth felt was that her mother would never see her second grandchild, would never be able to replace the first rejected one. But if this baby she carried was a girl she should be called Louise. That would be the final act of forgiveness.

CHAPTER 11

1949

The shoe-box prepared with love and heartbreak by Elizabeth and handed over to Kristall's new parents all those years ago was now safely hidden by Brenda at the bottom of an old blanket chest. Sheets and eiderdowns and other unwanted items were piled on top of it.

It was a thorn in Brenda's side, something she didn't want to think about but constantly did. She had put it in Kristall's bedroom cupboard at first, but that would never do now that the child was nearly ten years old and so curious about everything. She didn't want Bill finding it either. He'd been angry enough when she'd told him that Kristall was adopted. No need to remind him. As if he needed any reminding for that matter! He was always pointing out the difference between June and Kristall, the one so biddable, the other so difficult.

But what to do with the box? The child would have to know about it one day. Brenda would have it on her conscience forever if she kept it from her, got rid of it, for example. That wouldn't do at all. How about giving it to her for a birthday present? That way they wouldn't have to get anything else and she'd be as pleased as punch with it, wouldn't she? Bill would have to know of course, but if she told him he was going to save money it might make it all right.

Brenda waited until the night before the birthday and then she made sure that she gave her husband all his favourite things to eat. *To sweeten him up* she told herself nervously.

She always cooked him a substantial dinner when he came in at midday from the milk round, so this was just tea, but there were sandwiches and cakes, as much as she could provide on the ration. 'Only eight ounces of

258

sugar a week now, and four ounces of sweets, so stop moaning,' she had said to both her daughters recently. 'And that's four years after the end of the war too! We're still rationed because we've got to feed all those pesky Germans. Doesn't seem right somehow, seeing it was them that started it.'

Brenda considered that she did her best. She always felt a glow of satisfaction when she had managed a particularly good cake. She had to see that Bill was well fed. He usually had more than anyone else. A man needed it, didn't he! After all, he brought in the money. Often there was only bread and Marmite for Kristall and June and herself.

'What's in the blessed box, then?' Bill grunted when he had eaten, and after Brenda had cautiously mentioned its existence. She had stressed that they would save money on a present if they gave it to Kristall for her birthday. 'Why haven't you told me about it before?' he added, his voice definitely crabby now. 'Let's have a look.'

She suddenly remembered the bracelet. He mustn't see that. He might want to take it down the pawn-shop. Why hadn't she thought of it before she opened her silly mouth? *Stupid as usual*, she told herself angrily. *Nearly spoilt everything.* She must put him off somehow. 'It wasn't important,' she lied fearfully, 'I'd forgotten that we had it, really.'

However naughty and disagreeable Kristall was, and she seemed to be getting worse with every week that went by, she shouldn't

259

be deprived of that beautiful bracelet.

'Of course it's important,' he said, his voice rising ominously. 'I don't like you keeping secrets from me.'

She put her finger to her lips. 'Ssh,' she said. 'I don't want her to know until tomorrow. It wasn't meant as a secret, leastways, not from you. There's just an old baby dress and a couple of handkerchiefs. Nothing valuable. Nothing to interest a man.' She bent over him and kissed him on his bald head. 'Men aren't interested in things like that. I suddenly remembered it and thought she might like the dress for one of her dolls.' She handed him a mug of beer. She'd got a bottle in specially.

He took it, drank a long draught and appeared a little mollified. 'More likely to put it on that blessed guinea-pig,' he said with an unexpected attempt at humour. 'Do what you like then, woman. I've given up trying to understand the kid. Bad through and through if you ask me.'

Brenda sighed with relief, but she wouldn't let Kristall have the bracelet yet. Bill mustn't see her wearing it or he'd think she'd deceived him, and he'd be right of course. It would have to be hidden. A bracelet was easy to hide. She'd take it out of the box and put it somewhere safe, in her underwear drawer probably and Kristall could have the little nightdress and the handkerchiefs. No harm in that, nothing to anger Bill.

Brenda went into the scullery and started to wash up. She put hot water and soda into the enamel bowl and plunged a pile of plates in the

260

suds. She wished that Bill wouldn't keep saying that Kristall was bad through and through. The child had often heard him and that wasn't a good thing. Might make her even worse.

Brenda washed the dishes automatically, wincing now and then at the heat of the water on her already red and roughened skin. She reckoned she'd tried hard with Kristall even though Bill had turned against the child, but she had to admit that most of her efforts hadn't got her very far. All the early love she'd felt long ago had almost vanished, and now that she had June, her own precious little girl, she realised how stupid she'd been to keep on to David to adopt a baby. Kristall was too clever by far, and hard and unloving too. She was pretty enough, you had to admit that, with all those blonde curls and piercing blue eyes. Brenda didn't like those eyes at all, made you feel inferior and inadequate. They weighed you up and found you wanting! Yes, Kristall was a very uncomfortable child to have around. Not like chubby, happy little June, always wanting cuddles and kisses, always laughing. June would be starting school in September when she was five. Brenda was dreading that day.

Kristall opened her birthday cards, first one from Mummy and Bill-Daddy. She still refused to call him Daddy in her head. There was one from June, crayoned on a bit of paper torn out of her drawing book, and one from Sunday School. She propped them up on the sideboard and looked expectantly at her mother. She wasn't allowed to have a party now, hadn't had one for years and years, but there was usually a little present, some extra sweets perhaps or a ribbon for her hair.

'I've got a special present for you, now you're ten,' Brenda said nervously. She opened the cupboard beside the fireplace where she had put the box last night, took it out and handed it reverently to Kristall, reverently because she still had a feeling of awe over this box and perhaps a bit of sympathy for the unknown woman who had prepared these things so carefully. Prepared them with love too it seemed.

'What is it?' Kristall said. A shoe-box? She didn't want shoes for her birthday.

'It came with you.' It wasn't what Brenda had meant to say, but the words tumbled out in an embarrassed fashion.

'Came with me?'

'When we fetched you, when you were a baby, they gave us this box.'

Kristall stared at it quite stupefied for a moment. Then in a kind of slow motion she took it, placed it on the table, untied the ribbon, took off the lid and saw the little gown inside the yellowing tissue paper. 'You mean this is from my real mummy?'

Brenda felt a sudden and totally unexpected stab of rejection like a physical pain. Perhaps she still loved this child more than she thought. 'Yes,' she said quietly. 'From your first mummy. That's what you must call her, your *first* mummy.'

Kristall said nothing, replaced the lid and

silently walked up to her bedroom carrying the box in her arms, against her heart. It was the most precious thing she had ever been given. She sat on her bed and opened the box again, held the gown up so that the folds fell out and she could see the letters embroidered in golden thread on the little bodice. She traced them with her finger, a J and an E. What did it mean? Could it be that her mother and father had names starting with those letters? And they were done in gold, beautiful sparkling gold, gold for a princess. Her real mummy suddenly became a living person, a lady who had wanted her to have this. *She made this for me, for me, for me!*

She put the dress down on the bed, then took out the handkerchiefs, both delicate and lacy, never to be used. And at the bottom of the box there was an envelope with nothing in it, but on the front she read, *For Kristall, when she is grown.* She stared at it, looked inside again. There must have been something there. She took all the tissue paper out, shook the gown gently, looked on her bed and beneath it in case anything had been dropped. Then she took the envelope and ran down the stairs and waved it at her mother. 'What was in here?' she demanded. 'It's empty and look what it says on the front.'

Brenda's heart thumped and she felt hot colour rush to her face. How stupid she'd been to leave the envelope in the box. *Typical. I wish I had more sense.* 'I put it away for you,' she said. 'It's too valuable to wear. I thought ... I thought that your father might not let you have it.'

263

'What is it? Can I see? You can't stop me from having it now I know it's there.' Kristall imagined pearls, a ring, even gold sovereigns or pound notes.

'No, of course I can't. Sorry, love. I did it for the best.' Brenda plodded upstairs and Kristall followed her.

She opened her underwear drawer and took out the bracelet which she had wrapped in a pair of saucy black knickers which she never wore nowadays. 'Here you are, then. But you mustn't tell your dad. I'll help you find somewhere safe to keep it.'

'No,' Kristall said. 'You meant to steal it from me didn't you? Because it was from my real mummy.' She held it in the palm of her hand, saw the date, and the names inside, and because she had sharper sight than Brenda she read the three tiny words as well, *'Ich liebe dich'*. They meant nothing to her and she ignored them but the names seemed to jump at her, right into her heart. She ran into her own room and said them over and over again, 'Elizabeth and Julius, Elizabeth and Julius, Elizabeth and Julius, my parents.' Then to her own great surprise she began to cry. 'Why did you give me away,' she sobbed, addressing the bracelet as if it had life of its own. 'Was I bad even when I was little? Bill-Daddy says I'm bad through and through. Was that why?'

She put the bracelet on her arm but it was too big. She wanted to wear it always and she stared at it wondering what to do. Some of her tears fell upon its shiny silvery surface. Then she took the ribbon that had been around the box, put it through the bracelet and tied a strong knot. They did knots at Brownies so she knew all about how to make them safe. She wiped the tears away and slipped it round her neck and tucked the bracelet safely inside her liberty bodice. Bill-Daddy would never see it there and she'd only have to take it off once a week when she had her bath. It would remind her for ever and ever that somewhere she had real parents. She would try to be very, very good so that when she found them they would take her back.

She looked at the beautiful gown again. It was far too nice for a doll. She folded it as carefully as she could and put it back in the box with the lacy handkerchiefs and then she placed the box in the darkest corner of her cupboard with her toys and books on top. She mustn't risk Bill-Daddy or June finding it. She couldn't bear it if either of them even touched those lovely things. They were both out now, thank goodness, Bill-Daddy doing his milk round and June playing with the girl next door.

She didn't know that her mummy was crying too.

Kristall knew that she would never forget the day after her tenth birthday. She had been allowed to sleep at her friend's house for a special treat and she had paid June ten jelly babies just for making sure Henry's cage was fastened and the outside lavatory door locked last thing at night. Ten jelly babies were a lot out of the four ounces' sweet ration, but Kristall had worried about Henry nevertheless.

As soon as she got home she rushed through the house and out the back and there was the door wide open, and the cage door open too and no Henry to be seen. Then Mummy came out and said the most awful thing she'd ever heard. 'We'll get you another guinea-pig,' she said. 'We'll go to the pet shop tomorrow and you shall have a pretty baby one.'

'What happened?' Kristall screamed. 'Where is he? What happened?'

'I forgot to close the door,' she said. 'Next-door's dog got in and managed to get the cage—'

'No, it wasn't you. It was June. She promised me. It was June. I hate her. Where is she? I hate her, hate her, hate her a thousand, thousand times.'

Kristall knew where she'd be. Upstairs hiding in the cupboard, the big cupboard in the big bedroom that you could get right in. She ran up the stairs, two at a time—and flung the cupboard door open and yes there she was, behind her mother's dresses. Kristall grabbed her, pulled the dresses to the floor, trampled on them, pulled June out and hit her hard, dragged her across the room to the top of the stairs. 'I'll kill you,' she said. 'I'll kill you dead just like you've done to Henry.'

Brenda, coming upstairs as fast as she could, opened her arms and June fell into them, and both of them tumbled down the stairs, bouncing on each one like two bouncy cushions. Kristall stood at the top, white-faced, suddenly aware of the terrible thing that she had done. She ran down and stared at June's face, crumpled and bloodied. Her mother was quite still for a moment and then she opened her eyes and they were blank and frightening.

'Mummy, Mummy,' Kristall cried. 'I love you. I didn't mean it. I didn't mean to kill you both. Mummy, Mummy, wake up. Love me, love me.'

Slowly Brenda heaved herself into a sitting position and looked at both children. June was breathing. Thank God, June was breathing. She wiped the blood from the little girl's nose with her apron. Still the blood kept on coming. 'Get a tea towel, put cold water on it,' she managed.

Kristall clambered over both prostrate figures and ran to the scullery. When she came back she saw June held close in her mother's arms. 'My baby,' Brenda was saying as she rocked her gently holding her close to her ample chest. 'My precious, precious baby.'

Kristall handed over the wet tea towel and stood back and stared at them. Tears welled in her eyes and ran down her face like rain. Bad through and through. It was absolutely true. No one would ever love her now.

'I can't get up,' Mummy said. 'Go and get next door.'

Kristall did as she was told and was then sent to fetch the doctor. She made tea, fetched everything that was asked of her and the whole time she was quite numb, wishing that it was she who had fallen down the stairs, that she was dead like Henry. Poor, poor Henry. More tears fell like rain. And Mummy had not uttered one word of reproach.

June seemed not to remember anything that had happened. Her nose had stopped bleeding and that was the only thing that appeared to be the matter with her. 'Cushioned by her mummy,' she heard the doctor say. 'She is a lucky little girl. You have a badly sprained ankle, Mrs Hodgson, and a lot of bruises. You are lucky too. It could have been very much worse.' He was sitting on a stool, her mother's foot resting in his lap and he was binding it up stiffly. Kristall watched and listened as though it was all happening in a story book, as though nothing was real.

'How did it happen?' he asked.

There was a moment's pause and then Brenda said quite clearly. 'I slipped, doctor. Silly of me.'

'It will take a long time to mend and you will have to take it easy,' the doctor continued. 'Where's your husband?'

'Down the pub,' Brenda said, this time with a blush of shame. 'He always goes for a pint of a Sunday.'

'Then I suggest that you send a message to him. You'll need a lot of help for the next few days.' He turned to Kristall. 'You must go and tell your daddy what has happened,' he said. 'Tell him to come home.' He looked her up and down. 'You're a big girl. You'll have to do all the work.'

Kristall looked at her mother for confirmation. 'My sister lives in the next road,' she said.

'She'll come over. Run and tell Auntie Dorry, Kristall, and then go and tell your dad. Tell him to come home as soon as he can.'

And Kristall ran. Full of fear she ran. Bill-Daddy was sure to hear. He'd kill her for certain. June was the apple of his eye, just like it said in the Bible. When June remembered that she'd been hit and that her nose had bled so badly she'd tell him straight away and then he'd get out his strap and beat her until she was bleeding too, until she died.

Kristall ran to Auntie Dorry, shouted the news to her, 'Mum's been and fallen down the stairs. She wants you to go.' Then she ran on to the pub on the corner, pushed open the door and stared inside.

'No kids in here,' someone shouted.

She saw Bill-Daddy. 'Mum's hurt,' she yelled over the din. 'Fallen down the stairs. She wants you.'

She didn't wait for any response. She backed out of the door letting it bang behind her and she ran, faster than ever now, ran to the end of the road and down some more roads, not stopping until she came to the steep lane that led to the allotments. Just further on there was an empty shed. She had played there sometimes. Breathless and exhausted she crept in through the half open door, fell onto the earth floor and sobbed herself into a terrified nightmarish sleep.

Elizabeth was fond of the house that she and Philip had bought. It was convenient and spacious, had a pleasant garden, fields behind and a view down to Portishead at the front. The village was charming and she could cycle easily to Clifton, an agreeable ride when the weather was good. The road was fairly quiet and she particularly enjoyed cycling across the Suspension Bridge. Sometimes she would dismount and walk across. From up there the Portway far below was a toy road with toy motor cars and lorries. She loved to lean over the edge and watch them, imagine their drivers perhaps staring up at her, and occasionally she thought of the poor souls who had jumped off. This was a convenient spot to commit suicide!

But Elizabeth now felt reasonably happy and fulfilled, not in the least desirous of committing suicide! She had an adorable little son and a fairly satisfactory marriage. When occasionally she thought of the past, she saw Julius in her imagination with his fair, fat *Fraulein,* the estimable Liesel, and she told herself that, of course, she was very pleased for him!

There was news from Germany from time to time, just occasional short letters to Aunt Sophie from Julius, and now and then from Hans. Sophie, now living in her own small house in a Bristol suburb, passed on whatever information she received and often left the letters for Elizabeth and Emmi to read. Elizabeth would glance at them with false uninterest and seldom made any comment.

There had been confirmation that Heinrich and Helga had both been killed in the Dresden bombing, but Sophie had seemed not too upset or disturbed about this. The Berlin house was officially hers, but she was not very bothered about this either. Her legacy from her parents, safely invested in England for all the years she had lived in Germany, had given her enough to buy a house and to live comfortably. Julius, and Hans, who was out of prison now, would have to sort it out between them and hopefully send something for Emmi too.

But when Russia had cut off supplies from the British Sector of Berlin last year Sophie had been worried. 'There's nothing we can do about it though,' Elizabeth had said. 'Nothing at all. Leave it to the experts. They'll sort something out.'

And of course they did. There was the Air Lift, Allied aeroplanes delivering vital supplies to beleaguered Berliners for months. Food parcels dropped onto the Berlin streets instead of the bombs of a few short years before. Elizabeth read the newspaper reports, but mostly she tried to dismiss it all from her mind. Life was too full, too interesting. Germany belonged to a different existence. She didn't want to resurrect it. It was a Pandora's box that, once opened, might prove impossible to close.

One of her greatest joys was having Emmi living with her. She had nervously introduced Philip to her German relations when Aunt Sophie and Emmi had first arrived in England, and he had not been at all hostile, as she had expected. Aunt Sophie's charm had won him over, and to Elizabeth's amazement he had agreed to allow Emmi to come as nursemaid and help.

It was an admirable arrangement. With Isobel married now, there had been a gap in Elizabeth's life which Emmi filled abundantly. Emmi didn't want to think about Germany either. 'There are too many bad memories,' she said. 'I want to forget.' But she had offered to speak German to little Daniel. 'He might as well grow up bilingual,' she had suggested. 'It'll save him years of study later on.'

This had caused Philip's mother considerable outrage. 'My grandson must not speak that language,' she had snorted. 'French, now, would be more acceptable.'

'But Emmi doesn't speak French,' Elizabeth told her firmly. 'And German will be useful by the time he's grown up.'

'Never,' said Mildred Gibbons.

The redoubtable Mildred was the one thorn in Elizabeth's otherwise happy world. She had been furious when she discovered that her grandson was frequently strapped to the back of his mother's bicycle and taken to visit his other grandfather in Clifton. Richard Benson adored Daniel.

'If you would just ask, you could have Roberts and the car,' Mildred Gibbons was constantly saying. 'It's not safe to take my precious grandson on the back of a bicycle.' But Elizabeth always politely declined, always politely refused to be persuaded, and continued to cycle everywhere.

Even worse than going merely to Clifton, she

sometimes took Daniel on the much longer journey to visit her Jewish grandmother. Esther was well over seventy now but she seemed to have been rejuvenated by the formation of the new State of Israel. That had been in May 1948. Elizabeth would never forget her grandmother's joy. 'At last we have a country of our own,' she had said. 'Israel! The State of Israel. Doesn't it sound grand? I can hold up my head at last. I'm glad I've lived until now. I used to say, next year in Jerusalem, but I never thought it would happen, faithless old creature that I am! If I was a young girl again I should go and live on one of those kibbutzim that I've read about.' Her eyes had grown dreamy with longing. 'But a new, young country needs new, young pioneers. Perhaps my grandson will go one day.' She had watched the little boy playing with some building blocks and toy animals that she had bought for him and kept for his visits. 'Jewish blood runs in his veins after all!' she had said wistfully. 'And he has a good old-fashioned Jewish name.'

Jewish blood was something Mildred Gibbons certainly didn't want to know about, an absolute abomination in fact.

'She's as bad as Hitler,' Elizabeth had confided to Emmi one day.

'Don't joke about it, Lizzy,' Emmi had replied. 'There are too many terrible memories for me.'

When the Russian blockade of Berlin was finally lifted and the Western Allies declared that a new Federal and Democratic Republic of Germany would be born, Emmi read the news with mixed feelings. 'Will it really be democratic?' she said. 'Will they make sure that another Hitler never rises, do you think?'

Elizabeth had shaken her head. 'I'm sure that couldn't happen, and Germany is divided anyway. The Russians won't ever let go of their part, so each section will be smaller and pretty powerless. And the Allies are there, still in control.'

Emmi had continued to read, her brow creased in concentration and some disquiet. 'I see that Bonn is to be the capital of this new country, not Berlin.'

'That's a good thing,' Elizabeth said. 'Berlin has too many connections with ...' she thought of the Berlin she had known.

'With everything that was bad,' Emmi had finished for her.

'Where do you think Julius will settle? Dresden is in the East. Surely he won't go back there?'

'I have no idea,' Emmi had said implying that the matter was really of little concern to either of them, and of course it wasn't. *How unutterably stupid of me. Why did I mention his name? Is he still there in a corner of my heart after all? Yes of course he is. He always will be, however hard I try to cast him out.*

August 1949

Kristall's birthday, August 20th, was the one date in the year when Elizabeth felt justified in

274

allowing herself some nostalgia. Her daughter's existence was still a closely kept secret. With great difficulty she had managed to say nothing to Emmi or to Aunt Sophie about those terrible months when she returned to England just before the war. They had known that there had been a special friendship between Julius and herself but they had obviously assumed that it had come to nothing, that it had merely been a fleeting romance, snuffed out by long separation, all over long ago.

Sometimes Elizabeth, amazed at her own secrecy—deceit, perhaps, would be the better word—longed to tell, longed for a confidante, especially someone who knew Julius, had been part of that past, but some strange reticence stopped her. Would Emmi understand that all-consuming passion? Would anyone who had not experienced the heartache of loss ever be able to appreciate how it felt to give up your child to strangers?

Only her father and, of course, Isobel knew, and only with Isobel could she talk freely. But Isobel, busy with her own life, with husband, twins, and living in Scotland, was seldom available in person for the long hours of gossip, the sharing of mutual hurts and heartbreak that had been so welcome, so healing during the war years. They wrote often, however; closely written pages full of news and thoughts and ideas. These letters were Elizabeth's only link with the old memories. She often thought that if it were not for this precious friendship the past would seem as though it had never been.

The newspaper photograph of Kristall was hidden now, kept safely out of everyone's sight. Only on this day, and, of course, only if Philip was away at sea, did she allow herself the luxury of taking it from its tissue paper, looking at it, wondering about the small, rebellious face, wondering whether there was anything seriously the matter.

This year the day was extra special for it was the tenth birthday! Elizabeth yearned to buy a present, a doll perhaps. *Do little girls still play with dolls at ten? Does Kristall? Does she have any? How many? How does she look now? Is she any happier?*

Elizabeth had planned to cycle alone to Clifton today, to go into her favourite church and light a candle, make an extra special prayer and wallow a little in her thoughts, but Emmi looked at her apologetically at breakfast. 'I think that I should go back to bed,' she said. 'I feel hot and shivery. Summer 'flu or something. Do you mind, Lizzy?'

Of course she didn't mind. Emmi was very dear. She fussed around, made her a hot water bottle in spite of the August warmth, told her not to worry about a thing. It was time she had some fussing for a change.

So there could be no trip to Clifton today, no wallowing. It would have to wait until Emmi was better. Tomorrow was Sunday. Perhaps by Monday she might manage it.

When Kristall awoke from her short, exhausted sleep in the allotment shed, she was aware at

276

first only of a great weight of misery enveloping her. Where was she? She wanted to jump up and run out into the sunshine. Then she remembered, and the tears came again, and following them, black, dreadful despair. She rubbed earthy hands over her face and struggled to her feet.

Her mouth was dry and horrid. Water! She must have water if she was not to die. She had read adventure stories. You could live a long time without food, but water was vital. She knew there was a tap near the entrance to the allotments so that was all right. There would be some food too if she crept out at night and stole it. There was a row of runner beans quite close. They were nice to eat raw, and there were lettuces and radishes and carrots too. She knew all this because she had come here sometimes to get food for Henry. The men on the allotment were kind to her, gave her carrot tops and outside lettuce leaves, and sometimes a whole lettuce for her mummy. And there were lovely, juicy dandelion leaves in the hedge too. Henry loved those, but humans couldn't eat them, could they? She'd better be safe and just eat the proper things, even if she had to steal them.

She put one eye close to a crack between planks of the hut wall and squinted through it. There were only a few men working on their plots today because it was Sunday and you weren't supposed to work on God's day. But it was no good trying to get a drink now. She mustn't let anyone see her. They might think she'd just come to get something for Henry of course, but it was safer to wait until they'd all gone home. *Henry, Henry. You're dead. That growly next-door dog went and killed you. But it wasn't the dog's fault really was it? It was June, horrible, horrible June.*

She clenched her small fists and was overcome with hatred for her half-sister all over again. *No, not half-sister, of course, not sister at all, thank goodness. I never want to see you any more ever, ever.*

She looked around at the gloomy, cobwebby hut. How long could she stay here? If a policeman found her he'd take her straight back to Bill-Daddy and he'd be waiting with a big stick or his belt. He hadn't actually ever hit her with either, but he was always saying that he would, and surely now that she'd made horrible June all bloody and pushed Mummy down the stairs he really would do it.

What would it be like here in the dark? Could you really live on raw beans and carrots? She had been so frightened by her own bad temper and by what it had made her do that she hadn't thought any further than getting away, but now the difficulties and doubts came rushing in like a host of fearful goblins all intent on terrorising her to death. She flopped down onto the spidery earth again and put her hands over her face.

Then, like a sudden shaft of light a new thought came to her. Even though Jesus hadn't saved Henry, perhaps he'd help her now just like they said in Sunday School. She opened her eyes and considered it for a moment. Perhaps Jesus had thought that Henry was old and ought to be in Heaven. Jesus was good and couldn't let really terrible things happen after all. And He was kind, forgave people's sins. She had plenty of sins that needed blotting out before she asked for help, though.

She knew that it wasn't reverent to pray to Him sitting like this, especially when you'd been really bad and needed to be forgiven. She scrambled to her knees, and prayed earnestly that He wouldn't count all her terrible sins against her, but would forgive her just like the father did for the prodigal son in the Bible. That boy had been very bad, had run away from home and spent all his substance on riotous living. What was substance? She didn't know what riotous living meant either but it sounded pretty awful. Was it as bad as bloodying your sister and pushing your mother downstairs?

Kristall, with tears running down her cheeks, making clean rivulets through the grime, pleaded that Jesus would wash her in his precious blood and make her good, and that her real mummy and daddy would find her before Bill-Daddy.

'We're doing all we can,' the policeman said in a kindly voice to Brenda. 'We'll be in touch as soon as we find her.'

Bill was sitting in his usual chair, June on his lap. 'D'you want me to come and help search?'

'Not at the moment, sir. Like I said, we'll be in touch.'

When he had gone Brenda turned to him.

'If you hadn't been on at her all the time she wouldn't have run away.'

'What's that supposed to mean?' He put June on her feet and looked belligerently at his wife.

'Always saying you'll beat the living daylights out of her, telling her she's bad.' Brenda searched for a handkerchief in her overall pocket and when she found it wiped her eyes. 'Poor kid. She was really frightened of you.'

Bill shifted uneasily in the chair. 'I never touched her though. Not once. Why did she have to go and run away now, just when she's needed here? You with a gammy ankle and all. Selfish little cow.'

Brenda flinched. 'That's what I mean. You're always saying things like that, calling her names, things you'd never say to June and me.' She was quite staggered by her new-found bravery, speaking up to Bill. Perhaps things might have been better if she'd tried it before.

'She's not my real sister, is she?' June interrupted. 'I hope she never comes back.'

Brenda turned on her younger daughter with unusual anger. 'That's a wicked thing to say. If you ever say anything like it again I'll take my slipper to you, my girl.'

'Now who's threatening?' Bill said.

'She deserves it.'

'No I don't,' June whined. 'I never meant to leave Henry's cage open.' She wrinkled her lips petulantly. 'Did I Daddy?' she appealed to Bill.

'Course you didn't, love.' He knocked his

pipe out into the empty fireplace, refilled it thoughtfully and struck a match. 'But if Kristall comes back, perhaps we'd better try to be a bit kinder like your mummy says.'

Brenda's eyes filled with tears yet again. *'If she comes?* D'you mean that she might not?'

Bill got up, put on his jacket, 'I'm going out to see if I can find her,' he said.

It was the longest, most horrible day Kristall had ever known. Eventually, she heard the church bells ringing. It must be evening. The bells gave her a little tingling feeling inside. They sounded like God answering her prayers. Sunday was special. Mummy used to say *Better the day, better the deed.* Was running away on Sunday better than doing it on an ordinary day? Perhaps it was. She ought to have been in Sunday School this afternoon. Had her teacher missed her? Last week they'd had the story of the feeding of the five thousand. Jesus had made five loaves and two fishes enough for five thousand people. She wished she hadn't remembered that just now because it made her feel hungrier and hungrier.

She looked through the crack in the wall again. The men had all gone home now and she slowly opened the door and slid out. The runner beans were long and slender and they hung temptingly, waiting for her eager fingers. She picked one and ate it ravenously, then another and another. There was a row of carrots quite close too. She looked at the feathery tops, pulled the biggest and carried it to the tap. The men had turned the tap tightly and she had to use both hands to move it but after a lot of effort lovely sparkling water gushed out all over her feet. She picked up the carrot and washed it clean. It was scrunchy and delicious. When she was quite full of beans and carrots she put her head beneath the tap and drank as much as she could, water splashing all over her shoes again and down the front of her dress.

She looked around furtively. No one had come, no one had seen her. She slipped back into the safety of the hut and thought of Henry up in Heaven with Jesus. She supposed he was happy there, but if only he'd stayed with her a bit longer none of this would have happened. For one awful moment she wondered if Jesus really loved her after all. Certainly no one else did.

On Monday morning, Emmi pronounced herself quite over the 'flu and well enough to look after Daniel while Elizabeth went into Clifton. Anxious to get away as soon as possible for this precious yearly pilgrimage, Elizabeth pedalled as fast as she could along the country road. When she reached the Suspension Bridge she paid the small toll and hardly noticed the beauty of the Avon Gorge as she cycled across.

She went first to the church, propped her bicycle against the old stone wall, walked quietly up the aisle and lit a candle. She thought of Kristall as a baby, remembered the misery, wept a little, took the photograph from her handbag where she would keep it for just these few days, stared at it, knelt in one of the ancient wooden pews, prayed, and felt better. Then she left the church and went to see her father.

He was out so she let herself into his flat, picked up the local newspaper which lay on the mat, looked around with affection at the male disorderliness of everything, put the kettle on so that there would be coffee waiting when he got in, and then she sat down and opened the paper. Suddenly her attention was riveted. There was Kristall staring at her again, a different Kristall, older, a mature little face in a school gymslip. And underneath the stark message, CHILD MISSING. She read on as though in a nightmare. All the details were there: her name, Kristall Hodgson, the address in Bishopston, part of Bristol that Elizabeth knew slightly. She had run away from home on the day after her tenth birthday, the newspaper said. Then there was something about a dead guinea-pig. Elizabeth made little sense of the lesser facts. Just the picture, the description, fair curly hair, blue eyes, the child not seen since Sunday morning, search party out, the worst feared.

Dear God, dear God, I've just prayed to you for her. Don't let her be dead, oh, please don't let her die! My baby, my own precious baby. If Kristall is dead I shall be to blame. It will be my fault completely. I should never have listened to them, never have given you up. I'm coming, Kristall. Wait for me, don't die, I'm coming to find you.

She sprang up and collided with her father who had just arrived home. 'Look,' she screamed at him. 'This is Kristall. This is my baby. She's missing. She might be dead, murdered, drowned.'

He put his arms around her, held her tightly, let her beat her fists against his chest. Then when he could hold her no longer he picked up the fallen newspaper and read the account himself. 'I'll help you,' he said simply. There was ten years of guilt in his voice.

The policeman looked from one to the other and took the photographs from Elizabeth. A scowling child at a wedding, the other just an ordinary school snap, the one that had been circulated to all police stations.

'And what's your connection with the child?' he asked suspiciously. He put the photographs on the counter between them.

Elizabeth hesitated, all her anger and self-confidence suddenly evaporating. 'I just want to know if you've found her.'

He frowned. 'I'm afraid I can't tell you anything, madam.'

'Then she's still lost?'

He sighed. 'You're from the press I suppose? Thought we'd finished with all your lot for a bit.'

'No. I've nothing to do with the press.'

'Why are you so anxious to know, then?' His voice was brusque.

Elizabeth took a deep breath. 'I'm her mother,' she said. 'That's why I want to know.'

The policeman stared at her for a few moments and then grinned. He was less antagonistic and less formal now, more amused. 'Sorry, love, that won't wash. We've got a mother. Come on now, you'd better come clean.'

'She was adopted. I haven't seen her since she was a baby.' *He thinks I'm crazy. Perhaps I am.*

He nodded in the direction of her father. 'Who's this then?' he demanded.

'This is my daughter,' Richard Benson said quickly. 'The child is my granddaughter. We should be very grateful if you could give us some information.'

'How do you know that this is the right kid?' He tapped the photographs, still suspicious. 'You wouldn't know, would you, if you hadn't seen her for so long?'

'Her name! It's the name I gave her, an unusual one. They kept it.'

He sniffed doubtfully. 'That's as maybe, but even if what you say is true, you've no legal claim have you? There's nothing I can do. Sorry and all that.'

Elizabeth groped for a handkerchief and wiped her eyes. 'Couldn't you possibly just let me know when she's found?'

He stared at her, considering. 'Wait a minute,' he said. He disappeared into the office behind and when he returned some minutes later he was slightly more sympathetic. 'Leave your name and address.' His voice was gruff now, the brashness gone. 'We'll contact you when we have any more information. Can't do any harm.' He pushed a form across to them, indicated the

285

pen that was chained to the inkwell. 'There.'

Without thinking Elizabeth did as she was told, the nib scratchily forming the letters of her name, Philip's name, and the address of the Abbots Leigh house, his house. She stared at the words miserably, blotted them and passed the form back.

'We'll have to notify the real parents first of course,' he pronounced firmly.

Elizabeth looked at him, her eyes seeing not a simple English bobby, but seeing Julius, a summer house in a Berlin garden, a terrifying angry mob, broken glass, *Kristallnacht*, Kristall ... *We are her real parents* ...

She walked with her father through the quiet Clifton streets back to his flat. 'Perhaps you should have given my address,' he said, 'rather than your own.'

'Why?'

'To keep your anonymity.'

'From my own child?'

'Precisely. Philip doesn't know that she exists remember.'

'I want her back.'

'Think very carefully before you do anything foolish. You risk losing everything. Making the child unsettled too.'

Elizabeth felt angry. This was not the time for common sense, was it? It was the time for love and feelings and emotion to take over, wasn't it?

'He could turn you out. Have you thought of that? And no court would allow you to take Daniel. You would lose your son and probably not gain a daughter.'

Of course, of course, you are right, men so often are. In their own eyes anyway. How can I think of losing Daniel? What on earth shall I do? How can I possibly choose between my children?

CHAPTER 12

By Monday, Brenda was quite frantic, blaming herself, imagining Kristall dead, murdered, run over, drowned. She loved her more than she'd thought. Of course it was Bill who had caused all the doubts, made her see only the bad things. All children had temper tantrums, didn't they? And those piercing blue eyes that challenged her so often and so uncomfortably, they smiled as well. Frequently.

If she was safe and sound, and please God she was, she'd make up to her properly, cuddle her more, love her, really and truly love her like she did when she was a little thing just out of the home. Brenda remembered the day they'd fetched her, she and David. How happy they had been on that long ago autumn day with their new baby.

She brushed tears from her eyes, tried to concentrate on preparing vegetables for Bill's midday dinner, and for one revealing moment wondered why she'd ever married again. One man in a lifetime was enough to be doing with surely? She might have been happy, if only ... but then there was June. No Bill, no June! You had to put up with a man if you wanted little ones. That was the way of it. She sighed, peeled one more potato, plopped it into the pan, added a generous helping of salt, clamped the lid on and wiped her hands.

Bill had gone to work as usual. She was to contact him if there was any news. Of course he wouldn't have done the milk round if it was June who was missing. He'd be out there searching every open space, plaguing the police, making a complete nuisance of himself.

Her sprained ankle wasn't as bad as she had expected, thank goodness. It was possible to hobble about with the use of a stick, and she had to anyway, didn't she? Bill was no use, would never lift a finger to help, and her sister had a brood of her own to attend to. June was over there now playing with her cousins. It was a good thing she hadn't blurted out anything to her dad about Kristall hitting her. Perhaps she was still ashamed of leaving the guinea-pig cage open. Deliberately, Brenda thought. And didn't want to think!

Sunday night was the most fearsome, the most terrifying Kristall had ever spent. Hunger pains gnawed at her in spite of all the carrots and beans she had eaten. She was cold, and there were the mice! They scampered over her as she lay on the pile of sacks and at first she had screamed, then tried to think of the little white ones in the pet shop in the Hay Market and forced herself not to be afraid of them. She'd always wanted a pet mouse, after all! But what

288

was she to do? How was she to find her real mother and father, and what if they still didn't want her? Those fears were far more awful than a few little mice.

The worries went on and on. Even in her dreams they haunted her, and when she awoke they were more frightful still. She struggled to her feet and peeped out through the space in the wall. Bother! Two men had come early. No good trying to get a drink now or anything to eat. And she wanted the lavatory.

She couldn't stay here much longer. How about going to the church? God was there even on Mondays, and she had prayed to Him, so He was surely going to help. Quietly she slipped through the door, picked some dandelions so that the men should think she was just getting them for Henry. *Oh Henry, Henry. You're dead and gone and I'll never see you again. I hate that awful June.*

She walked up the lane and onto the road, and then along some more roads until she came to the big church. St Michael's, it was called, and the bells used to wake her up on Sunday mornings. This wasn't the Sunday School church. That was in a chapel and was a bit further on, but they kept that one closed except on Sundays. The church was always open. *A sanctuary,* her teacher had said once. *A sanctuary where people can go if they are in trouble, where no one can hurt them.* Well, she needed a sanctuary now, but more than that she needed a lavatory and there was one in the churchyard. She passed it on the way to school and it said WC on the door. Mum had told her it meant 'water closet'. Funny name for a lav.

There was a tap in the churchyard too and she washed her hands and face, dried them on her crumpled frock, and looked at some of the graves. This was where you went when you were dead, but poor little Henry didn't have a grave. He'd been eaten by that big boisterous dog. *I hate you, June. I'll hate you for ever and ever.*

She didn't realise that she had spoken the words aloud.

'It's very sad to hate someone!' The voice was male and low and kind.

Kristall spun round and stared at the tall man in the flowing dress thing. The vicar. Vicars wore those funny clothes because they were God's servants. 'She killed my Henry,' she said.

'Who is Henry?'

'He's dead. My guinea-pig. I loved him.' She felt hot tears on her face.

'That's sad too. Would you like to tell me about it?'

Kristall shook her head. 'No thank you.'

'Then you could come and have a cup of milk and some breakfast if you like. My wife is preparing mine just over there in the vicarage.' He nodded in the direction of the house next to the church.

Kristall had been told that she must never go with strangers, but surely God's servant was all right? And now that he had mentioned breakfast she was aware of the smell of bacon wafting over the old cemetery wall.

He held out his hand to her and after a moment she put hers trustingly in his. God must be answering her prayers after all.

The breakfast was scrumptious. She was never allowed two eggs at home. 'We have some kind old hens who lay them for us,' the vicar's wife said.

There was a cat sitting on the window-sill and another in the most comfortable armchair. They must be nice people if they had hens and cats. Kristall felt a glow of security and warmth spreading right through her, replacing the loneliness and the dark. Between mouthfuls she told them all about everything.

'So you ran away because you are afraid of your daddy,' the vicar said when the bacon and egg were quite finished and she was tucking into a third piece of toast.

'Bill-Daddy hates me because I'm adopted.'

Neither of them said anything about this. Kristall looked from one to the other expecting shock or denial. Instead the kind lady said, 'Your mummy will be very worried. Would you let me tell her at least that you are safe?'

Kristall had been doing a bit of thinking while she was telling her story, coming to her senses perhaps. She knew that she hadn't been kind to Mum at all, had been horrid in fact. And there was another thing that she had decided. Brenda was to be called Mum from now on. Mummy would be reserved for the real one, the one called Elizabeth.

'I want Mum to know that I'm all right,' she compromised.

'Would you like me to tell them?'

She frowned, considering this idea. 'All right. But not to tell them where I am yet.'

'Very well, not if you don't wish it,' the vicar said. 'But they'll have to know eventually.'

Of course they would. Of course she would have to go back. She realised now that there was nowhere else to go. She wasn't living in a fairy story any more. She had run away on the spur of the moment just yesterday. And yesterday she had been a little girl. In twenty-four hours she had grown up!

She finished the last piece of toast, wiped her mouth carefully with the big linen serviette that the vicar's wife had given her and smiled weakly at them both.

'I should like you to tell my mum I'm sorry, and that I'll come home if Dad won't hit me ... if she really wants me back,' she added with a sorrowful sniff.

'I'm sure she wants you. Does your daddy often hit you?'

'No, he never has.'

'Then why ...?'

'He's always saying that he will and he says I'm bad through and through and he'll have to beat it out of me one day, and now that I've hit June and made her fall down the stairs he's bound to do it, isn't he?'

Margaret Wiltshire shook her head and smiled reassuringly at her. 'If he has never hit you at all then I don't suppose he will now, and no one is bad through and through. At least I have never met any little girl who was. Sometimes a little bit naughty perhaps, but that's all.'

'My real parents gave me away because I was bad through and through,' Kristall said.

'No, no, my dear. You must never think that. I'm sure that your mother loved you very much and parted with you because she believed you would have a better life.'

Kristall thought about this. 'So I'm not really bad?'

'Of course you're not.'

She hoped they were right. She wasn't too sure though. You couldn't change your thoughts about yourself as quickly as that however much you tried. From bad through and through to just a little bit naughty was a very big jump to make!

Suddenly she remembered the bracelet round her neck. She pulled it up and held it out on its ribbon. 'My first mother left this for me.' She struggled to untie the knot and then handed it to the lady.

'*Elizabeth and Julius, 25.12.37,*' Margaret read. She peered more closely. '*Ich liebe dich.* I love you, in German. How very interesting.' She passed it to her husband. 'See, in very small italic letters, *Ich liebe dich.* I don't expect you can read it.'

He held it this way and that. 'No, my dear. Can't make out a thing.'

Alarmed, Kristall looked from one to the other. 'I couldn't understand those funny words. Are they really German? Germans are wicked. My real parents aren't Germans.'

Margaret immediately regretted reading the

293

inscription aloud. 'They are lovely words,' she said, trying to repair the damage. *Ich liebe dich* means I love you.'

James glared at his wife. 'No,' he said, turning to Kristall. 'I don't suppose for one minute that your parents are German. But not all Germans are wicked, you know. They were terribly misled by their leader. This is a very beautiful thing. You must take great care of it. The German words may not be significant at all. Perhaps it was bought in Germany. A lot of English people went there for holidays before the war. You see ...' he indicated the inscription again, '... the date is Christmas Day 1937. I expect they were having a Christmas holiday in Germany. And Elizabeth is a good old English name, anyway.'

He handed the bracelet to Kristall and she took it gingerly and stared at the words. There was something ominous about them now. In spite of the reassuring remarks she was terrified. 'Don't tell Bill-Daddy about the bracelet. He doesn't know I've got it, and he really hates Germans.' She put her finger over the threatening inscription. The words had meant nothing to her before but now they made the bracelet seem mysterious and alarming. She threaded the ribbon through it and tied it round her neck, tucked it away inside her grubby dress. 'You won't tell?' she repeated, more anxious than ever now.

'Of course we won't tell, my dear. The words show you something rather beautiful about your real parents though, don't they?'

294

'What?'

'That they loved each other.'

'That just makes it worse,' Kristall sniffed. 'If they loved each other why didn't they love me too?'

'They may have been separated by the war. A lot of people were,' the vicar said. 'But the words on the bracelet will be our secret, yours and ours, just between you and us.' He put his finger on his lips.

His wife made an attempt to lighten the atmosphere. 'What is it my grandson says when he makes a promise?' she said. 'Something horrid like, "cross my heart and hope to die".' She laughed and made the sign on her neck. 'There! Your secret is perfectly safe with us, my dear, and now I suggest that you have a nice warm bath, and put on some of the clothes that I keep here for my granddaughter and I'll wash your things. It's a bright blowy day. You can help me to mangle them and they'll dry in a trice.'

Gratefully, Kristall allowed herself to be comforted, to be mothered and looked after. Gradually the horrors of the previous night and the day before it began to fade. 'I wish you were my mummy,' she whispered as Margaret wrapped her in a big fluffy towel.

Margaret laughed. 'Granny perhaps. Would you like me for an adopted Granny?'

'That would be lovely,' said Kristall.

Later that morning Brenda, beside herself with anxiety, heard a knock on the door. Her heart pounded rapidly and she rushed through from the kitchen to answer it. A clergyman! This was it then. The worst had happened. Kristall was dead. Otherwise why would they send a vicar? She gripped the door, and the little front garden seemed to sway around her. She was going to faint. 'What happened?' she whispered.

'She's safe,' the man said quickly. 'My wife is looking after her.'

She couldn't believe it at first, and then the sudden relief was almost as shattering as the fear and the panic. 'Thank the dear Lord,' she said piously.

'May I come in?' he said. He was standing there looking at her.

She tried to come to her senses. 'Yes, yes of course, sir.' She led the way into the little front parlour and he stood awkwardly before the empty fireplace.

'I found her in the churchyard,' he said, 'this morning. She was hungry and my wife gave her some breakfast.'

'You haven't brought her back, then?' Brenda looked vaguely towards the bay window.

'She asked me to come and talk to you first,' he said. 'She's very frightened of her father.'

'He's never touched her.' There was slight indignation in Brenda's voice now. 'Never!'

'So I believe. She told me that. Could I speak to him?'

'He'll be back later. He starts the milk round early and comes in about midday, then he has his dinner and a sleep.'

'I'll bring her home around two o'clock if that suits?'

Brenda nodded. Bill would have finished dinner by then, be in a good mood. A meal and a beer always put him to rights.

'She's adopted, I believe?'

Brenda could feel herself blushing. Why did Kristall have to tell him that? She nodded. 'My first hubby and me couldn't have children. I've got one of my own now though, a girl, June. Bill and me, I mean. He's my second hubby.'

'And, of course, Kristall is jealous,' her visitor said. 'It happens in most families when another baby comes along.'

'I'll try to make it up to her when you bring her back.'

'I'm sure you will. And now I must go straight to the police station. I should have gone there first, of course.'

Brenda nodded. 'Yes. They've been searching everywhere.'

'I shall tell them how I found her, that she is well and unharmed, and that I'm bringing her back this afternoon.' He stood up, held out his hand. 'You've had a bad time, Mrs Hodgson,' he said. 'But it's all over now. Rest assured.'

Brenda shook his hand and felt comforted and relieved. It was truly the end, or nearly the end of a frightful experience and she had learned her lesson. 'Thank you, sir. Thank you very much indeed for all you've done for us,' she said.

She showed him to the door and watched as his little Austin chugged off down the road.

James Wiltshire went next to the police station as he had said he would. When all the official reports had been made, the policeman leaned over the desk and whispered confidentially to him, 'The other mother came in, you know.'

'You mean the real one?'

'So she said.'

James suddenly felt quite out of his depth. 'How did she come to know about it?'

'Search me!' The policeman glanced down at his notes. 'Oh yes, something about the name. She said that it was the one she had chosen and that it was so unusual that the kid must be hers.'

'And do you mean to say that she's here, in Bristol?'

'Lives in Abbots Leigh.' He shuffled through his papers and drew one sheet out. 'Yes, here it is. Mrs Elizabeth Gibbons. Very well spoken and all that. Surprising really. I felt sorry for her. She was very upset. Came in with her father. She's been on my mind ever since.'

Elizabeth! The name on the bracelet! So it was probably true, then. 'What are you going to do?' he asked.

'Nothing official. She's got no proof of relationship. I should like her to know the kid's safe though.'

'Would you like me to tell her?'

The policeman looked considerably relieved. 'Best thing all round if you did,' he said. 'That way I'm not stepping out of my line of duty so to speak. She's on the telephone so that makes it easier.' He passed the paper across the counter.

298

'I wouldn't give you this information if I didn't know you and if you weren't a clergyman, of course. But I reckon you'll know how to deal with it.'

As he drove home James considered the policeman's remark. Clergymen were supposed to be paragons of virtue and repositories of wisdom, yet he was in quite a quandary about what he should do next. It wasn't his business at all to interfere in adoption cases. Adoptive parents had rights and one of them must surely be to remain incognito, especially to the real parents. The policeman shouldn't have revealed what he knew, of course. Surprising really. He must have been very impressed by the real mother to hand over the address like that. Mother? Which one of the two anguished women deserved compassion? Both, of course. A quick telephone call was probably the best thing, revealing nothing, just that Kristall was safe.

He clumped into the house and there she was, playing with their granddaughter's dolls and dressed in their granddaughter's frock. It gave him a shock to see her like that. She might have been their own. The pathetic little waif he'd rescued earlier had given way to a very pretty child.

She looked at him as he came into the kitchen. 'Did you see my mum? Is she very cross?'

'She isn't cross at all,' he said. 'She was just very, very happy to know that you are safe. You gave her a lot of worry. She wants you back.' He smiled reassuringly.

Kristall looked down at the doll she was tucking into the big black pram. 'What about Dad?'

'I promised to take you home after he's had his dinner. Your mummy assured me that he would be in a good mood then. I'll stay with you as long as you like. I'm quite sure that he won't be cross.'

'I bet he will be. Will you really come right in with me?'

'Of course I will.'

Elizabeth returned home earlier than usual. Emmi was preparing lunch for herself and Daniel. 'You're back very quickly,' she said. 'I thought you intended to have lunch with your father. You need not have rushed. I'm quite recovered.'

'It wasn't that.' Elizabeth took her jacket off and sat down heavily at the kitchen table. If only, oh if only Isobel was here instead of her cousin! Guiltily she tried to replace that unworthy thought with gratitude that at least she had Emmi. 'I have to talk to you,' she said.

'Go ahead. Can you talk while I finish these potatoes?'

'If you promise to concentrate. Where is Daniel?'

'In the garden with next-door's dog. They're playing tug-of-war or something.'

'Emmi ... I don't know how to tell you.'

Emmi stopped, potato in one hand and peeler in the other. 'Whatever is the matter? You look as pale as death.'

300

'I feel like death. For pity's sake come and sit down and listen to me. Emmi, please put that bloody potato in the sink and *listen*. And give me a cigarette.'

She didn't smoke, hated it, but now she puffed and choked and coughed. Then she reached for a saucer and stubbed the cigarette out. 'I'm worried silly, full of shame and reproach, and I don't know what the hell to do.'

Emmi dried her hands and sat down opposite her. 'Tell me,' she said.

Without preamble she dropped her bombshell. 'I have a child, a daughter, ten years old, adopted and she lives here in Bristol.'

It was Emmi's turn to feel as though all the blood in her body was draining away into the floor. She put her hands over her mouth in horror and could make no sensible response.

'Julius's child,' Elizabeth said. 'I was pregnant when I came back from Germany in 1938. He doesn't know. He must never know. You must promise never to tell him.'

Emmi stared at her cousin, eyes wide with amazement and horror. 'Why?' she managed. 'Why did you leave him, Lizzy? And in Heaven's name, how could you have kept it a secret from all of us?'

'I wonder at that constantly now, but then I thought he was a Nazi. I really did. Do you know the terrible things he said on *Kristallnacht*? *Jews, only Jews*. He shouted those words as though the people being set upon, beaten senseless in front of our eyes, didn't matter one jot. And I believed that he meant it! I called his daughter Kristall, so that I should always remember, always reject her. Oh God, Emmi how could I have been so foolish, so wicked and so impossibly blind?'

Emmi rose, pushed her chair back and went to the cupboard, took a bottle of brandy and poured a measure into each of two glasses. She pushed one across the table to Elizabeth. 'Drink it!'

Both women were quiet for a moment, the fiery liquid burning in their throats, bringing temporary relief.

'I deserve everything that has happened. I've brought it all on myself,' Elizabeth said.

'I guessed that he was no Nazi,' Emmi said. 'If only you had talked to me about it I might have been able to put your mind at rest. But why are you telling me all this now, at this particular moment?'

'Because she has run away from her adopted parents, because she's lost, might be dead even. It's in the paper.' Elizabeth fumbled in her handbag, pushed the crumpled photograph over to Emmi.

Emmi smoothed it out, stared at the child, and all colour drained from her face for the second time. 'She's so like Julius,' she whispered.

'And Philip doesn't know either,' Elizabeth said grimly. 'He told me that he wanted to hear nothing of my previous men friends so I took him at his word and didn't tell him that I had had a child. I was wrong wasn't I? Deceitful and wicked. What on earth am I going to do?'

'Nothing.' Emmi, shocked to her roots, nevertheless summoned all her common sense to the rescue. 'You say that neither of them know? Then it's too late to tell them now. Nothing would be gained.'

'I know where she lives,' Elizabeth murmured. 'It's in the newspaper. I can't keep away, Emmi. If she's found I must know whether she's happy and why she ran away.'

'You shouldn't, Lizzy. You'll only upset her. She probably doesn't know that she's adopted and you'll mean nothing at all to her. She isn't your child any more.'

Elizabeth was angry now. She clenched her fists. 'How can you say that? You've never had a child. You can't possibly know how it feels. She's flesh of my flesh, blood of my blood, *my baby.*' She got up and stalked out of the room, went upstairs to her bedroom and threw herself on the bed, thought of Philip and then of Julius. *What an unholy mess I've made of my life. Can I ever put any little part of it right?*

The telephone rang eventually and she ran downstairs, eager to reach it before Emmi did. A strange voice, a cultured, friendly voice asked for her. 'I am Mrs Elizabeth Gibbons,' she said. 'Have you any ...?' She paused. She must be careful, mustn't say anything else. This was obviously not the policeman she had spoken to at the station. She stood rigid and tense, waiting.

'Kristall is safe,' the voice said. 'I am taking her home this afternoon. Her parents have been worried about her.'

'How? Where is she now? Why did she do it?'

'Because her guinea-pig had been killed,' he said. 'That seems to be almost all it was about. Please don't worry, Mrs Gibbons. I found her in my churchyard this morning. I am the vicar of St Michael's church.'

Elizabeth clutched the telephone with both hands, pressed it to her ear. 'And are you sure that she's all right?'

'Perfectly. Please let matters rest. The police told me of your identity and, believe me, I do realise how you must feel.'

'Do you? How can you possibly know how I feel?' Anger replaced gratitude.

There was a moment's silence on the line, then a cough, and then the polite well-bred voice said, 'I am very sorry indeed Mrs Gibbons if I sounded glib. Forgive me. You must do whatever you feel is best, of course, but I believe that nothing can be gained by your intervention.'

'I understand,' she said coldly. 'Thank you very much for letting me know.' She put the receiver back onto its cradle and walked into the kitchen in a dream. Emmi and Daniel were about to have their lunch.

'Was that Daddy?' Daniel said.

'No, not Daddy.'

Emmi looked at her, wide-eyed, anxious.

'She's all right,' Elizabeth managed. 'Going home this afternoon.'

'Who's all right?' Daniel asked.

'A little girl who was lost.'

'Why was she lost?'

'I've no idea,' said Elizabeth and then she turned and ran out of the room, went into the lavatory and cried as though her heart would break all over again.

They stood at the front door together, Kristall gripping the clergyman's hand, never wanting to let go. He was the grandfather she had never had, a new and unexpected bastion of safety in her small, uncertain world. She heard quick footsteps and the door was flung open and before she knew what was happening she was in her mum's arms.

'You're safe, you're safe, thank goodness,' she said and Kristall, when she had managed to extricate herself saw tears on her mother's face, speedily brushed away.

Then they were inside and Bill-Daddy was there finishing his dinner. She stood quite still and looked at him, wondered why she had ever called him that silly baby name. He was Dad. Just Dad. It wasn't an important name, not like Daddy or Father. She would keep those names safe in her head for when she found the real one.

'Hello,' he said. 'You did a stupid thing didn't you, frightening your poor mum out of her wits?'

'Sorry.'

'I should think so. You need a good hiding my girl, but I suppose I'll overlook it. Never run off again mind or you'll feel my belt.'

It was at that moment that Kristall's fear of

Bill Hodgson evaporated like summer rain. She discovered quite suddenly that he was just a big-mouth, a nasty word the boys at school used sometimes, but it really was true. He liked to talk big and important and threaten to do horrible things, but inside he was a softy, not too bad at all really, not someone you could look up to, but not someone to be frightened of either. The feeling gave her an immediate sense of superiority. She already felt like that about Mum, knew herself to be much cleverer and able to manage her, and now it was the same for Dad too. She had just realised another thing as well. She was quite fond of Mum. That had been a surprise, but it was nice really. And Mum seemed to like her more than she'd thought. But Dad? Could she ever be fond of him? She doubted it very much.

She pulled herself to her full four-feet-five inches. 'I won't run away again. It was horrid. There were spiders and mice, and I was hungry.'

'I suppose you want me to buy you another guinea-pig?' Dad said.

She looked at him witheringly. 'No thank you. I don't want any more pets, ever. I should be frightened of June doing something nasty to them again.'

'That's not a very kind thing to say.' This was from Mum. Sadly.

Kristall shook her head. 'Well, it wasn't kind to leave his cage open.'

June was there too, sitting on the rug playing with her toy farm. She had been quiet, just

306

watching and listening. She picked up a lead cow and a tree. 'You can have these if you like,' she said. 'Instead of Henry.'

Kristall looked at them scornfully. 'I don't want them.'

'Give your sister a kiss and say you're sorry,' Brenda said firmly to her younger child.

June got to her feet knocking over most of her farm animals. She put her arms around Kristall. 'Sorry,' she said.

James Wiltshire smiled. So all was well that ended well then. It had all been a storm in a teacup. Mr Hodgson didn't seem so bad and Mrs Hodgson obviously loved the child. He hoped the other mother wouldn't do anything foolish to spoil things.

'Well, I'll be off then,' he said. 'And, Kristall, if your mummy and daddy will allow it, Mrs Wiltshire and I should like you to come to tea one Sunday afternoon.'

Kristall smiled at him. 'You are my new granny and grandfather. I should love to come to tea.'

The following day, Daniel was playing in his sand pit in the garden. 'Come and look at my castle, Mummy,' he called. 'There's a moat all round and Aunt Emmi brought me some water for it but it won't stay in.'

'Lovely,' Elizabeth said, preoccupied.

'No, not lovely,' Daniel objected. 'You're not looking properly. I can't make the water stay, but I've made it strong to keep the Germans out and there's our flag on top.' He scrambled to his feet, ran to her and grabbed her hand. 'Come and see.'

Elizabeth allowed herself to be taken across the lawn. 'Why do you want to keep the Germans out?'

' 'Cause they're our enemies, silly.'

'Not any more, darling. Have you forgotten something?'

'What?'

'Aunt Emmi is German.'

'Only half, and it's different because she's a lady. Ladies don't count. They can't fight.' He released her hand and made some minor repairs to the castle wall.

'Germans aren't our enemies any more,' she repeated.

'Daddy fought them.'

'Yes he did, but they're our friends now.'

'I call that stupid.' He looked up at her. 'When's Daddy coming home? I'm going to ask him about it.' He stood up, brushed sand from his hands. 'I wish he'd come home soon. He promised to buy me a big present next time. I want a puppy.'

Elizabeth smiled at his rapid change of subject. 'Let's go in and have a drink and one of those delicious little cakes that Aunt Emmi made yesterday,' she suggested.

'Yummy, yummy,' said Daniel.

Later, when she and Emmi were alone, Daniel back in the garden kicking his football around the lawn, Elizabeth said, 'I intend to see her, Emmi. Soon.'

Emmi paused in her ironing, and a frown

creased her normally happy unruffled features. 'I don't think you should, Lizzy. When we talked about it yesterday I thought you had agreed not to do anything.'

'That was yesterday!' Elizabeth was washing up. She scrubbed viciously at the burnt-on brown marks around the edge of a Pyrex casserole. 'All these years I presumed that she was happy and I tried to put her out of my mind for much of the time. But now absolutely everything has changed. She ran away, didn't she? A child doesn't do that for nothing. I've been awake most of the night going over it in my mind. They say it was because of a guinea-pig. I can't accept that it was only that.' She looked up from the sink, 'For goodness' sake, Emmi! Can you ask me to go on being wise and sensible? I can't rest until I'm sure that she's happy, unless I know why she did it. Supposing they're cruel to her? I must be quite sure that she wants to stay with them.'

'If she was legally adopted, as you say she was, there won't be any choice though, will there?'

'I don't care a damn about that. Kristall is my baby and if she's being cruelly treated, then I shall have to do something about it.'

Emmi changed irons, putting the cool one on the Aga to heat up again. 'I thought the vicar who telephoned said that everything was all right now.'

'I have to see for myself,' Elizabeth said obstinately. 'I shall not say who I am. I shall go to the house and pretend to be doing a survey or something. But I must get a glimpse of her. Please, Emmi, try to understand.'

'Have you thought about Philip and Daniel?'

'Constantly. My father told me that Philip might turn me out if he discovered that I'd had a child. And that if he did, I'd lose Daniel.'

'Then how can you possibly even contemplate going to see Kristall?'

'I don't know. I honestly don't know. I'm not going to think about the risks. Philip could never separate me from Daniel.'

'Don't underestimate him. In Germany the law was always on the side of the man,' Emmi said. 'I don't know how it is in England, Lizzy, but be careful. For everyone's sake be careful.'

It was June who opened the front door to her. Elizabeth gazed at the chubby, unprepossessing little girl. 'Is your mummy in?' she asked, heart thumping. Surely this wasn't ... no of course not, much too young and not a bit like the photograph in the newspaper.

A plumpish and pleasant looking woman followed the child to the door. 'Good afternoon. Are you from the insurance?'

'No,' Elizabeth said. 'Sorry. Could I come inside?'

'If it's the newspapers, I haven't got anything more to say.' Her voice was defensive now. 'She only ran away because next-door's dog killed her precious guinea-pig and everyone knows about that. I've said it a hundred times.'

'No,' said Elizabeth again. 'I'm not from the newspapers either.' Faced with the woman whom she had often hated in her mind but

310

who now seemed so vulnerable, so ordinary, her plan to lie about her visit suddenly became despicable. She was ashamed. 'I'm not official at all. I should just like to talk to you for a few minutes.'

'What about?'

'I should prefer to come in first.'

The woman looked nonplussed. 'All right then,' she said unwillingly. 'Only for a few minutes mind.' She stood back and indicated an open door just inside. 'I'm in the middle of baking.'

The little front parlour had a musty smell. Elizabeth stared at the small tiled fireplace, the neatly placed three-piece suite that appeared never to have been sat upon. There was nothing homely or welcoming about the room. She straightened her skirt, pulled at her jacket and put her hand to her hair. The grips had come out during the long and windy cycle ride and she felt untidy and hot and impossibly nervous. 'I'm sorry I'm such a mess,' she apologised. 'I've cycled right over from Abbots Leigh.'

Puzzled, Brenda frowned. Abbots Leigh! That was the posh village over the other side of the Suspension Bridge. Why should someone want to cycle all that way to visit her?

Elizabeth, heart still thumping like a piston, said quickly, 'You are Mrs Hodgson, I believe. My name is Elizabeth Gibbons.'

Then Brenda knew. She put her hand on the arm of the sofa to steady herself, wished she had a fan like those Spanish ladies in the painting above the fireplace, wished she

311

could faint away, wished that the ground would open up and swallow her. She stared at this dishevelled stranger and saw Kristall in the fair complexion, the curling hair, the upper-class manner. 'Julius and Elizabeth,' she whispered. 'On the bracelet!'

The bracelet! Elizabeth's hand went automatically to her wrist where Julius had placed that solid silver band so long ago, the bracelet that she had put in the shoe-box along with her tears and her love. *Ich liebe dich.* She could hear Julius's voice speaking those wonderful, magical words, made even more poignant now with the distance of years and language between them.

She nodded, felt tears threatening. 'Yes. I am Elizabeth. I ... I'm sorry to come like this, without any warning, but—'

'But you saw the newspapers? It crossed my mind that you might because her name is so unusual. I should've changed it, nearly did, but I liked it. It's given the game away though hasn't it!' Brenda clasped her hands together, agitated, talking too much as usual when she was nervous. 'You live in Bristol, then?'

'Yes. Since I married. Abbots Leigh. Can I ... can I see her? I won't say anything, and I'll not make any trouble for you Mrs Hodgson. I promise. I only want to see her, just once.' All Elizabeth's resentment towards this unassuming little woman had disappeared. She was the supplicant now, the one at fault ... at fault in every particular.

'Sit down,' Brenda said. 'If you really won't let on who you are I'll get her.'

312

Elizabeth shook her head, fumbled for a handkerchief. 'Thank you. I've been so worried. Just give me a moment.' She brushed tears away, tried to compose herself.

'Yes, I suppose you must have been worried.' Brenda wondered how she would feel if her precious June ... well, that didn't bear thinking about and she'd never have given her away in the first place. She looked coldly at Elizabeth, felt slightly superior for the first time since this unwelcome visitor had arrived on her doorstep. 'I don't know that it's a good thing, mind you,' she said, 'but if you really want to see her ... well, I suppose you'd better, but be careful what you say. She's bright, tumbles to things in no time. Tell her you're ... oh, anything but not who you really are. That's what I've been dreading from the day we got her, David and me.' She sniffed noisily. 'She's too brainy for me and Bill. Her being so smart and clever is what's made it difficult sometimes. She's like you, I suppose.' She went to the door. 'Kristall,' she shouted. 'Come on down. There's a lady to see you. Wants to ask you about school,' she added with sudden inspiration.

After interminable minutes during which the two women fidgeted and found nothing to say there was a clattering on the stairs, and then a tall, thin child stood there and looked at Elizabeth, looked with Julius's eyes and later with Julius's smile, and Elizabeth felt the years melt away and she was back in a Berlin garden on a golden winter afternoon nearly eleven years ago. She sprang to her feet, tried to gather

her wits together, tried to smile. What on earth to say? How to ask questions that might sound sensible to this intelligent ten-year-old, questions about school, for goodness' sake. She wanted to cross the room to her, wrap her arms around her, and then jump onto the next train, bus, boat, whatever, rush across still-devastated Europe and find ... *Stop being so melodramatic, so feeble!*

'Hello, Kristall,' she said. 'What a pretty name. Do you know what it means?' *It means Kristallnacht: suffering, death, horror, sparkling broken glass crunching beneath my feet. It means a little girl in a blue dressing gown watching her father dragged off to a terrible death ... dear God it means all those frightful things ... why did I choose such a name for my precious daughter?*

'It's glass, special glass that glitters and shines,' Kristall said. 'That's what my teacher told me. The spelling is wrong though. I don't know about that.'

'Do you like school?' This was safer ground.

'It's all right. I quite like it.'

'What are your favourite subjects?'

'Sums and problems and reading, of course.'

'Do you read a lot?'

'Always got her head stuck in a book,' Brenda interrupted. 'Not like me and Bill. We never read books.'

Elizabeth saw the scornful look that flashed momentarily across the child's face. She was like a fish out of water here, didn't fit at all. The thought gave her pain, like a knife

314

sliding between her ribs, twisting and torturing, accusing.

'I don't know *your* name.' Kristall suddenly said, and before she could think, and because she was so nervous, Elizabeth had replied. 'Mrs Gibbons, Elizabeth Gibbons, Elizabeth after the princess. Well not quite because I am older than she is.'

Then, like Brenda a few minutes before, Kristall suddenly knew. She knew! It was clear as clear. She stared, wanted to cry, wanted to strike out with both fists and hit them, real mummy and Mum, both sitting there so stupidly, thinking that she was stupid too, thinking that they could deceive her, thinking that she wouldn't guess. But this Elizabeth wasn't beautiful, wasn't wearing lovely clothes, wasn't ... wasn't what? Nothing was as she had imagined it might be. And where was her real father? *Where was he?* He should be here as well, tall and handsome, smiling and sensible, not asking silly questions about school. 'Why did you ask me about my name?' she said, tears brimming. 'You chose it, didn't you?'

To Elizabeth the shock was terrible, like a torrent of freezing water thrown suddenly without warning, a monstrous, unexpected thing to happen and she felt quite unable to do anything at all, tongue clamped to her teeth, hands clenched round the strap of her handbag, eyes staring. Everything was happening too soon, no time to go gently as she had planned.

Surprisingly it was Brenda who came to the rescue, who seemed suddenly dispassionate and

315

self-possessed. 'We weren't going to tell you, but now you've guessed. I might have known you would.' She looked from one to the other, mother and daughter, two strangers standing there in her parlour, facing one another, awkward and tense, no words or understanding between them. She had rehearsed this dreaded meeting many times in her head. Perhaps that was why she was outwardly so calm. But it had never been quite like this. 'This is your first mummy, Kristall,' she managed. 'She saw your photograph in the newspaper, and she was very worried because you had run away. She came to find out whether you were safe.' An uncomfortable silence, and then she added quickly because she could think of nothing more to say, 'Are you going to give her a kiss?'

Elizabeth took a step forward. *A kiss! A kiss to make up for ten years of love and cuddles and care. A kiss to atone for my sins.* She held out her arms, mutely pleading, still saying nothing at all. Apart from the ticking clock on the mantelpiece there was complete silence. To Elizabeth the whole world was holding its breath.

Then Kristall came into her arms and Elizabeth held the stiff, slight little figure for a moment, planted a kiss on her golden, curly head, tried to remember the baby she had held ten years ago, and released her. They backed away from each other and Elizabeth smiled uncertainly. 'Perhaps we can be friends.' *That's all I can hope for and that will be a bonus, a wonderful, wonderful gift, all I deserve.*

Kristall nodded. 'All right. Have you got a

motor car? The vicar who found me gave me a ride in his. It was lovely.'

Elizabeth wanted to laugh hysterically. 'I can get one,' she said.

'Will you take me out in it? I want to go to the zoo.'

Brenda looked shocked. 'Kristall! Don't be so cheeky.'

The tension was broken at last. Elizabeth, still trembling, still not thinking logically at all, said, 'If your mummy agrees I should love to take you to the zoo.'

'Oh, Mum will agree.'

This was spoken with such confidence and with such an air of condescension that Elizabeth felt stirrings of doubt and inadequacy. Would she be able to manage this bright, forceful child? Yes, of course she would! Kristall was Julius's daughter. She must always remember that. The spirit of rebellion that she now knew had enabled him to stand firmly for the things he believed in, to face prison, likely death, and then to triumph over the loss of his legs, that wonderful spirit was obviously strong in this child of his to whom she had given birth. *If only I had possessed just a little of that courage I should have defied my mother, gone back to Berlin. Kristall might have been born there.* Then another frightening thought. *But my grandmother is Jewish. What would have become of us all in Hitler's Germany?* She looked at the small, defiant figure of her daughter, remembered the child in the blue dressing gown and shivered. 'I'll arrange the motor car and telephone you

317

about a suitable day, then,' she said.

'We haven't got a telephone,' Brenda said.

'Then I'll write.' *Why on earth did I mention the telephone? It's upper class. No, they wouldn't have one. The possession of a telephone sets me apart ... the last thing I want.*

'Won't you stay and have a cup of tea?' Brenda asked unwillingly.

'No, thank you. I must get back to my little boy.'

'You've got a boy?' Kristall's voice was immediately hostile.

Why did I say that? 'Yes. Daniel. He's three and a half.'

'Is he my brother, then?'

'Yes. Yes, of course he is. Your half-brother.'

A frown crossed Kristall's face and then the question that Elizabeth, strangely, had not expected, was not at all prepared for.

'Where is my father?'

Hot colour flooded her face. She looked down in confusion and then weakly at Brenda, but no help came from that direction this time, just an embarrassed stare. 'A long way from here,' she managed. 'In another country.'

Kristall's frown deepened. 'His name was Julius. It's on the bracelet.'

'Yes. So you have it?'

'I keep it round my neck on a ribbon beneath my liberty bodice. Dad mustn't see it. I want to find my real father. If you know where he is why can't you take me there?'

'That's enough, Kristall,' Brenda said feebly. 'Don't bother Mrs Gibbons any more.'

'But I want to know.'

Elizabeth took a deep breath. 'I'll tell you as much as I can when I take you to the zoo.'

'There's something I do know,' Kristall said. 'Something that's awful. Mrs Wiltshire, she's the vicar's wife, told me about the German words inside. *Ich liebe dich.* She understood them. My father isn't a German, is he?'

Pictures of Germany swam into Elizabeth's bemused brain, Berlin, the good times, the bad, the concentration camps, the great Nazi rallies. 'There are many very good Germans,' she said. 'Your father was one of those.'

'I don't believe you,' Kristall said angrily. 'I've seen them at the pictures. We fought them in the war, didn't we? How can they be good?' She paused and looked from one woman to the other. 'So he is a German, isn't he? I don't want a German father.' She turned and ran out of the room. Elizabeth heard her footsteps quick on the stairs and then the slam of a door, deliberately loud and violent.

Brenda was exceedingly shocked. 'Is it true? That he was German?'

Helplessly Elizabeth nodded. 'That was why I couldn't marry him,' she said. 'It was 1938!'

'We'd have thought twice about taking her if we'd known. Even my first hubby might have been a bit put off.' There was condemnation in Brenda's voice. 'To think we've harboured a little Jerry all these years.'

Elizabeth put her face in her hands, wanted to run upstairs after her child, gather her into her arms as if she had been a baby, and for the second time that afternoon wished to run away from here, run far from such terrible ignorance and intolerance.

'Her father was working to overthrow Hitler and the Nazis,' she said. 'He was put in prison for his efforts, then he was made to work in a punishment squad and had both his legs blown off by a mine. He was a very brave man and a very good one too.' *Was! Why am I talking of him in the past tense? He's not dead. Dead to me perhaps, but not dead to Kristall, not dead to Liesel!* She looked at Brenda defiantly.

'I'll not tell the hubby,' was all Brenda said. 'He hates Germans.'

'And you'll not hold it against Kristall?' Elizabeth was angry now.

'No. I wouldn't do that, especially if it's true about her dad getting his legs blown off. Fancy having German blood in your veins, though. Whether it's good blood or bad blood doesn't come into it really does it? Poor little soul! No, I'll not hold it against her, and as long as the hubby doesn't find out we'll be all right. If he does, if she ever spills the beans to him, then I should think he'd want you to take her back right away. Funny things, men aren't they? He'd not want a German in the house even if she does have good blood.'

Elizabeth cycled the long miles home, glad of the exercise, hoping it would still some of the conflicting emotions that filled her head. Kristall, the child of ten years of dreams had materialised into a defiant little figure with a

320

multitude of problems, a child who would be difficult to manage, hard to get to know, and ... hard to love? Oh no, a thousand times no. Love would be easy, understanding would be more difficult.

Kristall had been called downstairs again a few moments before Elizabeth had left. Brenda had told her to blow a kiss and she had obeyed. Even though it was not a spontaneous gesture it was precious, something to treasure. Elizabeth knew that their relationship in the future might be uncertain but a beginning had been made, the dream had become the reality.

At home Daniel was having his tea. 'Emmi made more cakes,' he said. 'Cakes with sweeties on.' He held one out to her.

'Thank you, darling.' There was a jelly baby lying across a tiny dollop of precious icing sugar on the top. Elizabeth thought of Kristall, wondered if she had jelly baby cakes for tea.

CHAPTER 13

Elizabeth and Emmi had no chance to talk until Daniel was in bed. 'He's asleep at last,' Elizabeth said as she came into the kitchen where Emmi was finishing the dishes. 'I have never felt so unwilling to read about Pooh Bear as tonight. And even that increases my feelings of guilt. I am absolutely riddled with guilt about everything.'

Emmi put the tea-towel carefully over the Aga rail and sat down at the big scrubbed table. 'Women often are riddled with guilt. It's how we are made. And now please, Lizzy, are you going to tell me what happened? I've been dying to know ever since you came home.'

'It's been a wonderful, traumatic day. I don't know where to begin.' Elizabeth took off her cardigan and threw it over a chair. 'Gosh, Emmi, it's boiling in here with that thing belching out heat. Can we go into the garden?'

Outside the air was still warm and full of the scent of honeysuckle. Pears and apples were ripening on the trees that Philip had planted when he first bought the house and the hydrangea hedge was in full bloom. Everywhere there was beauty and order. Elizabeth stared at the lovely, familiar things and was immediately filled with a sense of impending catastrophe.

'What am I doing, Emmi?' she said. 'I've brought such predicaments into my life, haven't I?'

'It's not been all your fault. For goodness' sake stop being so hard on yourself, stop pitying yourself. Tell me what happened today.' Emmi's voice was firm, slightly impatient.

They sat on an old wooden seat close to the house so that they should hear Daniel if he woke and Elizabeth related every detail. Finally she said, 'And she wants to go to the zoo! In a motor car. And I've promised to take her!'

Emmi listened to the whole story without comment. Julius's child! She still found it difficult to get used to the idea. 'I should think the zoo would be a good idea actually,' she said when the telling was over.

'Is that all you have to say?'

'What more is there? You've made up your mind.'

'What shall I do about Daniel? Shall I tell Philip? Is my father right? Will Philip be so angry that he'll ask for a separation? Am I ruining our lives, Philip's and Daniel's as well as mine and possibly yours? Emmi, help me. What am I to do?'

Emmi lit a cigarette, inhaled deeply before she replied. 'I'm not very wise, Elizabeth. I'm younger than you. I've not been married, not had a child. Of what use is my advice?'

'You can look in from the outside. Not being emotionally involved you might be able to see things more clearly.'

'All right then. You've made the first move. I didn't agree with that, but you've done it. You'll have to take her to the zoo. You can't reject her all over again, can you?'

Of course she couldn't! Those last few words from Emmi went straight home to Elizabeth's troubled conscience, galvanised her mind.

'I'm going to buy a car,' she said. 'I'll have to. I've been thinking about it for a while actually. I can't take Kristall out in mother-in-law's Bentley with mother-in-law's chauffeur, can I?'

'Hardly. A motor car? Are you serious?'

'I need the freedom, Emmi. Especially now, and I have the money. My mother left me some, and that will be the final irony won't it? I shall use her money to visit the daughter she made me reject!'

'How will you go about it?'

'My father tried to persuade me into getting one long before all this happened. He hates my cycling so much, worries about accidents and things. He'll do the buying and everything.'

'Can you drive?'

'Yes. I learnt at the end of the war. No problem there.'

'And petrol? It's still rationed.'

'Stop being so negative. My father to the rescue again. He hardly uses any of his allowance.'

It took more than three weeks for the purchase to be completed and the car delivered. Elizabeth waited anxiously during that time, wrote to Kristall telling her exactly what was happening, and in spite of her confident remarks to Emmi, asked her mother-in-law's chauffeur to give her some refresher driving lessons.

'Come to your senses at last, then,' Roberts said. 'Giving up that bicycle are you?'

'Possibly,' Elizabeth said and wondered what on earth he would say if she told him the truth: *I have a daughter. I am buying a car so that I can visit her secretly!* Even more shattering would be Mildred Gibbons' reaction. In spite of her anxiety, she smiled to herself more than once when she thought about this.

It was a Ford Prefect. On the appointed day Elizabeth drove nervously from home, across the Suspension Bridge and round the Clifton Downs. She passed the zoo to which she would soon be returning, stared briefly at the entrance gates, remembered suddenly the time she and Philip had come here before they were married. And now she was to bring her daughter! A miracle? Perhaps she believed in miracles after all.

She pulled up outside the terraced house and sat for a moment to compose herself.

Kristall had been standing at the front window watching anxiously for the past hour. She rushed to the door as soon as she saw the car, followed by a flustered Brenda.

'She's all ready,' Brenda said. 'My, what a lovely, shiny new car, Kristall. Fancy you going in a car like that.' She bent and kissed her on the cheek. Kristall kissed her back with more fervour than usual.

Elizabeth opened the little front gate, held out her hands to her daughter. 'Hello, Kristall,' she said. She smiled at Brenda. 'We'll be back in about two or three hours' time. That all right?'

'Fine, just fine. No need to rush.'

'I've only ridden in a motor car twice before,' Kristall said. 'That was the vicar's. I went to tea with them last Sunday.'

'They must be very kind people.' Elizabeth opened the front passenger door for her, marvelling at the easy friendliness. She hadn't expected this so soon.

'Yes they are. I call them my adopted grandfather and granny.' Silence for a while and then, 'Have I any real grandparents?'

'Yes. Yes you have. My father lives in Clifton.'

'Can I see him?'

'Not today, but soon.'

'Promise?'

'Yes, of course I promise. He's longing to see you.'

'What about my grandmother?'

'She died a few years ago.'

'Did she know about me?'

'Yes, Kristall, she knew about you.'

Elizabeth drove slowly, carefully, hoped there would be no more questions like that last one. 'What are the things you like most to do?' she asked, abruptly changing the subject.

'Reading. I told you about that. I read and read. And I collect stamps too. We swop them at school. I've got some really valuable ones. One is worth ten shillings and sixpence. At least that's what the Stanley Gibbons book says. That's your name isn't it? Gibbons? Was he a relation of yours?'

Elizabeth laughed. 'No, I don't think he was. Do you have a stamp album?'

'Only a sort of exercise book. I'm saving up for a proper one.'

'I might be able to give you some foreign stamps. I think I have a lot at home.'

'Thank you.'

There was a silence between them then for a long time. Conversation was difficult and Elizabeth was relieved when they arrived at their destination. 'Here we are,' she said. 'Out you get.'

The first cage was Alfred's. Kristall stared at the young gorilla. 'Poor thing,' she said. 'I don't think he ought to be all on his own, do you?'

'I've never really thought about it. Perhaps you're right though. And his cage is a bit small for so large an animal, isn't it?'

'I think it's cruel.'

They walked on towards the lions. The two beasts paced their cage, backwards and forwards incessantly. 'I'm glad they can't get out, but I bet they'd rather be in Africa,' Kristall said. 'Have you ever been to Africa?'

'No. I don't think I want to go either.'

'I do. I want to go just about everywhere.'

Elizabeth laughed. 'You obviously have a great spirit of adventure. You must be very brave. Not at all like me.'

'Was my father like that?'

Elizabeth's heart missed a beat. Why had she not realised that she would probably have to face endless questions about Julius, Julius whom she wanted so desperately to forget. 'Yes, I suppose he was.'

'You promised to tell me about him.'

Best be honest. This is my daughter. She is intelligent and, hopefully, kind. 'He was very good and very brave. Do you mind if we don't talk about him just now? It makes me sad and I want to enjoy our first outing together.'

Kristall looked up at her. This was the first time an adult had treated her as an equal. Mum never did, and certainly Dad didn't. She tried to think of this strange woman as a person in her own right and not merely as her mother.

'All right then,' she said. 'But you'll tell me all about him some time very soon won't you?'

Elizabeth nodded. 'Of course I will. And I shall take you to meet Aunt Emmi. She knew your father throughout the war. She can tell you more than I can.'

'Who is Aunt Emmi?'

'My cousin. She lived in Germany during the war. My mother's sister, my Aunt Sophie, married a German you see. She and Emmi, that's her daughter, came home to England as soon as they could when the war was over.'

The next question took Elizabeth completely by surprise. 'I suppose she speaks German, then. Would she teach me?'

'Well, yes. I expect she would. Why do you want to learn German?'

'When I'm old enough I'm going to find my father!' Then as another thought struck her. 'He is still alive isn't he?'

'Yes, he is.' They were walking towards the tall railings of the giraffe house. 'He suffered because he was involved in a plot to get rid of Hitler.'

'What do you mean?'

'I thought we weren't going to talk about him now.'

'Please?'

Elizabeth stared at the giraffes, enormous but graceful beasts. There was a young one too, nervous, close to its mother. She was not really seeing the animals, but seeing instead a young man with no legs, with tin ones, struggling with sticks. She had never seen him like that in real life, only in imagination. *Julius, Julius, how are you managing without legs? Your daughter is here with me, asking me about you. What shall I tell her? You don't know she exists. I want her to know you, to be proud of you.* The big giraffe started to eat from a rack of hay and leaves fastened high up on the wall.

'How did he suffer?' Kristall pulled urgently at Elizabeth's sleeve.

'He was imprisoned because he was in a plot to overthrow Hitler. That wasn't allowed in Germany, of course. Then they put him into a very dangerous unit of the Army. He had a bad accident to his legs.'

'Are you sure he's all right?'

'Yes, Kristall. I'm sure he's all right. And for now, no more about Julius. Let's go and get an ice-cream.'

They bought cornets and wandered towards the monkey temple. Kristall wanted to hear lots more about this unknown and fascinating father, but Mother had a closed-up look about her. It wouldn't do to ask any more questions. Perhaps another time! She tried to think of something else.

They both stopped and leaned over the railings of the monkey enclosure.

'Do monkeys really live in temples?' she asked staring at the amusing antics of the animals in front of them.

Elizabeth was nonplussed. She had no idea whether wild monkeys lived in temples and just at the moment the question seemed totally irrelevant. In fact the idea of monkeys in temples was quite fantastic when you came to think about it. It had never crossed her mind before. 'I suppose they must, otherwise the zoo wouldn't have built one,' she said.

'Why do they live in temples?'

'I really don't know. In India a temple is a kind of church. Perhaps they live in ruined ones.' Elizabeth struggled to take an interest in this strange conversation while her mind was swamped with the wonder of this day, of being here with her daughter, actually with Kristall after all these years of longing and fantasy. She had to keep turning to look at her to make sure that she was really and truly there, that it wasn't a dream from which she would wake to find herself alone and Kristall's presence just an illusion.

Kristall licked her ice-cream carefully all round the edge of the cornet so that it should not drip down the front of her cardigan. 'Look at the big ones grooming each other. Why are they doing that do you think?'

'I believe they are looking for fleas,' Elizabeth said. She remembered her mother telling her this when she was a little girl. 'See, they're eating them!'

'Ugh, how horrible! And there's a baby monkey on its mother's back.' Abruptly she turned to Elizabeth and said, 'What can I call you? My other mother is just Mum.'

Startled, Elizabeth said, 'I don't know. What do you suggest? You could call me Elizabeth if you liked.'

Kristall was considerably shocked. 'But you're a grown-up. I couldn't call you by your first name.'

'That's a pity. I suppose you wouldn't consider Mummy?'

Kristall was silent for a moment or two. 'That was what I had decided, but it doesn't seem sort of proper somehow. Would Mother be all right? Just Mother?'

'Lovely,' said Elizabeth. 'Because that's what I am.'

'Mum says that I must call you my first mother.'

'Sensible of her. She seems very nice.'

'She is. I pushed her and June down the stairs you know. Did you know?'

'Not really. You don't have to tell me if you don't want to.'

They walked on towards the kangaroo and wallaby enclosure. 'It was June I was really cross with. She'd left Henry's cage open and he was killed. I wanted to kill her too!'

'Henry was your pet guinea-pig, wasn't he?'

'Yes. I thought then that no one but Henry loved me.'

'And now you've discovered that you were wrong.'

Kristall sniffed. 'Mum didn't say one angry word to me and I might have killed her and June. She didn't tell Dad either. She loves June best of course, but she loves me too. She must do mustn't she?'

'Yes. I'm sure she must.'

'Look at that baby in the mother's pouch.

You can just see his head.' Kristall pointed at one of the wallabies.

Elizabeth looked. 'She keeps him warm there until he can run and hop about on his own.'

'Why did you give me away? I used to think that it was because I was bad through and through. That's what Bill-Daddy always said. I called him that when I was little. Stupid really. Now he's just Dad. I don't like him much. In fact I don't like him at all.'

'Of course you're not bad. What an awful thing to say.'

'I'm glad it's not true, but why did you?'

Oh, Kristall, Kristall, why did I? The question I've asked myself a hundred times. 'I loved you very very much. I wanted to keep you, of course. It broke my heart to give you up, but I couldn't marry your father.'

'Why not?'

'He lived in Germany and there was going to be a war.'

'Is that why you don't want to talk about him?'

'Yes. I've already told you. It makes me sad.'

Kristall suddenly felt strong and grown up. She was beginning to understand things now. All the uncertainties of her life were being resolved one by one. 'You won't mind if I go to Germany when I'm bigger and find him will you?'

Elizabeth gripped Kristall's hand, smiled at her, and shook her head. 'It'll be a long time before you're big enough to do that,' she said.

'I don't suppose I shall mind then.' But she wondered, with infinite pain and guilt how she could possibly tell this earnest and intense little girl that her father was quite ignorant of her very existence.

Julius was sometimes tempted to wonder who had really won this dreadful war. He had just received one of Sophie's occasional letters from England. He read it for the second time and glanced at Liesel who was sitting opposite him with a piece of mending in her hands. 'Some things are still rationed over there,' he said. 'It doesn't seem right somehow. They were the victors, after all.'

'What's rationed?'

'She says that the children only have four ounces of sweets a week. That's just a little bag.' He put the closely written page on his lap and cupped his hands to show how much.

Liesel had no benevolent feelings for her country's conquerors. Dresden had seen to that. She shrugged her shoulders. 'I really don't care about English children one little bit,' she said coldly.

Julius looked at her and remembered Elizabeth, as he increasingly did lately. Remembered her smile, her eyes staring at him in incomprehension on that terrible night, the night of the broken glass, the night when she thought he had betrayed everything that she believed of him, the night he had pretended he was a Nazi. He remembered the afternoon of that day too. Remembered the feel of her as if it had been yesterday, her young body lying in his arms, hesitant at first, and then gradually giving herself fully and gladly to him. He remembered the rapture of that first love, a devotion that he had thought could overcome everything.

His lips creased in bitterness as he recalled the letters in which he had poured out all his deepest feelings and his hopes for their future. She had replied at first, had told him that she loved him, but there had been reserve in those lines, and he had guessed that she still thought him a Nazi, despised him for it. He had felt so powerless. He could feel the censor's eyes reading his every word, and so there was no way to tell her of his involvement in the plots against Hitler, of the duplicity into which he was forced. Then her replies had ceased coming and a few months later the great chasm of their countries' war had opened between them.

A blackness swept over him now. What a mess those years had made of his life! Yet he knew that he was lucky. Yes, lucky. Compared with the millions who had perished, and in so many terrible ways too, he had been fortunate. Liesel was always telling him so.

'Well,' she said, biting the thread of her sewing and adding it to the pile on the table at her side, 'I suppose as you're so keen on the English you will want to stay here in Berlin.'

'Do you really want to live under the communists?' Julius said wearily. 'Especially after what they did?' He thought of the raping, murdering soldiers of the Red Army taking their revenge on a defeated Germany.

334

'It's not like that now,' she said. 'Dresden is being rebuilt. It's my town, Julius. I belong there whatever has happened to it. I'm young and enthusiastic. I want to be part of it again, to help rebuild. Here I feel that I am in some sort of prison camp. Everything we get in West Berlin is a hand-out from the British or the Americans.'

Her discontent worried Julius. They had moved out from his father's house since Hans had come home from prison. 'I can't sleep under the same roof as my half-brother,' he had told her. But the flat he had found was small and damp and he dreaded the winter.

He picked up the letter again, turned the page over. Elizabeth had settled happily in Bristol, Sophie wrote. Her little son was three years old, and Philip had bought them a nice house in a pleasant village on the outskirts. Emmi was still living with them. *Philip.* Julius said the name to himself, said it in anger. A naval officer, damn him. With all that gold braid and two good legs! He screwed the piece of paper into a tight ball in his hands, crushed it with unnecessary force as though it were this unknown Philip. Liesel stared at him in surprise.

'Why are you doing that?'

He shrugged. 'Just anger,' he said.

'About what?'

'Nothing and everything.'

'I'll make us some coffee,' she said.

He watched her fold her sewing, walk into the tiny kitchen. He knew he should be grateful he had found her, that he was alive, that Germany

335

was beginning to pick up the pieces of its life again. And Dresden? Yes, if she wanted to go so much they would go, start a new life there. It had been his home too, and the communist regime couldn't last for ever surely? After all, when you had survived the horrors of the Third Reich, you could surely survive anything that life might throw at you. 'We'll go to Dresden,' he said when she returned.

She put the coffee cups on the table and dropped her bombshell. 'I shall go, Julius, but I want to go alone.'

He stared at her, unbelieving, expecting to be filled with a vast sense of loss, but to his surprise all he felt was relief.

'Any reason?' he managed.

She cradled the cup in her hands. 'Lots of reasons, I suppose. Do you mind too much, Julius?'

He shook his head. 'Mind? Do I mind? That's not an easy question to answer, Liesel.' Then after a pause, his voice full of bitterness, he said, 'Is it my legs? Do you want someone with two sound legs?'

She stared at him, angry now. 'How dare you ask that of me. Of course it's not your legs. In fact rather the reverse.'

'You mean that you've only stayed because ...'

'Not that either. Stop torturing yourself and me. We're not right for each other, simply that. The war threw us together and now it's over we have to remake our lives in our own way.'

'And you really want to go to Dresden alone?'

He could hardly believe it.

'Yes. That's what I want. I've contacts, and I believe in communism. It's the right thing for the world, Julius. I know you don't agree.'

'No I don't, but I would have put up with it somehow.'

'That's no good for me.'

He heard the fanaticism in her voice, wondered why he hadn't noticed it before.

'It'll be our own German brand of socialism, not a Russian copy. I'm sorry, Julius, but this is how it has to be.'

He drank his coffee and inexplicably thought of Hans. He shivered slightly and smiled at her. 'I shall always remember you, Liesel. When will you go?'

'I've had a letter,' she said. 'I'm expected in a few days' time.'

November! Sparklers, a bonfire in the garden, potatoes with crisp black skins burning your fingers, sausages on sticks, lots of fun. And Elizabeth had taken the risk of asking Kristall to join them.

'Who is Kristall?' Daniel had said.

'A little girl I know.'

'Why do we have to have a girl? I don't want her.'

'You'll like her.'

'No I won't. I don't like girls. Can't we have a boy?'

'All the little boys we know have their own bonfires.'

To Kristall, Elizabeth had said, 'I'd love

you to come, dear, but there's one important thing.'

'What's that?'

'I don't want Daniel to know that you are my daughter.'

'He's my brother isn't he?'

'Your half-brother, yes.'

'Why can't he know?'

'Because he'll probably say something in front of his father and I have to tell Captain Gibbons very carefully.'

'Why?'

'Because he doesn't like to think that I ever had another boyfriend.'

'I didn't think you could have babies if you weren't married.'

'You shouldn't. Babies need a mummy and a daddy, but sometimes when you love someone very much you don't think about that. I loved your father, Kristall, just as if we were married. We couldn't stay together because it was in Germany and lots of terrible things were happening there. I've told you this before. You know about Hitler don't you?'

'Of course I do. I've seen it at the pictures.'

'Then you know how awful it was. I couldn't stay in Germany and bring you up there.'

'So you left my father all on his own.'

'I had to. He was German. It was his country.'

Kristall had nodded thoughtfully. 'All right then. I won't say anything about who I am. I quite like secrets. Who do you want me to be?'

338

'Just a friend,' Elizabeth said. 'A friend who can't have a bonfire because her garden is too small.'

'Well, that isn't a lie anyway,' said Kristall. 'We'd burn the house down if we set fire to old Guy Fawkes on our titchy little bit of grass!'

This time Elizabeth took Emmi and Daniel with her when she fetched Kristall. Daniel, in the back of the car, sat very still, sulking a little. 'I hope this girl isn't bossy,' he said. 'I don't like bossy girls.'

'I'm sure she won't be bossy,' Emmi said. She too was feeling nervous. Julius's daughter! The thought was somewhat frightening, certainly bewildering. And it brought back too many painful memories. She had been slightly in love with Julius herself long ago before the war. She had not known then that he was her half-brother, the son of her father's mistress. She remembered the day on which she had realised that he and Elizabeth were in love, the day they had come back from their walk beside the lake, *Kristallnacht!* And this child they were about to meet was the result of that afternoon! Her very name was evocative of a past which Emmi longed to forget.

They pulled up outside the little terraced house and Elizabeth got out of the car. 'You two stay there,' she directed. 'I won't be a minute. I expect she's ready.'

As before, Kristall had been waiting in the cold, musty parlour, staring impatiently from behind the net curtains. 'They're here, Mum,' she called. She dashed to the front door, flung it open and then paused, suddenly shy.

Brenda hurried to join her, wiping soda-reddened hands on her apron. 'Now, be a good girl,' she said. 'And remember your secret.' They had talked about Daniel and about keeping her identity hidden. Brenda had been slightly indignant about this at first, but she had gradually accepted that it was all for the best. If Captain Gibbons got to know and didn't mind about it too much Kristall might want to go and live with them, and that would be awful. Since the running away episode Brenda had revised all her feelings about her adopted daughter, didn't want to lose her now. Best if she and her first mother were just friends, nothing more.

'Yes, okay, Mum, I'll remember.' Kristall was out of the door without a backward glance.

'This is Aunt Emmi,' Elizabeth said, 'and Daniel.'

Emmi climbed out of the car and smiled at the little girl. 'I'm glad you could come, Kristall,' she said.

'Thank you. My ... Mrs Gibbons says you speak German.'

'Yes, I do. I hear that you want to learn.'

'Could you teach me?'

'Probably. It's a hard language, though.'

Daniel had wound down the window and was leaning dangerously out. 'I speak it,' he said importantly. 'I speak lots of words. *Meiner name ist Daniel.*'

Emmi joined him in the back seat.

'We thought that you would like to sit in the

340

front,' Elizabeth said.

'Thank you.' Kristall settled herself quickly but turned round to the other two. 'What does that mean?' She repeated the words. *'Meiner name ist Daniel.'*

'It means my name is Daniel, silly,' he said.

'Meiner name ist Kristall,' she said, and Elizabeth felt her heart beat furiously. Julius's child speaking her first German words!

'Bravo,' said Emmi. 'The word *meiner* is a bit different for you because you're feminine. You say, *Meine name ist Kristall.* It sounds almost the same but the spelling is different.'

Kristall said the words again and again, then to Emmi, 'I really do want to learn. It sounds nice. I think I'll soon manage it.'

They were to shop in Park Street, and then have tea before going home. Emmi took Daniel into the museum while Elizabeth and Kristall looked at dresses. 'I shall buy you one,' Elizabeth announced.

'I like your long skirts,' Kristall said. 'I think the New Look is lovely. Mum won't wear it.'

Elizabeth grinned to herself in spite of her nervousness. The tight-waisted full-skirted fashion that had so recently swept the country by storm after the shortages of the war years, wasn't quite the right attire for someone of such short and tubby proportions as Brenda Hodgson. 'Perhaps it wouldn't suit her,' she said. 'You need to be tallish.'

'I'm tall, like you.'

'Yes, you are. Do you want a frock with a full skirt?'

Kristall nodded. 'I want to look like you.'

When they had made their choice they went into the museum, past the stuffed animals, the ancient pottery and the shrunken heads.

'Are those really heads of people?' Kristall said. She frowned at the small grisly faces.

'I think so. It says they are.'

'How awful. I wouldn't like my head put in a glass case when I'm dead.'

They laughed together and Elizabeth felt her tension disappearing. Buying your daughter a pretty frock, talking about simple things together, laughing, these were surely amongst the loveliest pleasures of life. She had thought it would all be so difficult, but it was easy, wonderful! If only ... But those two little words could spoil the nicest things. She determined to cast them right out of her mind. 'We're going to meet the others in the British Restaurant along there,' she said. 'It's at the back, behind the staircase. I expect Daniel is already tucking into one of the biggest cream cakes they have. Don't forget our secret, will you?'

'No, don't worry,' Kristall said in the most grown-up voice she could muster. 'I told you, I like secrets, and I do understand, really.'

The restaurant was quite full and they joined the queue at the counter. Emmi and Daniel waved and they saw that there were two spare seats at their table. Elizabeth bought a cup of tea for herself and milk for Kristall. They chose spam sandwiches, a custard slice and greasy doughnut and Elizabeth carried the tray gingerly between the crowded tables.

342

'Yummy yummy,' Kristall said. 'That dough-nut looks really wizard.'

Not to be outdone Daniel glared at her. 'Mine was wizard too,' he declared.

The bonfire party was as great a success as the shopping expedition and the tea, but later, on the way home when they were alone together, Kristall was very quiet.

'Have you enjoyed yourself?' Elizabeth questioned anxiously.

'Yes, very much thank you.' The tone was prim.

'We might have to wait a few weeks before I can take you out again. I'm sorry, but Daniel's daddy will be home, and ...' Elizabeth was driving along the wide road flanking the Durdham Downs.

'I know,' Kristall said. Then, changing the subject rapidly, something she frequently did and which Elizabeth had at first found disconcerting, she continued, 'The Red Maids School is along this road. I want to go there when I'm eleven, but I'll have to work hard for a scholarship.'

'I'm sure you'll manage it, Kristall. The next time I take you out, when it's in the daytime, we'll drive round that way if you like.'

'But that won't be for ages.'

There was a gloominess in her voice that upset Elizabeth considerably. 'I'll see what I can do. The time will pass quickly though.'

Then another swift change of subject. 'I like Aunt Emmi, and Daniel is okay. It's funny having a brother and not being able to tell him that he is.'

'I'm very sorry about that, Kristall. One day it'll all come right, I'm sure.'

'Did you know that Aunt Emmi gave me some stamps for my collection?'

'She said that she was going to. And I shall buy you a splendid album to put them in.'

'Can I have it for Christmas? I won't stick these new stamps in my old one if you're going to give it to me then. I'll wait for the proper album.'

'For Christmas. I promise.'

That night, in her room, keeping them a secret from Dad, Kristall spread out her new stamps. They were all German. He wouldn't like that, might ask difficult questions. There were a lot of stamps still on the envelopes, and all addressed to Mrs Sophie Kleist, Aunt Emmi's mother apparently, the lady who had married a German a long time ago. What a strange thing to do, marry a German. But real Daddy was German! She was beginning to get used to the idea now. Julius von Brandt. If Mother had stayed in Germany and married him she'd be German, wouldn't she? You were only English if you were born in England she had read, so it followed that if you were born in Germany you'd be German. The thought made her shiver.

She said the name over and over to herself. 'Julius von Brandt.' She had persuaded Mother to tell her his full name when they were on their own together earlier this afternoon. It sounded strange and exciting.

She turned the envelopes over and then her heart started to beat wildly, great thumps so that she could hardly breathe. There in sloping black letters was that name, and an address written all across the top. The envelope had been roughly torn open and she smoothed the ragged edges of paper together so that she could see each word. *An address! Clear as clear!* Her own real father had written those words. Why hadn't Aunt Emmi told her that she knew where he was, that they had letters from him? Perhaps she would have done so later on. But it didn't matter now. She stared at the words as if suddenly hypnotised. *She knew where her father was!* It was the most marvellous, wonderful thing, next to meeting Mother, that had ever happened to her.

She held the envelope in her hand as though it was the real living person, as though it had breath and life, clutched it to her breast, and then she put it back with all the others in the paper bag that Aunt Emmi had handed to her after the bonfire party. She walked across the room, lifted the linoleum from the corner of her bedroom floor and slipped the package underneath. She pulled a chair across and stared at the place. Neither Mum nor Dad, nor real Mother either, should know that she knew. When the time was right, she would write him a letter, a letter to Julius von Brandt! She would have to learn German fast.

CHAPTER 14

November 1949

'Mama and I put flowers on Werner's grave yesterday,' Emmi said. 'The cemetery was particularly peaceful. Perhaps it was the weather, so still and grey.'

'I have never been there.' Elizabeth's voice was thoughtful, full of guilt. She looked at her cousin across the bed which they were making together. 'Do you think very badly of me for that?'

'I've wondered frequently why you don't go.' Emmi smoothed the sheet carefully on her side of the bed. 'There's nothing threatening about it.'

Elizabeth shook her head. 'I wonder too. Constantly. I should have gone when your mother first told me that he was buried here. I've been putting it off for four years, haven't I?'

'You and Werner were fond of each other,' Emmi said. 'I remember feeling very jealous sometimes. He was my brother and I adored him, yet he always brightened up in a special way when you came to stay. I had to take second place during your visits.'

'Gosh, Emmi dear. How awful. I'd no idea. I suppose that you were just the little sister, always there. I was English and only an occasional visitor. That gave me a bit of added glamour, probably.' She tucked the bottom sheet in tightly, expertly. 'But he loved you very much, Emmi. He was always very protective towards you. I remember that.'

Emmi shrugged. 'Brothers usually are, aren't they?'

'I don't know. I never had any, unfortunately. That was why I looked forward to staying with you all in Berlin so much. Werner was the brother I always wanted. We were very close. I remember fancying myself in love with him in the early days, but he was a cousin and it didn't seem quite right. Then of course there was Julius!'

Emmi grabbed a pillow and wrenched off its used cover, throwing it onto the floor. She wanted to say, *you had them both, didn't you!* She took a clean pillow case and pushed the pillow into it, shook it and punched it angrily. 'I miss him still, even after all this time. When I go to the cemetery it helps a little. I just stand there looking at his name on the stone, and at the others too, his crew and some other *Luftwaffe* fliers, and a few RAF graves as well, British and Polish. And there are the graves of those who were killed on the same day, killed by Werner's bombs.'

'Don't get too introspective and gloomy will you, Emmi? It was a long time ago. You have to look forward not back.'

Emmi smiled at her. 'Don't worry. I'm not going crazy. I go with Mama as you know,

347

then we find a nice little restaurant and cheer ourselves up with huge creamy cakes.'

'Well that's a relief. But you make me feel very guilty. I'll make a point of going very soon. Perhaps I've kept putting it off because I wanted to remember Werner alive, as my friend, not as my enemy. It takes a lot of courage to acknowledge a German cousin who bombed your own town.'

'I suppose it might,' Emmi said, 'but I don't have that problem. Being in Germany right to the end drove those kind of doubts out of my head. I saw Berlin a mass of rubble don't forget. The morality of it all, the rights and wrongs, don't seem to matter very much, not to me anyway. I just grieve for a brother lost, and all the others as well.' She took the other pillow, changed its cover, put it on the bed. 'They are all Hitler's victims whichever side they were on.'

'Yes. Of course you're right. You make me feel absolutely shame-faced.' Elizabeth took a crisply ironed top sheet and shook it out over the bed. Then she paused for a moment and looked through the window at the November sky and remembered vividly other days, other skies and the menacing throb of the German bombers that came so regularly during that long summer which seemed a lifetime away now. She had thought of Werner every time they came, thought of him with bewilderment, but now she remembered him as he had been before the war, full of fun, full of life. That was how he would be for her when she went

348

at last to visit his grave. 'I should like to go alone to the cemetery,' she said. 'For my first visit anyway. Do you mind?'

Emmi straightened the sheet, tucked her side in carefully, shook her head. 'Of course not.'

'There's another thing,' Elizabeth said. 'An odd coincidence, something Kristall said. Apparently her first adoptive father was killed in one of the big daylight raids over Bristol. He was in the shelter at the BAC that had a direct hit. When I checked up I discovered that it was the same day that Werner was shot down, September 25th 1940. So one of Werner's bombs probably killed Kristall's father! Later her mother ... her adoptive mother, married again and Kristall became unhappy. If all that hadn't happened she wouldn't have had any need to run away and I should never have discovered her. That's too awful to think about now.'

They spread blankets on the bed, tucked them in beneath the heavy mattress, turned down the top sheet, added cover and eiderdown and then stood up. Both simultaneously straightened their backs and looked at each other.

'Strange coincidence,' was all Emmi said.

'Do you think it's just coincidence?'

'It must be. There's no pattern to anything is there? The war has made a great gigantic muddle everywhere.'

Elizabeth frowned a little. 'A muddle! Well that's the understatement of the year.' But then she suddenly thought of a day years ago on the farm, an event that had remained in her memory ever since. She and Isobel had been working in the hay field when a great gust of wind had come unexpectedly out of the calm summer sky. It had caught up the hay and whirled it around above their heads and then had deposited it in another field and all over the place, to the delight of the cows and to the amazement of herself and Isobel. She remembered standing there quite helpless watching the currents of air swirling hay and dust and debris over their heads. Perhaps Emmi was right. The war was like that. It had made a terrifying muddle of everything. It was like a whirlwind. It had caught up everyone in its path and altered the course of their lives.

But now, suddenly, she wanted to see where her cousin was buried, take flowers, make atonement. And she must go alone. It was not too far away and she had just enough petrol. There was still a week before Philip was due home on leave. This was to be a longer leave than usual, four whole weeks he had said. She would have to go immediately or put it off yet again.

The cemetery was huge, full of grey angels pointing to the skies with grey hands and a hope of immortality, gnarled crosses and lovely old trees. She wandered down the central path staring at the multitude of pious sentiments and heartbreaking lines.

'Beth, loved daughter of Mary and Seth,
died aged five years 1895–1900.
Safe in Jesus' bosom.'

'Susanah, precious wife of Martin Jones, died 1895 aged 20 years and John Henry, son of the above, died 1895 aged two days. Both sadly mourned.'

Elizabeth paused now and then to stare and contemplate. She had not spent much time in cemeteries before today. Her mother was buried in the local churchyard, a small, personal place where she went with her father occasionally to leave flowers, but these vast acres were quite different, a city of the dead, yet peaceful and beautiful in a way that she had not thought possible. The weak November sun was filtering gently through branches of beech and oak almost bare of leaves now and a row of yews stood in sombre guard near the Chapel of Rest. Here and there amongst the grass were brilliant patches of autumn crocus.

Then she saw it, a great stone cross and around it well-tended graves in straight rows as though the men resting there were still on the parade ground, still standing to attention. She quickened her pace and read some of the names.

'Captain John Bennet, Royal West Kent Regiment, 4th June 1940. Age 29. Sadly missed.'

'Pilot Officer Thomas Jones. A pilot of the Royal Air Force 25th September 1940. Aged 25. Much loved son of Betty and Richard Jones. Remembered with pride.'

There were so many, and all so young. Polish names stood out amongst the British, all members of the RAF, and then separated just a little by a mere strip of grass were the German graves, a dozen or more. She stared at them, bemused, read the names one by one. They made her think of her cousin's friends, children she had played with in those carefree long-ago days in the big Berlin garden. Franz, Karl, Johann, Ernst, Gerhard, and then the one she sought. It was set at the end of a row, the German cross cut into the stone like all the others, a symbol that made her shiver with distaste. And then the inscription,

WERNER KLEIST
14.2.20–25.9.40

There was nothing more, no Bible verse, no 'loved son of' nothing! Just the stark facts. And the date of his death was the awful, condemning thing: 25th September 1940, the very day of the frightful raid in which hundreds had died, Kristall's adoptive father amongst them.

How did Aunt Sophie deal with this knowledge? Did she feel embarrassed when she brought flowers? Did she look around to make sure that no one saw her? There was a small wreath of red carnations at the foot of the stone now. Elizabeth stared at them and wondered if her aunt had visited recently, put them here for next week's Remembrance Day, perhaps? Did she come more often than she admitted?

She thought of her own little son and wondered how you coped if your child had brought destruction and death to your own people. She felt fresh compassion for her aunt. Werner had been a model son, never headstrong or cruel like Hans. Elizabeth had not known him to do anything in anger. He was a gentle person, like a much loved brother to her for so long. How could he have flown bombers over his mother's country? It was a mystery she would never solve, a question without an answer. She knelt on the damp grass, put her hands on the headstone and spoke softly, 'I loved you, Werner, as my brother while I was growing up. Where are you now? Do you know I am here? Are you sad about what you did?'

She heard footsteps on the gravel, turned to look up.

'You knew 'im then?' The voice was unfriendly and Elizabeth scrambled to her feet, embarrassed to have been overheard.

'My cousin,' she said. 'He was a good man.'

'Bloody Jerries,' the man said. 'There ain't no good Germans. I was in the trenches the first time round. The Somme.'

Elizabeth groped for her handkerchief, wiped tears from her eyes.

'Keep yer tears for all our lads over there.' He nodded towards the British graves. 'And for them Jews in them bloody camps. Don't waste time on a bloody Jerry.'

He shambled off and Elizabeth stared after him, considerably shaken, thinking suddenly of Julius and of Kristall, of Germany, exciting and

353

beautiful before the war. How could it all have turned so sour? She looked at Werner's grave again. Then she turned away and knew that she would never return. Yet strangely it was Julius who had become more real because of this visit. The past had suddenly become the present, and the present, the past.

Armistice Day, November 11th, and Philip was due home. She was to meet him from the railway station.

'Can I come, Mummy?' Daniel said, all excitement. 'You promised that I could go out in your motor lots of times. I like trains too. I want to see the trains.'

'I thought you wanted to see Daddy?' Elizabeth laughed at him, momentarily putting her worries aside.

'Yes, 'course I do. We're not taking Kristall are we?'

'No.' Her voice was sharper than she intended.

'She's got her own daddy. She can't have mine. She told me about him when we had the fireworks.'

'What did she say?' Elizabeth was alarmed.

'Just that she doesn't like him much, and that he likes her sister best.'

She breathed a sigh of relief. 'I don't want you to talk about Kristall when we see Daddy. Let's keep it a secret for a bit shall we?'

'Okay,' he said.

The train was due at twelve o'clock. 'Remember that you are not to say a word about

Kristall,' Elizabeth reminded Daniel on the way to the station. 'You like secrets don't you? Well this is a very special secret.'

'Why is it?'

'Because he might not like the idea of us taking her out and all that. We'll wait until the right time to tell him.'

'Why?'

'He doesn't know about her yet and we don't want him to be cross just as he arrives do we?'

'No. He'll have presents for us.'

Elizabeth was driving very carefully, taking a long time. Philip's leave would certainly he traumatic. How did you confess to your husband that you had a daughter, a ten-year-old, and you wanted to see her frequently, have her in your home, and that her father was German? *How will he take it? What will he do? Will he rage and storm, throw me out?* Her hands were clammy on the steering wheel, her heart thumping irregularly, frighteningly.

'He promised me a puppy.'

'Yes, he did. But he won't have one with him.'

'I know he won't. We'll get one tomorrow.' Daniel had obviously forgotten about Kristall for now. A puppy was of far greater importance.

'Don't forget the secret.'

'Okay.'

She drove up the Temple Meads incline and parked close to the station entrance. For a moment she sat quite still in the car. Until Kristall had been catapulted into her life again she had been longing for this day as she always looked forward to Philip's rare times at home. But now ...

'Come on, Mummy,' said Daniel impatiently. 'I want to see what Daddy has brought.'

The remark irritated her. 'He's brought himself,' she said. 'Isn't that enough?'

Daniel rattled the door handle. 'Want to get out. Want to meet Daddy.'

Half an hour later she saw him striding along the platform towards her, waving, smiling, handsome, oh, so handsome in that glorious uniform. He put his luggage down, held out his arms to both of them, and there was room for Daniel and for herself in his embrace. Then he stood back and looked at them. 'My, what a big boy,' he said. 'What a great big handsome boy for Daddy.'

And Elizabeth suddenly felt tears in her eyes and wondered how she could ever let anything as insubstantial as a dream spoil this happiness. *But Kristall is not insubstantial, not a dream. Julius may be, but his daughter is not.*

'Mummy has bought a motor car,' Daniel said. 'Ladies can't drive but Mummy can.'

Philip laughed, caught his son up in his arms, held him high above his head. 'Why can't ladies drive, then?'

' 'Cause cars are only for men.'

'Oh dear. Where did you get that idea from?'

'From Grandma. Ladies are special and have chauffeurs.'

Grandma! Elizabeth frowned. Now that Philip

356

was home she would have to see more of her mother-in-law, and Mildred Gibbons knew nothing yet about Kristall. Another terrifying milestone!

Philip turned to Elizabeth. 'A car? What sort?'

'A Ford,' she said. 'I've only had it a short time. I didn't tell you. I wanted it to be a surprise. You can drive it home if you like.'

Philip retrieved his luggage. 'Well,' he said, 'I shall have to get used to an emancipated wife I suppose. Right then, lead on. The rest of my stuff is being sent. I can't wait to be home.'

They walked through the subway and out into the soft November sunshine. 'There it is,' said Daniel, pointing, 'and what's 'mancipated?'

'Clever!' Philip winked at Elizabeth. He stowed his luggage and took the key that Elizabeth held out to him. 'Sure you want me to drive? It's yours after all.'

'Not so emancipated,' she said. 'I should be terrified driving with you in the car.' *And I'm terrified anyway. Terrified of seeing you change when you know about my daughter.*

'I want to sit in the front,' Daniel demanded. 'I can, can't I, Daddy?'

'Only if you sit very still.'

'I promise,' said Daniel.

Philip started the engine. 'Nice little car. I'm glad you decided to get one in the end. I suggested it, if you remember?'

In the back seat she smiled a little to herself. He always liked to think that every innovation was his idea. 'Your mother kept threatening

357

me with Roberts and the Bentley. I needed to feel free.'

'Of course. We must call on the parents this evening. I telephoned last night.'

And you didn't telephone me! Game and match to my mother-in-law! 'Must we, on your first night?'

'I think so, darling. You don't mind, do you?'

Mind! Do I mind? I want to strangle them, at least, her, and perhaps you too, Philip. Elizabeth's momentary happiness and the fear which had followed it faded rapidly, both emotions giving way to anger and frustration. 'I suppose not,' she lied. *I mustn't antagonise him over this. Just now. More important things are at stake.*

'That's good, then. I presume that Emmi is still with us?'

'Yes. She'll look after Daniel while we are out.'

'Aunt Emmi talks funny to me. It's German. She's going to teach Kristall to talk funny too.'

'Daniel!'

They were driving round the tramway centre, Philip concentrating, keeping his eyes firmly on the road ahead. 'Who is Kristall?' he said.

Daniel looked at his mother, clapped his hands over his mouth.

'A little girl we know.' Elizabeth hoped her voice sounded matter-of-fact.

'I wasn't supposed to tell,' Daniel said. 'It's a secret.'

Philip was driving up Park Street now. 'Why's that, then?'

358

'We'll tell you all about it later. Daniel hopes that you are going to buy him a puppy tomorrow.' Elizabeth desperately changed the subject.

'Yes, I promised, didn't I? It's okay as long as Mummy agrees. Have you any particular one in mind?'

Elizabeth relaxed. Safe for now anyway.

'I want a great big dog,' Daniel said. 'A big huge, huge one.'

Philip laughed. 'We'll see what we can do.'

The evening was long and tedious, Mildred Gibbons at her most nauseating, Philip trying valiantly and unsuccessfully to please both wife and mother, his father tediously jaunty. The new motor car was a cause of great discord. 'Women who can afford a chauffeur should never drive themselves,' Mildred declared, not realising that she was twenty or more years out of date. 'You could have had Roberts and the Bentley any time you wanted.'

On the way home Elizabeth laughed nervously about this particular phobia of her mother-in-law. 'She lives in cloud cuckoo-land,' she said. 'Does she realise that it's 1949?'

'She regrets the passing of the agreeable years before the war. The twenties were golden years for her and the thirties were pretty good. She wants servants and gracious living again.'

'They might have been agreeable for her,' Elizabeth said, 'but not for millions of others. What about poverty and unemployment?'

'Those things were fine if you were rich, a

good source of cheap labour.' He paused, turned the corner into their road. 'But try not to be too hard on her. She means well. She'd do anything for me.'

'That's the trouble,' Elizabeth said half under her breath and then wished she had not.

'Let's change the subject. No disagreements on my first night home. You were going to tell me about this little girl. What was her name? Daughter of friends I suppose?'

Elizabeth took a deep breath. 'No, Philip. She isn't the daughter of friends.'

He pulled up at the end of their drive, got out of the car to open the gates, climbed in again and drove carefully through, parked in front of the garage. 'We'll have to have another one now we've two cars.'

'Another one?' Elizabeth was thinking of babies, of Kristall.

'Another garage.'

'Oh yes. Of course.' She tried to concentrate. 'I'll shut the gates,' she said, anxious to put off the betraying moment. She walked down the drive in her uncomfortable high heels, every step click-clacking on the concrete. When she returned he had the front door open and Emmi was there to greet them.

'Nice evening?'

Elizabeth shrugged. 'So-so.' She grinned at Emmi. 'Daniel gone to sleep?'

'Yes, after a bit. He's excited about getting a puppy tomorrow.'

'I hope we can.'

They went into the kitchen, made a cup of

360

tea, stood around the Aga drinking it and then Emmi said, 'I'm going to bed. I want to finish my book. There's nothing like reading in bed. It's one of my little pleasures.' She swilled the cups, put them to drain, filled a hot water bottle, smiled at Elizabeth and went quietly upstairs.

'She's being tactful,' Elizabeth said. 'Doesn't want to intrude on our first evening together.'

Philip searched for his cigarettes. 'I'll have a smoke first. Want to join me?'

She shook her head. 'No thank you. I still can't get used to the things.'

'Then come into the drawing room and talk to me. I need to catch up on all the news. So Daniel is having German lessons! A bit young, isn't he?'

'The younger the better. Emmi just prattles away to him and he's picking it up naturally.'

'French would be more acceptable.'

'That's just what your mother said. But Emmi doesn't speak French.'

'A pity. German has so many bad memories for such a lot of people.' He thought of U-boats, of machine-gun fire, of hours in the water clinging to the side of an over-full little lifeboat, of watching his friends slip beneath the oily turbulent surface of the Atlantic, unable to stand the cold any longer. He thought of photographs of Auschwitz and Dachau. 'Well, never mind,' he said. 'Having another language is always a good idea, any language, I suppose.'

She nodded. 'He seems to enjoy it anyway.'

'And of course, you speak German too.' He looked at her strangely. 'I had almost forgotten your German connections.'

They were sitting either side of the drawing room fire now. Elizabeth added some coal, poked it to a flame.

'Does Emmi offer German lessons as a paying concern? Daniel mentioned this little girl whom she teaches. Any others? I shouldn't think it was very popular option so soon after the war.'

Elizabeth shook her head. 'No nothing like that. It's quite informal, not proper lessons.'

'Who is she, then? You were going to tell me.'

She clasped her hands together on her lap, unclasped them, twisted her wedding ring and the engagement ring with its huge diamond round and round on her finger. 'She's rather special, Philip. I've just ... just found her.'

He looked up, startled. 'What do you mean, found her?'

'I don't know how to tell you this.'

'Go on. I won't mind. I'm pleased that Daniel has a friend. Perhaps we can take her with us tomorrow to choose this puppy?'

Elizabeth stared into the fire. 'You remember when you asked me to marry you? You asked me about my past and then said that you didn't want to know, that it hurt you to think of me with another man?'

'Yes, and you said that he had been German. That it was all over.' He stood up slowly and stared down at her. 'My God, Elizabeth, are you trying to tell me you've been unfaithful to me while I've been at sea?' He stubbed out his cigarette, threw it into the fire, clenched his fists.

She didn't move, didn't look at him. 'No, Philip, nothing like that. I have been completely faithful to you ever since that day at Weston when I promised to marry you, to pray for you. With all the temptations of wartime, the GIs, everything, I never looked at another man. And I have prayed for you, every single night as I promised I would.'

'Then what are you talking about? Why are you so ... so petrified?'

'Kristall is ten, Philip. Ten years old. She's my daughter. She was born long before I met you, in 1939 and I was forced to have her adopted.'

He stared at her as if he had seen a ghost. The colour drained from his face. Then he got up, crossed to the sideboard and poured a large whisky, drank it in one go. 'So you have deceived me all these years.'

'Not deceived you.' She shook her head. 'You knew that ... that I had had a lover. I told you. But you didn't want to know any more. It was 1938. I was young, foolish, thought I was in love. Philip, you can't condemn me for something which happened so long ago, years before we met.'

'You're telling me that this child is yours and his, a half-German bastard and you've "found" her. Bloody clever of you. How long has it been going on?'

'Has what been going on?'

He didn't reply.

'She was unhappy. She ran away from home. That's how I found her. I saw her photograph in the newspaper.'

'How long, I said?'

'Since August.'

'Then it's got to stop.' He lit another cigarette, stood with his back to the fire.

'What do you mean?'

'I won't allow you to see her again.'

Elizabeth stared at him with fear and sudden repugnance. 'You can't say that.'

'I've said it. I'm the master in my house and you'll obey me. You'll not see her any more. I'll have no remembrance of your sordid little affair in my home, no reminders of your unprincipled past life to pollute my son. Is that clear?'

She was furious now. 'How dare you refer to my love for her father as a sordid little affair. It was no such thing. Yes, I loved him and he may have been German but he fought against Hitler as much as you did.' She clenched her fists. 'It was a long time ago and it's truly in the past. You've no need to be jealous. But Kristall is not in the past. She's a lovely little girl, my child, Philip. My child as much as Daniel is. I love her. She's beginning to love me a little. I abandoned her once. I can't do it all over again.'

'Of course she's not *your child*. She has parents, hasn't she? You gave her away. You've no claim on her, no claim at all, and nor should you have.'

'They are willing to let me see her.'

'But I most definitely am not.' He stormed

out of the room banging the door furiously. She heard him unbolt the front door, slam that one too and then start her car, not his. She listened to the familiar sounds, the front gates being opened, and then the sound of the engine dying away in the distance.

She sat there for a long time and eventually the door handle turned slowly and Emmi, in curlers and dressing gown, came into the room. 'Whatever has happened, Lizzy?' she said.

'I've told him about Kristall.'

Philip drove fast and furiously with no idea where he was going or for how long he drove. All he could think of was his wife giving birth to another man's bastard child. He had known about the German, but had preferred not to think about it, had been able to banish the knowledge for much of the time, but a child for God's sake! That was something else, something quite else!

Would he have married her if he had known? Probably not. He remembered their first meeting and then the day at Weston-super-Mare. He had been so anxious to marry. He winced a little at the remembrance of his youthful enthusiasms and certainties, those foolish things he had said. But the marriage had worked on the whole. Daniel's birth had been wonderful, of more importance perhaps than all the prestige of his naval career.

But now this! Her body had produced another child for another man! He couldn't bear it, couldn't endure the humiliation, for that was how it felt. His property had been violated. And she expected him to see this child, to allow her into his home. It was the most preposterous, the most repugnant thing he had ever heard. It couldn't be countenanced at all.

When he eventually returned home he thought of using the spare bedroom. Could he ever touch her again, let alone make love to her? He downed another whisky and then another, went upstairs slowly, pondering. Then sudden resolution filled him. His pulse quickened. Elizabeth was his wife and by God he'd make love to her tonight if it was the last thing he did. Perhaps they'd have another child to cast out the misbegotten one. He opened the bedroom door noisily, undressed and threw his clothes onto the floor, wrenched back the tightly tucked-in bedclothes and pulled her into his arms roughly, hardly thinking what he was doing.

'Philip,' she said. 'Philip ...' He covered her mouth with his lips, forced his tongue between her teeth viciously as he had never done before. He was filled with anger and lust, the desire to overpower and subdue. He pulled her nightdress savagely away, so savagely that he could feel the flimsy material rip in his hands. He forced himself into her with no word of love or kindness or apology.

She resisted him at first but was no match for his strength and when it was all over he lay on his back and stared at the moon shining between the branches of the tree outside the window. She was crying. Well, let her cry. He put the bedside light on, lit a cigarette and lay there smoking. He could hardly accept that he had done what he had done, yet he was triumphant rather than ashamed. He had raped his wife! It was completely out of character, went against everything he had ever believed of himself. But his body and his honour were satisfied, for the moment anyway. He finished his cigarette, switched out the light, turned away from her, and slept.

Elizabeth, eyes red from weeping, head aching, and a hundred quandaries unresolved, crept from bed early the following morning and ran a bath. She soaked her violated body in scented water and tried to banish the memory of her humiliation. Above all else she wanted to talk to Isobel, wanted to drive to the station and get the next train to Scotland. Emmi was sweet, Emmi was a good friend, but there was no one in the world to equal Isobel.

She had carried her clothes into the bathroom. Fully dressed she would feel less at a disadvantage and it would deter him from attempting to make love to her again. Make love! What a mockery for the anger and aggression of last night. She shuddered as she wiped herself dry. She shook *L'Aimant* talcum powder over her skin with unusual recklessness so that it lay on the pink carpet like a scattering of fine snowflakes and she scuffed it into the deep pile with her bare feet, enjoying the heady scent and then sneezing uncontrollably into the towel.

In the kitchen she made a cup of tea and tried to regain a measure of self-control and calm, listened for signs of life from upstairs. It was Daniel who bounced into the room first. He ran over to her, threw his arms around her neck. 'We're going to get my puppy today aren't we, Mummy? Daddy promised.'

She held him close, kissed his shining hair, smelt the clean, lovely smell of him, and knew that her heart would break for the second time in her life if she had to give up this precious child. 'Yes, darling. I hope so. Have some breakfast and we'll see about it.'

Of course she could not go to Scotland, could not pour out her heart to Isobel, could not rush out to see her father or her grandmother, and above all else could not visit Kristall. *I am a prisoner here in my house, a prisoner because I love my son. Because of Daniel I must give in to my husband's demands, agree to his rules, and today I must go and choose a puppy just as though everything is right in my life!*

CHAPTER 15

Kristall stared at the parcel on the kitchen table.

'Well, go on, open it.'

'I've never had a parcel before, not in the post.'

'Of course you haven't. I've been dying to know what's inside. Nearly opened it myself.' Brenda picked it up, turned it this way and that as she had done many times since the postman had delivered it halfway through the morning. 'Here's the scissors,' she said impatiently.

Kristall cut the string that was tied securely with a lot of knots. Then she slowly pulled back the brown paper and there it was, a large green stamp album and a letter. 'It's from Mother. She was going to give it to me for Christmas.'

'Well, you're a lucky girl. You don't have to wait. See what she says, then.'

Kristall opened the envelope and read the letter silently.

'My dear Kristall,

I do hope you will like this stamp album and have a lot of fun putting all your stamps in it. I've enclosed some stamp hinges too because you'll need lots of those. It was to be a Christmas present, but I want to give it to you now instead.

I am afraid that I have some bad news. We shall have to wait for quite a while before we can go out together again and I shall not be able to invite you here as I had hoped. It's very hard to explain. As soon as Captain Gibbons goes back to sea I shall come to see you, but that probably won't be until after Christmas. His ship needs a lot of extra things done to it so he will be home for a few weeks yet.

Please don't write. Captain Gibbons would prefer us not to meet while he is at home and although I am very sad about this I have to do what he says.

Daniel sends you a kiss and so does Emmi,

and I send you lots and lots of kisses with this letter.

And a lot of love too, my precious Kristall.

From Mother.'

Kristall read it again and then again, and she felt angry tears in her eyes. Quickly she brushed them away. She threw the letter onto the table and without looking at Mum she ran upstairs to her bedroom. She slammed the door shut and flopped onto the bed. How dare she? How dare she do it all over again? To give your very own daughter away once was awful, but to do it twice was absolutely horrible. Kristall pulled her teddy bear into her arms and scrunched him to her breast so that he was almost flattened. Then she heard Mum plodding along the landing. The bedroom door opened a crack and Kristall sprang to her feet. No one must know how hurt she was.

'Cheer up, lovey,' Brenda said opening the door wider. 'It's a splendid stamp album, what you've always wanted.'

'Well I don't want it now!'

'Yes you do, of course you do.' Brenda came right into the room, the album in her hands. 'I've had a quick look. There's every country in the world in here, and some have more than one page.' She opened it enticingly. 'And it's got pictures of the stamps to help you. Here's Egypt with pyramids on and France and it's even got two pages for Germany. You've got some German stamps haven't you?'

Kristall nodded.

'And here's Greece and Holland. My good-ness, Krissy, you'll be really clever when you've learnt about all these places.'

'She gave it to me because she doesn't want to see me any more.'

Brenda put the book down, sat on the bed and patted the space beside her. 'I read the letter after you threw it down. It isn't like that at all. She loves you, but it's her hubby who's laid down the law. He's jealous most likely. She can't help it, love. I expect she's as sad as you are.'

Kristall sat down beside her and felt a comforting arm thrown around her shoulders. She snuggled close and let the tears come, unrestrained now. 'But why does she have to do what he says? She's got a motor car of her own and all that. She could have spared some time to come instead of posting it.'

'Men are the bosses, and that's the truth of it.' Brenda sighed and thought of her own life. 'It oughtn't to be, and perhaps one day things might change, but for now, well, we've just got to put up with it.'

'I'm not going to put up with it, not ever,' Kristall said. She searched for a handkerchief and wiped her eyes and her nose. 'I'll never get married.'

Brenda smiled. 'That's as maybe, but mean-while, don't be too hard on your first mum. You get busy and stick all those stamps you've got into this nice album and then you'll have it ready to show her when she does come to see you.'

'I might.' Kristall's tone was grudging. She pulled the book towards her and flipped through the pages. 'Where's Sierra Leone? I've never heard of that.'

Brenda shook her head. 'I don't rightly know. Sounds like Africa. I reckon I ought to save up and buy you an atlas to go with the stamp album, and then we'll have a real little clever clogs in the house.'

Clever clogs! Kristall liked that. She'd never heard it before. Oh well, perhaps she'd use the stamp album after all. She wanted to anyway.

Every week Kristall and June went to Sunday School. 'Can I take my stamp album?' Kristall asked Brenda one Sunday afternoon. 'I've finished putting the stamps in and I want to show it to my teacher.'

Brenda, at the sink, washing up greasy dinner plates, grinned to herself. The stamp album had proved too big an attraction to be rejected and Kristall seemed to have recovered from her displeasure with her first mum. Brenda was glad about that. She couldn't bear to see the child so upset and disappointed. It was cruel of Mrs Gibbons to cast her off a second time, of course, but perhaps she had no choice. Women often hadn't.

'Put it in a bag, then,' she said. 'You don't want to spoil it after all the time you've spent on it, do you? And keep hold of June's hand when you cross the road.'

Kristall was entrusted with the care of her younger sister on Sundays. 'All right,' she said.

She found a paper carrier with BENDLES STORES written across it and she put the album carefully inside. She had some German envelopes with their stamps still on too. She had read in the Gibbons catalogue that sometimes stamps were more valuable like that. But the special one with *Julius von Brandt* and the precious address written on the back, was still safely hidden beneath the carpet. She took it out now and then and looked at it, brushed her fingers across the magic letters, but always returned it to its secret hiding place and did nothing. The German lessons had stopped, of course, and couldn't be started again until that bothersome Captain Gibbons was safely away at sea once more. And anyway, she couldn't pluck up enough courage to actually write to this mysterious father of hers, even in English. The thought was too frightening. Best keep it just a dream for now, a dream that she could make into real life at any time she chose, any time she was brave enough!

Kristall looked forward to Sundays, mostly because she really loved her Sunday School teacher. Miss Fischer was young and pretty with dark curling hair and sparkling brown eyes. The children sat together in a big hall for the first half an hour and sang hymns, said prayers, and listened to a Bible story. Then they split into small groups of six or so, each with their own teacher. This was the special time that Kristall liked best. She hadn't to bother about June because she was in another room with the little ones. The children were all ten and eleven years old in Kristall's group and they talked about important things, grown-up things sometimes. It was supposed to be about the story they had just heard, but it was easy to get Miss Fischer to tell them all sorts of other things. Today the story had been about how King David had been chosen to be king of Israel.

'You can draw him with his harp and his sheep if you like,' Anna Fischer told them. She gave out wax crayons and paper.

They knelt on the floor and put the paper on the seat of the little wooden chairs if they wanted to draw.

'That's sissy,' one of the boys said. 'I'm going to draw him cutting off Goliath's head with his sword.'

'David didn't have a sword, only a sling and stones,' a girl objected.

'It was Goliath's sword that he used, stupid!' came the quick reply.

Kristall looked from one child to the other. It was a babyish conversation even though they were ten years old. She didn't want to talk about such silly things or do a drawing either. 'I've brought my stamp album to show you,' she said shyly to the teacher. 'There isn't a page for Israel. If David was the king of it there must have been one once. I haven't got any Israelite stamps either.'

'Israeli stamps,' Anna corrected. 'There hasn't been an Israel for nearly two thousand years. There is now, though.'

Kristall looked critically at her album. 'The

countries are in alphabetical order,' she said. 'Look, here's Iraq and then it goes straight to Italy.'

'You'll have to put a page in and write ISRAEL at the top.'

'Why has Israel only just started?'

Miss Fischer laughed. 'Started again, you should say. It was there two thousand years ago. You can see if you look at the old maps at the back of your Bible. Now Israel is there once more, just since last year, 1948. It's partly happened because of all the terrible things that Germany did to the Jews.'

Kristall felt a small niggle of disquiet. She always did when anyone talked about how bad Germany had been. 'It was Hitler, wasn't it?' she said anxiously.

The boy who was jubilantly colouring a bloody picture of a decapitated Goliath joined in. 'Pity King David wasn't around to chop off Hitler's head. That would have served him right.'

'I've got some German stamps and some German envelopes,' Kristall said. She pulled them out of the paper carrier.

'How did you get those?' Anna Fischer's cheerful, friendly voice changed, became suddenly wary.

Kristall stared at her in surprise and then looked down again at the stamps and envelopes of which she had been so proud. Perhaps it was wrong to boast about German stamps. Perhaps they reminded people too much of the war. 'Someone gave them to me,' she said, unwilling to acknowledge any personal connection.

'Please put them away, Kristall. I don't want to look at them.'

'I'm sorry,' Kristall said. Embarrassed, she pushed them quickly back into the carrier. She had been so proud of them and now they were quite spoiled as though they had suddenly become bad, tainted with Hitler's horribleness. She hadn't thought of it like that before.

'I'll walk along with you afterwards,' Anna said, sounding a little contrite. 'And I'll try to explain.'

'All right,' she said. 'We'll wait outside for you.'

'I thought your stamp album was lovely,' Anna Fischer said later as they left the building. She pulled on her gloves and slung her bag over her shoulder. 'I'm sorry if I upset you about the envelopes and stamps from Germany.'

They walked quickly because of the cold and Kristall didn't know what to say. At least Miss Fischer was her normal friendly self again, but why should simple envelopes have made her so upset?

'I lived in Germany until I was seven years old,' Anna Fischer said. 'It was a bad time for my family. I hate to remember it. One day my father's shop was attacked, and he was taken away.'

Kristall's eyes opened wide in astonishment. 'What had he done?'

'Nothing. He was Jewish. It was *Kristallnacht*, the night of the broken glass. They call it that because all the Jewish shops were smashed and

376

there was glass all over the place.'

'*Kristallnacht,*' Kristall repeated slowly. 'That's like my name. Mum said that it means shining glass.'

'*Kristall.* Of course. And you spell it the German way too don't you? I wondered about that when I first saw it on something you had written.'

Kristall felt cold, an icy chill that had nothing to do with the November weather. She was aware of a sudden creeping blackness as though there was something horrible all around her that she didn't understand, something in which she had some unknown part and yet was powerless to do anything about. She didn't want to talk about herself or to say that she was adopted. 'What happened to your father?' she asked.

'He was sent to a concentration camp. He died.'

June had been silent so far. She let go of Kristall's hand and skipped ahead a little and then waited for the other two to catch up. 'Where's your mummy?' she said.

'Here in England. She managed to escape with me and my little brother. She's English, and she's not Jewish either, so it was fairly easy to get the papers and things.' Anna looked down at the two little girls. 'I don't suppose you understand much of all this that I'm telling you, do you? It doesn't matter really, but I wanted you to know that thinking about Germany brings back memories of that awful night. It was the last time I saw my father and I get very sad and very angry. That was why I

377

didn't want to look at your German envelopes and stamps.'

'Sorry,' Kristall whispered.

Anna smiled. 'You couldn't have known.' They had reached the corner where their routes parted. 'It's I who should be sorry really. I've been so gloomy.'

Kristall shook her head. 'You haven't.' Then she remembered something that Mother had told her. It hadn't meant much at the time, but now it seemed important. 'My great-grandmother is Jewish,' she said. 'I'm glad that she didn't live in Germany in the war.'

Anna looked at her with fresh interest. 'So you're a little bit Jewish like me!'

'Am I? I suppose I must be.' It was a new idea to Kristall. She was half-German and a bit Jewish too! What a mix up. Better not tell Dad. He probably didn't like Jews any more than he liked Germans.

'Your great-gran was one of the lucky ones,' Anna said. 'To be in England, I mean. You must tell me more about her next week. I've got to rush now.' She smiled at them. 'See you next Sunday.'

Kristall stood quite still and stared after her. How was she going to explain that she had never met her Jewish great-grandmother? Perhaps she could say that she was dead. She must be very very old if she was Mother's gran. Oh dear! It was just dreadful being adopted. You felt sort of split, like two separate people.

'What's a concentration camp?' June said. 'Is it like my Brownie camp?'

Kristall shook her head. 'No, nothing like that. A kind of prison, I think.' The blackness was still with her. Why had they called her Kristall if it meant such an awful thing? *Kristallnacht!* She said the word to herself again just as Anna had said it and it sounded threatening and strange. It meant something bad and not lovely sparkling glass after all. Would it be any good asking Mum about it? Probably not. Mum didn't know much about things like that. It would have to wait until she saw Mother again, and that wouldn't be until after Christmas. Or perhaps she could ask adopted Granny and Grandfather? They would know. The Reverend and Mrs Wiltshire knew just about everything.

'Yes, Kristall. We know about *Kristallnacht,*' Mrs Wiltshire said. 'It was a night in Germany in 1938 before the war when hundreds of Jewish shops were attacked and all the glass broken. It lay all over the streets and so it came to be known as Crystal Night.'

'Why did the Germans do that?'

'Because Hitler believed that the Jews were a problem in Germany. He wanted to get rid of them.'

Kristall thought about this. 'But he was wrong, wasn't he?'

'Yes, of course he was. Very wrong and very wicked.'

'Why do you think my name is Kristall? My Sunday School teacher said that it's spelt in the German way.'

'I've no idea, my dear. But we know that

your father was German, don't we? You must ask Mrs Gibbons.'

'I can't see her until horrid Captain Gibbons goes back to his ship, and that'll be January.' Kristall thought of the envelope beneath her carpet and of the Berlin address. She wanted to say *I know my father's name and where he lives,* but she kept her lips firmly shut. She wasn't sure enough even of good, kind Mrs Wiltshire to tell that secret.

There was another thing she knew about her father though, and it made up for all the terrible things that people kept saying about Germany. Mother had told her that he was a good man and hadn't agreed with Hitler, and he'd suffered because of it. Julius von Brandt wasn't one of the wicked Germans at all. She must hold on to that every time anyone said anything nasty about the war.

1950

Philip Gibbons did not rejoin his ship in early January as he had expected. With bags packed—and Elizabeth, this time, secretly rejoicing over his imminent departure the following day—he suddenly complained of stomach pains. He woke her in the night, threw himself out of bed and staggered into the bathroom. She heard him heaving, being sick. He had never been ill, took great pride in his health and fitness. She pulled on her dressing gown and went to investigate.

380

'Think it's appendicitis,' he gabbled. He was kneeling on the floor, both hands gripping the edge of the lavatory pan. 'Pull the chain, for God's sake. I can't get up.'

She did as he asked then held him firmly beneath his arms and pulled him to his feet. 'You must go back to bed. I'll ring for the doctor,' she said. He was hot, dripping with perspiration. She helped him along the landing and back into their bed. She mopped his face, shook the pillows, made him comfortable, and fetched a bucket in case he should be sick again.

'Appendicitis is in the family,' he gasped. 'Both parents had it.' He clutched his stomach. 'Thank God it didn't happen in the war.'

Her heart sank. His leave had already been longer than they had expected and it had only been just bearable, so different from all the others. He had not relented at all over Kristall, had refused utterly to see her and he had told Elizabeth again that she must sever the connection completely.

'I cannot possibly do that,' she had said. 'But I'll compromise. I won't see her while you are at home. When you are away I shall do as I please.'

This had infuriated him, but he had heard the stubbornness in her voice, was aware of the determination and firm resolve. 'Perhaps I can compromise too,' he had said eventually. 'You may meet her at your father's flat or at your grandmother's house. I will allow you to take her out if you wish, but don't bring her here,

381

and don't let her meet Daniel.'

Elizabeth had wanted to hit him, to throw everything in sight at his handsome, smug face. This was a side of him that she had not known existed. It reminded her of his mother. How she hated Mildred Gibbons! She had thought him gentle, good-natured, altogether admirable. The rape had dented this opinion somewhat. He had made love to her again but she had felt used, just a vehicle for his satisfaction.

And now he was ill, very ill probably, and wouldn't be able to go back to sea for weeks. She wept tears of angry frustration, called the doctor, and wondered how she would survive, and more important, what on earth she could say to Kristall.

When Kristall received yet another letter from Mother telling her of this latest catastrophe she wanted to cry and cry with indignation and misery, but instead she gritted her teeth and decided to do something else instead. Mother was really and truly letting her down so there was only one thing to be done now. She couldn't wait to learn German. She would write to her real father in English now, right away. She couldn't live on dreams any longer. She had to make them come true.

Berlin—January 1950

Julius stood transfixed. He held the photograph in one hand and the piece of paper in the other.

He closed his eyes, opened them again, read the page again, stared at the neat childish writing on the wide-lined paper. Surely he was dreaming this? He flopped down on the nearest chair. It was a mistake. It was meant for someone else! For the third time he read,

'Dear Mr Brandt,

I hope this letter reaches you safely. My name is Kristall Hodgson and I am your daughter. I was born in England in 1939 and my mother is Mrs Elizabeth Gibbons. She couldn't keep me so I was adopted, but she found me a few months ago and we have seen each other three times. She's nice, but her husband doesn't like me and won't let her see me when he is home. He's a captain in the Royal Navy.

I should like to see you one day and I should like to have a photograph of you so that I know what you look like. I am sending one of me that was taken at school.

Could you tell me why I'm called Kristall? Is it because of *Kristallnacht?* My Sunday School teacher told me about that. I didn't know how to spell the end bit of the word but Mrs Wiltshire told me. She's a friend of mine and she knows a lot of things. She said it was German for night. Aunt Emmi is teaching me German but I've only had two lessons so far.

I have a bracelet that you gave to my real mother. I wear it round my neck under my liberty-bodice. It says *Ich liebe dich* inside. I know what that means.

I do hope you understand English and can read this. Please don't tell my real mother (Mrs Elizabeth Gibbons) that I have written to you. I think she would be cross.

From your loving daughter,
Kristall xxxxxx'

A little girl stared at him from the photograph, a child with curly hair tied into two plaits, one over each shoulder. It was Elizabeth, wasn't it? An Elizabeth he remembered from long ago. But she had never had plaits like that. And there was something else too about the small face. At first he couldn't think quite what, and then he saw. It was his mother. There had been a photograph something like this in her flat in Dresden, a little girl in a silver frame, fair plaits over each shoulder.

Dear God in Heaven! Elizabeth! The summer house! A November afternoon of enchantment and love, yes real love such as he could feel for no one else. And to be followed by what? By the obscenity of *Kristallnacht*. He suddenly realised the significance of the name. Kristall! Kristall! How could Elizabeth have done such a thing? To have called her that, and to abandon her! Was it some sick joke? Surely not.

Anger was followed swiftly by remorse and self-reproach. *Oh, Elizabeth, why didn't you tell me? Why didn't you come back to me when you found out? I would have come to England to look after you if you had wanted that. You loved me. I am quite sure that you loved me. But why then didn't you answer my letters?*

It had been 1938! Hitler! The horrors of the Third Reich! He shuddered and then he wept.

He asked for the rest of the day off and took the tram to the old house, Sophie's house, for it was still hers and he had told her that he would keep an eye on it for her. Hans was there, but it was a shattered and disconsolate Hans who sat alone in the cold rooms and spent his time reading or doing nothing at all. Julius despised him, almost hated him, but just lately he had found himself pitying him a little.

He let himself in, shivered at the dank, musty smell, the coldness, and peopled it in his imagination with all the family, with noise and warmth and love. He had been happy here all those years ago although he had been the usurper, the bastard child. He could see them all, almost hear them, their shadows appeared to him from every gloomy corner. There was Werner talking about flying, Emmi gentle and quiet, half-sister and good friend, Hans strutting about in his new SS uniform, the shiny black boots resounding on the stone floor. He thought of his father, jovial, kind, generous. And there was Elizabeth too of course, young, so very English and so very dear.

But Hans was no shadow. He was, as usual, sitting in the conservatory wrapped in an old blanket. 'Why don't you get outside and do something?' Julius said, thinking of the garden that had become an impenetrable jungle, and thinking bitterly too of his own inability to do anything about it. 'If I had a couple of decent legs I'd knock it into shape in no time.'

Hans looked up at him. His eyes were vacant, holding neither anger nor friendliness. 'Perhaps I will,' he muttered. 'One day.'

Julius sat down opposite him. He needed to talk and there was no one else. He sighed for the ghosts who inhabited these lonely rooms, sighed for his mother too, lost utterly in the fireball of Dresden. 'I've had a letter from England,' he said.

'My mother?' Hans seldom wrote to his mother, had ignored her overtures of reconciliation.

Julius shook his head. 'Aunt Sophie and Emmi are well, but it was not from them.'

'Who then?'

'From a child. From a child I didn't know existed. From my daughter!'

This shocked Hans into some slight movement. He sat up straight and the blanket fell to the ground. 'What did you say?'

'Elizabeth and I have a daughter!'

'You filthy bastard!'

Julius had not expected this reaction. 'You're a fine one to say a thing like that.'

'I never fucked a girl and then deserted her.'

Julius felt shivers of distaste run up and down his spine. 'I didn't desert her, for God's sake. I wanted to marry her. She ran away from me. Remember when it was? Remember, Hans! 1938. *Kristallnacht*, the camps, the killings, the obscenities of the things you and your ilk were so proud of!' He wanted to get up and strangle his half-brother there and then with his bare hands.

Hans retrieved his blanket, sank back into the cushions again. 'Yes, I remember. Remember too bloody well. How can I ever forget? I've done my prison sentence but that wipes out nothing, especially when bastards like you remind me again and again. I wish they had let me swing for the things I did. There'd be no remembering then.'

Julius flinched at the word bastard. Its very truth always distressed him. 'I'm going outside,' he said reaching for his stick. 'The smell in here disgusts me.'

He walked through the January garden, pushing aside branches of brambles and bare, damp undergrowth. The summer house was still there. He stared at it, at the irony of it. Half of Germany in ruins still and this little place survives. He went inside. Eleven years and more had passed since he and Elizabeth had given themselves to each other here. The wraiths of the two people they had been then seemed to be judging him. He shivered. What terrible years they had been, the most frightful in the history of the world it was said, and all because of his country, Germany, of which he had once been so proud. The old memories belonged to another life, another existence.

Suddenly he knew what he must do. Go to England, of course. Because of his job as translator with the British Army he could probably get the necessary pass. He would find his daughter, see that she was happy. Bring her back to Germany? No, probably not, but he must acknowledge her, perhaps adopt her if that could be done. He thought of his mother who had always longed for a daughter. *Well, you have a granddaughter now, Mother. I shall try to make you proud of her!*

He went outside again, pulled the door shut, and looked up at the grey sky and smiled in spite of the great well of sadness that always filled him when he thought of his mother. He walked slowly back to the house and told Hans what he intended to do.

'Please, Julius, let me come with you,' Hans said. 'It's the only way I can face the future. I must see my mother and make my peace with her face to face. Letters won't do.'

It was the last thing Julius had expected or wanted. To be in Hans's company for long nauseated him. Yet this was no longer the proud Nazi he was looking at, was it? Hans was a broken man, his half-brother after all, his father's legitimate son, and the only son left to Aunt Sophie. Could he do it? Could he actually put up with him for days on end?

Probably not.

Elizabeth! Of course if he went to England he would see Elizabeth. *Du hast meiner Herz* he said silently. Yes, she had his heart still. But she belonged to another man, a man with two legs and an abundance of gold braid, damn and blast him. Why did Kristall say that Elizabeth must not be told? He frowned, troubled, perplexed.

'Would it be difficult to get me a pass too?'

388

Hans persisted nervously.

Julius shrugged. 'I don't know. I'd have to see. It might be possible, and it might not. I'll let you know.'

CHAPTER 16

'For God's sake, Hans, speak English. Remember where you are. You used to be more fluent than me.'

Hans grunted as he followed Julius from the train. He had spent most of the journey from London in silence, struggling to make sense of a copy of *The Times,* but twice he had addressed Julius in German, only to receive suspicious stares from the other occupants of the carriage. 'I haven't spoken English for years,' he grumbled.

'Then get your memory going fast,' Julius directed. 'I seem to remember that Aunt Sophie wouldn't have any other language spoken in the house when we were children. You were quite fluent then.'

'Long time ago. English wasn't exactly welcomed in my outfit!'

Julius looked at him in disgust. He had been struggling throughout the journey to find some charity in his heart but it didn't come easily. Outside they hailed a taxi. 'Got your mother's address handy?' he said, determined that Hans should make some effort.

'I know it,' he said, and self-consciously recited the English words to the driver.

Julius juggled stick and luggage and cursed his legs as always when he was in a new situation, but as the taxi lumbered through the Bristol streets he forgot about himself and stared glumly at the bomb-damaged buildings. It was nearly five years now since the end of the war and still the city had a decrepit look, as though no one had the heart to do anything much about the ruins except clear the sites up a bit. He had not visited Bristol since 1936 and he thought nostalgically of those days when he was very young and life was good. *The past is more real to me than the present much of the time. The past and Elizabeth!* He sat up straighter, made an effort to pull himself together. Thinking like that was rank stupidity. *The present is what matters and I am about to meet my daughter.*

He felt a shiver of excitement and apprehension too. Perhaps she would not like him? Perhaps he would be a disappointment to her, or she to him? *Kristall von Brandt!* He couldn't resist giving her his name in his mind. A daughter, his child, ten years old! It was unreal, almost too amazing to grasp.

Hans was quite still and silent beside him. Julius wondered what he was thinking. Was he nervous too? If so it would be for quite different reasons. He knew that Hans was longing desperately for a reconciliation with his mother. Julius hoped that he would receive it.

The taxi took them up Park Street and then on towards Clifton, and suddenly, unexpectedly,

Julius was quite overwhelmed with the need to see Elizabeth. Why had she not replied to his letters back in 1938? The old, unanswered question hovered still, as it had done repeatedly throughout the years. And now there was this bigger one. Why in God's name had she given their baby away? He was outraged at the thought yet, perversely, he wanted her in his arms. And he hated his artificial legs more fiercely than at any time since he had lost the real ones.

He remembered making love to Liesel. He had been so embarrassed, so ashamed but she had been kind to him, had helped him so that in the end it didn't matter. But she too had left him, had rushed off to Dresden and left him alone in Berlin just as Elizabeth had done years before. He clenched his fists in frustration and anger, and then reminded himself yet again that he was not here to see Elizabeth. She had another man and another child. He lit a cigarette with fumbling unsteady fingers.

The car was slowing down, stopping. He looked up at the tall, three-storey house, a pretty house with a small garden in front. So this was where Aunt Sophie lived now. He had written to her here many times, reporting on the concerns of her property and affairs in Berlin which she had left in his hands. And in her last letter she had told him that of course she would receive him gladly and Hans too if the necessary passes could be managed.

The taxi-driver opened the door for him and he stumbled out, groped for the money and tried to remember how it went. Then he and Hans were standing outside in the cold, and swiftly the door was opened and Aunt Sophie, dear, kind Aunt Sophie whom his father had wronged, was there with a welcome for both of them.

'I had your telegram,' she said. 'Come in.'

There was a meal ready, and afterwards they sat close to the fire and talked, talked until there was little more to say, all explanations made, and Hans forgiven.

'I shall drive you over to Kristall's house the day after tomorrow,' Sophie said. 'That will give time to write a postcard and tell them to expect you.' She added another piece of coal to the fire and smiled at him. 'I haven't met her myself yet, but Emmi assures me that she is a charming and clever little girl.'

Julius stared into the dancing, comforting flames. 'It's the most amazing thing that has ever happened to me,' he said. 'Do you think we shall like each other, Aunt?'

'Of course you will.' Her voice was breezy, full of confidence.

'What about telling Emmi and Elizabeth that Hans and I are here? How shall we do it?'

Sophie pursed her lips. 'I've said nothing, as you asked in your letter. Elizabeth was always adamant that you shouldn't know of Kristall's existence. Suddenly hearing that you not only know, but have made contact with each other and that you are actually here in England, in my house, is going to be a shock.' She looked at him steadily. 'Are you still in love with her, Julius?'

He had not expected this question, yet he had

pondered it a thousand times in his heart.

He nodded.

'It will be difficult for both of you,' Sophie said. 'Remember that she is married and that she has a son.'

'I'm not likely to forget either of those things,' he said bitterly.

Two days later Julius stood in the rain and waited outside the small terraced house in Bishop Road. Sophie had driven him over in her little car. 'I have just enough petrol,' she had said. 'It's still rationed here and only supposed to be used for journeys of national importance.' She had laughed. 'I think this is of national importance, don't you?' Now she said to him, 'Go on then, Julius. I'll wait in the car.'

He stared at the front door bell as if hypnotised. He drew a deep breath, pushed it and could hear its strident peel inside the house.

Then the door opened and the world stood still. There she was, Kristall von Brandt, his daughter, a little girl who reminded him of his mother and yes, Elizabeth too. 'Kristall?' he said. 'I am Julius.'

She stared at him, wanted to cry, but if she allowed those tears to come they would be tears of pure joy. There he was at last. A dream come true. She took a few steps forward and he held out his arms to her. She went into them, felt the rough tweed of his long overcoat. 'Daddy,' she whispered.

He held her for a long time and then put her away from him, studied her face. 'You are like my mother,' he said. 'She was beautiful. And you are like your own mother too.' He drew her into his arms again and it seemed to Kristall as though he never wanted to let her go. She was really loved at last. It was one of the nicest feelings she could remember.

Mum was hovering in the background. 'Are you going to come in and have a cup of tea, Mr ...?'

He released Kristall and smiled, a charming smile that quite won Brenda's heart.

'Thank you, Mrs Hodgson. That would be nice. My aunt is in the car. May she come in too?'

' 'Course she may. I'll put the kettle on. Kristall, show the lady and gentleman into the parlour.'

Brenda hurried out to the scullery, busied herself with the best china, the best teapot. *Fancy! Just fancy that! Me, entertaining Germans right here in my house. But the lady isn't German, is she? Kristall said she'd married a German years ago. Silly thing to do!* She carried the tray through, poured tea, handed biscuits round.

The conversation was formal and stilted. Kristall sat on the edge of her chair glancing as often as she dared at the tall, handsome man who was her father, her real, real father. It was like a fairy tale. The only thing that didn't fit was the stick that he needed to walk. He'd had to put it down when he'd held out his arms to her. She'd noticed that, and she had picked it up for him and he'd smiled a strange, sad little smile. Whatever was it like not to have any legs? She couldn't bring herself to look at his trousers with the tin ones inside.

At last the difficult half an hour was at an end and they were out in the sunshine, for the rain had stopped. They drove up to Clifton, to the Downs. 'You must show your daddy the Suspension Bridge,' Aunt Sophie said. 'I shall go home now and I shall return at three o'clock to pick you both up. We'll go to my house for tea and after that I'll take you home, Kristall.'

They watched Sophie's little car disappear and then they walked across the famous bridge, stared down at the tiny motor cars on the Portway far below, and wondered what to say to each other. They crossed the road and walked back on the other side and then found a restaurant and, advised by Kristall, Julius ordered cottage pie and peas, with apple tart and custard to follow.

'Cottage pie. I've never had that before,' Julius said.

'It's wizard, my very favourite.'

He grinned. If cottage pie brought her such pleasure what fun life was going to be in the future with so many wonderful things to show her and to give her.

When they had finished the first course and were waiting for the second he said, 'Well then, Kristall. Are you going to tell me all about yourself? We've a great number of years to catch up on.'

'Ten and a half,' she said. 'Well p'raps not

that many. Babies don't talk much for about two years do they? June didn't.'

'Eight and a half then,' he said, laughing. 'You'd better get started.'

And then the first shyness disappeared and the words began to flow. She wanted to tell him everything, all the important things in her life and those that weren't so important too. He was such fun to be with, so kind, so handsome, her father, her real, real father. She told him about Henry, about pushing June down the stairs and then running away, about Mother discovering where she was, about the stamp album and the envelope with the address on the back.

She knew that he was listening, really listening. It was something that grown-ups seldom did. 'And I hope that I shall get a scholarship,' she finished eventually. 'To a grammar school. Mum is going to put me in for the boarder's exam for the Red Maids School too. It's very hard, but she thinks that I might be clever enough. If I pass I shall be able to go there and sleep. She doesn't really want me to go, but she says it's the best school in Bristol and I'll do well there if I work hard. I intend to work very very hard and go to university.'

Julius smiled, his heart full of love and pain and bereavement. 'So you don't want to come back to Germany with me, then?'

She shook her head. 'Could I come for holidays sometimes? That would be the best thing. I don't think I want to leave Mum for ever. She loves me, you know. Well, she loves June best because she's her real daughter, but she loves me too, and I love her quite a bit.'

'And what about your ...?' He didn't know what to call Elizabeth, was embarrassed and full of pain at the thought of her rejecting this bright, entrancing child.

'My first mother? I call her Mother. I can't live with her because of Captain Gibbons. That's her husband. But like I said, I don't truly think that I want to anyway. She's nice, but she didn't bring me up, did she?'

'No. No she didn't. So you're quite happy with things as they are?'

They had finished their meal and were walking along the Clifton Mall now and Kristall slipped her hand into Julius's. 'Yes. I suppose I am. At least I shall be when rotten old Captain Gibbons goes back to his ship and I can see Mother sometimes.' She stopped and stared at the draper's shop which they were passing. 'Mother bought me a pretty frock when we were out a few weeks ago. It was fun. She wears pretty dresses, the New Look. I don't suppose you know about that.'

He shook his head. 'I don't think we have that in Germany. If we do, I don't know about it.'

She stared up at him. 'Haven't you got a wife or anything?'

'No. No wife or anything.'

'That's sad. I wish you could have Mother. She'd like that. If you loved one another once, like it says on my bracelet, why don't you any more?' She frowned. 'Are you going to see her while you are here?'

'You said in your letter that you didn't want

her to know that you had written to me. She doesn't know that I'm in England.'

'She didn't tell you about me being born did she?'

Julius hadn't expected such perceptive questions. This was dangerous ground. How to explain? Blame the war? Yes, perhaps that was the safest thing, and it was the truth too. 'She couldn't tell me. It was wartime. You know all about that, don't you?'

'Yes. Your country and mine fought each other. You didn't like Hitler though, did you?'

'No. Let's not talk about the war. Do you mind if Elizabeth knows that you've written to me and that I'm here and we've met each other?'

Kristall considered this question. She had been thinking about it ever since she had written and she was quite worried. She didn't want to upset Mother or make her angry. 'I'm a bit frightened,' she confessed. 'I should have told her shouldn't I? I wrote to you in a hurry because I was so upset about Captain Gibbons being disagreeable and all that.'

'Don't be frightened.' Julius wanted to scoop her up in his arms and comfort her, but he refrained. He hadn't a father's rights yet, perhaps he never would have. 'I'll try to see her, and then you and I will meet again and everything will be all right.'

'Perhaps all three of us could go out somewhere together?'

He smiled and pressed her hand in his. 'Perhaps,' he said. 'But with Captain Gibbons still at home that might be a bit unwise, don't you think?'

Kristall wasn't sure about this, but she nodded anyway. 'I suppose so. It would be nice though.'

'Very very nice indeed,' he said quietly, half to himself. It was the biggest understatement of the day.

'Come on then, tell me all about it,' Brenda demanded when Kristall arrived home. 'I thought he was very personable and charming for a German. Is he rich? Can he get about much on those tin legs? Where did you go?'

Kristall took off her coat, put it on the hall stand and followed her mum through to the scullery. 'Yes, he can walk really well and he's quite lovely, lovely, lovely.' She did a little twirl and nearly knocked the ironing board right over. 'We went across the Suspension Bridge and then came back and had some dinner in a café and went for another walk and talked about things, and after that Aunt Sophie met us again and drove us to her house. I haven't been there before. That's where my daddy is staying.'

'You can wipe a few dishes while you're talking,' said Brenda, who was washing up. 'Your Aunt Sophie seemed very pleasant too.'

'Yes, she is. She's my great-aunt actually, my grandmother's sister. I told you that she married a German, didn't I? That's how it all started.'

'How what started?'

Kristall went to the cupboard and took a clean tea-towel from the shelf. 'All the German things.

She had three children. They are sort of cousins, I suppose.'

'And where does your real dad fit into all this?'

Kristall wasn't quite sure. She hadn't got that clear yet. 'I think he is a distant relation.'

'What happened to the three children?'

'Aunt Emmi lives with Mother and helps her. Then there's Hans. He came over with my father. He's nice too. I met him this afternoon. He's a bit shy and doesn't talk much. He was something not very good in the war and they told me not to ask him about it.'

'Oh, and what was that then?' Brenda was immediately suspicious.

'I told you, I don't know and I mustn't try to find out. And there's Werner.'

'Who's he when he's at home? Another nasty Jerry name by the sound of it.'

Kristall wiped the plates very carefully, drying each one at least twice over. 'Well, you won't like this. He was in the *Luftwaffe*. That's the German air force. He's buried in a cemetery here in Bristol.'

Brenda lifted her hands from the soap suds and stared at Kristall. 'You mean he bombed us and got shot down?'

Kristall nodded, speechless.

'Well, of all the things. Just to think that all the time you and me were in the cupboard under the stairs listening to the Jerry bombers overhead, one of the blighters was your relation!'

'It's terrible,' Kristall agreed. 'Supposing we'd known! And they all said how nice he was. Aunt

Sophie has a photograph of him in his uniform on her sideboard.'

'Your dad, the one that adopted you,' Brenda said, 'got killed in one of those raids. The Jerries went and dropped a bomb right on the air-raid shelter at his works. I'm glad I didn't know about your Werner then.'

Kristall put the plates in the cupboard and started on the cutlery. It was all very hard to understand. Why couldn't everything be simple and straightforward? How could Werner have done such a thing? 'Aunt Emmi is going to take me to see his grave one day,' she said. 'He was her brother. You'll let me go, won't you? I do want to. I want to try and understand the war and everything.'

Brenda laughed hollowly. 'Well, there's a thing! Going to visit a Jerry grave. Not a healthy place for a child. No, I don't think you ought to go.'

'Please,' Kristall said. 'I like Aunt Emmi and she's teaching me German.'

'Ye gods!' Brenda said. She had heard this expletive recently on the wireless and liked it. It relieved her feelings and wasn't blasphemy like, *God*, or *good God*, or any of the other much worse things that you could say. 'Ye gods,' she repeated. 'Whatever shall I hear next? You'll be wanting to go and live in Germany one day, I suppose.'

Kristall shook her head, placed the dried cutlery carefully away in the correct places in the shallow drawer beneath the kitchen table and then went to Brenda who was washing up the pans now. Standing behind her she put her arms right around her and said, 'No, Mum. I'm not going to Germany. Not till I'm grown up anyway. I want to stay here with you for ages and ages. Although I've discovered my real father and my real first mother I'd rather stay with you for now.'

Brenda dropped the pan back into the bowl of water with a splash. She wiped her hands on her apron and turned around to look at Kristall. 'Well now, that's a lovely thing to say.' She gave her a hug and kissed the top of her head. 'Perhaps it was a good thing, you running away. Brought us to our senses, didn't it!'

Kristall smiled and returned her hug with enthusiasm. Mum treated her quite grown up sometimes, talked to her as though they were equals. And yes, she often thought about how much her life had changed since that awful weekend. Things at home were much better. Even Dad was inclined to be friendly now and then, and June had been so sorry about Henry that she had been quite nice for ages.

And best of all, of course, it was because of running away that she'd found out who her real parents were. There was no more dreaming about princes and princesses and silly baby things like that. They were both nice real people and her daddy was absolutely wizard in spite of being a German. He was a good German anyway.

'So you'll let me go and see Uncle Werner's grave one day, then?' she said making the most of the goodwill that seemed to be flowing in abundance.

'I suppose so, but don't say anything to your dad about cemeteries and Germans and things like that. He wouldn't like it at all.'

'My Sunday School teacher lived in Germany before the war,' Kristall said, suddenly remembering this piece of interesting information.

'Germany, Germany! I don't want to hear anything else about Germany, Miss. And when you've finished the drying up you can read a story to June for me. She's been plaguing my life out to finish her latest Enid Blyton.'

'Okay,' Kristall said. She was really, really happy. No one should look down on her for being adopted any more. She was Kristall von Brandt, a much better name than boring old Kristall Hodgson!

Emmi called on her mother the following day and nearly fainted with shock when she saw her brother and half-brother there.

'Why all the secrecy?' she said when she had recovered a little, and after she had welcomed each, Julius with enthusiasm and Hans more hesitantly. 'Why didn't we know? Why so sudden? And what about Elizabeth?'

'Sit down, dear, and I'll explain,' Sophie said. 'It's quite a long story.'

When Sophie had finished Emmi was full of remorse. 'So it was my fault? Do you mean to say that one of those envelopes I gave to Kristall had your address on it, Julius?'

He nodded. 'That's right. She wrote to me

403

and I had the surprise of my life. She asked me not to tell Elizabeth she had written, and so far I haven't.'

'How could I have been so stupid?'

'It was a good mistake, Emmi.' Julius emphasised the word 'good'. 'Because of it I've found my daughter.'

'I suppose so.' Emmi was still doubtful, still considering all the implications.

'It must have been meant,' said Sophie a trifle piously.

'But what about Elizabeth?' Quite at a loss Emmi turned to her mother. 'How on earth are we going to tell Elizabeth?'

'I thought you could do it.'

'Me?'

'Yes, dear.' Her tone was matter-of-fact. 'You live there. It would look odd if I turned up out of the blue. You know that I only visit when I am invited. Julius cannot possibly go and neither could Hans. You are the only one. You are returning there this afternoon. It's obvious that you must tell her.'

'I couldn't.'

Julius crossed to the sofa where she was sitting, took her hands in his. 'Do it for me, Emmi. I need to see Elizabeth. You will have to be our go-between.'

Full of apprehension, Emmi cycled home just before dark. She usually loved this peaceful journey across the Suspension Bridge and along the Portishead road to their village, but today she pedalled swiftly, unwilling to confront Elizabeth, yet wanting to get it over with as soon as possible.

Julius had walked with her to the gate of her mother's house when she was leaving, had thanked her profusely and had watched as she tied her headscarf tightly beneath her chin. He had looked at her bicycle with some concern. 'Will you be all right on that?' he had said. 'How far is it?'

'A few miles. I do it frequently, every time we need some shopping in fact.'

'Sorry to have to ask you to do this for me,' he had said. He had kissed her on the cheek as he always used to do.

'I don't know how Elizabeth will take it, but I'll do my best for you, Julius.' She had wobbled unsteadily away, waving to him just before she turned the corner.

She put her gloved hand on the place where he had kissed her, wobbling again as she did so. There could be no possible future for Elizabeth and Julius could there? Why was she helping them to meet? Was it the right thing to do?

When she reached home she put her bicycle into the shed and opened the back door which led directly into the kitchen. She threw off her coat. Pedalling so fast had made her hot and out of breath and she felt considerably sorry for herself.

Elizabeth was in the kitchen preparing vegetables. 'Had a nice time?' she enquired.

'So-so. Where's Daniel?'

'Upstairs with Philip. The last time I looked in they were playing snakes and ladders.'

'Is Philip getting up?'

'He thinks that he shouldn't. Temperature up a bit. Daniel keeps him amused.'

'That's good. I'm going to make some Ovaltine,' Emmi said. 'Want some?'

'Please.' Elizabeth took potato peelings from the wide stone sink and carried them to the bin which stood just outside the kitchen door. 'Is Aunt Sophie all right?' she asked, closing the door again.

Emmi poured milk into a pan. 'Yes. Fine. She has visitors.'

'Visitors?'

She put the milk onto the Aga, stood staring at it, mesmerised, wondering how on earth to tell what she had to tell.

'From Germany.'

Elizabeth turned incredulous eyes upon her. 'Germany? Who on earth?'

Emmi swallowed. 'Hans and ... and Julius!'

Elizabeth gripped the table for support. 'What? What did you say?'

'Hans and Julius.'

There was a breathless silence in the room and then the milk rose to the top of the pan, ran over the edge, sizzled onto the hot-plate.

Elizabeth shook her head. 'No, oh no. He can't be here, Emmi. Not like this, not without telling me. Why? Dear God in Heaven, why did no one tell me?'

Emmi removed the pan to the draining board and wouldn't look at Elizabeth. 'Kristall wrote to him. She found the address on one of those envelopes I gave her. She wanted the German stamps. Remember? I didn't notice the address on the back. It was an oversight.'

'Oversight! My God I should say it was. So he knows about her?'

'Yes. He knows.'

Elizabeth flopped into the rocking chair, gripped its arms, stared at Emmi's back. 'I don't believe it. After all the years that I've struggled to hide the facts. To think that he should find out like this! It's too awful. How could Kristall have done such a thing without asking me about it first?'

Emmi turned and looked at her. 'Quite easily, I imagine. If I was adopted and suddenly found myself in possession of my real father's address I think I should want to get in touch with him straight away.'

'No you wouldn't. There might be frightful complications.'

'Kristall is only a child. She wouldn't see any problems.'

'If only she had told me first! We could have talked about it, made proper arrangements.'

'Remember,' Emmi said, 'that you weren't going to see her again until Captain Gibbons had recovered and had gone back to his ship. That would be a long time to a child. Perhaps that was the reason.'

'Oh God, what a mess!' Elizabeth was filled with remorse. 'What a fool I've been. So selfish.' Then as another thought struck her. 'Is that woman here with Julius? Liesel or whatever her name was?'

Emmi shook her head. 'Just Julius and Hans.'

'Is he married or anything?'

Another shake of the head. 'I've no idea. He didn't say.'

'Is he angry?'

'Angry?'

'Because I kept Kristall's existence a secret? Now it seems such a frightful thing to have done. I'm frightened, Emmi.'

'You mustn't be. My mother has explained everything to him. She's helped him to understand how it was when Kristall was born.'

'Dear Aunt Sophie,' Elizabeth said. 'What a wonderful person she is.' She tried to take herself in hand, endeavoured to marshal her thoughts and feelings. How many years since she had seen Julius? Ten? Eleven? And now she suspected that she was pregnant again with Philip's child. The child of that awful rape. Rape? Did you call it rape when it was between husband and wife? Probably not.

The agonising thoughts chased each other through her head and still she sat there rocking forwards and backwards, wondering what on earth to do, how to cope with the staggering news that Emmi had thrust at her. Julius, Julius of the tall, willowy body, the fine artistic hands, the blue eyes, the smile, *Julius, my daughter's father, Julius whom I love and have loved for so long.* 'When can I see him? Help me, Emmi.'

'He wants to see you, of course. He knows that you are happily married, though, and that you have a son.'

Elizabeth stared at her again. Happily married?

Did Emmi really think that? Had she and Philip been able to put up such a good front before her and Daniel? 'Could you arrange a meeting for us? Can you find an excuse to go over there again tomorrow? If Philip asks, you could say that your mother is ill, anything. I can't wait, Emmi. I want to be with him when he first meets Kristall.'

Emmi put more milk to heat, made two cups of Ovaltine, stirred generous amounts of sugar into each. She handed one to Elizabeth. 'He already has. They spent half a day together.'

Elizabeth stared at her as if she were a ghost. 'Oh, Emmi, Emmi, that's awful.'

Emmi looked at her coldly. 'Why awful?'

'Because, because? Oh, I don't know why. Because I'm selfish I suppose. Because I wanted to be the one to introduce them to each other.' She drank some of the scalding liquid and then put her drink on the floor beside her chair and wiped her eyes. 'I can't bear it, Emmi. I should have been there. I know that I refused to tell him about her, yet in my secret heart I've dreamed a thousand times of the moment when they would meet. Just a fantasy really.' She took her cup again, cradled it in her hands, sipped gingerly now and then. 'By giving her up when she was born, by not telling Julius I've given up all my rights though, haven't I? And now it's all happened without me.'

Emmi's anger disappeared. She felt sorry for her. 'I'll go over again tomorrow,' she said. 'I'll try to arrange for you to see Julius. My mother will fix something.' She went to her cousin and put her arms around her, hugged her tightly. 'Stop torturing yourself, Lizzy. It'll all come right in the end.' Her words were more optimistic than she felt.

'The best place for you to meet Elizabeth will be the cemetery, the one where Werner is buried,' Sophie said to Julius. 'I expect you want to be alone and you won't be disturbed there. I shall take you over, and Elizabeth can drop you off here afterwards.'

Julius looked at her in amazement. It all seemed so simple, so cut and dried. The second traumatic event of this incredible visit to England was to take place in a cemetery, at his half-brother's grave! 'Thank you, Aunt Sophie,' he said. 'I'm very grateful.' *Grateful? Yes but vastly anxious and tense too. How on earth can I face her? How to ask all the questions that have boiled and frothed in my mind for the past eleven years, and those new and even more important questions too that have been added to the others since I heard about Kristall's birth?*

'It's all arranged,' Emmi said to Elizabeth the following day. 'You are to go to the cemetery, to Werner's grave on Sunday afternoon. Julius will be there at three o'clock. Philip won't query it. Sunday afternoon is the time for visiting cemeteries and you can say you're going to my mother's for tea.'

'What about Daniel?'

'Easy. Tell Philip that cemeteries are not suitable places to take children. He'll be glad

410

to have him here at home anyway.'

Sunday afternoon, a wintry sun, bare trees, cold frosty wind, and for the second time Elizabeth stood silently, staring at the simple headstone. There had been no flowers to bring. A recent sharp frost had killed off the last of the chrysanthemums so instead she had taken secateurs and cut small pieces of branch from the newly blossoming witch hazel that grew at the end of her garden. This tree was always a fragrant joy during these bleak January months when there was little else to lift the heart.

She had come early. She walked on the wet grass, placed some of the bright yellow sprigs on the bare earth beneath her cousin's name, Werner Kleist. She bowed her head and thought of him alive, laughing. Then she walked across the gravel path to some other graves, also simple headstones, but with English names and English messages inscribed. There was one with no name. 'A pilot of the Royal Air Force', it said. She put the remaining blossoms there and bowed her head again. *Why do I feel as I do? Why am I doing this on one of the most momentous occasions of my life? To show how foolish war is, perhaps?* She looked at her watch. Fifteen minutes to go.

He walked between the avenue of yew trees which stretched the length of the cemetery, his stick tapping on the Tarmac. Her heart went out to him in pity. *Pity? I don't wish to feel pity. He must be the strong one. I need strength and support in the man I love.*

411

He was wearing a long overcoat and a trilby. He was older. Of course he was older, eleven years and a deadly war older. It showed in the slight stoop of his shoulders, the stick, the shaming, horrible stick. *Shaming. No never shaming! How can I possibly think so? If there is any shame it is mine!*

She went towards him her arms ready now to welcome and support.

He needed no support. He smiled at her. 'Hello, Elizabeth.'

Silence for a second, then her arms outstretched and the space between them swiftly crossed.

He let his stick fall, took both her hands in his. 'A strange place to meet isn't it, after so long?' He spoke in German and his voice was the same as she remembered, deep, resonant, setting her heart on fire.

Tears filled her eyes. 'Perhaps the most appropriate place,' she whispered.

He bent to kiss her gently on the lips, without passion, with love and concern. 'I've seen our daughter,' he said simply, and his words held no condemnation. 'Thank you for her, Elizabeth.'

They sat down on an old mossy seat and there amidst the graves she wept all the shame and misery of the years. They talked and held each other until Elizabeth had expunged all her guilt and fears, until she knew she was completely forgiven. The cold of the January day encased them both and Elizabeth felt that she would never be warm again. Yet the coldness of her body was in stark contrast to the warm glow in her heart. She knew that their love was just as real and as wonderful as it had been long ago in the Berlin garden.

But then reality intruded and she was filled with the old heartache, a heartache that Julius's closeness did nothing to lift but rather made more intense.

'We can do nothing about it,' she said. 'I am pregnant, Julius. I can't desert my children. I cannot do the same terrible thing again. To give a child away once is too big a sin to bear. I can't repeat it.'

There were birds in the branches above their heads. They rustled the few dead leaves that remained so that some fell to the ground. 'Like our love,' she said. 'Dead leaves falling.'

'I can't let you go like this,' he said. 'Come back to Germany with me. I'll bring up your other two children.'

'Do you think Philip would allow that? No, Julius, for now there is no other way.' Her voice was low, controlled, full of grief. 'Perhaps in the future there might be. We must keep in touch this time though. Now that I've found you again I don't want to lose you.'

'That might not be easy for either of us.'

'Why do you say that?'

He shook his head and held her thickly gloved hand more closely. 'Just practicalities. You have a husband.'

'Yes. Yes of course I have.'

'I want to think that you are happy. Will you be happy for my sake, Elizabeth?'

She looked at him, her eyes full of doubt

413

and misery. 'Happiness seems a very long way off just at the moment.' But then she felt his despair and made an effort. 'Perhaps in time I shall be content. Who knows? And what about you, Julius?'

'How can I be happy without my heart?'

'That's a lovely thing to say,' she whispered. 'But you mustn't say it or think it.' She rose quickly to her feet knowing, unwillingly, that this wonderful unbelievable hour must come to an end. She watched him reach for his stick and forced herself to remark as casually as she could manage, 'You'll find someone else and forget all about me. What happened to Liesel?'

'She has gone back to Dresden.'

'Your city. Will you go back too?'

They walked close together beneath the darkening sky.

'I might. I shall go wherever I can find a university place. I was training to be a doctor, remember?'

'But Dresden? Isn't that in the Russian-occupied part of Germany?'

He winced. 'Yes, unfortunately. But it's also my town. I love it and it's in ruins. I want to help rebuild. It was very, very beautiful, still is in a strange way.'

'So you won't mind living under the communists?'

They reached the cemetery gates. 'I might. I haven't made up my mind yet.'

'I'll drive you back to Aunt Sophie's,' she said.

They drove in silence most of the way and

outside Sophie's house he took her in his arms again. 'I want you and Kristall with me forever,' he whispered.

She kissed him, passionately this time, then leaned across and opened the car door. 'One day, Julius, I shall come to you. Or you will come to me. I know it in my heart. Go now, quickly. I can't bear any more.'

With difficulty he climbed out of the vehicle and she watched him go into the house. He looked back only once, then the door closed and there was nothing, nothing in her heart but a cold empty space.

She drove back to Daniel and to Philip. *I am doing the right thing. I must not repeat my first wickedness. I can never leave Daniel. A second betrayal would be the ultimate wrong. And by the end of the year there will be another child. Forgive me, Kristall, please, please forgive me, Julius. Whether I can forgive myself is quite another matter.*

CHAPTER 17

August 1950

'It would have been a little girl.' The words came to Elizabeth from a long distance through a fog of incomprehension. She opened her eyes and the room swam in confusion. A little girl, Kristall, a child she couldn't keep. No, that was wrong.

This wasn't Kristall. She could keep this one, a daughter, a sister for Daniel. She tried to sit up. 'Can I see her?'

A white-coated figure bent over her. 'Not at the moment, Mrs Gibbons. Just rest.'

She felt a needle in her arm, the walls would not be still, then she was asleep, dreaming. *Kristall, where are you? Why are they taking you away?*

Philip Gibbons, summoned hastily from Scotland where his ship mercifully had just docked was standing beside her bed. He stared at the doctor in disbelief. 'Don't let her die. For Heaven's sake don't let her die.' The words were wrung from him in anguish. Memories of the night he had raped her, raped his own wife for God's sake, had been chasing through his mind ever since he had received the telegram. His newly born child was dead, his wife nearly so. Perhaps it was a punishment. Dear God in Heaven, let it not be.

'Kristall!' Her voice was weak, tormented. 'Kristall. Why are they taking you away?' She said the same words over and over again. She came out of sleep for brief moments into the bewilderment of delirium. 'Would have been a little girl,' she muttered. 'Kristall, dead. No no, not Kristall.'

'Who is Kristall?' The young doctor looked at Philip, perplexed, anxious.

He hesitated. 'Her daughter. She was born before we were married.'

'Your wife has been calling that name

416

repeatedly. She seems very agitated. It might help if she could see the child. Is that possible?'

Philip was jolted out of his anguish. Kristall to come here? It was unthinkable. He tried to grasp at some excuse. 'I thought you didn't allow children in the wards.'

'How old is she? I expect we could make an exception. Especially as your wife has a private room.'

He tried to think logically. 'Eleven or so.'

The doctor nodded. 'That would be all right, then. It might ease your wife's mind, might make all the difference. She equates the baby she has just lost with this other daughter. Could you bring her in?'

Philip was appalled. He had never met the child, didn't want to meet her, and as for driving to wherever she lived and ... it was absolutely unimaginable.

'I don't know that I can.'

'It could save your wife's life. I cannot put it more strongly. Patients frequently make a sudden, dramatic recovery when some problem or other in their lives is resolved. The power of the mind is immense, Captain Gibbons, as I am sure you know.'

Philip nodded. 'I'll see what I can do.'

'Make it speedy then. There's little time to lose.'

'I don't want to leave her.'

'Can you telephone? Is that possible?'

He breathed a sigh of relief. Emmi! Of course. The excellent and reliable Emmi! She would know where Kristall lived, would do all that was necessary.

'Get a taxi,' he commanded astonishingly over the telephone. 'Bring the child here as soon as you can.'

Kristall was called from her classroom. 'Your mother is very ill and is asking for you,' the headmistress said. 'Your Aunt Emmi is here.'

Kristall pulled on her blazer. Mother? Why was Mother ill? Was it Mum or Mother? If Aunt Emmi was here it must be Mother.

Daniel was in the car too. 'Mummy has had a baby who's died,' he said. 'She wants to see you. They won't let me go in because they say I'm too young. Stupid if you ask me.'

'No one is asking you,' Emmi said, short-tempered because of her anxiety.

'Who told you to get me?' Kristall asked.

'Captain Gibbons.'

'What? He doesn't like me. I've never seen him.'

'Well, never mind about that now. When we get to the hospital you must just go in there and hold your mother's hand. She keeps asking for you, apparently.'

'Is she going to die?'

Emmi shook her head. 'I don't know, Kristall. I don't know. We must pray hard that she doesn't.'

Philip Gibbons stood up when a nurse brought Kristall into the small side ward. He looked at her awkwardly.

'So you are Kristall,' he said. 'Your mother is very ill.'

Kristall ignored him. She walked quietly over to the bed and stared down at Elizabeth lying there, her eyes shut and her face so frighteningly pale. 'Mother,' she whispered. She took the limp hand in both of hers and held it firmly for a moment and then she put it to her lips. 'Don't go away and leave me, Mother. Don't leave me again.' She stood quite still for a long time, and then the nurse brought a chair and she sank down upon it without letting go of her mother's hand for an instant. She stroked the fingers gently, willing life into them, willing her to respond.

At last Elizabeth's eyelids fluttered and she opened her eyes and stared blankly. Then, 'Kristall? Have they brought you back?' The words were faint but clear enough.

'Yes, Mummy. Yes. I'm here.'

Suddenly Elizabeth appeared to relax. 'That's all right, then,' she said. She stared around as if looking for someone else. 'Isobel? You see. I was right. I told you I wouldn't lose her for ever.' Her eyes closed again and her breathing was even and calm, but Kristall was frightened.

'Who is Isobel?' she said. 'She seemed to be speaking to someone who isn't here.'

Philip thought for a moment. 'Must be her wartime friend, Isobel MacDonald. They were in the Land Army together.'

'So this Isobel knows about me?'

'I suppose she does.'

The nurse approached, brisk and competent. She took Elizabeth's pulse, put a thermometer into her mouth and finally smiled at Kristall. 'I think she'll be fine now,' she said. 'She's been very worried about you for some reason. Now that she knows you are here she'll sleep peacefully, and tomorrow she will be much better.'

'Can I stay a bit longer and can I come tomorrow?'

'I'm sure you can, but just now you go downstairs with your daddy, Kristall, and get a cup of tea and by the time you come back she might be awake.'

Kristall turned towards Philip. She was about to say, *he isn't my daddy at all,* but, surprise, surprise, he held out his hand to her and the words froze on her lips.

'Thank you for coming, Kristall,' he said. 'Let's go and see if we can find Emmi and Daniel and something to eat, shall we?'

They went down the stone steps together, saying nothing to each other.

Daniel, sitting impatiently in the hall on the ground floor, saw them coming. He turned to Emmi. 'Gosh. Daddy and Kristall are here,' he whispered. 'I thought he didn't like her.'

Kristall was fetched by taxi every evening to visit Elizabeth.

'Well, there's a turn up for the books,' Brenda commented when they were waiting for this impressive transport to arrive on the fifth evening. 'Fancy that grumpy old Captain

Gibbons sending for you like this.'

'He doesn't seem to be grumpy any more,' Kristall said.

'I hope he's not going to ask you to go and live with them?'

Kristall was silent.

'He hasn't has he?' Brenda's voice was full of alarm.

'He said I could if I wanted to.'

Brenda flopped into a chair. 'Oh, my dear life. I bring you up and give you everything and slave away for you morning, noon and night and then off you go to a posh house in Abbots Leigh, just like that.'

Kristall turned to her and threw her arms around her, kissed her enthusiastically. 'I didn't say I was going, did I?'

'No, you didn't, come to think of it.'

'Well, I'm not!'

Brenda was quite overwhelmed. 'And why not, madam? They're rich.'

'I know they are. I shall go for holidays sometimes, and perhaps once a week for tea.'

'So you'll have the best of both worlds!'

'Yes I shall. Isn't that wizard!'

They heard the taxi arrive and Kristall went to the front door and opened it. Then she turned back to Brenda who had followed her through the passage. 'I love you, Mum. I love my other mother too and my nice German father. I'm very very lucky, aren't I?'

Brenda adjusted Kristall's beret and scarf. 'Yes. I suppose you are.'

Elizabeth was sitting in the day room when Kristall arrived. 'I'm going home in a few days' time,' she said. 'I'm quite well now and looking forward to leaving here.'

Kristall kissed her. 'And I can really and truly come and see you in your house once a week, can I?'

'You can come as often as you like,' Elizabeth said. 'Captain Gibbons stressed again that he wouldn't mind if you came to live with us. I've never seen a man change so quickly. You've completely charmed him, Kristall. It's a miracle.'

'It was because you got better as soon as I came to see you.'

Elizabeth smiled to herself. Perhaps that was it. Philip had always been a romantic, a believer in omens and miracles. His tough naval officer exterior was just a cover for that other side of him. She remembered with affection that he had said something about carrying her favours into battle when they became engaged all those years ago. She had been slightly amused then. He had asked her to pray for him too, and she had done so every night during the war.

And now all the problems and worries of her life seemed to be resolving themselves. Philip had apologised to her and she to him. They were completely reconciled. The loss of their baby had brought them wonderfully together, and in losing one daughter they had found another. Philip had amazingly said something like that after Kristall's third visit.

'I couldn't leave Mum for ever,' Kristall said.

'But I'd like to come to your house for tea on Saturdays.'

'Then that's fine. That's what we'll do.'

'Are you sad about the baby?'

'Very sad, but because she died Captain Gibbons has discovered you. So something good has come out of it.'

'Just like when I ran away. Lots of good came out of that.'

'That's how it often is.'

'And what about Julius?' Kristall called him Julius now. It seemed easier than Father or Daddy. 'Do you think he'll come to England again?'

A pang of sadness dented Elizabeth's composure. 'I shouldn't think so. Aunt Sophie had a letter from him. He's going to Dresden to live and he's been awarded a place in the university there. He wants to be a doctor.'

'Why does that stop him from coming to England?'

'Because it's in the Eastern part of Germany. They call it the GDR now. That stands for German Democratic Republic and they don't like their people to travel?'

'Seems silly to me,' Kristall said. 'Silly to choose to live there too.'

'It's his city. He always loved it.'

'Oh well, perhaps I'll go and see him one day when I've learnt enough German.'

'Perhaps you will,' Elizabeth said.

'Will you go?'

Elizabeth shook her head. 'No, Kristall. I shall not go to Germany for many many years. Your father will make a new life for himself and perhaps he'll marry one day. I hope so. I want him to be happy. You can write to him and tell him about us all occasionally, but I must forget him now, at last.'

Kristall looked at her wonderingly. Being a grown-up seemed so complicated. How could you truly forget a man like Julius who had once said *Ich liebe dich* to you and had put it on a bracelet? She sighed and felt sad. But her sadness only lasted for a moment or two. The future lay ahead of her, a gleaming exciting path. 'Now that I've got my scholarship to the grammar school, I've decided that I should like to be a doctor too,' she said. 'Or maybe a vet. I like animals better than people. Do you think my father would be pleased if I was either of those things?'

'He'd be delighted,' Elizabeth said. 'Absolutely delighted, and so would I.'

'I'd be following in his footsteps wouldn't I?'

'Of course you would. You'll have to work hard.'

'I mean to. I shall work very very hard and make him proud of me.'

'He's proud of you already.'

Kristall was filled with contentment. She thought she must be the happiest child in the whole world.

EPILOGUE

They walked hand in hand beside the grey waters of the Elbe.

'Dresden has risen from the ashes,' Julius said, 'like the mythological phoenix. Now that Germany is reunited and we have the wealth and expertise of the West we shall be able to do much more. There are plans to reconstruct many of the buildings just as they were.'

'Rather like our lives,' Elizabeth said. 'Rising from the ashes, I mean.'

He laughed. 'Hardly ashes. Have you been happy all these years, Elizabeth?'

'Yes, much of the time. I've had my children, and grandchildren. They are very good to me, Kristall and her family especially. I don't deserve her.'

'Our daughter,' he said. 'I'm so proud of her. But now the future is completely ours. Every golden hour of it. No distractions, no problems, just us.'

'You and me together forever.'

They swung their joined hands and walked as briskly as he could manage across the *Augustusbrücke,* enjoying the bright winter sun, the glint of frost on grass and each other's company.

425

'One of the best views of Dresden is from here,' Julius said when they reached the end of the bridge. 'This panorama has been painted by artists for centuries.'

'I wish you had brought me here before the war.'

'It will be just as beautiful again.'

'In our lifetime?'

He smiled at her. 'Perhaps. We have a lot of living to do, Elizabeth.'

'And we can do just what we want, please ourselves for the rest of our lives,' she said. 'We are free, free, free. Where shall we live, Julius?'

'We could go to America.'

'Or Australia and permanent sunshine. One of Kristall's sons is there, our joint grandson.'

'Or the South of France,' he said. 'I've always fancied a villa on the Med. We could have a boat.'

They came to a wooden seat and sat for a time staring at the little craft and the paddle steamers on the river.

'Do you really want a boat? I've always been sea-sick.' They both laughed and simultaneously leaned closer together and kissed, kissed with the hunger of all the separated years. 'Not here,' Elizabeth objected weakly. 'Surely we can wait until we get home.'

'Home? My apartment? Do you really feel it's home?'

'Just for now. Just until we have decided where we shall live. What a gloriously frivolous decision to have to make!'

Suddenly Julius was serious. 'Frivolous? Not quite the right word for me. After years of living under communist rule you can't possibly imagine what that freedom means. I'm not used to the idea yet.'

'Perhaps we should stay here and watch the rebuilding of your lovely city.'

'Perhaps. But I think not. We'll make a new start. Together. Somewhere with no memories.'

'Memories!' Elizabeth said thoughtfully. 'We had so few letters from you over the years, Julius. Fill me in now with all the details.'

He stared across the river at the splendour of the Semper Opera House. 'It was reduced to a heap of rubble in 1945,' he said, nodding in its direction. 'Now it's almost as beautiful as before.'

'But I want to know about you,' she said. 'You never married. We knew that much.'

'I had a couple of friendships.' He smiled. 'Nothing permanent, but enough.'

'What about the girl you met in the ruins?'

'Liesel? She returned to Dresden too and we met from time to time. She was a fanatical communist.'

'Is she still?'

'I've no idea. She married and we lost touch a long time ago.'

'Your life seems to have been very uneventful.'

'Kristall came to see me three years ago as you know. That was a big event for me.'

'With that funny travel agency. What was it called?'

'The Berolina. They did conducted tours, very

427

restricted and ordered. We had little time alone together. There were tourist guides hovering all the time.'

'Yes. She told me. Philip was ill then or I might have come as well. He was ill for a long time. I nursed him at home and couldn't leave him even for a day. They were difficult years.'

'My poor Elizabeth.'

She shook her head. 'No, don't call me that. I wanted to make those last months totally happy for him. It was a sort of reparation in my mind for all the times I had thought about you, Julius, all the times I was unfaithful to him in my imagination.'

'But you were happy weren't you?'

'Yes. I was happy. We had a good marriage on the whole. We were friends and that's important. After he died I felt that my world had fallen apart, and then ... just a few months later ...'

'The wall came down, the East was free,' he finished for her.

'And I thought of you, Julius. I thought of you then with hope and excitement.'

'And now here we are!'

Elizabeth suddenly took off her glove, pushed up her sleeve and held her hand out to him. 'Kristall gave me this just before I left,' she said. 'She has worn it for years and now said that I must have it.'

'Ich liebe dich,' he whispered. He touched the bracelet and then lifted her hand to his lips. 'The words mean as much now as when I had them engraved for you.'

'Do they really, Julius?'

'Of course they do.'

Unexpectedly she laughed. 'There's one difference though.'

'And what is that?'

'Then we could read the words. Now I need a magnifying glass as well as my glasses!'

He laughed too. 'That's the only difference.' Suddenly he was grave. 'No it's not. I had forgotten.'

'Forgotten?'

'I have no legs!'

She put her arms around him, pulled his head down to hers. 'I love you more for that.'

'More?'

'Of course, more. It's a wonderful badge of honour isn't it? You opposed the most evil regime on earth and I'm proud of you for it, Julius. As Kristall was, as she still is.'

'Do you mean that?'

'Of course I mean it.'

It was cold. They stood up and walked again. He could manage without his stick now.

'Dare I ask you to marry me then, Elizabeth?' he said.

'Try me.'

'Will you marry me, Mrs Gibbons? Do you fancy changing Gibbons to von Brandt?'

She nodded. 'Yes. I'll marry you, *Herr* von Brandt. It's taken us a long time, but yes, I'll marry you just as soon as you like.'

'Tomorrow?'

They laughed again. They were always laughing.

'Any time. As soon as it can be arranged.'

'And we can live anywhere in the whole world. What a simply stupendous thought.'

'No we can't. I've just thought of something.'

'What?'

'I'm not totally free.'

He looked at her anxiously for a moment. 'Oh, why not?'

'There's Caro.'

'Caro?'

'My dog!'

'Then we'll have to live in England.'

'Would you like that?'

'Absolutely perfect,' he said.

The publishers hope that this book has given you enjoyable reading. Large Print Books are especially designed to be as easy to see and hold as possible. If you wish a complete list of our books, please ask at your local library or write directly to: Magna Large Print Books, Long Preston, North Yorkshire, BD23 4ND, England.

This Large Print Book for the Partially
sighted, who cannot read normal print, is
published under the auspices of

THE ULVERSCROFT FOUNDATION